FREED

LACEY LEHOTZKY

First paperback edition October 2024

ISBN 979-8-9915584-0-2 (paperback)

ISBN 979-8-9883620-9-8 (e-book)

ISBN 979-8-9915584-1-9 (hardback)

Book cover by Beholden Book Covers

Edited by Kaitlin Ugolik Phillips

Published by The Lehotzky Group LLC

www.laceylehotzky.com

MORE BY LACEY LEHOTZKY

A Choice of Light and Dark

Chained

Light

Dark

Freed

PRONUNCIATION GUIDE

Agrenak - AG-ren-ak
Aress - AH-ress
Béke - BE-k
Blire - B-lire
Cazius - KAZ-ius
Drazen - Dray-zen
Domi - do-mi
Endre - EN-dre
Északi - EE-sah-kee
Este - esh-te
Félvér - fell-ver
Izidora - iz-i-dawr-uh
Kazimir - kaz-imir
Kaztar - kaz-tar
Kirigin - ki-ri-gin
Kriztof - KRIS-tof
Liliana - lil-i-ana
Radence - RAY-dense
Ruslan - ROO-slahn
Ryza - RYE-zah

Telivér - tell-i-ver
Vaenor - VAE-nor
Vadim - vaa-deem
Valynor - VAL-noor
Vasvain - vas-vain
Vaszoly - vaas-o-ly
Vlisa - vlis-a
Viktor - vik-tor
Zalan - ZA-lan
Zekari - zek-AR-i
Zheka - zeh-kah
Zuriel - ZUR-iel

CONTENT WARNING

Freed is suitable for audiences of 18+. It contains scenes that sensitive readers might find disturbing. Your mental health matters, and you should make the choice with which you feel most comfortable.

This is by no means an exhaustive list of trigger warnings, and you can check the author's website for the most up to date list.

Trigger warnings: Torture, kidnapping, mentions of rape and sexual assault, nightmares, flashbacks, panic attacks, suicidal ideation, graphic violence, death, and mentions of physical, verbal, mental, emotional, and child abuse. The explicit sexual content in this book contains group sex scenes, orgies, anal play, impact play, breath play, and more.

Északi
Iron Realm
Day Realm

Night Realm
Crystal Realm

A CHOICE OF LIGHT AND DARK
PLAYLIST

Hunting Season - Ice Nine Kills
Watch The World Burn - Falling in Reverse
There's Fear In Letting Go - I Prevail
Werewolf - Motionless in White
Masterpiece - Motionless in White
No Masters - Bad Wolves
I Will Not Bow - Breaking Benjamin
Fallen Angel - Three Days Grace
Infinite - Silverstein, Aaron Gillespie
Riot - Three Days Grace
TRIALS - STARSET
Don't Stay - Linkin Park
Face Everything And Rise - Papa Roach
Say You'll Haunt Me - Stone Sour
Last to Know - Three Days Grace
Without You - Breaking Benjamin
Pain - Three Days Grace
Whispers in the Dark - Skillet
Take Me Back To Eden - Sleep Token
Whatever It Takes - Stephen Stanley

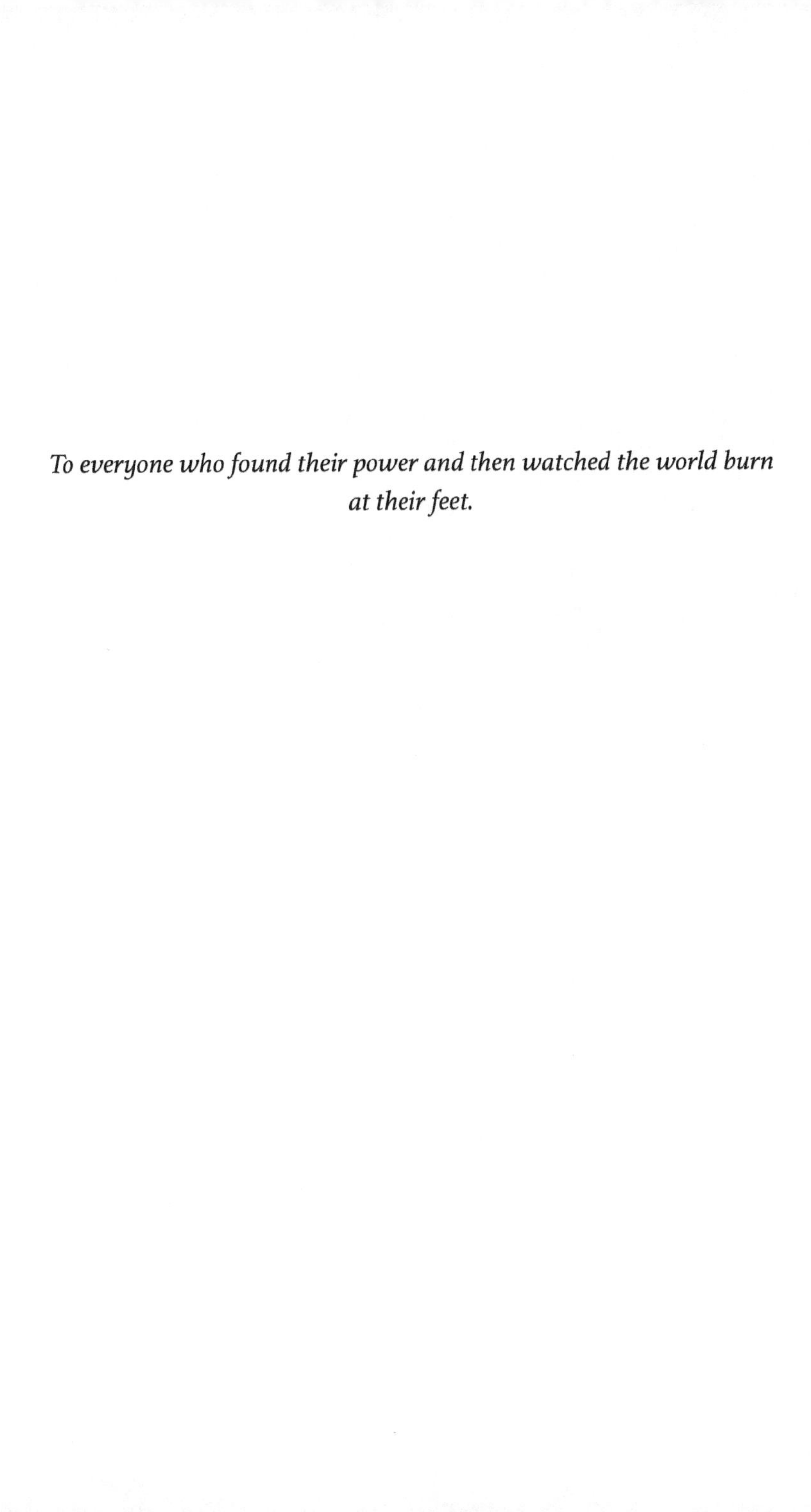

*To everyone who found their power and then watched the world burn
at their feet.*

***

PROLOGUE

Black flames filled his palms as he stalked forward, staring down his opponent. Fury, hotter than anything he could conjure, burned through his veins as he hurled a fist straight toward the white-haired male. Smooth as water, his opponent dodged the blow, circling back to face the enraged male. "Come on, hit me. You know you want to, Ruslan," the Angel taunted.

That only angered Ruslan more, and he charged again, only to meet air where the Angel had once stood. A growl rumbled from his chest as he squared his shoulders. He needed something, anything, to slake this rage that never seemed to dim. It had been weeks since his mate had woken with a smile on her lips, weeks since he'd heard her bright voice.

"Stand fucking still then, Zuriel," Ruslan snarled, feinting a jab and following it up with a powerful cross.

But Zuriel knew what he planned and easily slipped to the side, countering with a swift punch to the ribs. On instinct, Ruslan lashed out and slipped Zuriel on the jaw, sending him stumbling back. A grin spread across the Angel's face as he rubbed the spot. Zuriel knew this was what Ruslan needed to cope – at least for now. He had to calm the male so the events that needed to happen would unfold, and if he had to suffer a few blows for it, so be it.

Ruslan attacked again, and the two fell into a wickedly fast dance, limbs flying almost too quickly for an onlooker to observe. Sweat slicked both of their torsos, and wild bits of hair fell around their faces as they finally slowed their movements. Ruslan braced his hands on his thighs, sucking down air, while Zuriel wrapped his around the back of his neck and stared up at the sky.

Blue spots adorned the ribs of both males, and blood dripped from a cut just above Ruslan's right brow. Zuriel's left eye was purple and quickly swelling. "Feel better now?" the Angel asked, dropping his arms.

Ruslan straightened, slicking his hair back with one hand. "Yes."

Zuriel stepped forward and locked Ruslan in his gaze. "Good. Because you need to keep it together. For Izidora."

Guilt settled like a heavy stone in Ruslan's belly. He glanced away, toward the lonely mountains that called to him. Beyond them, the male responsible for his mate's continued absence roamed freely, *alive*. Every night, Ruslan drifted off to dreams of how he would peel the skin from his bones, forcing him to suffer a thousand tiny cuts, just to feel a glimmer of pain like the one that consumed him every waking moment.

He knew that he needed to pull himself together. She deserved better than the male he had been. Not only that, but he *wanted* to be a better male for her. He would deliver on all the promises he'd made to her – to unite the realms, to empower her, to kill Kazimir together when the time came.

To do that, he needed to regain control of himself and his emotions. Heaving out a breath, he said, "I know." Then, he straightened his spine, grabbed his shirt, and whispered the words that would ferry him to Ryza Citadel, where he would finally step up and be the king he wanted to be.

———

WHITE FLAMES FILLED her palms as she wandered through the darkness, hunting for every shadow, hurling her fire into them with an anguished scream.

"Why me?" she yelled into the void, over and over and over, her throat going raw from the depth of her torment.

"Why, Goddess, why did you give me this burden to bear? I've suffered enough for a thousand lifetimes." The flames fell away as she clutched her hands in her hair, fisting the chestnut strands in an attempt to feel *something* other than utter agony and despair.

Tears raced down her face in an attempt to reach the dark below her bare feet, running away from her sorrow.

"Why do I have to suffer at the hands of others?" she whispered, her voice broken as she sank to the ground.

"What did I do to deserve this?" Curling in on herself, she buried her head in her arms, sobs wracking her chest as she allowed herself to feel the unending pain.

The Goddess never answered her when she asked these questions. In fact, no one answered her at all. She was utterly alone, abandoned to suffer in the void. There was no explanation for why she was chosen to change the course of history; no, she simply had to accept the role and move on with her life.

She was exhausted, angry, and thirsty for vengeance. The blood she had spilled before did not dim the screaming in her head telling her she needed to fight back against the powers that harmed her time and time again.

But she was also lost, and she didn't know how to find her

way back to the world of the living – or if she wanted to. There, only pain awaited her.

Picking her head up, she gazed into the endless black around her. "Will there even be happiness for me in the end? Or will I lose him too once I go back?"

Through the fog of darkness, a beacon of light stepped forward. He glided in her direction, his white hair flowing behind him on an invisible breeze. "There will be happiness for you, Izidora. Come, it is time for you to return to the land of the living. You are needed."

"How do you know?" she said, her voice so small and weak as she gazed up at her cousin.

He proffered his hand, and she accepted it, allowing him to pull her to her feet.

"Because your story is not finished, not yet. You will write the ending how you want it to be."

I

THE AWAKENING

1

RUSLAN

Six months had passed since that fateful day Kazimir had tried to kill Izidora, and my mate remained lost in the void between worlds, not quite living, but not quite dying. Every morning that she did not wake with me, another piece of my heart broke, turning to ash and blowing away on the breeze. The need to drain Kazimir of every drop of blood, torture him in every sadistic, demented way until he begged for death, was a constant roar in the back of my mind, never slaked by the pain I inflicted on myself or others.

The wood-paneled office in Ryza Citadel had become my personal prison, and as I sat through another parade of people who needed something from me, I couldn't help but wish Izidora had taken me into that void with her. At least then I wouldn't feel this utter emptiness where the other half of my soul should be. Even now, I found myself reaching down our bond to speak with her when I triumphed or when I was frustrated with someone – which was far too often given how thin my patience had worn.

What would our world look like when she finally woke?

My chair creaked as I shifted my weight, resting my temple

on my fisted hand as Rares began a long-winded explanation of his recent experiments. Zuriel was notably absent from the meeting, given that it was his day to watch over my mate while she slumbered. He and Gozzak, one of the Demons that had been captured with him, had been overseeing Rares as he continued his work. I didn't trust the old Mage not to try some underhanded or sneaky shit while I was preoccupied with Izidora's condition. He might be sworn to obey and defend the Iron Crown, but I'd experienced enough of his twisted words to know better.

By the dark circles bruising all our eyes, the whole Iron Realm knew none of us slept well, too focused on the rise and fall of Izidora's chest, the fluttering of lashes that too often turned out to be nothing but still offered a semblance of hope.

I cut Rares off, wanting him to get straight to the point. "So have you figured out how to prevent Kazimir's binding magic from blocking access to ours, or not?"

The gnarled hands wrung themselves as he hesitated to answer. Not that I could blame him – I'd lost my temper more than once when he appeared in my office without a solution. We needed to work around that obstacle, given that was what rendered Izidora incapable of defending herself. "Not exactly. This time I had more progress. I think if I could just see it in action–"

My fists banged into the desk, and I was on my feet in an instant. "I am not risking anyone's life for your observations. Try another way."

"There is no way to know for certain unless we have someone with binding magic to use," he protested, shrinking back into his chair.

I cocked my head to the side. "And you cannot find such a person on another continent? Or you aren't able to recreate it yourself?"

"My attempts at recreating it have failed so far, you know this. As for the other continents... well, a person with binding magic tends to keep themselves hidden. The Fates don't often gift it, and madness is a common side effect of it. As we've seen."

Gozzak cleared his throat, his red eyes darting between the two of us. "If I may, I served under General Rapp, who possessed this magic, in the Great War between the Angels and Demons. He was a touch crazy, yes, but the madness of which you speak only affects those with Goddess-gifted magic. Demon magic is Fates-gifted."

The Demon looked as if he wanted to say something else. "Go on," I encouraged.

"During the war, the Goddess often gifted counter magic to ensure that whatever the Fates offered us, the Angels could manage, at least in part. I never saw anything that could nullify General Rapp's magic, but I saw plenty of magics in equal and opposite power to it. Perhaps that is the better route to take, rather than blocking it," he offered.

I slunk back into my chair, mulling over what Gozzak had said. Then I scrutinized the man who had a hand in creating me with a little less irritation. "Work with Gozzak in creating counters for it or new inventions that would make a substantial impact should our magic be locked down."

The old Mage's dark eyes brightened for a moment, and that toothy grin I despised flashed across his face. I was giving him what he wanted, but stopping Kazimir was more important than stopping Rares's twisted experiments.

I swiveled in my chair, gazing out at the summer sun casting its rays over the stone buildings spanning Radence, the capital of the Iron Realm. Well, not only the Iron Realm – not anymore.

I had kept my promise to Izidora and united the realms, not that they needed much convincing once they heard what Kazimir had done. When Izidora woke, she'd be the empress of the Északi Empire, consisting of the Iron, Crystal, and Day Realms. I'd allowed the other monarchs to keep their titles and positions, needing them to watch over their realms while I managed my own. The continent was too vast for one person to oversee all operations, and I'd quickly learned the importance of delegating and snap decision-making.

At least the deluge of work kept me mostly distracted from the unending pain. I'd taken to numbing my emotions just to get through the day, lest I be consumed by my thirst for vengeance and make a rash decision as I drowned in despair.

Izidora would wake. I just had to keep believing it.

I'd also offered the other monarchs access to all the innovation the Iron Realm had achieved, and Iron Fae and Félvér spread across the realms installing lifts, hot springs, tracks, and more – free of charge, of course, a gift from the new, *generous* emperor. The tracks beneath the Agrenak Mountains that divided our continent remained a closely guarded secret, however. The last thing I wanted was for the Night Realm to discover them and use them against us.

"What of the other endeavor?" I finally asked Rares.

"I have succeeded in pushing the full shift."

Whipping around, I dropped my hand away from my face and narrowed my eyes upon Rares's self-important grin. "How?"

"A potion finally did the trick. The Félvér who cannot already complete a full shift will need to drink it one hour prior to the change. It should remain effective for a few hours at least. We'll need to continue testing to be sure of the exact timing, and it will likely differ for each type of breeding. The Dragons will need a higher dose more often than the Wolves, for example."

A slow, sadistic smile pulled my lips as that victory sunk in. None of the Félvér with Dragon Shifter heritage had more than wings, claws, and horns – myself included – and being able to shift into a Dragon? That would be fucking incredible. "I'd like to test this potion on myself as soon as possible."

"I will prepare another batch. It takes time to brew. I'll also be needing more ingredients," he added.

"Buy whatever you need and start brewing as many batches as you can. We'll need a stockpile for what's ahead," I commanded, my thoughts drifting again to soaring among the skies as a fully shifted Dragon – a dream I'd had since I was a child and yet never thought possible.

"Emperor." A voice tore me from my thoughts, and the ghostly image of one of the Mages appeared off to my left. Rares was forgotten as his protege shifted from foot to foot.

"What is it, Katrina?" I asked, my tone bland and bored. I'd sent Mages to Vlisa, the capital of the Crystal Realm, and Zheka, the capital of the Day Realm, because their spells allowed them to communicate across great distances quickly.

"Queen Viktoria has just given birth to a healthy babe. The little princess is resting peacefully and will make an appearance before the Day Realm in two months."

"Send my well wishes to the royal family and inform them we'll be in attendance for her introduction to the empire." Rares shot me a sidelong glance, but I ignored it.

"Yes, My Emperor. Shall I inform Desmond?" Her translucent form waved slightly before she muttered a spell under her breath, re-forming her image.

"Yes, King Airre and Queen Immonen will want to hear the news as soon as possible. That will be all, unless you have other information to relay?" I glanced at Rares, and he subtly shook his head.

"That is all, sir. I will check in with you later this week at our usual time," Katrina said before her shimmering form disappeared from my office.

"That is excellent news regarding the queen of the Day Realm," the old Mage commented.

"Indeed it is. You were speaking of–" My words were drowned out by the slam of wood on wood, and I jerked out of my seat, ready to fight the intruder.

Liliana stood in the doorway, seafoam green eyes alight, chocolate brown hair sticking in every direction with black feathered wings still protruding from her back like she had flown as fast as she could to my office. When she opened her mouth to speak, those three words I'd been dying to hear for six months spilled from her lips.

"Izidora is awake."

2

ENDRE

Wanton sounds slipped beneath the heavy wood door, and I sighed, bracing my forearm against it before letting my head rest there.

"Do you want me to tell him?" Viktor asked from behind me.

"No, I can manage. I just don't want to walk in and see him fucking them again. He barely attends council meetings anymore, and more often than not, my father sends me to drag him to them," I replied, pushing off the wood and facing Viktor.

"After everything that happened, he's just a bit obsessed with his legacy. It will pass," Viktor defended him, and I nodded, too tired to argue.

More than anything, my soul ached for Liliana. It had been six months since I kissed her goodbye, and that kiss still burned my lips, calling me from sleep night after night as I thought about her, wondering if she was safe and wondering if I'd ever see her again. The ravens I'd surreptitiously sent to Radence had gone unanswered.

A cry of pleasure tore me from thoughts of her, and sucking

down a steadying breath, I counted to ten and then opened the door.

Kazimir was balls deep in Taya, not slowing his furious pace as Viktor and I entered the room that smelled of sex and smoke. The haze that hung in the room gave it an atmosphere of sultriness, but my stomach only turned at the sight of Kazimir's harem splayed out over chaises and beds. The circular room was hidden away at the top of one of Este Castle's spires, leaving them undisturbed unless someone dared brave Kazimir's ire to interrupt them.

A few days into our retreat from the Iron Realm, a large Wolf had charged us, and in our fear of the massive beast, we'd nearly killed Taya before she shifted back into her Fae form. She was as obsessed with Kazimir as Kazimir had been with Izidora, which I figured worked out for him in the end.

"Kazimir," I called out, hoping to draw his attention.

He didn't even look at me as he growled, "What?"

"Queen Viktoria has had her babe. It's a female."

His movements slowed, and he pushed Taya away, facing us with his dick still hard. "And when will she be presented?"

"I don't think we're going to be welcome for that," Viktor said, saving me from having to admit the truth.

"I am a king on this continent. Of course I will be welcome," he scoffed, sliding off the bed and throwing on a robe to cover himself. He ran a hand through his dark hair, smoothing the sex-tousled strands.

Viktor and I shared a look, having learned not to argue over how he was viewed outside of the Night Realm in the past six months. "We should probably start preparing to leave, then. She'll be presented in two months' time."

"Don't tell them we're coming. I want it to be a surprise. I have a gift for the child and I wouldn't want anyone to spoil it."

A wicked grin broke out across his face, and his dark emerald eyes gleamed with something sinister.

"Of course, My King." I sketched a bow, then hurried from the room before he moved on to one of the other females he'd hunted the Night Realm for. All the females in his harem had hair with a reddish tint, and the symbolism was not lost on me.

"We are going to send word, yeah?" I said to Viktor as we wound down the spiral staircase.

"Kazimir said he didn't want to," Viktor shrugged.

"Yeah, but sending word is the right thing to do," I challenged. "You know the other monarchs are going to be pissed when he shows up."

"We're not at war, so it's not like an explicit 'you're not welcome' in lieu of an invitation. Besides, if they didn't want us to show up, why would Desmond tell us Queen Viktoria had her baby?"

The Mage assigned to the Crystal Realm was hard to read, and while Ruslan had not offered the ease of communication to the Night Realm that he had given the others in his empire, Desmond had taken it upon himself to relay important information anyway. I couldn't quite figure out his motivations, and when I brought it up to Viktor, he blew me off. It wasn't like Viktor to be so unconcerned about something this important, and I got the sense that maybe his father was padding the pockets of the Mage.

Our fathers, along with Vadim's and Kaztar, had been running the Night Realm smoothly since Kazimir had executed High Lords Luzak and Valintin after his coronation. Their plot against Izidora and Kazimir was not forgotten in the months we'd spent away from Vaenor, the capital of the Night Realm, on our way to Béke and back. It was then that my wariness of my best friend had grown, for the merciful male his father had crafted him to be slipped away faster than the wind through my fingers.

We spotted Vadim in the hall of the Royal Wing as we descended the final stair from the harem's tower. His unkempt beard had grown shaggier in the months we'd been back, and his long hair was a mess piled on top of his head.

"Where are you headed?" Viktor asked him, and he stopped short, falling in stride with us.

"Back out to the training field. We've got a new batch of recruits coming in today."

"Have you had a chance to assess them yet?" Viktor smoothed his already perfectly styled hair, a nervous habit he'd had since childhood.

"No, but they're young, which means they're more trainable than the older recruits we've been getting."

Our boots echoed in the deserted hall as we wound our way to the front of the castle.

"What number does that put the army at?" Viktor questioned.

"Nearly three hundred thousand. The new conscription rules are pulling younglings in from across the realm. I'm struggling to find housing for them all," Vadim replied, tugging on his beard.

"Let my father know. He's working on getting some new buildings erected outside the city walls," I said.

"I should ask Tibor to build me a small city out there, then I can have the training fields next to them. Would be better for everyone involved," Vadim chuckled. "Can't have the young ones in the taverns every night and then too hungover to train in the morning.

"That's not a bad idea," Viktor mused.

Vadim laughed. "I know. I came up with it. I'll speak to Tibor this evening."

We arrived in the grand entrance hall, and Viktor and I needed to begin arranging for our departure. "See you later, Vadim," I said, and we parted ways in front of the massive double doors that led into the summer air.

"Do we really need three hundred thousand soldiers?" I grumbled, brushing my hair out of my face.

Viktor's sage eyes hardened. "We need to protect our realm. It's now three against one on the continent and only a matter of time before Ruslan shows up on our doorstep with an army of his own. You know he's not going to let go of what Kazimir did to Izidora."

From what Desmond had told us, Izidora was still locked between the land of the living and the land of the dead. I was certain it was her state of limbo that had kept Ruslan away from the Night Realm as of yet.

Not that anyone in the Night Realm, outside of the ones who attended Béke, knew about the events that had come to pass at the end. We'd all covered for Kazimir when we returned from Béke, an act that still left a bitter taste on my tongue.

The story was that Izidora had chosen Ruslan, Liliana had chosen to stay with Izidora, and we'd left with strained tensions and with Kazimir's grief lodged even deeper into his heart. When he wanted to, he played the heartsick rejected mate well, garnering sympathy from all Night Fae.

How did I never see the darkness that lurked within?

I never thought my best friend was capable of the things I had witnessed while we were in the Iron Realm, and honestly, I couldn't lie to myself and say it was all due to the mating bond. The binding magic had an effect on him too, but I was questioning everything, including some of his actions prior to Izidora's rescue, and even more after.

But I was alone in my opinion. Viktor, Vadim, and Kaztar refused to hear my concerns. So I kept my innermost thoughts to myself, hoping that by remaining by his side I could prevent the worst of the madness as it sank its claws into him.

After the turmoil of the past year, the Night Realm needed stability, and the cause of the many was greater than the cause of the few.

3

IZIDORA

The world came into focus slowly, as if I were waking from a lazy afternoon nap. A gauzy overhead canopy became clear, the dark fabric highlighted by the golden sun. I blinked softly as my eyes adjusted to the light.

Where was I?

I tried to lift my hand, but the motion was stopped by something soft.

Sheets? Was I in a bed?

How did I get here?

I must have made a noise, because a heartbeat later, Zuriel stood over me.

"Izidora," he breathed, his icy blue eyes bruised and his white hair spilling over his shoulders as he leaned down to examine me.

"Wha–" I tried to speak, but my voice was rougher than sand.

"Shh, don't strain yourself. Let me help you sit up so you can drink some water." My cousin took great care in slipping his arm beneath me, lightly wrapping the other across my middle and scooting me backward so I leaned against a stack of pillows.

My brain was still in a fog, and confusion pulled at every thread of thought I tried to conjure. Zuriel lifted a glass to my lips, and as I reached up to steady it, I found my hands shaking uncontrollably.

"It's alright, I've got it," Zuriel soothed, tipping the glass. I parted my lips, allowing the cool liquid to pass across my parched tongue. After several sips, he took the glass away, and I sucked in a deep breath.

"What happened?" I croaked, questions popping into my mind in rapid succession as the water lifted the haze.

"What is the last thing you remember?" he asked, his eyes roaming me as if he searched for any sign of pain or injury.

Pausing to scan my memories, I thought back to the masquerade, the lantern festival where the white fire burst from within and shrouded everything as far as the eye could see in light, the parade...

The parade.

Kazimir.

My fall.

Ruslan flying to my rescue.

The knife.

I clutched my chest, ripping at the fabric there as my heart thundered faster than any hoofbeats. Zuriel clutched my hands to still my frantic movements, dropping his voice into a soothing tone. "You are safe now. We healed you."

I shook my head, unable to believe the words spilling from his mouth. Whipping my head around, I found no sign of my mate, and my stomach immediately turned over, causing me to heave.

"Breathe, cousin," Zuriel pleaded, as he rubbed my back and I doubled over, desperate for air and answers.

"Ruslan..." The hoarseness in my voice was only increased by the agony I felt at my mate being gone.

"Is at Ryza Citadel. I will send Liliana to fetch him now if you can promise me you'll be okay for a few moments as I slip out?"

Then, my head cleared enough that I sensed our bond awakening, filling me with an ache to rival that of my head. I nodded furiously, trying to regain control of myself, and Zuriel sprinted from the room, flinging open a heavy wooden door Ruslan had once carried me through when he'd shown me around the palace he'd built for us.

"Fetch Ruslan. Now," I heard him say in the distance.

"What's wrong?" the bubbly voice drifted through the door.

"She's awake."

"Oh, shit, I will go right now," she replied. Liliana. My best friend was still here.

A moment later, a bang reverberated across the ceiling, and Zuriel was by my side, holding a bowl containing a thick substance. "Do you think you can eat?"

I crinkled my nose at the goopy liquid. "Maybe something other than that. Cinnamon rolls?"

The smile that broke across the Angel's face was filled with relief. "I should have guessed. Don't move. I'll be back momentarily." Again he sprinted from the room, and I waited patiently for his return.

I felt weak – so fucking weak – as I tried to shift to make myself more comfortable. Tears sprang to my eyes in time with my rising frustration, and I gritted my teeth before pushing my body higher.

How long had I been asleep?

I recognized that I was in our bed at Roc Palace, and craning my neck, I studied the wall-length fresco depicting an epic love story between an Angel and a Demon. Around the bed, various chairs and chaises had been dragged into the room, some still containing rumpled pillows and blankets. Books lay scattered in haphazard piles, and the fires were only embers in the hearths.

Outside, the sun shone brilliantly, and not a hint of snow was visible in the distant capital city.

Zuriel interrupted my examination with his return, carrying a plate filled with steaming pastries along with a ruby red drink. The sweet scent drifted in my direction, vanilla and cinnamon making my mouth water. He placed both on the table beside the bed before crouching down and retrieving a tray. He settled it across my lap, and my stomach released a rather large rumble as he placed the plate in front of me.

"Eat slowly," he warned. "It's been a while since you had solid food."

My brows pinched, and I narrowed my eyes on my cousin before I asked, "How long?"

His face remained neutral, unreadable as ever. "I'll let Ruslan explain everything when he arrives. Eat, you need your strength."

Dissatisfied with his caginess, I made a noise of annoyance before turning my attention to the food, lifting the roll with shaking hands and taking a small bite. Zuriel hovered like a worried mother, on the precipice of jumping forward should I need assistance. Chewing slowly, I savored the delicious flavors that warmed my mouth, then bit into it again and again until the first roll was nothing more than icing on my fingers.

By the time I finished the second roll, my head was clearing rapidly, and my hands no longer shook. Sucking my fingers clean, I studied the ruby liquid on the corner of the tray. "What's this?"

"It's to help with your strength," Zuriel said, once again as nonspecific as possible.

Before I had a chance to express my annoyance, a voice popped into my head.

"Sprite?"

My heart leaped as my mate's voice flitted through my mind, though it was frantic and strained with worry.

"Ruslan, please, I need you."

"I'll be right there."

I didn't even have time to take a breath before Ruslan and Liliana appeared in the doorway, and moments later my mate crushed me to him, a sob wracking his chest. "Sprite, sprite, sprite," he repeated through his relief, stroking my hair as he soothed both himself and me. The power of his emotion traveled down our bond, and tears streaked down my face as I shared his feelings. "I thought I'd lost you forever. My soul has been empty since that day. Oh, fuck, I don't even know what to say other than I am so fucking in love with you, Izidora, and I will never, ever let anything happen to you again."

Lifting my arms, I wrapped myself around him as much as I could, needing him with the same intensity as he needed me. The moment I woke and feared he had died played over in my mind, and I dug my nails into him as if I could bring him even closer so we were fused from head to toe, never to be separated again. Tears tracked down my face as every ounce of anguish on both ends of our bond flooded it, and it wasn't until the forcefulness of this eased that I dared to extricate myself from his hold. I needed to breathe and dry my nose and eyes so I could gaze upon Ruslan's handsome face, the one that would always be my true home.

His smoky eyes swirled with so much devotion, I nearly drowned in it. Beneath them, dark circles told me just how much he had worried, though the rest of him was carefully groomed as he had always been. His dark hair was slicked back, and matching stubbled coated his strong jaw. This close, the faint scar across his temple was visible, as well as the tattoos that climbed up his neck.

I touched his face, brushing my fingers across the soft hairs and then my thumb across his cheekbone. He captured my hand with his, turning into it to kiss my palm. "Sprite," he croaked, and it was as if the whole world fell away, and all we could see was each other. A hand captured the back of my head, pulling it forward so he could plant a kiss on my forehead. I closed my eyes and savored the feeling of fire racing to where his lips touched me.

Without missing a beat, he chucked off his boots and carefully removed the pillows propping me up before replacing them with his hard body, allowing me to lean against his chest as he enveloped me in his embrace.

Liliana and Zuriel hovered near the bed, the latter holding the untouched red drink, and I shot them both a watery smile before turning serious. "Can someone please tell me what's going on? How long was I asleep?"

Ruslan rubbed the sides of my arms, soothing my turmoil. The breath he blew out was hot on the top of my head. "It's been a little over six months since Kazimir tried to kill you."

Six months.

Another chunk of my lifetime *wasted* by some male who thought he should have control over my life. My fists clenched around the sheets covering my legs, and another wave of hot tears spilled over my eyes.

"I'll fucking kill him," I swore, my body tingling with the depths of my rage.

He deserved it for what he did to me.

Without hesitation, I reached for the drink that Zuriel promised would make me strong, yanking it from his grasp and tipping it back. I gulped it before my mind and body reconnected, but when they did, I tasted the hint of metal cutting through the citrus drink.

Sensing my hesitation, Ruslan murmured, "Finish the whole thing."

I obeyed, though Liliana and Zuriel shared a knowing look. Once it was completely drained, I wiped my mouth with the back of my hand. "Someone tell me what was in that." It wasn't a question, but an order that carried the force of my fury.

"Demon blood," Ruslan answered immediately, and bile rose in my throat. "We've been giving it to you while you slept to maintain your strength. No one knew how long you would be out, and, well, I knew you wouldn't want to be as weak as you were when you left the cave when you woke up."

His consideration doused my anger like pouring water over a burning blaze.

"The Demons offered it up willingly for you after they heard what happened," Zuriel added, and Liliana nodded her confirmation.

It was then that I realized I hadn't addressed my best friend. "You stayed." My voice cracked in time with her stoic facade, and she pushed past Ruslan to embrace me. A soft chuckle vibrated against my backside as he witnessed our reunion.

"Of course I stayed. You're my best friend, and someone with a brain needed to take care of you. You can't trust these males to know anything about female care. I washed your hair and trimmed your nails, even painted them when I was bored." I glanced down at my hands to find a black varnish there.

"Thank you," I whispered, hugging her back even tighter.

When she pulled away, she swiped at her seafoam green eyes, clearing them of salty tears.

"You haven't been alone for a second these last six months," Ruslan told me, and I understood then the meaning of the extra chairs, pillows, and blankets. "Drazen has been here too."

"Where is he now?" I asked, wanting to see the half-Dragon as much as my cousin, best friend, and mate.

"Surveying our army. We're preparing our empire for an attack from the Night Realm," Ruslan explained.

"Empire?" My brows dipped together.

I felt him smile against my back. "The Északi Empire belongs to us. You, my mate, will be its empress. We united the Iron, Crystal, and Day realms."

The world swayed around me as I spun to face my mate in my excitement. Staring into those smoky grays that had captivated me since the moment I laid eyes on him, I saw the truth of his words, and a wide grin stretched across his lips. "Without bloodshed?"

"Without bloodshed," he confirmed, hands moving to either side of my face as he pulled me in for a deep, bruising kiss. I moaned into his mouth, my body coming alight under his touch – a touch I had been deprived of for half a year.

He broke our kiss, leaning his forehead against mine, and the ache down our bond eased with our reunion. "After the other monarchs heard what happened to you, it wasn't hard to convince them to band together. We'd already made it clear that the Iron Realm had enough power to overthrow them, and when I sweetened the deal with offers of access to those innovations they saw during Béke, they came willingly into the empire."

My stomach rumbled again, and before anyone opened their mouth to speak, Zuriel was trotting off, no doubt in search of more food.

"Do you want to try to get out of bed? The sooner we get you moving around, the better," Ruslan asked me.

"Surely I didn't sleep for six months because of a knife to the chest," I said by way of answer.

"No. Rares said you almost broke your spine. It took him a long time to heal it properly so you wouldn't be paralyzed."

The memory hit me like a punch to the gut, and I was suddenly transported to the moment I'd broken my bond with Kazimir. The explosion of magic that had knocked me backward. The snow scattering in a thousand directions. The boulder that knocked the air from my lungs and sent pain ricocheting through my body. Using every drop of magic in me to heal myself and try to save my mate. Closing in on burnout.

"Yes," I managed to say as a tremble wracked my frame.

I was in Ruslan's arms. I was safe.

Queen Immonen had been right – the moment I broke the bond with Kazimir, everything went dark. Her words were no mere metaphor; instead, they had been my reality since that fateful day.

Ruslan sensed the turmoil rising within me through our mating bond and pulled me to his chest, cradling me like I was the most precious gemstone in the world.

"First the cave, now this. How will you ever forgive me for not protecting you?" he murmured, rocking me.

"There is nothing to forgive. You were right there, and Kazimir managed to kidnap me from under your nose. All of this is his fault," I swore, lips pressing into a line as more memories returned to me – how my necklace had fallen off and how I'd gone to fetch it from beneath the stands where we'd watched the parade.

Had he been the cause of the broken chain?

Zuriel returned with a healthier selection of food – a rainbow of fruit, chicken, cured meats, cheese, and some bread – and my stomach growled with the ferocity of a cat at the sight. Liliana crawled onto the end of the bed after he arranged the tray, stealing a handful of fat grapes for herself. I patted a spot on the bed across from me, indicating Zuriel should join us in it. My cousin kicked off his shoes and scooted around Liliana, the four of us forming a haphazard circle around the food I perused with gusto.

"Eat the chicken," Ruslan encouraged, pinching the seasoned slice between his fingers and bringing it to my lips. I opened my mouth and allowed him to place the meat inside, savoring the herbs coating the skin.

"So what else has happened in the last six months?" I asked around my food, covering my mouth with my hand so I didn't send crumbs spilling into the blankets.

"Right before Liliana burst into my office, Katrina, the Mage I assigned to the Day Realm, appeared with news of the Day Realm's new princess," Ruslan said, reaching around me for a chunk of cheese.

Liliana squealed, clapping her hands excitedly. "I'm so happy for them. When will she be presented to the world? Are we invited?"

"In a few months, and yes we are invited. Which means," Ruslan rubbed my arms reassuringly, "we need to get you moving and strong again, sprite. I won't allow you to leave the Iron Realm until I know you can defend yourself again."

After drinking the Demon blood concoction and eating, I did feel better than when Zuriel had first propped me up against the pillows. The room did not spin, and my hands steadied, allowing me to lift grape after grape to my mouth with ease.

More than anything, I wanted to be strong again. The next time Kazimir tried some shit would be his last – I would make sure of it.

"Then get out of my way," I stated, with a fierceness beginning to blossom in my chest. Ruslan scooted back, unwrapping himself from around me and landing lightly on the floor beside the bed. Bracing my hands on the mattress, I pushed myself from underneath the tray, then swung my legs toward the side of the bed.

Ruslan held out his hands, offering me support in lowering myself to the floor. "Careful, sprite, you haven't walked on them in a while."

The loose pants I wore tumbled to my ankles as I slid from

the high bed, and my legs swayed beneath me when my bare feet hit the stone. Ruslan immediately grasped my shoulders to keep me upright, the worry in his gray eyes intensifying as I blinked rapidly. The world around me spun again, and I waited for the gray fuzziness to retreat before saying, "Hold my hands, please."

He grasped them firmly and then retreated so I had space to move. Liliana and Zuriel held their breath behind me, and I lifted one foot, wobbling momentarily, then set it on the floor. I managed ten paces before I had to stop, and a wide grin broke out across my mate's face. Liliana released a whooping cheer as I turned around, Ruslan hovering behind me in case I needed support. By the time I reached the bed again, my legs trembled from the effort, and I collapsed against it, sweat pouring from my temples. But I grinned like a maniac because I'd pushed through and done it.

Fuck these males who thought they could keep me down.

I was Izidora Valynor, future empress of Északi, a survivor, and an insidious bloom.

They would not see how sharp and deadly my thorns were until I was slicing them to ribbons with my killing blows.

4

DRAZEN

The sound of metal boots striking the packed earth rang in my ears long after the Iron Realm's army finished marching for the day. Gem-encrusted pommels glinted in the sunlight, and the swish of the delicate, light chainmail covering the chests of the winged warriors filled the air overhead as I made my way to the war tent on the outskirts of the army's camp. In the distance, Ryza Citadel's black spires pierced the sky in defiance of the Goddess for daring to give the Iron Realm less power. A wry grin tugged at the corners of my mouth as I surveyed the legion of Félvér – those of us born in the Iron Realm with mixed blood – off to one side. From the ones with wings who could take to the sky to the ones who could shift into another form and everyone in between, we were powerful, unstoppable, and ready to take our place in this world.

Artur, my second-in-command, ducked through the opening followed by a handful of the emperor's personal guard and the two Félvér High Lords, Anton and Slavian, who had all been selected for major positions in the army. Kriath, who shifted into an Eagle, would lead the winged Félvér, while Savich, who shifted into a Bear, would lead the grounded

Félvér. Artur and I could monitor from high above with our massive Dragon wings, though neither of us possessed the ability to fully shift into a Dragon – not yet anyway. Anton and Slavian would manage smaller, specialized units filled with Wolves and Demon Félvér who worked shadow magic, respectively.

I'd poured over all the texts I could find on war during many of my shifts watching Izidora slumber, studying every scrap of information found in Ruslan's library and implementing the strategies of world-famous generals of the past. I was immensely pleased with the structure borne of those hours of study.

Ruslan had been pissed enough at Kazimir that he allowed Rares to begin experimenting – on willing participants – to push for a full Dragon shift, among other things, because bringing the massive beasts forth from within could turn the tide of the war. Not that we needed it. The Night Realm was as good as done with the pent-up rage Ruslan carried, along with our secret weapons – the tunnels, the full numbers of the Félvér, and other shit Rares had concocted. Rares was a bastard, but his twisted ideas would serve us well in destroying the Night Realm.

Even some of the Telivér – the full-blooded races from other continents – that remained in the Iron Realm volunteered to assist in the army. Konsteon, a Centaur Shifter, volunteered for the cavalry, and the Demons all wanted to fight in the infantry.

"Artur, what news do you have?" I asked, stopping him as he passed.

"General," they all saluted in unison before Artur addressed me.

"Emperor Ruslan has sent word to gather a small force to be deployed to the Day Realm. Queen Viktoria has given birth and they are expected to be in attendance for the little princess's presentation to the world. He would prefer that the force is already present and settled when they arrive."

I raised an eyebrow. "Is the emperor seriously going to leave his unconscious mate to travel to the Day Realm?"

"You haven't heard?" Artur's dark brow furrowed.

"Heard what?" I challenged.

"She's awake."

"For fuck's sake, why didn't you lead with that?" I cursed, taking a quick survey of the army around me. Artur could command them for the remainder of the day – after all, I'd had my share of days sitting by Izidora's bedside these past six months. Then I kicked myself for being so far out of pocket that my second-in-command heard the news before I did. "Why did no one fetch me immediately?"

"He just sent word a few moments ago," Artur reassured me.

"Handle everything for the rest of the day." Without waiting for a response, I shot into the sky, my lapis lazuli colored wings casting a blue shadow through their membranes as I banked toward Roc Palace. The sun dipped below the peaks of the Agrenak Mountains that ringed the Iron Realm by the time I landed on the roof of the palace built into the side of the mountain. I banged on the hatch for someone to let me in. When no one appeared for a few moments, I tried the handle, finding it unlocked. Banishing my wings, I dropped onto the landing below, shutting and latching it behind me. Shaking my head at someone's forgetfulness, I jogged down the stairs and into the living area of the suite that had nearly become my second home.

"Drazen!" Izidora's bright voice greeted me as I hit the stone floor, and across the room, she sat in front of a roaring fire, Liliana, Zuriel, and Ruslan all hovering nearby.

Racing across the room, I skidded to a stop in front of her, taking her small hands in mine and sighing with relief. It felt as if a weight had been removed from my chest seeing her grin up at me. The memory of that knife impaling her, then blood draining from her limp body as I sat helplessly, had plagued my nightmares for months. Worries that she'd never wake had creeped in despite my best efforts to maintain a positive attitude about the whole situation.

"It's good to hear your voice," I said, checking her over for any injury. Not that she would have any under our watchful eyes. Whoever sat with her during the day ensured she was taken care of, and I'd tried to keep up her muscles by moving her through various positions with Liliana's help a few times a week.

I looked at the Night Fae female I'd grown more than close with in her time in the Iron Realm, her seafoam green eyes shining as if she couldn't believe it was finally happening.

"We have to get you back into training as soon as possible," I told her, earning a laugh.

"I can't tell you how many times I've already heard that and it's only been a few hours." She tucked a lock of chestnut hair behind her ear with a playful glance in her mate's direction.

"Well, it's true. We'll go back to our normal routine. Strength with Ruslan in the morning, sparring after lunch, and magic with Zuriel in the evening."

She exhaled, long and slow. "You have no idea how much I want everything to be normal again. I'll do whatever it takes."

I quickly checked in with Ruslan, who nodded in confirmation of what I suspected. "I'll make sure Rares is mixing his Demon blood drinks more frequently. Xorrek and Gozzak won't mind offering more blood."

She nodded, and finally I dropped her hands and settled my attention on Ruslan. "I hear we're also going to the Day Realm?"

"With Izidora awake now, I want to go with protection. Who knows what kind of shit the Night Realm will pull. I have no doubt they'll find out and show up," Ruslan growled, clenching the back of the couch so hard that his knuckles turned white.

"Do you plan on moving us or will we ride the whole way?" I clarified.

He cracked his neck, vertebrae by vertebrae. "Half and half. I don't want to exhaust my magic in case we need it, but I want more time with her here." The look he offered Izidora could have melted even the most dug-in glaciers in the Agrenak Mountains.

"Noted. In the meantime, we'll get Izidora strong again." Rising to my feet, I surveyed my little family, the people I would gladly give my life for – Liliana included. Winking at her, I asked the group, "Who wants to celebrate?"

5

☾

KAZIMIR

Taya whined the entire time I packed my bags to leave for Zheka, the capital of the Day Realm, where the little princess was to be presented to the world in two months' time. The worn leather saddlebags I'd used for years groaned as I stuffed clothes into them, followed by the jewelry I'd claimed as my own from the Royal Treasury. Impressions were important, after all. And Taya was not giving me a good one as she begged once again.

"Why won't you make me your queen? I don't care that you want to fuck the others. We have so much fun as a group," she purred, running a sharp nail along my arm.

"I don't have time for this conversation right now," I grumbled in response, buckling the strap to secure the opening of one of the bags.

"If you made me your queen, you'd be able to take me along to events like these," she continued, ignoring the warning in my tone.

I was on her in an instant, pinning her beneath my weight while she sank into my bed. My hand formed a ring around her neck, and her golden eyes flashed with desire. "First, carry my child, and I'll consider it."

She spread her legs wide, wrapping them around my hips and pulling me in closer. "Come inside me again before you go, then."

My cock was harder than my sword as she whispered those words through the constriction on her throat. Angrily, I used my free hand to unbutton my pants and free my cock, only lifting my weight long enough to flip up her dress and insert myself inside her. She wore nothing beneath the thin dress, and I growled my approval as her pussy soaked my cock.

The thrusts I delivered were so brutal that they threw her backward on the bed, and I had to chase her to it to keep fucking her. "You want my seed?"

"Yes," she whimpered when I released her neck.

In my mind, aquamarine eyes replaced gold, and the red ribbons that fanned around her head darkened to a deep chestnut. Her breasts bounced in the thin straps that held them up, and I leaned my head down to bite the pebbles peeking through them. She cried out, and I slapped her before capturing her chin in my hands.

"Who do you belong to?" My voice dropped to a sinister level.

"You," she panted, her walls beginning to flutter around my cock. "Harder."

I obliged her plea, forcing her mouth open and my fingers inside it while I speared into her, seating myself to the hilt and circling my hips. She gagged as I forced my hand deeper, but she did not ask me to stop. Instead, she pushed her hips into mine to deepen our connection.

"Good girl," I praised, removing my fingers from her throat and allowing her to breathe again. "Your breath is mine. Your body is mine. I own you."

She nodded, her eyes blown out with lust. I slapped her again. "Say it."

"You own me," she repeated back, giving me the words I needed to hear to come.

My balls tightened, cock thickening inside her. Her moans became erratic as we chased our releases, and with a roar, I found mine, filling her with ropes of hot seed.

The pulsating sensation sent her over the edge, and she cried my name. "Kazimir!"

Her pussy milked every last drop from me, and it wasn't until I was certain every bit of me was so deep inside it wouldn't come out that I pulled away. "Stay there." I growled the warning, tucking away my cock before continuing to pack. She obediently remained, tracing lazy circles over her pebbled nipples and down to her bare stomach as she watched me.

"How long will you be gone?" she asked after silence reigned for too many minutes.

"A few months," I said, gritting my teeth around the words. It wasn't necessarily the truth, but no one here knew of my plans to earn us some fucking respect on this continent again.

She sighed, a lazy, disappointed sound that had me narrowing my eyes on her. "I'll miss you."

I didn't deign to respond as the last of my things were packed away, and I hefted the bag over my shoulder. We'd have to travel light since we'd be cutting it close with our arrival anyway. Taya made to rise from my bed when I snapped, "I said don't move. I want you pregnant by the time I return."

She whined, her wolfish side emerging momentarily, but remained in place. Raking a hand over my face, I crossed to her side and planted a kiss on her forehead before brushing her red hair back. "I'll see you when I get back."

Those golden eyes shone as she nodded, and I almost felt bad about leaving her.

Almost.

Before she could say anything else, I slipped from my room and trekked through the halls of Este Castle – my Goddess damned castle – toward the stables where the Nighthounds waited for me. What was left of them anyway.

"It's all yoursssss..." the three-stranded voice whispered in my head.

The Fates had been speaking to me more and more frequently since I had left the Iron Realm, coaxing me along the path to glory and victory. I was their vessel, chosen to carry out their wishes, and in return, I'd have everything I wanted.

"Yessss..." the voice hissed again.

But as I turned down the hall outside the massive ballroom, I was struck with a wave of grief. My walk ground to a halt, and I gritted my teeth as I paused at the spot where Kriztof, Krigin, Zekari, and my father's lifeless bodies had lain. The Fates couldn't return them to the land of the living, so I'd seek vengeance against the Iron Realm in their names instead.

As with every time the thought of my fallen brethren entered my mind, I wanted a drink. Or a fuck. Preferably both at the same time.

The waning summer sun caressed my face as I emerged from my castle, and I was reminded of a day, very much like this one, a year prior when my father, Viktor, Endre, and myself had set out toward the Agrenak Mountains with hope in our hearts to recover the lost princess. Vadim, Kriztof, and the twins met us along the way with the very last piece of information we needed to find her.

And then? She fucking chose Ruslan over me.

I searched for her. I saved her. I fixed her. She had been mine long before I laid eyes on her. That fucking bitch would rue the day she'd broken our bond.

Viktor snapped me out of my ruminating thoughts, handing

me Fek's reins. The black stallion tossed his mane, nearly as restless as I felt being stuck in Vaenor for months on end. "Where are the others?" I asked, scanning the bustling stables for Endre and Vadim.

"They're speaking with Tibor about constructing some new housing outside Vaenor's walls, among the trees so our army has a dedicated place to stay," he replied. "They'll join us in a moment."

"Fucking Fates, we need to get going," I spat out, checking the angle of the sun to gauge the time.

Viktor's sage eyes swept over me, taking in my rumpled attire. "Have fun saying goodbye to Taya?"

A wolfish grin spread across my lips. "You could say that."

The courtyard in front of Este Castle buzzed with activity, and my skin itched with the need to be on our way. Endre and Vadim appeared moments later, but only Endre led a horse. The council would rule in my stead while we were gone, and as usual, the High Lords had given their sons permission to represent their interests while we met with the other realms.

"Where is your horse, Vadim?" I frowned.

"I need to stay behind and manage the army. The three of you will travel faster without me," he replied, rubbing a hand against his scraggly beard.

I scanned the three of them, all wearing identical hardened expressions. With the looming threat of the Iron Realm marching on us, everyone's stress was at an all-time high. Not that anyone but us knew *exactly* why they would respond with such ferocity. Since our return, I'd had to do a damn good job of fanning the flames of fear and snuffing out whispered questions as to why we should be afraid. Not that anyone really questioned me anymore. I'd made a show of strength from the moment I returned as their rightful king.

That included creating this army. Vadim staying behind to oversee the development of our fighters wasn't the worst idea.

"Fine. Let's get going," I said, stomping my foot into the stirrup and swinging my leg over my stallion's back. My friends joined me in their saddles, and I tapped Fek's sides with my heels to move him along, steering him in the direction of the open gate. The Night Fae stopped in their tracks as we passed, some wide-eyed in awe of their king. I waved to them, casually adjusting the Night Crown so it glinted in the summer sun.

The streets of Vaenor were overcrowded, and in every direction warriors clad in leather armor dipped in and out of taverns and shops. But the Night Fae parted for their king, and we had a clear path through with my subjects bowing to me along the main thoroughfare out of town.

This all too familiar ride seemed to bring with it more and more pain, and I gritted my teeth until we finally crossed the bridge leading out of Vaenor and into the woods beyond. My two closest friends and I wasted no time bringing our horses to a gallop and speeding off into the woods in the direction of the Crystal Realm, and beyond, the Day Realm, where a new little princess would soon be introduced to the world.

And my plans would begin to unfold.

6

IZIDORA

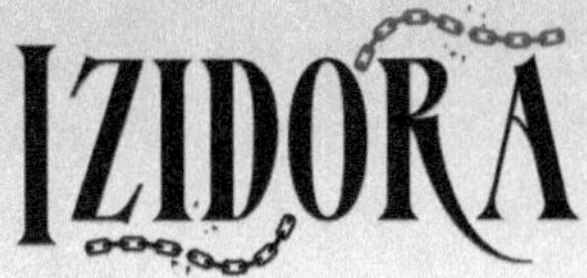

A flicker of flame from dying embers held my attention as I rested on my side, Ruslan curled around me. In the dead of night, I remained awake, long after Ruslan had finally drifted off to the land of dreams. Yet the thought of closing my eyes and losing myself to the endless void seized my stomach, and I refused to succumb to the desire for sleep. Too long, I had waded through the endless dark. In Ruslan's arms, I was safe. The slow rise and fall of his breath brushed steadily against my spine as my thoughts swirled and spiraled.

Because in the quiet, my mind *raged*.

With no distractions, no one watching me, I had only myself and the memories that continued to haunt me to contend with. So I stared into the reddened wood cocooned by soot-stained stone, reliving the horror of the final moments of my memory prior to my long slumber. I wanted every drop of wrath imbued in my bones so that when the time came, I could draw on my magic and slaughter Kazimir without a second thought.

Because, upon tapping into the white flame and moonlight-wrapped crystal in my chest again, I discovered the light had vanished.

In its place, darkness reigned.

I swallowed a bitter laugh. Queen Immonen had been right – everything did go dark after I broke my bond with Kazimir. Dark, for the comatose state I slept in; dark, for the emotions in my source of magic; dark, for my bloodthirsty thoughts.

Absently, I stroked Ruslan's arm with a lazy, light touch that contrasted the heaviness and force of my thoughts. What would my mate think if he knew that there was no light left in me?

As the first rays of dawn snuck beneath the heavy curtains blocking the wall-sized windows in front of me, Ruslan stirred. His arms twitched around me, and I finally tore my gaze from the fire to my mate. He blinked slowly, his dark lashes fanning against his skin before those smoky grays sucked me into their depths, unveiling the emotions of his soul. I didn't need to be an empath to feel the profoundness of his devotion. With a single look, he made me feel as if I were the very sun shining beneath the curtains, the air he needed to breathe, and the water he needed to drink.

He would love me no matter what.

"Morning, sprite," he murmured, that raspy voice of his sending tingles across my skin. The hand resting on my hip began kneading the muscle there, and I groaned under his touch.

"Morning, mate," I replied once the movements stopped. I nudged him in a signal to continue, and he obliged, moving his ministrations up my back until his large hand cupped the back of my head.

"I love hearing you say that. I missed the sound of your voice so much," he whispered, pulling my face to his and sucking my bottom lip into his mouth. "I missed kissing your perfect lips. I missed you being flush against my body like this." He hooked his leg over mine and pulled me closer to emphasize his point.

His hardness dug into my stomach, and I closed my eyes, appreciating the feel of his hot skin against mine, the cedarwood scent that filled my nostrils, and how safe I felt beside his bulk.

My eyes popped open as he moved me to my back, his muscles rippling as he caged me beneath him. My fingers ghosted over his shoulders, then down his torso and over his cut abs until I reached the V that led me to his morning erection. The moan that escaped him was primal and filled with longing when I wrapped my hand around him, savoring the velvety feel of his skin. "It must have been so hard for you to watch the time pass. I had no idea. I only wandered endlessly in the darkness. There was no time – no anything."

"I told you once that I would die without you, Izidora. That is more true than ever. Should you leave this earth, I will follow you moments later. There is no me without you." The ferocity in his tone sent goosebumps skittering across my skin, and I shivered as the force of his feelings traveled through our bond.

I opened my mouth to speak, but he shook his head. His eyes swirled with so much emotion, but deeper than the rest was a profound sorrow. "I am so sorry I didn't protect you, sprite. That I let you wander off on your own. I should have gone with you. I should have done *anything* other than what I did. It is because of me that he hurt you."

"It's not your fault. Kazimir made his choices, and you had no way of knowing."

"Why did you throw that shield in front of me instead of yourself?" Ruslan asked, searching my eyes for the answer. The thought must have plagued him for some time given how desperately he assessed me.

My throat worked as I fought against the rising tide of emotion. "I thought he was going to throw the dagger at you. In the heartbeat of time between Kazimir throwing that knife and creating that shield, I realized that I would die without you too and that I'd never told you that. I *should* have told you that. It was my final thought before everything went dark."

Ruslan crushed me against his chest, enveloping me in his warmth and cedarwood scent. "I know. I've always known, even if you didn't say it, Izidora. That's why I tried so hard for you while you were sleeping. I wanted to be worthy of you when you awoke."

Tears welled in my eyes, and I cupped his cheek, scratching at the hair that coated his strong jaw. "You are so worthy of me, Ruslan. You are so worthy of love."

His throat worked, and then he exhaled, his whole body seeming to relax with my words. "I still should have done more, and I swear to you I won't let that happen again. You'll never leave my sight."

I shook my head. "You have always empowered me, given me the space and freedom to become strong on my own. Coddling me *now* is not what I want. You would burn the world down for me, slaughter anyone who dared lay a hand on me. Don't force me behind a wall out of your own guilt. Let me be free."

His head dropped, resting in the center of my bare chest. Ruslan trembled as he sucked in a few shaky breaths. "Reconciling the two is difficult sometimes," he admitted quietly. "Especially as I watched over you all those months. How am I supposed to give you both protection and freedom?"

"By doing what you've always done – training me. Pushing me past my limits so they grow. Supporting me on the days my emotions are overwhelming. Being by my side when I need you. Educating me and ensuring I am not reliant on you for everything." My voice grew stronger as I listed all the ways Ruslan had helped me. "I love you, Ruslan. The reason I returned from the dark is because I knew that all the pain that awaited me here would be worth it, so long as I had you."

He lifted his head, showing me the redness rimming his eyes. "I am so glad you returned to me. I can't tell you how many times I debated moving myself to Este Castle to slit Kazimir's throat while he slept. How many times I've bloodied my knuckles trying to ease the ache of your absence. How many bottles I emptied alone to numb the pain. All this time, I tried to hold myself together, to be the male you deserved when you finally woke. I never doubted that you would. I knew you just needed time to heal."

I ran my fingers from his jaw to his hair and smoothed back the long strands. "I'm so sorry you suffered for so long."

"And I am sorry you are still suffering," he whispered.

"I still have more healing to do, I think," I said. Twin tears tracked down the sides of my face and plopped against the soft sheets.

"Whatever you need, I am here," he swore.

Swallowing down the lump in my throat, I nodded. I was just so fucking happy to be with my mate again. We'd find a way forward, together, that soothed our traumas.

Bending his head to me, he skimmed his nose along my neck until he reached the sensitive underside of my ear. "Marry me. Tomorrow."

I threaded my fingers into the hair at the nape of his neck and scratched his scalp. "Not now. Not when I can barely stand on my own. When I marry you, I want it to be the biggest celebration the Iron Realm has ever seen. I want everyone in attendance to see how strong I am. How powerful we are together."

And not when I was still so lost in the dark, with vengeance in my veins. Not when my thoughts were consumed with images of my twin blades flaying my enemies.

He shot back, his eyes flaming with black fire, and I smiled sweetly up at him. My heart raced when he braced himself with one hand and brought the other to rest on my neck, his thumb running over my bottom lip. "Maybe I should drag you before the High Priestess today and we can celebrate later."

"Is that a challenge?" I taunted, my low belly heating as his head dipped closer to mine.

"There's my sprite," he growled, capturing my mouth and forcing his tongue past the seam of my lips. It explored carefully for a few moments, tasting me, teasing me as it twined with mine. But when I arched my back into him, scratching the nape of his neck, he lost all semblance of control. His movements became wild, frantic, as he touched me everywhere but my heating center and my hardening nipples.

The way his tongue moved against mine, like this was our last kiss and he wanted it to last lifetimes, had me melting even further into him, desperate for what we'd both been missing for the past six months.

When he broke away from me, chest heaving and cock dripping onto my stomach, it felt as if my heart had been stabbed again. "Don't stop," I begged, tears springing to my eyes.

"I don't want to hurt you," he groaned, feeling the same pain as me.

"When have you ever treated me as fragile? Don't start now."

The growl that rumbled in his chest vibrated against my own, stirring a longing deep inside me. "You are not fragile – never have been. You are a fucking diamond, forged in the depths of hell and pulled from the earth ready to shine. But I don't mistake that shine for weakness. That shine is a distraction from what really lies beneath your pretty exterior – a will of fucking iron and a dark side that wants to be let out to play. And, oh, sprite, how we'll play."

At his words, tears pricked my eyes, spilling over the sides and tracing a path to the rumpled sheets beneath me. "I am an insidious bloom," I murmured, repeating my version of the words Kazimir had said to me. He'd called me deadly, but I was insidious, and I'd proven that with the way Ruslan and I had worked his alliance right out from under him. The war we'd wage against him would be no different. I'd trap him in my orbit, slowly but surely tugging him down the path I wanted, and at the end, it would be my sword that sliced through him, ending his pathetic life.

"That's right. Now show me those thorns, sprite. I want to feel your pain," he ground out as he ground into me.

My nails scratched a bloody trail into his back, the metallic scent filling the air around us as he threw his head back and moaned. "Spread those pretty legs for me."

I obliged, my core already dripping as my body called out to his. Aligning himself with my entrance, he pushed in slowly, hissing through his teeth. "You're so tight. Gonna have to stretch you back out."

I gasped as he sank deeper, feeling so deliciously full. I never wanted to be without him again. When he seated himself fully, white and black sparks danced around us, our magic flaring to life at our deep connection.

"Oh!" I gasped, looking around us as the embers danced and played in the half-darkness. Ruslan stilled his movements to admire them with me, grinning wildly as his black sparks chased my white ones.

It was still white on the outside.

"Even our magic missed each other," he murmured, leaning down to kiss me. He circled his hips, earning a groan of pleasure from me.

"I didn't know our magic could do that," I breathed around his lips.

"Mate magic has a will of its own," he said, grinding in so deep more stars sparked to life overhead. My eyes rolled back as the sensation overwhelmed me, and I gasped for breath once he started moving faster. My walls tightened around him, already so close to coming with his thickness sliding through me. Wetness coated my thighs as my body melted for him, and my nails dug deeper into his back, grasping for purchase as he pounded into me.

The sounds that slipped from my lips were filled with pleasure. "Ruslan, I need more."

"More what?" he asked, pausing so his smoky gray eyes swirled above me, pupils dark with lust.

A noise of protest caught in my throat at his stillness. "More pain. More pleasure."

Without hesitation, he plucked a hardened nipple between his thumb and forefinger, pinching it harshly and causing me to cry out. "Yes!"

He repeated the motion, resuming grinding his hips against mine, and I pushed back into him, wanting him deeper. "Play with yourself, sprite. I want to feel your pussy clenching around me as you scream my name."

Obliging him, I dipped a hand between us, finding that sensitive bundle of nerves and circling my fingers over it. My hips bucked at the added sensation, and Ruslan grounded me with another tweak of my nipple. A tingle spread from the top of my head to the tips of my toes, those sparks flying around us increasing their fervor.

"That's it, come for me," Ruslan groaned, his thrusts becoming erratic as he chased his release.

With a cry, my whole body spasmed, my pussy clenching around his cock as my back arched off the mattress, and I clung to him like he was the only thing saving me from falling into the abyss. "Ruslan, oh fuck–"

With a grunt, he pulled out of my center, leaving me aching and empty, then spilled his cum onto my stomach, panting heavily as his cock twitched and finally stilled. He reached over the side of the bed and found a discarded towel, using it to clean me off before tossing it away again.

"I'll make sure you get a contraceptive tea this morning," he finally managed to say, sweat dripping between both of us. Despite that, he pulled me into him as he laid on his side, cradling me with a tenderness I'd come to expect from the male who had always been known as a ruthless prince. Only I got to see this side of him, and I preened under the knowledge that he reserved this only for me.

Our hearts beat in sync as we laid there, spent from making love for the first time in far too long. "So, about the wedding..."

"Yes?" He perked up immediately behind me.

"I want to be strong enough to walk on my own in front of our people. I want them to see me as powerful, not to pity me." The conviction was strong in my voice, leaving no room for argument.

Thankfully, Ruslan didn't try to sway me. "You will show them how powerful you are. Nothing has ever stopped you or broken you before, and this is no exception."

A wave of sadness washed over me, the vague memories of wandering in the dark rising on the tide of it. "Ruslan... when I was... sleeping, I wanted to give up. I wondered what the point of returning was, if there was only going to be pain for me. There's just been so much of it..." Tears burned my eyes, blurring the form of my mate.

Sucking in a shuddering breath, I asked, "What did I do to deserve this pain?"

A rough palm cupped my cheek, thumb swiping away the salty tears that overflowed as I began crying uncontrollably. Voicing that one question broke me in a way I never knew possible. The whips that had rained upon my back in the cave did not compare to the pain of thinking that somewhere along the way I had done something that brought this pain upon myself – pain that seemed as endless as the night sky. The kind of pain that dragged me to the dark depths of despair where the only way out was death.

The raspiness to Ruslan's voice thickened as I shattered to pieces, clinging to him like the lifeline that he was. "Sprite, you have done *nothing* to deserve this pain. The Goddess and the Fates wove this path for you – for us – long before either of us were born. It is them you should be blaming, not yourself. We are only pawns in some fucked up game they are playing, and the prophecy is proof of that."

I lifted my soaked face from his bare chest, and he brushed the chestnut locks away from my face, showing me the strength of his conviction. The words from the prophecy floated to the front of my mind, and I let them fall in time with my tears.

> *"The ones that are part of all will be born under a full moon*
> *Her white light will fill the land*
> *But her mates' darkness will rise*
> *Kings will fall*
> *Rivers will run with blood*
> *There is a choice*
> *Follow the light*
> *Descend into the dark*
> *The harrowing pass decides it all"*

I'd made my choice – Ruslan. The mark between my shoulder blades demonstrated that for those who could not feel this incredible bond that threaded our fates, our souls, together.

But there was one more choice the prophecy mentioned – light and dark. And with what I'd discovered when I woke, I wondered if that was the heart of the matter. "Ruslan, there's one more thing."

The skin across his face tensed as if he sensed my trepidation. "Yes?"

Swallowing, I admitted the truth. "My magic... inside, it's no longer white."

"What do you mean?" he asked, brows dipping slightly.

"Before Kazimir tried to kill me, when I called on a positive emotion, the crystal in my magic well turned white. The crystal itself had been clear before. Now, only dark fills the black crystal there," I whispered, tugging my bottom lip between my teeth.

He thumbed it away. "Sprite, are you worried I will think differently of you because of that?"

I nodded, nose and eyes pricking. Hurriedly, I swiped at them both.

A growl rumbled from his chest, pressing into mine. "There is *nothing* that could make me love you less, Izidora." The toned muscles of his arms flexed around me, as if he could show me through his physical strength alone that he'd never stop. "In fact, watching you embrace that darkness as we slaughtered the males who abused you was one of the memories I slipped into whenever I laid here with you, waiting for you to wake. The sheer ferocity you displayed that night, the way you reclaimed your power slice by slice... I was in awe of you. Still am. So don't fear the darkness, sprite. Embrace it. Hone it. Use it as the weapon it can be for you. Claim its power as your own and don't let anyone tell you there is something wrong with that."

The hard set of his mouth as his gray eyes roamed mine told me he meant every word.

"Especially yourself. We'll face the darkness together, head on." His fingers tightened across my spine, his words falling from his mouth with renewed fervor. "We'll *become* it. Make the world *fear* us for it. Kazimir has *nothing* compared to our combined might."

The last of my tears dried as I felt the strength of Ruslan's conviction through our bond. The worry bled from his eyes, morphing into pride as I straightened, steeling myself with what I needed to do to make that happen. It was time for kings to fall and for us to make rivers run with blood.

"Let's go train."

7

—

☽

ENDRE

The fire popped and crackled as I allowed it to lull me into a meditative state. The flow of being was a welcome reprieve from the anxiety that had gripped me as we neared the border with the Crystal Realm. Kazimir, Viktor, and I had been riding hard in an attempt to reach the Day Realm in time for the little princess's announcement, and yet sleep did not call for me as the stars winked into existence overhead. Only the smell of smoke that filled my nostrils and the heat licking across my skin kept me company, my friends having dipped into their tents to rest. I didn't trust that this close to the border, we'd be safe from attack.

My hair fell into my eyes and I brushed it back, no doubt leaving a trail of dirt along my already sweat-soaked and stained skin. We were used to living like this on the road, bathing in the rivers and occasional lakes that popped up in the Night Realm, but the insanity of the last year had me yearning for a bed, bath, and roof over my head.

An owl hooted above me, startling me from my reverie, and I glanced around our small camp to see what disturbed it. Nothing moved in my line of vision, though the leaves on the trees around us ruffled with a light breeze. Grasping my wine-skin, I gulped down several mouthfuls, trying to still my beating heart and put myself to sleep.

Viktor snored off to my left, and I sighed, dropping back against my rolled up pack. The stars were brilliant through the canopy, enhanced by the lack of light from the moon. I tried counting them in a halfhearted attempt to distract myself from thoughts of Liliana. Every night when I closed my eyes, no matter where we were, there she was, her white smile flashing in my direction, her head tipping back in laughter, or her seafoam green eyes sparkling with mischief.

I understood how Kazimir had felt when Izidora was in the Iron Realm and we traversed a very similar path through the other realms to find her.

Was Liliana safe? Had she moved on from me?

The last letter I'd sent her was as much a warning as it was a plea. I had no idea if I'd see her in the Day Realm, but with every fiber of me, I hoped I would. Vadim worried for her too, though he'd never admit to it. And High Lord and High Lady Arzeni had nearly collapsed when we returned without her. If I could bring them news of her good health and happiness, it would ease their pain.

My mind ran circles until the first hint of day began banishing the stars one by one. The fire had died to embers, merely smoldering at my feet. I couldn't bring myself to move, to face the day we entered the Crystal Realm. But if I didn't wake Kazimir at first light, he'd be pissed about us losing time.

What could he possibly think would happen when we arrived?

Taking a lazy overhead stretch, I yawned wide, my jaw popping with the effort, then sat upright. Rubbing my eyes with the heels of my palms, I tried to ease the tiredness that lingered there. "Kazimir, Viktor, it's time to get going," I groaned, muscles and joints protesting as I pushed to my feet.

Muffled sounds drifted from their tents, and I fished out some dried meat from my bags to chew on while we packed camp. Viktor stumbled out first, looking as though he was still asleep, and from muscle memory alone broke down his tent and rolled it up to tie behind his saddle. Kazimir emerged looking fresh and rested, then strode around our encampment with ease.

Must be nice to feel so invincible that sleep came easy no matter where we were.

I paid him no further attention as I readied our mounts, throwing our heavy packs across their backs and buckling saddles around their bellies. Within a dozen minutes, we were astride our horses and angling them back toward the road that led to the Crystal Realm.

No one had spoken, and for that I was grateful. I wanted to hear any potential hoofbeats racing in our direction, and more than that, speaking would give away our location. A sidelong glance at Viktor revealed his lips pressed together and his shoulders tense beneath the fighting leathers he wore. The two of us were dressed for battle because, honestly, we could face one at any moment. Though Viktor disagreed in words, his choice of attire spoke volumes.

The sun drifted higher in the sky, and the trees began to thin, signaling our arrival into the Crystal Realm. We hugged the foothills of the Agrenak Mountains, and on this side of them, the glaciers shone from the top layer that melted and ran off the sides, filling the lakes with their icy, fresh water. Thousands of waterfalls flowed over cliffs, some merely a trickle, others mighty in their strength, but all breathtaking. Viewing them from this distance was incredible, and it looked like the mountains had been painted with them by the expert hand of a master artisan.

As we closed in on one particularly large waterfall, the

crashing water overtook my ears, and we did not hear or see the Crystal Realm's soldiers until we were nearly upon them.

"Stop where you are!" A tall male with dark blond hair called, standing in his stirrups to make himself known. The white horse pranced beneath him, but with the grace of the Crystal Fae, he hardly swayed.

Yanking on my reins, I slowed my horse, coming to a stop in line with Viktor and Kazimir. Both my friends stared straight ahead, and I returned my attention to the approaching party. "Who seeks passage through the Crystal Realm of the Északi Empire?"

Clearing his throat and pasting on a disarming smile, Kazimir shouted, "King Kazimir of the Night Realm, along with High Lords Endre Zadik and Viktor Adimik!"

The cavalry eyed us warily, but there was no denying we were Night Fae. Whether they believed we were noble was a different story. "Where are your papers?" the leader questioned.

"Papers?" Kazimir said with a light laugh. "I need no papers. I am the king of the Night Realm."

"All those seeking entry into the Crystal Realm are to have papers granting permission to enter. If you do not possess them, we cannot let you pass," he explained, a hand hovering near the sheath strapped to his saddle. Behind him, three mounted archers tightened their grip on their bows, drawing back the strings ever so slightly.

With a furious glance toward Viktor, I tried to convey my confusion and concern, but he ignored me. The distant look in his eye told me his mind was churning over a way out of our predicament.

"Why wasn't the Night Realm informed of this change? We do, after all, share a border." Kazimir's voice hardened, the deep timbre resonating with a hint of fury – one that usually did not bode well.

"Recent orders," the leader explained, hand twitching. "Now, if you'll please return to the Night Realm and come back when you have the proper paperwork."

Had Liliana revealed the contents of my note?

My stomach plummeted as Kazimir flicked his fingers, the imperceptible movement that signaled he was about to use his magic.

"Kaz–" I started, but was cut off when Viktor voiced his opinion.

"Vaenor is a month's ride from here, so if the change was 'recent,' as you say, we would not have had sufficient notice to obtain the new paperwork. If I remember correctly, the Crystal Realm has a grace period for all new laws enacted to give ample time for word to spread throughout the large kingdom. Surely we fall within that grace period."

The Crystal Fae's eyes narrowed on him. "You still can't prove who you are. How do I know you aren't another group of refugees?"

Refugees?

With a flourish, Kazimir produced the Night Crown from his bag and placed it on his brow. "Is *this* proof enough?" The emerald color in his eyes deepened to black, and I waited with bated breath to see if he would unleash his binding magic should the male challenge him again.

With a backward glance at his companions, the Crystal Fae grumbled and settled into his saddle. "Niilo, send a raven to Blire Palace immediately, notifying them of the king's entry into the Crystal Realm."

Kazimir made to move forward, and the archers lifted their bows in one smooth motion. "You haven't been dismissed," the leader said smoothly. Another soldier, Niilo I assumed, slid from his saddle and scribbled on a piece of parchment against his horse's hide. Then he opened a small cage hanging there, quickly securing the note to the leg of the bird inside, and threw the creature into the air.

The tension rolling off Kazimir was palpable, and I tried my best not to shift in my saddle as we waited for the Crystal Realm's warriors to settle and release us. Niilo lifted his hands to the sky, and the bird zoomed away on the artificial wind propelling it. Once it was out of sight, the soldier remounted his horse, nodding to his commander.

"Right, here's how it's going to go. That raven has sent word into the Day Realm of your entry and that we will be escorting you until we reach the border. We've requested another unit to replace our station. Don't try anything, or you won't like what happens when you reach the Day Realm." Without waiting for a response, he turned his horse and kicked him into a gallop.

The growl that rumbled from Kazimir's chest was animalistic, though he spurred his horse on in pursuit of our escort's leader. Viktor and I followed, the remaining Crystal Fae taking up position behind and around us as we raced around the foothills of the Agrenak Mountains.

I tightened my grip on my reins and glanced sidelong at Viktor. My oldest friend stared straight ahead, into Kazimir's back, and refused to look at me. With gritted teeth, I returned my attention forward. I didn't trust Kazimir not to unleash his binding magic on the Crystal Fae who would be escorting us, endangering Viktor and me. He cared for nothing and no one but himself these days, and maybe it was my lack of sleep, but I was running out of patience for it. Tired of walking on eggshells around him. Exhausted from biting my tongue.

I wanted my friend back, the one who'd lived at my house while Cazius was off searching for Izidora. The one who was strong, calm, brave. The one who'd earned my trust and loyalty in the years riding across the continent together.

Was he gone forever, or was there still a chance for him?

The question lingered, louder than the waterfalls and the hoofbeats in my mind, as we hugged the path through the Crystal Realm. Thank the Goddess it was a short one, otherwise, we might be fucked by the time we arrived at the Day Realm's border.

8

IZIDORA

Pain threaded through my teeth as I gritted them, forcing myself to take another step forward. The wood beams parallel with my forehead inched by as I fought with everything I had to just fucking reach the end of the training ring. Sweat soaked my hair, my clothes, my entire body as I managed to move my trembling muscles one last time before collapsing forward on hands and knees. My chest heaved from the force of my efforts, and cheers erupted around me, from the guards it seemed I'd sparred with only days before.

But it fucking wasn't days since I'd held a sword and won my weight class at Béke.

The darkened crystal flared alongside my rage. Tears mixed with sweat and dropped onto the dusty ground beneath me as I lamented the loss of the strength I once had. Digging my nails into the dirt, I allowed that grief to flow through me and bend to my will, then shoved myself upright, swaying slightly.

I was not done yet.

Drazen, Ruslan, and Zuriel watched me with bated breath, but I ignored them and pushed on, the edge of the ring only steps away. Liliana stood there with another metallic cocktail of

Demon blood, and the moment I reached her, I snatched it and downed the entire glass. A trail of red joined with my sweat and tears, and I was grateful that my back was to the rest of the onlookers, because I was certain I looked insane.

"You did it!" Liliana exclaimed, overjoyed for my weakness. But her bubbly face fell as more tears did from my eyes. "What's wrong?"

"I feel so helpless," I ground out, blinking at the sky as I tried to regain control of my emotions. Even the sunny blue day couldn't brighten my mood. It was my first summer out of the cave, and here I was, trying to jam together the pieces of me that wanted to shatter when I should have been laughing with my mate and enjoying the warm wind that gusted down from the mountains. I was weaker than I had been taking my first steps into the world beyond.

And here I thought I couldn't regress any further than that.

She laughed and smacked me on the shoulder, causing me to jerk my head forward and shoot her a confused expression. "Of course you're weak, you laid in bed for half a year. But you know what? You're a fighter, and before the week is up, you'll be ready for a sword again. We've got to show these dumb males who're really in charge here."

Her unabashed confidence pulled a grin from me, and I swiped my face with the bottom of my tunic. "You're right. They think they're so powerful, but we can bring them to their knees anytime," I quipped, some of the heaviness that clung to me like a winter cloak lifting.

"Exactly," she giggled, glancing over my shoulder at the pack of males hovering like mother hens.

Zuriel's melodic voice floated over the din of clashing swords and into my ear. "Well done, cousin. Ready for magic lessons now?"

"Ugh," I replied, making a face and earning a snicker from

Liliana. The three came into view as I faced them, stoking the white fire that wrapped itself protectively around the rest of my magic. At least the sun still made this new mixture of white and black undulate wildly in my chest. "Can I have something to eat first?" I groaned, my stomach making its wants known with a rumble loud enough to echo around the Agrenak Mountains.

"I'll have Cedomir bring some food to the suite. You can practice magic on the roof," Ruslan suggested. A hint of guilt trickled down our bond, and I knew, because there were no barriers between us anymore, that he blamed himself for what had happened to me. Hence, his eagerness to take care of me in any way possible.

Batting my lashes at him to take advantage of that fact, I asked, "Will you fly me up there?"

Liliana snorted beside me, covering her mouth and whispering, "Case in point."

Ruslan unfurled his black wings, the leathery membrane nearly translucent in the summer sun. His wingspan was enormous, nearly knocking Drazen and Zuriel back as he showed them off. The former rolled his eyes as Ruslan snatched my waist and tucked me into his body. "I won't marry you until you fly yourself up and down."

This had become our joke over the past week, new conditions to schedule our vows that had been so rudely interrupted by Kazimir trying to fucking kill me. It wasn't that I didn't want to be married to Ruslan – no, my hesitation came from the lack of space in my head for responsibilities as empress. The only thoughts I could entertain for any length of time were of revenge.

Of blood dripping down my blades.

Before I could tease out a retort, he leaped into the air, stealing my breath and a scream from my lips. The laugh that followed the sound was maniacal, and I banged weakly against his chest in mock defiance. Moments later, we hovered over the palace built into the side of the mountain, and my mate set me ever so gently on my feet. The wind from our friends' wings buffeted us as they landed in various positions around the smoothed rock roof. Liliana, Drazen, and Ruslan disappeared through the hatch a moment later.

Stepping to the balustrade, I took a moment to admire the breathtaking view.

The Iron Realm spread before me, the high peaks spearing into the sky like they had every right to be as angry as I was at the way my life had been unfolding. Even in the summer, the peaks still wore caps of snow, the whiteness of them nearly blinding as the midday sun reflected off of them. They were sentries to the valley below, nestling the capital of the Iron Realm in a protective embrace and preventing any unwanted intruders from penetrating the peace within. The sun was even stronger higher into the range, bringing with it a joy I had only felt since leaving the cave where I had been chained for most of my life. As the light kissed my skin, I tipped my head back, breathing deeply in the fresh mountain air, and the white flame that lived inside my chest flared to life, filling me with power and banishing the lingering frustration with my inability to do more than walk around.

At least my magic felt more powerful than ever, despite the darkened crystal.

The ethereal beauty had not weakened or dried up during my time wandering in the void. If anything, the well of magic was deeper, fueled by the rage of having more of my life stolen from me. It felt as if that white flame would consume everything inside me, then burst forth and engulf the world around me in a blaze so furious someone might *finally* see this pain that felt all-consuming.

Some day, and soon, they would face my wrath.

Zuriel stepped beside me, joining me in gazing across the realm that would soon be as much mine as Ruslan's. The white locks of his hair lifted in a pine-scented breeze as it dusted across the mountain at our backs.

"It is beautiful," he commented after a moment of silence.

"What is Keleti like?" I asked my cousin, thinking of his homeland across the ocean where he and my father, Ithuriel, had been captured along with some Demons.

"There are mountains like these that divide the continent in two. On one side, everything is lush and green, while on the other, it is a desert that stretches endlessly until it reaches the sea," he murmured, his icy blue eyes taking on a wistful absence from the world around us.

"Do you ever miss it?" I asked quietly. Curiosity and something that felt a lot like sorrow filled me at the thought of the continent where my mother and father had tried to flee for safety so the mated pair could be together, without the blades of the kings of Északi hanging over their heads.

Was it possible to long for something one had never known?

The Angel blinked rapidly, clearing his eyes and mind of wherever he'd wandered. "I do, sometimes. But my place is here, with you."

He offered no more commentary, and I sensed that he wanted to speak of it no further. My cousin had his secrets, and he would share them in due time, as always. Checking over my shoulder, I realized we were alone on the rooftop. I stepped away from the railing, squaring my shoulders over my shaky legs.

Pinning Zuriel in my fierce gaze, I loosed a long breath and pronounced, "I want to practice immobilizing my opponents."

The air inflating Zuriel's lungs stilled, along with the whispering wind, as if the world was watching, waiting, for what would happen next. For me to embrace the darkness.

For Zuriel to help me do it.

Ruslan had vowed to stand hand in hand in the dark with me so I wouldn't have to face it alone. He'd already spent enough time there that it was as familiar as his own name. Darkness, after all, had been my only friend in the cave. This was merely a different aspect of what inky blackness had to offer. A dark twist on my Goddess-gifted magic.

Was there really such a thing as light and dark? Or was everything merely a shade of gray, as Liliana had once said? Certainly, I could use my magic for good. For healing. For removing the pain, the burdens others carried like sacks of stones.

I could also use it to sow pain, discord, and strife.

It all came down to how I *chose* to use it. How I wanted to bend the magic to my will.

And in that moment, I was *choosing* to use it in an insidious way I'd sworn off before. Days ago, I'd decided I would never place limits on myself again, that *nothing* would hinder the full strength of my Goddess-gifted power.

Not me, not stupid principles, and certainly no male.

If I wanted the world to burn at my feet for what it did to me, I had to embrace every part of myself, utilize every scrap of magic and ingenuity I had, and plummet into an endless well of power. But that well would only deepen with repetition, with utilizing the magic in the sinister ways I wanted, over and over and over.

A thin line formed between Zuriel's white eyebrows. "Are you certain?"

An affirmative dip of my chin was all I offered in response. Steeling my spine, I called on the threads of magic in my chest and brought them just below the surface of my skin.

The air finally fled my cousin's lungs, and he nodded. "You will tell me when you tire. It will likely drain you faster than you realize, given how long it's been since you last accessed the talent."

He didn't have to add that my current weakened state wouldn't help matters either.

"I will," I promised, rooting my feet into the rock.

Using a leather strap, Zuriel tied back his white hair, though a few stray strands fell into his face as the wind whipped through the mountains once again. "Prevent me from walking," he commanded, his voice level and calm. Then, he lifted a booted foot and made to step toward the center of the roof.

Yanking on the threads of my hatred for Kazimir, I slammed it into the earth with enough force that his eyebrows shot up his head and the ground trembled beneath my feet. I pitched to the side, losing my hold on him immediately.

"Is everything okay?" Ruslan asked down our bond.

I winced, realizing I'd likely startled everyone in the suite below. *"Just dropped something."*

"Cedomir will have food ready shortly. Don't strain yourself too much," Ruslan murmured, his tone soothing and filled with tender care.

"Thank you," I sent back down the bond, then closed my mind to everything but Zuriel, who had righted himself again.

"That was quite forceful, Izidora," he commented, head tilting ever so slightly to the side as he studied me.

"Well, I have a lot of anger to pull from," I growled, flexing my fingers.

Without missing a beat, Zuriel began to move toward the center of the roof. "Again," he said, eyeing me closely. He made it three steps before I called my empath power forward again, sticking his boots to the stone, though with less force this time. He nodded his approval, and I dropped the magic.

Despite the cooling breeze kissing my face, sweat beaded my temples. Glancing over my shoulder, I found one of the tables set haphazardly a few paces away. Gritting my teeth, I walked to it, then leaned my rear against it for extra support.

"We can stop if you are tired," Zuriel offered, worry leaching into his eyes.

"No," I snapped, diving into my magic again. "My well won't deepen if I don't push my limits. I just need a little support standing."

His lips thinned as if he wanted to protest my declaration, but he must have thought better of trying to convince me otherwise. "Alright, stop me from flying away then."

Massive white feathered wings, so much like my own, sprung from his back. In two flaps, he was airborne, racing higher into the sky. The dark crystal flared to life as I imagined his feet slamming into the stone roof, blending the image with the tangled knot of emotions in my chest. In a heartbeat, he was plummeting, and I only barely managed to release my hold before he collided with the roof.

A laugh escaped me as he touched lightly to the ground, grinning. "I appreciate you not hauling me into the suite via a rock tunnel."

"It certainly would have startled the others." My lips curled into a smile. "Maybe we should do it anyway. I could go for a bit of fun." Everyone had been hovering so close since I woke, and I honestly wanted to do *anything* other than have Ruslan, Liliana, Drazen, and Zuriel staring at me, as they doubtlessly had the entire time they waited for me to wake.

Zuriel shook his head, a few more strands of white falling loose. "Perhaps another day, when you don't look like you're going to faint on your feet." He closed the distance between us, and I made to follow him. Only, the world swam when I pushed off the table, and gray spots danced in my vision. I didn't realize I was falling until Zuriel was hauling me upright again by my upper arm.

"I can make it," I protested, but another step told both of us that was a lie.

He chuckled, then looped his arm through mine and supported me the rest of the way to the hatch that led to the suite. As if he sensed my need for him, Ruslan was there, arms outstretched, to accept me from my cousin.

"I don't need–" I started to protest, but Ruslan cut me off.

"Yes, you do. At least for now."

He tucked me against his chest, and I rested my ear against the steady thrum of his heart as we spiraled down, down, down to the living space. The iron lid banged closed a moment after the thump of Zuriel's boots met the landing overhead. Liliana and Drazen were already splaying our feast across the dining table, and Ruslan settled us into two chairs on one end while they finished and Zuriel joined us.

Once my family was seated, we dug voraciously into our food, laughing, teasing, and even tossing bread at one another as insults were flung. For just a little while, I forgot all about the darkness, the rage, the thirst for blood, and simply let myself *be* with the people I loved the most.

9

RUSLAN

Rares handed me a sludgy drink, which I immediately sniffed with caution. "What the fuck is this?"

"This is how you will shift into a Dragon," he huffed, displeased with my lack of enthusiasm. Given our history and all the shit he had experimented on me as a child, I had every right to be wary – even if I'd requested that he mix me this very drink.

Drazen stood beside me, crinkling his nose after the disgusting scent hit his nostrils, too. "The other Dragon Félvér really drank this?"

Artur, Drazen's second in command, looked like he was going to be sick from the smell alone, and his throat worked as he held the drink at arm's length. All the Dragon Shifter Félvér in the Iron Realm had gathered in this valley far away from Radence, and the ones who had allowed Rares to test his potions on them nodded in affirmation, a few plugging their noses before they downed the liquid.

Izidora, Liliana, and Zuriel perched on an overhang nearby, watching the scene unfold from above. The valley was secluded enough that all the Félvér could shift and fly without being spotted by unwanted voyeurs, and hilly enough to give us a running start in our fully shifted forms. Taking off from two legs was easy, but four? Well, none of us had done it before.

"Cheers," I said, lifting the drink in Drazen's direction before following the lead of the other Dragons and plugging my nose. The liquid was thick as it coated my tongue, and despite holding my breath, the bitter taste still hit my senses, nearly making me gag as the concoction entered my throat. I managed to get it down, though for a moment I thought I might not *keep* it down. "Fuck, Rares, can we at least get a chaser?" I griped as the threat of gagging subsided.

"Shit, really," Drazen spluttered beside me, wiping his mouth with the back of his hand. "That was disgusting."

The old Mage rolled his eyes. "You wanted it to work, not to taste good."

"Why can't we have both?" Artur muttered, looking green and clutching his stomach.

"Hold that shit down," Drazen ordered, noticing the pallor of his second in command's skin.

Empty containers were collected and placed in a bag near the tethered horses while we waited for the potion to take effect. Rares had told us that it could be anywhere from half an hour to an hour, and that we'd start to itch uncontrollably when the time was right. We mingled about, some lounging in the grass, others tossing a ball back and forth while we waited for the inevitable. I winked at Izidora, sending her a wave of passion down our bond. She sent one right back, and I grinned like a maniac as I gazed up at my mate.

She was beginning to look like the female I'd first met. With the help of the Demon drinks, her muscle tone was reforming quickly, and her normally pale skin was tanned from time spent in the sun. Every day, she and Liliana lay on the roof and forbade us from flying up or popping through the hatch. Side by side, the two females were stunning with their sun-kissed skin.

The itch started between my shoulder blades, and I smirked as the potion began to take effect.

"Do you feel it?" Drazen asked, reading my expression.

"Fuck yeah," I replied, ripping my shirt over my head and tossing it aside. The bond heated as my mate perused my muscled torso covered in tattoos. Drazen's teeth flashed with the thrill of the power rushing through us, and he stripped moments later, his own change overtaking him faster than mine. Blue scales erupted across his skin, and a moment later he was running, trying to get clear of everyone surrounding us. Without taking my eyes off him, I shucked off my pants and raced down the hillside.

Drazen reached a low cliff just in time for his wings to unfurl, and in the blink of an eye, an enormous lapis lazuli dragon burst from his skin, flapping its massive wings and lifting him into the air. The roar he released echoed around the peaks, and I felt my own inner Dragon rising to meet his. My skin felt like someone was peeling it away with pumice stone, the desire to claw at it nearly unbearable. I focused on breathing as I raced toward the ledge, hearing several pairs of footsteps following in my wake. Plush grass gave way to rock, and I closed in on the edge. Releasing a roar of joy, the shift tore through me, and I was airborne, soaring among the peaks in a way I'd never been able to do before.

"You are breathtaking," Izidora said down our bond, her voice brimming with wonder and awe.

"Show me what you are seeing."

Izidora projected the image soaring in front of her eyes into my mind. Two massive Dragons flew through the sky, one blue, the other blacker than the night during a new moon. My Dragon form seemed to swallow the light around it, and my scales shone with a dark luster. Beside me, Drazen glittered like a gemstone, the light catching the iridescence of his blue scales. We roared together, releasing blue and black flame into the sky above us as we soared higher and higher. Beneath us, the Félvér shifted and leaped, joining us in the sky. Within a minute, a horde of Dragons flapped their wings wildly to catch up to their leaders.

"We're going to win." Izidora's pride and thrill were palpable down our bond.

"If what you're showing me is true, we absolutely will, sprite."

"Can I ride you?"

The snort that ripped through my nostrils contained a hint of smoke. *"Think you can hold on?"*

"I thought you said you would always be there to catch me if I fall?"

If my Dragon form could smile, that was what I would have been doing as her words soothed that part of me that felt responsible for everything that happened to her.

"Be prepared to jump on."

Her inner squeal was headier than any herb or whisky, and I snapped my wings shut, plummeting toward the earth in a dizzying spiral that left me wanting more of the thrill.

Who needed pain when this exhilaration existed?

Banking hard to my left, I floated on a draft toward where Izidora, Liliana, and Zuriel perched. My mate leaped to her feet, her white wings appearing at her back, and she stood, poised and ready for the leap as I passed by.

"He's going to let you ride him?" Liliana exclaimed, her mouth popping open, and I chuckled to myself at her jealousy. Maybe Drazen would get the hint once he saw Izidora on my back.

"Ready, sprite?"

"Ready."

Flaring my wings, I slowed my pace slightly, drifting as close as I could without clipping my much larger than normal wings against the rock. Just as I was about to pass, I tucked my wings close, and Izidora pushed off the ground with all her might, feathered wings flapping as she sailed through the air and landed atop my back with a heavy thud.

"Find something to hold on to."

She scrambled across my back, and with as much care as I could, I snapped my wings out, catching a drift and allowing her time to settle.

"All good now."

"I'm not going slow."

"You always say that."

"This time I mean it."

And truly, I did. There was nothing like being fully shifted into a Dragon, and I wanted to suck every bit of time out of this potion. Well, there was one thing that was better – my mate riding me. Our bond hummed excitedly as my wings beat faster, sending us climbing into the sky. A scream tore from her lips, and I smelled her fear and her arousal, the perfect cocktail for my nose.

Glancing below us, I saw dozens of other Dragons drifting lazily through the valley, learning their new forms and preparing for battle. It was unfortunate that we could not communicate with one another in this form, and I would have to put Rares and Drazen to work on a solution.

"This is incredible," Izidora said, shifting to one side to peer down with me.

"The second most incredible sight I've ever seen."

"What's the first?"

"You. On your hands and knees. Crawling toward me."

The scent of her arousal flared, and I knew she was thinking about it too.

"Later we'll have to play. I need to be inside you after a day like this."

"Play how?" Even speaking mind to mind, the lust was thick in her voice.

"You tell me. Your body is strong enough for a lot now."

Leaving her to her wild imagination, I roared at the Dragons below me, and they all looked up simultaneously at their alpha. I dipped my head and started climbing, hoping they'd understand that I wanted them to follow.

Drazen scooped up Liliana, leaving Zuriel and Rares alone on the ground as he raced to join me. A loose formation formed behind me as Dragons took their place based on rank, and we soared together past snow-capped peaks, banking together like we would have in our Fae forms. Izidora and Liliana alternated between screaming in excitement and screaming in fear, both of which pleased me greatly.

Circling back to the valley, I began a slow descent, allowing the group to fall in line as we landed in various positions throughout. The thud as one Dragon after another landed shook the ground beneath my talons, and I craned my long neck around to ensure everyone had arrived and landed safely.

"Tell everyone I want to practice taking off and landing from here until the potions wear off. We have no other way of communicating."

Izidora stood on my back, balancing between the spikes on my spine, and shouted, "Your emperor wants you to practice taking off and landing until your potion wears off!"

Dragon heads dipped in acknowledgement, and Izidora and Liliana both slid down our scales and onto the plush green grass. Lowering my head to her level, I realized just how massive our shifted forms were. My head was nearly as big as her petite frame, and one giant gray eye was the size of her head.

"Your scales are so pretty," she cooed, stroking them lovingly.

I growled low. *"I am not one of your horses. I am a fearsome beast."*

"Sure," she said, planting a kiss on my nose. Then she patted it and walked away, pressing her lips together to hide a smile.

Lashing out, I hooked a fang onto her loose tunic and tugged her back to me. Her heart skittered against her ribs, even more audible in my fully shifted form. *"How about now?"*

"You proved your point," she said, smacking me on the nose after I released her. But the smile that spread across her face told me she liked when I pushed her limits, and I planned on pushing them again that night.

I waited for her and Liliana to rejoin Zuriel before beginning my own practice, propelling myself airborne with the force of my claws against the earth, using my larger wingspan to force my heavy body higher. Around me, the Félvér began to fade one by one, their bodies shrinking in on themselves until only a dusting of scales covered their bodies and they searched for their clothes.

Drazen and I were some of the last to fade, and as my Fae body returned to me, the high of the shift came crashing down. "Rares!" I barked, scanning for the Mage.

He appeared moments later, notebook in hand. "What?"

"You will address your emperor with respect," I growled, not in the mood for his usual bullshit.

"What, My Emperor?" he replied, finally lifting his gaze.

"Find a way to make the full shift ability permanent, instead of potion-dependent. And we need a way to communicate in our shifted forms. I am assuming the others are having a similar issue?" I raised a brow, waiting for his response.

It was Drazen who confirmed my suspicion. "That has been a major complaint from the new units, yes. You can still communicate with Izidora through your bond, yeah?"

I nodded, glancing at the female watching us closely.

"A few of the other Félvér shifters have mates too. We should utilize them for now to help with direction. That will give us time to find another solution," Drazen suggested.

"I agree with Drazen," Rares commented. "As for permanent... I'll work on it." He sighed as if it were a chore to him, when really, it would be a major accomplishment in his experiments. The Mages on Nugati would laud his praises across the ocean, and for centuries to come. Even I could acknowledge that would be impressive.

"Fine. These abilities will turn the tide for us. We'll need to leave soon for the Day Realm, but while we are gone, put all your effort into it, Rares." Izidora stole my attention as she approached with my clothes in her hands. "I think we're done for the day. See to it that everyone makes it back to Radence."

I strode in my mate's direction, snatching her into my arms and kissing her roughly, not caring that my cock hardened for all to see. Her mouth tasted like vanilla, undoubtedly from all the cinnamon rolls she'd eaten this morning, and I groaned into her sweetness. Breaking our kiss, I whispered, "I need you to ride me in another way."

The flush that graced her cheeks was divine, and I murmured the spell that bent space and time and allowed us to move quickly to our bedroom at Roc Palace. The second our feet touched the polished floor, I grasped her waist and threw her onto our bed, following immediately with my body and pinning her beneath me.

"Ruslan," she panted, lifting her hips to meet mine. There were far too many clothes between us. I shifted one finger into a talon and shredded every bit of fabric covering her flushed skin. Her pants I ripped away first, not caring where they landed so long as my mate's soaking center was bared to me.

"So fucking wet already. Did flying atop my back turn you on?" I purred, dipping between her thighs while the light tunic she wore slipped away from her breasts, the torn lace beneath thin enough to expose her hardened nipples.

"Yes," she admitted, scooting her hips close to my face in a silent plea to touch her there.

My fingers clutched the insides of her thighs, massaging the tense muscles as my hot breath fluttered against her perfect pink slit. "Did you think of how you'd like to play?"

Her pussy visibly clenched, and a wicked smirk spread across my face. "Can we go to Steel?"

"Mmm," I replied, planting my lips above my hands but nowhere close to where she ached for me. "What do you want to do there?"

"I want to watch–" I interrupted her words with a flick of my tongue against her clit, eliciting a gasping breath.

"Watch what?" I said, my lips hovering over her most sensitive spot.

"Watch the others fuck," she moaned, wiggling beneath me in an attempt to relieve the tension coiling inside her as she remembered what had happened during Béke.

I rewarded her honesty by sucking her clit into my mouth, then flattening my tongue and working it over and over until her chest heaved with pleasure.

"Please, I need more," she begged, pushing back into my face.

Izidora was absolutely soaked, her arousal coating my mouth and stubble, but I still needed more of her delectable taste. Dropping my tongue away from her sensitive nerves, I parted her folds and dove inside her core, lapping directly from the source of my light.

"Oh Goddess," she swore, back arching off the bed.

I paused my ministrations, causing her to whimper. "She's not here to save you, sprite. You will fall apart by the hands of your dark God, and it is my name that will slip past those pretty lips."

And with those words, I dipped two fingers inside her, stretching her out as my tongue worked every inch of flesh between her thighs. The sounds she made were intoxicating, and my cock was painfully hard as it dug into the soft mattress. Her walls began fluttering, signaling she was close to coming.

My fingers moved faster, curling against the spongy spot that I knew would cause her to soak my face further. "Scream my name as you break over my fingers."

And she did, arching off the bed with the force of her orgasm, and I did not stop stroking her until she trembled beneath me. "Good girl," I praised, capturing her mouth in mine and forcing her to taste herself. She moaned into my mouth, and I stole her air with a swipe of my tongue across hers.

"Ride me," I ordered, lifting my weight off her and flipping to my back. The tip of my dick was soaked from my own arousal, and when Izidora grasped it to line it with her entrance, I thought I might die from pleasure.

"Fuck, yes, sprite, I need to feel you."

She ran the tip along her sopping center, teasing me in the worst way. "Maybe I should wait a moment."

My blood heated and a wicked grin formed on my face. "Do you think you're in control here?" Like lightning, two hands dug into her ass and I impaled her on my cock. "Because you're not." I bucked my hips, sending her head snapping back and a moan catching in her throat. "When I say ride me, I expect you to ride me." She whimpered as I brutally thrust up into her, our skin making a slapping sound. "Tell me you understand."

"I understand," she panted, sweat beginning to form on her brow.

"Good girl. Take the rest of your clothes off and ride me like you did my Dragon form."

She wasted no time throwing off her shirt and the lace underneath, baring her breasts to me. Goosebumps skittered across her skin as the cool air touched it, hardening her nipples. She circled her hips, taking me deeper, and I groaned as her pussy clenched around my cock. Between thumb and forefinger, I grasped each nipple and tugged, sending her a hint of pain to mix with her pleasure, just the way she liked it.

"Mate," she moaned, and a word had never sounded so good to my ears.

I repeated my actions, earning another breathy word. She bounced up and down on me, and sliding in and out of her felt even better than soaring among the peaks in my Dragon form. "That's it, ride me, mate."

I moved a hand to her hip to help guide her, and each time she sank down, her clit ground against my abdomen. "Touch me," she begged, her brow furrowing in concentration.

Releasing her nipple, I placed the pads of my fingers against her sensitive bud. She shamelessly ground into my hand and cock at the same time, bracing her hands on my shoulders to get just the right angle. The hand on her hip migrated further behind her until my fingers dipped toward her puckered hole, rubbing it lightly in time with her clit.

"Ruslan!" she gasped as I applied pressure, and I smirked, loving that she wanted the extra sensation to get off.

"Fuck my cock and hands," I commanded, and she obeyed like the good girl she was. Her movements became erratic as she chased another release, and my balls tightened as her pleasure heightened. She was so damn beautiful moving above me, her chestnut hair falling in pieces out of her intricate braids, and the way her breasts bounced with her movements was hypnotic.

"I'm going to-" she started, her breath hitching as her orgasm tore through her. Maintaining pressure against her holes, I thrust up into her, allowing her nails to dig into my tattooed chest as wave after wave of pleasure rocked her body. Her walls milked my cock, and with a roar, I shot hot ropes of liquid inside her, throbbing with the strength of my release.

Breathless, our gazes collided, and our bond hummed contentedly, satiated at least for the moment. "You ride me so well, sprite," I praised before lifting her off of me and strolling to the bathroom to clean up. I returned with a glass of water and towel for her, smoothing her sweaty hair and kissing her forehead. She looked up at me with sleepy aquamarine eyes that stole my breath and made me want to burn the world down to avenge the wrongs done to her.

Crawling into bed beside her, I tucked her against my chest, rubbing soothing circles into her back as she drifted off. She'd never admit it, but she forced herself to stay awake far too often, and she needed the rest to recover from all the training she'd been doing. When her breath finally softened, I allowed my eyes to close as I drifted to the land of sleep, with the lazy afternoon sun spilling across us.

10

LILIANA

The black raven blinked at me as it proffered its leg, waiting patiently for me to lift the scroll attached there. The sigh that slipped past my lips carried the ache in my heart because there was only one person who sent me ravens – Endre. I reached for the bird's leg, gingerly untying the string that held his note in place. The scroll was shorter than the last few had been, and I wondered if Endre was starting to give up because of my continued silence.

Unrolling the parchment, I checked over my shoulder to ensure the others were occupied in the training ring.

Liliana,

Kazimir insisted we attend the new princess's announcement to the world. Viktor, Kazimir, and myself are departing today and bringing no one else. I hope I will see you in the Day Realm. You are my first thought every morning and the last thought before I go to sleep. I miss the feeling of you beside me at night and your beautiful eyes when you wake in the morning. Nothing is the same without you.

Always yours,

Endre

The scroll snapped shut as I blinked through the hot tears

that threatened to spill down my cheeks. I did not cry – not for any male. But my heart whispered a different story, one that said no matter what, Endre's soul would always call for mine. Swallowing down the feelings, I straightened, and the bird cocked its head as if it expected me to pen a reply and attach it before it took off. Like every other time, I smoothed its blue-black feathers and offered it a morsel. It picked the seed from my hand, then flapped its wings and let the wind lift it high into the sky, disappearing into the mountains beyond. I watched it go until my keen Fae eyes could no longer discern the black dot in the distance.

"Who was that from?" Izidora's bright voice startled me, and I nearly jumped out of my skin when I found her standing beside me, peering into the distance.

Clearing the thickness from my throat, I murmured, "Endre."

"And you didn't write back?" she clarified, lifting a dark brow. The color had returned to her skin, and she was able to walk around with ease, though she was soaked in sweat, and rivulets dripped from the tendrils of hair that had escaped her chestnut braids.

"I never do." I lifted a shoulder in a half shrug, trying to act as though I didn't care. But my best friend was an empath, and nothing got by her.

"Mmm," she responded, her lips twitching as she suppressed a smile. "And why is that?"

"Ugh, Izidora, I can't get into it," I said, my throat catching on the words.

She wrapped an arm around my waist, and I rested my head on her shoulder. "You've supported me all this time. Let me support you."

From her touch, the fear of voicing my true emotions aloud melted away, and my tense shoulders dropped in time with the sigh that allowed my feelings to flee. "I wanted him to choose me. The letters he sends tell me how much he misses me, but he's still there."

I wanted Endre to show me I was all that mattered to him in the world, and no matter what I did, he would always love me.

A warm feeling ghosted over my skin, and love flowed from my best friend and into me. "It makes sense that you want him to put you first and that you're angry he isn't. You deserve someone who worships the ground you walk on."

"Fucking right I do," I choked out as Izidora dissolved the barrier around my emotions, allowing me to feel them without fear of them overwhelming me.

"What about Drazen?" she asked, not releasing me.

Goddess, she was fucking perceptive.

"Drazen knows my feelings are complicated. He says that he'll take what parts of me he can get." Swiping at my eyes, I lifted my head from her shoulder and faced my friend.

A wide, mischievous grin stretched across her face as she took my hands in hers. "Remember how you said that you thought you needed two males to keep you in line?"

A mirror grin spread across my face as I recalled our conversation from the night of the masquerade ball. "I do."

"I think you need three," she laughed, her tone light and teasing, and it was everything I needed to shift out of my self-pity.

"Why stop at three? I could have four," I joked, linking my arm with hers and strolling in the direction of the training ring where sweaty males of all mixes sparred. "Do you feel up to some hand to hand combat?"

Two full red cocktails rested against the fence, and she bent to grab one before popping off the lid and sipping from it. "If we go slow."

"Don't worry, you set the pace and I'll follow," I reassured her, not wanting Izidora to push herself too hard, and at the same time knowing she needed – wanted – to test her limits.

We leaped over the fence, and Drazen caught my attention from across the ring. His ocean blue eyes raked across my sweaty form, sending heat between my thighs. The hunger in his gaze was undeniable. As was how good he was in bed.

Zuriel stood beside him, along with Xorrek and Gozzak, two of the Demons who had evidently been captured alongside him and offered their blood willingly to Izidora. The whole situation was a bit odd, but every time I asked Zuriel about it, he dodged my question in his typical mysterious fashion.

Izidora and I squared up, raising our fists to shoulder level in preparation to strike. My friend was a few inches shorter than me, so I had the reach advantage, but she was fast and I knew better than to leave my sides open too long. I struck first, throwing out a quick jab to gauge her reaction. It was slower than it used to be, but she slipped her head to the side, rolling her shoulder to defend it. She returned with a flurry of fast strikes, all landing lightly as we began the dance. I sidestepped, and Izidora tossed a quick kick toward my ribs. I caught her foot, causing her to grin and hop.

"Pull it out!" Ruslan called from somewhere off to the side.

"That's what she said!" I hollered back, and Izidora laughed before extracting her foot from my grasp.

Her breathing was already labored, so I slowed down and waited for her next move. She feinted like she was going to throw a combination of strikes at my head, and I raised my hands instinctively, falling for her trap. Without hesitation, she dove for my middle, locking her hands around my waist and sticking a foot behind mine, sending us tumbling toward the dirt. I tucked my chin and slapped the ground to ease my fall, lifting my legs and encircling her waist so she couldn't pass around me.

"Nice trip," I laughed.

"I've still got it," she panted with a smile.

We turned serious moments later when she began her slippery assault, wiggling out of my grasp and popping to her feet while she trapped one of my legs between hers. Pinning my hip to the ground with one hand, she walked my legs to the side in an attempt to smash them into the ground and hop around them. I twisted onto my side, bracing my hands on her shoulder and knee, trying to prevent her from coming forward. She switched tactics, hopping to my other side, bracing her hand on my hip and bracing her shoulder against my knee. The other was smashed against the ground, and I allowed her to slide through until she was perpendicular on top of me.

Sweat poured from us both as she locked her hands around my head and shoulder, panting to catch her breath. "We can stop at any time," I reminded her.

"Nope, I want to keep going," she said through gritted teeth.

"Slide your knee across," Ruslan instructed from wherever he watched.

"Hey! No one is coaching me over here," I protested.

"Prevent her from sliding her knee across!" Drazen yelled, his voice drawing nearer.

I rolled my eyes. Males.

As Izidora went to slide her knee, I pushed off her, spinning in the dirt on my back until my feet pushed against her hips and flung her backward. Scrambling to my feet, I dusted myself off as she laughed and did the same. Izidora's face was a violent shade of red from her exertion, and she swayed slightly upon straightening. "Okay, I think that's enough for me," she admitted, though the tightness in her jaw spoke to her frustration.

Ruslan appeared beside her faster than anyone should be allowed to move and clutched his mate to him. "You're doing so well, sprite. I'm so proud of you."

She craned her neck to look at him, eyes shining with the type of love I wanted for myself one day. Drazen bumped his arm into mine, signaling his arrival.

"I think I'm ready to face the world again," Izidora told Ruslan, sending a smirk across his lips and darkening his eyes.

"Are you?" he replied. "Because I haven't even seen you practice flying up and down from the palace roof yet."

Izidora chewed her lip, then pushed out of his hold and fetched the half-empty red cocktail, draining it in a few gulps. Her glittering white wings burst from her back as she tossed the glass away, and with a devious smile, she shot into the sky.

The look of panic that crossed Ruslan's face was priceless.

His leathery black wings burst forth and he shot into the sky after her, staying within range of his mate as she flew hundreds of feet into the air.

"Bet she makes it," Drazen said, our attention following them.

"Of course she'll make it, Drazen. Come up with something more interesting."

"Fine. I'll wager she makes it to the top, then tries to fly down but gets scared and Ruslan has to carry her the rest of the way."

"I'll wager that Ruslan tries to help her when she falters but she yells at him and then makes it to the ground on her own."

Drazen held out his hand, and we shook on our deal. The two winged Félvér disappeared over the ledge that served as the roof of the palace built into the mountain. Silence stretched between us, though with Drazen the silence was never uneasy. His laid back attitude was a comfort more often than not, balancing out my excitable personality. A finger caressed my waist as we stood there, and I subtly leaned into the comforting touch.

Two dots appeared high above us, and I held my breath as Izidora and Ruslan began their descent to the ground.

"She looks scared," Drazen teased, his Dragon senses giving him an advantage over my Fae ones.

"She'll be fine," I replied, though I couldn't lie to myself and say the drop from the roof to the ground didn't make me wildly uncomfortable. It was a long way down, even with wings to safeguard me and a lifetime of flying practice.

They dropped lower, finally coming into focus for me. Izidora's brow was furrowed in concentration, and her white wings reflected the midday sun, making her truly look like an Angel from the nursery tales my mother told me as a child, descending from the heavens. Ruslan's hands hovered in front of him as he watched over her, allowing her the space she needed to succeed but offering support should she require it.

About halfway down, Izidora's wings faltered, and she dropped severely. I gasped, bringing my hands to my mouth as all I could do was watch as she fell. Ruslan snapped his wings shut and dove to catch her, but moments before he reached her, those white wings spread wide again and caught a draft. Her furious descent halted, and a fierce, determined look reappeared on her face.

"Thank the Goddess," I breathed, watching as Izidora whipped her head toward her mate and they exchanged words.

"I guess you win," Drazen teased, bumping me again with his shoulder. "The usual reward?"

I snickered as the two made their final drop to the ground. "You know it."

Izidora beamed with pride as her feet touched land, and she collapsed onto her ass, breathless and giddy. Drazen and I jogged toward them, and Drazen released a whooping cheer.

"Guess you both can be finished with training today," Ruslan smirked, snaking his arms around Izidora's waist and lifting her into the air as he captured her mouth.

"As if I need your permission," I scoffed, trying to worm my way between them so I could steal my best friend, not caring they were mid-kiss.

Ruslan growled at me, but I didn't relinquish my position, especially as Izidora laughed. Drazen snorted behind us, and I raised a brow at Ruslan, waiting for admonishment. He only sighed, looked between me and his mate, and said, "Go have fun."

I snatched Izidora's hand, giggles bubbling over for both of us as I tugged her toward the hidden passage that led to the lift. Ruslan and Drazen's heavy footsteps followed, echoing off the rock until Ruslan pushed past us to open the door. The four of us piled into the pillar in the mountain, and with the slowness he knew Izidora preferred, Ruslan lifted us to the top of the palace, directly onto the floor that held the giant suite that had become like a home.

"Ruslan, we really should build a wing for our friends to sleep in," Izidora said as she stepped into the foyer that barred entry into the suite unless you were magically granted access to come and go.

"But they'd never get any sleep," he grinned down at her, opening the door for us to enter the large living space. If Izidora's face wasn't already so red, the blush that covered her cheeks would have been more evident.

I grinned to myself as the four of us entered the enormous bathroom. Being around my friends made me forget that my blood family was in the Night Realm, serving a mad king, and I was in the Iron Realm, enjoying the luxuries offered to me.

If only Endre could see what I did in Kazimir, then he would be here, with us.

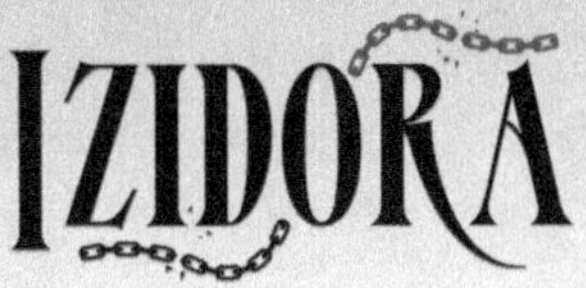 IZIDORA

For the first time since I'd awoken, I was blissfully, utterly alone. Not that I didn't appreciate Ruslan, Liliana, Drazen, and Zuriel's constant support. No, it was that I felt like I was suffocating from all their care, their attention, and pretending to be strong and keep moving forward, when sometimes all I wanted to do was scream into the mountains until my throat bled and my voice abandoned me, unable to bear the anguish that still clung to me.

Drazen and Zuriel had swept off early this morning to meet with some of the other army leaders. And Liliana had waved me off, begging for more sleep when I appeared in her apartments at Ryza Citadel.

When I'd told Ruslan what I wanted to do while he attended his duties today, he'd seemed hesitant at first, but since no one outside the Iron Realm knew I had awoken, we decided it would be safe enough for me to go alone. So I'd ridden Mistik out of the city with a promise to Ruslan to check in with him every so often. I knew exactly where I needed to go, but that didn't make the trek any easier.

With shaking hands, I pulled my beautiful dapple gray mare

to a stop when we breached the first plateau into the Agrenak Mountains, the very same spot where Kazimir had taken me after he kidnapped me. This time, the snow was absent, and a few wildflowers poked through the scattered rocks. The sight of their colorful petals swaying in the light breeze made me clench my teeth.

"I'm here, but I'm going to barricade my mind so you don't have to bear the depth of my emotion," I told Ruslan down our bond.

"Sprite, you are never a burden to me, nor are your emotions. Feel what you need to feel and do not worry for a second about me. But I am only a thought away if you need me."

"I love you."

"And I love you more."

With a thud, I leaped to the ground, not bothering to secure Mistik. My faithful horse wouldn't go anywhere. The large boulder that had cracked my spine when I'd landed against it after breaking off my bond with Kazimir cast a long shadow pointed directly at me, as if it were beckoning me to relive the nightmare of that experience.

My next step was a flash back to the moment I'd pushed every last ounce of magic I possessed into a shield for my mate. Next was the replay of the blade sailing past him. Then was the excruciating pain of it slicing into my chest. By the time I flattened my hands on the rock, I was panting, fighting with my brain to get my emotions under control.

The dark crystal in my chest *fed* on the anguish ripping me apart.

A laugh escaped my lips as images of the blade were ousted by one of Queen Immonen's frightened, frantic face after she'd had a vision in the dress shop.

"Everything will go dark," she had said.

If only she'd known just how deep that darkness would go. I'd tried to see if I could recall that white light, to pull on the happiest of my emotions and change the color. All I'd succeeded in doing was morphing it into a smoky gray that reminded me of Ruslan's eyes.

Even the sun seemed to mock me as it beat into my eyes. I glared at it, like I could unleash my ire in its direction and somehow find relief. This anger, this pure, unfettered *rage* at everything life had put me through was too much for my tiny body to bear. It needed to explode from me like a volcanic eruption, turned into a molten river that would consume everything in its path.

How could one person manage such enormous emotions?

And so that laugh morphed into a scream as I clawed and beat the rock, imagining it was Kazimir's fucking face. King Zalan's. King Azim's. The guards'. The list of people who had hurt me felt *endless* and despite the fact that all but one were dead, it wasn't enough. Killing all those males with Ruslan was intoxicating, yet it only served to intensify my thirst for more.

Would it ever be? Would there ever be a time where I'd be abundantly happy, without the claws of something traumatic sinking into me?

I hadn't done any more sessions with Zuriel since awakening, though perhaps I should. Twenty-one years was a long time to have those terrors build up with no way to release them.

Tears blurred my vision, and I released one last choked cry. The echo of it remained in my ears as I dropped my head and tried to regain my breath. The salty drops plummeted to the dusty earth, an offering to the tiny blossoms rooted there.

I was an insidious bloom.

Kazimir had underestimated me. King Zalan had underestimated me. King Azim had underestimated me. These fucking kings of Északi were *useless*. They had no idea the power contained within females, and that it was by our mercy that we allowed them dominion over us.

Ruslan never scorched the earth where I planted myself; instead, he nurtured it so I could bloom.

Chest heaving, I sank to the ground, resting my back against the boulder and soaking in the shade.

How poignant it was to be bathed in darkness with the light just out of reach. How ironic that over half a year later I was braced against the monumental stone of my own volition.

Heart thundering against my ribcage, I tried to suck down serrated breaths, searching for a semblance of calm amid the raging storm in my mind. But I was dragged back to the moment Kazimir's hand had clamped over my mouth, cloaking us in invisibility and preventing anyone from witnessing him kidnapping me. I squeezed my eyes shut like the action would wring the memory from my mind.

It didn't.

A light rustling pricked my ears, and I opened my eyes, watching through blurred vision as Zuriel dropped from the cloudless blue sky. With the lightest of touches, he landed, coming to kneel just outside the shadow that engulfed me. The corners of his icy blue eyes were tight, and they scanned me with hurried movements.

"Are you okay, cousin?" he asked gently, banishing his white feathered wings.

It was as if my thoughts of our sessions had summoned him, and I didn't bother to ask how he knew where I was. He had this keen sense of knowing when I needed him most, and in that moment, I was grateful he was there.

"No," I choked out around the lump in my throat.

Zuriel remained motionless, waiting for me to continue.

After curling and uncurling my fingers a few times, I managed to get out, "I thought I could handle him on my own. I *wanted* to handle him on my own, to prove that I didn't need anyone to take care of me. But then I couldn't."

My cousin's eyes softened even more. "Oh, Izidora–"

I shook my head, cutting him off. I needed to get the words out. "I was so scared, not being able to use my power." Hot tears spilled over and raced down my cheeks. Then, the truth of the matter slipped free after them. "I want someone to protect me, but I want to be strong on my own. I want to feel safe, to feel like I have the freedom to relax, but every time I turn around, there's some new threat that sweeps those feelings just out of reach. Will anything I do ever be enough? Or will I be forever cursed to vacillate between stolen moments of peace and fear?"

Zuriel scooted closer, then switched to sitting cross-legged. Curving his spine, he lowered his head to meet mine and took my hands. "You can be strong on your own and still have the protection of others, cousin. You do not have to rely solely on yourself. Nor do you have to prove anything by doing so. No one will think you weak if you remain tucked in the net of safety that the people who love you provide. Ruslan tortured himself for months after he allowed you to wander off on your own because he thinks he should have been the one to retrieve the necklace for you."

I nodded, more heat searing my cheeks as tears continued to fall. None of it was Ruslan's fault, despite the blame he placed on himself. He'd done everything to protect me, and I'd still insisted on being independent.

How could I have both?

As if Zuriel was reading my mind, he said, "In this coming war, he will not let you out of his sight, of that I am certain. But you are strong, and you can fight with us on the battlefield. The two of you are mated and possess unique powers because of it. Utilize that advantage and find the overlap where Ruslan's protection allows you to tap into the immense well of magic in your chest."

With the backs of my hands, I dried my eyes. "He's exactly what I needed."

A small half-smile tugged up the corner of Zuriel's mouth. "I know."

"But these emotions..." I trailed off, closing my fist over my heart and giving my chest a thump. Dropping my head, I sucked in a serrated breath. "I don't want to have to hold all this myself. Don't think I can. It's going to consume me."

"Let me help you bear the burden," Zuriel said quietly, and I lifted my gaze to meet his sincere one.

"Another session?" I asked.

"If that is what you wish, then we shall do it," he replied, straightening.

The work would be hard, but worth it, especially if it could provide me with a modicum of relief from the feeling of Kazimir's hands on my skin, his mouth searing into mine as he forced a kiss on me. So, I crossed my arms over my chest and began to tap.

Down I delved into the memory of what had happened there in the winter, the moments coming back with the same clarity as the open sky above us. As if I was there again, a crisp breeze caressed my face, turning biting as we raced, blind, into the Agrenak Mountains. Hoofbeats filled my ears.

And I *trembled.*

"I couldn't access my magic," I whimpered, terror flooding me anew. The tapping quickened as the feeling of being gagged returned. "I tried and tried and tried. I didn't want to have to be saved again. I didn't want to be a victim again."

Sweat beaded on the back of my neck, then dripped cold down my spine.

"Kazimir always made me feel like I needed to be saved by him. That I should have been grateful to be saved by him. I didn't realize the difference between him and Ruslan until so much later. Didn't realize how fucked up his actions and words were when I had nothing else to compare them to. How was I supposed to know it wasn't healthy?" A choked sob slipped out with my question.

"Keep going," Zuriel encouraged, his tone soft like a warm caress.

"Thank me for saving you. Call me your hero," Kazimir had commanded while we had sex on more than one occasion. Memories of him moving inside me while those praises breathed in his direction made my skin crawl.

"Why didn't I see it?" I whimpered as the tangled web of my relationship with Kazimir began unfurling.

Kazimir went from being my savior to my kidnapper. Ruslan went from being my kidnapper to my empowerer. One set me free only to try to chain me. The other chained me in order to set me free.

"How could you have seen it?" Zuriel challenged, though bite was absent from his tone.

"I couldn't," I whispered, and he nodded.

"Can you forgive yourself for that?"

His question slammed into me and stole my breath. I was blaming myself for so many things that happened that were outside of my control. Kazimir's depravity was not my fault. His manipulations were not my fault. He took advantage of my naivete and didn't think twice about it. Didn't even try to deny it when I confronted him about it.

"I forgive myself for trusting him." Saying the words aloud opened something in the space between my ribs, relieving a profound ache I hadn't known existed. The tapping continued with more fervency as I tried to rid myself of this blame. "I forgive myself for not doing more to protect myself because I was already doing everything within my power." I dragged in another breath. "I forgive myself for placing the fault on my own shoulders rather than where it deserves to be laid."

Chest continuing to expand, I repeated my affirmations, "I am safe. I am strong. I am powerful. I am an insidious bloom."

"Yes, you are," Zuriel added pointedly. "And with all of those things, you will have your revenge, cousin. You need not rewrite the ending of what happened to you here today. That day is coming, and soon."

I ceased the tapping and dropped my arms to my sides, bracing my palms against the dusty earth. "Then, I will finally be free." Pushing myself to stand, I steeled my spine and faced the world once again.

Zuriel rose too, lithe and graceful. "Come, let's train with the army today so you can feel just how protected you will be on the battlefield."

Mistik was exactly where I'd left her, munching on some grass. Her head perked up, ears flicking forward as Zuriel and I approached. A soft nicker slipped from her throat as I flattened my palm on the side of her face and stroked the fur there. She bumped my belly with her nose, making me laugh. Zuriel patted her hide too. "When the war is over, you should breed horses, like High Lady Domi of the Night Realm. You have a gift with animals."

I flashed him a smile. "I think I would like that."

My cousin's eyes held a sadness to them as he looked down at me, but it was gone before I could comment on it. "You ride, I will fly. They aren't training far from here currently."

Circling to Mistik's side, I gripped the saddle with both hands and planted my boot in the stirrup. Swinging my leg over her back, I settled in for a short ride. "Lead the way."

12

KAZIMIR

I clenched my jaw so hard I thought a tooth might crack as we stopped *again* to camp with a fucking escort of Crystal Fae. They said nothing to us, but forced themselves in a ring around our tents, ensuring that we couldn't escape into the night. The dark beast that raged in my chest begged to be released, to kill them all and satiate my anger with their blood pooling at my feet.

The crashing of the waterfalls in the distance did nothing to suppress the cacophony of my thoughts, and it took every ounce of my willpower to quiet the binding magic that nearly consumed the tendrils of moonlight in my chest. Viktor and Endre were grim faced as they sat with me near the fire. The changing of seasons brought with it cooler nights that beckoned all closer to the warmth.

Fucking Fates, a year ago we'd been preparing to launch our air assault on Vasvain, the highest peak in Északi, to rescue Izidora, and on this night I was surrounded by idiots who didn't understand what I needed to do. Picking up a stick and working it through my fingers, I tried to give my hand something to do other than strangle the Crystal Fae around us.

They would fucking pay.

"So, Elo," I had learned the leader of the regiment's name at least, "how much longer until you drop us off in the Day Realm?"

The male shot me a nasty side eye, then continued stirring the pot over the fire.

"Not soon enough," another Crystal Fae muttered in the background, intentionally loud enough for his words to drift into our ears.

Elo looked between the two of us before responding. "Only a few more days if we keep up the pace. Which I would very much like to do."

"Tired of us already?" I mocked, not a hint of real teasing in my tone.

"Kazimir," Endre warned under his breath, but I silenced him with a wave of my hand.

"You should be thrilled to escort another monarch. It is a great honor, after all." I continued to goad him, wanting to get the rise I very much needed as an excuse to unleash the binding magic.

But like every night, he didn't deign to respond to my prodding, merely filling bowls and passing them around the camp. Groups of Crystal Fae clustered together and enjoyed their meal, reminding me far too much of traveling with the Nighthounds. The thought of our group brought another wave of grief, and like every time, I suppressed the need to confront the loss of my father, Kriztof, and the twins. I didn't have the time to deal with the heaviness of that day. I couldn't save them, I couldn't stop Ruslan from taking my mate, and my all around failure had caused me to lose everything – even if I'd gained a crown in the process.

Where were you, Fates?

They'd gifted me with the magic I thought would get me

back everything I wanted, and yet I sat beneath the stars again instead of ruling the Night Realm alongside Izidora. A crazed smile tried to break my face, but I clamped down on it lest anyone see the madness entombed with all my other dark secrets – like the obsession I had carried since before we ever found Izidora. I couldn't let it go even after she broke our mating bond. My soul felt tattered and burned in a way that wasn't reparable.

Was I upset with myself for trying to kill her? At first maybe, but not anymore. The moment she shattered our bond, I felt like a knife had dug into my chest and carved out a piece of me. The pain, the fucking blinding anguish that made me feel like I was about to die, forced me to lash out. Sure, Ruslan had been there too, but I didn't want him to have her. He didn't *deserve* her. She was mine – to save, to have, to covet. His mongrel blood made him even less worthy of her.

The longer we rode toward the Day Realm and the other monarchs, the more I thought that maybe I was entitled to making them feel the depths of the pain they'd caused me too.

Tossing the broken stick into the dirt, I stalked toward the sparse trees that dotted the foothills. A rushing waterfall waited just beyond our encampment. As I suspected, several Crystal Fae scrambled to their feet and chased after me. I ignored them, striding straight toward the shallow pool formed by years of relentless beating from the glacial melt. Kicking off my boots, I entered the water, the ice cold biting into my bare skin as I waded deeper. Stripping off my leather armor piece by piece, I tossed them into the grass, shooting a teasing grin over my shoulder at the soldiers who followed me.

"Hope you don't mind my nudity," I commented, stripping off my half-soaked pants and mostly dry tunic until I was naked in the knee-deep water. The waterfall was almost like a makeshift shower, so I stood beneath it, letting the icy spray wash away weeks of grime as I faced them.

"Oh don't be shy, come on in," I purred at the waiting group, who shifted from foot to foot, but didn't take their eyes off me for a second. "Suit yourself." I shrugged, tipping my head back and wetting my hair. The pressure of the water was a little too much for my taste on top of it being freezing fucking cold, but the absolutely uncomfortable expressions the Crystal Fae wore were worth every biting drop.

When I reopened my eyes, Endre and Viktor both stood on the edges of the shore, looking between me and my guards. Viktor then looked to Endre and shrugged, shucking off his clothes and wading in to join me.

"See, we could have quite a lot of fun if you loosened up a bit," I called out to them, but they remained stoic as ever.

Endre pressed his lips together and looked away from Viktor and me before running a hand through his hair and stripping off his armor.

"Fucking Fates it's cold," Viktor griped, joining me beneath the falls and scrubbing dirt off himself in a hurry. I could barely hear him over the rushing in my ears, which meant if we spoke softly we might have a few private words.

I waited for Endre to join us before I turned my back to the Crystal Fae and dropped my tone. "We need to ditch our escort. Any thoughts?"

Viktor responded first. "That's all I've been thinking about since they picked us up, but I don't see a way out of it."

Endre interrupted him. "You wanted to visit the Day Realm for the new princess's announcement, so we might have to play nice for the moment."

I scoffed, annoyed that the greatest strategist in the Night Realm had nothing better than 'I don't know' to offer up and that my sensitive friend felt the need to remind me of the purpose of this trek.

Gritting my teeth as I scrubbed my skin with some moss I'd found growing nearby, I replied, "Fine. We'll tolerate them."

Viktor and Endre both dipped out of the icy falls before I did. The freezing water cooled me off in a way I so desperately needed if I was going to keep my shit together for the foreseeable future. Finally shoving off the slippery rock, I waded back through the pool toward the Crystal Fae who stood in matching arms-crossed, stone-faced stances. As I walked – fully nude – to the line of tethered horses, I grinned at the males following me, ensuring they each got a nice good look at the crown jewels. From my bag, I grabbed decently fresh clothes, then winked and pulled them on. Rather than lose the semblance of inner peace I'd found, I disappeared into my tent for the rest of the night, trying to pretend the Crystal Fae weren't feet away and ready to run me through.

I didn't even think of Taya as I drifted off to sleep beneath a layer of warm blankets.

13

IZIDORA

Creatures fell from the skies around me, dropping like rain to the battlefield below. Whipping around, I searched for light-sucking black and iridescent blue among the skies, but found none. The roar of soldiers around me couldn't stop the panic that clawed up my throat, and I tried to sprint away from the fray and to higher ground. Each step felt like I was moving through quicksand, and tears burned my eyes as I fought to run.

"Please, please please," I begged anyone who would listen. But it was no use. My limbs were nothing more than stone while the leather-clad soldiers surrounding me moved like the wind. Suddenly, the sun was blotted out by a thousand black dots, and movement returned long enough for me to observe the new addition to the battle. A thousand pairs of black feathered wings circled above, most carrying longbows with arrows already notched. It was only then that I realized a circle of soldiers had formed around our group, and we backed together, defenseless from all sides.

"Why!" I screamed, tearing my throat with the force of my agony as the first arrows twanged into the air.

With a gulping gasp, I bolted upright, throwing Ruslan's arm off my waist in the process. I clutched my chest, my heart being out of control as the absolute terror from my nightmare carried over into my waking existence. Ruslan was upright within a breath and yanking me into his embrace. The gentle rocking motion he offered still did not soothe me. "You're safe, here in our bed. I've got you."

Twisting my fingers in the white sheets beneath me, I tried to ground myself to the present, but the lingering bits of the nightmare clutched at me until I used my other senses to regain control. The sun set behind the sharp peaks in the distance, darkening the room that smelled of sex and wood and roses. Ruslan's warmth at my back relaxed the tense muscles there, and finally, I sank into his hold.

"Do you want to talk about it?" he murmured, his raspy voice gentle, but through our bond I felt his worry.

"It was a battlefield... we were surrounded." I shook my head as if I could banish the last of the violent images. "Everyone was going to die."

"We have the advantage, Izidora. I won't let that happen," Ruslan promised, and I believed him. Wholeheartedly. After witnessing the Dragons in the sky today, in addition to the ferocity of the Iron Realm's army, and Rares' continued experiments with non-magic weaponry, I couldn't imagine a way in which we would lose. Nothing the Night Fae could conjure would match the might of the Iron Realm.

Blowing out a breath, I nodded. "Especially because of the Dragons."

Nuzzling the top of my head, Ruslan responded, "Especially that." We remained locked in the tender embrace until the dying sun disappeared behind the mountains. "Do you still want to go to Steel tonight?"

My cheeks and core heated at the thought. "Yes," I whispered. "Should we invite Liliana and Drazen?"

"Why not? Though I'm fairly certain they'll be there given

that it's one of the busier nights of the week at Steel," Ruslan murmured, planting a tender kiss on my hair.

Extracting myself from Ruslan's arms, I yawned, stretching my stiff limbs and working movement back into my body. "Do I have time for a bath before we go?"

"Absolutely. You stay here and I will draw it for you." Ruslan hopped from the bed, making his way to the bathroom. I raked my eyes across his naked form until he disappeared around the corner. Turning over, I sprawled out as I rummaged through the bedside table in search of something to read while I bathed. I was still slow, especially since I'd had a chunk of time without reading at all, but Ruslan had been working with me every night, just like we used to before Béke.

Water splashed into the deep soaking tub, and the earthy scents of lavender and rose wafted to the bedroom, enticing me to wander to the bathroom. Candles floated in the water and lined the sides of the tub, Ruslan lighting them one by one with his magic. It was a peaceful oasis, and just what I needed after the nightmare of nearly dying on the battlefield.

"I'm going to shower and look over some paperwork while you bathe," he commented, straightening when he noticed my entrance. "I've got to take care of a few things before we leave for the Day Realm. And I'll definitely be too busy after our wedding to do them." He smirked suggestively, and I grinned in response, my belly fluttering under his heated gaze.

"How many days?" I asked, padding toward him and running a nail down the center of his muscled torso.

"Too many," he growled, capturing my finger and nipping the pad of it. "You will be my mate, my wife, and my empress. All will bow before our might and our wrath."

"The two most powerful Fae to ever live," I repeated his words from so long ago back to him.

"That's right. Now, hop in and relax, sprite. You deserve it."

He released me, and I stepped lightly over the lip of the tub, groaning as the heat soaked into my body. Sighing, I leaned my head against a rolled up towel on the edge.

Ruslan thought of everything.

The sound of cascading water filled the bathroom as I allowed my gaze to soften and linger on the landscape before me. Basking in the bath, I relaxed, letting go of everything and simply *being* for a moment. We were always so busy, so on the go, that moments like this were rare.

When my mind had enough of nothing, I lifted the book from its safe place on the edge of the tub and cracked its pages. I lost myself in the mystery until the water grew cold enough to warrant my attention, and only when I could stand it no longer did I blow out the dark flames surrounding me. The water sloshed as I reached for a towel to dry myself, and I wrapped it around me before I wandered our suite in search of my mate. I found him in the living area, bent over a pile of papers and scratching away. Leaning against the doorframe in nothing but a towel, I watched him work, loving the way the muscles rippled across his back.

Without looking up, he said, "In the back of the closet you'll find some dresses for warmer weather."

Of course, sneaking up on a mate was nearly impossible with the bond acting like a beacon to one another. "Thanks," I replied, strolling to the closet in search of something fun to wear to Steel. If I'd learned anything in my time in the Iron Realm, it was that despite the cold, skin was the norm. And with the summer temperatures, I could only assume that meant clothing was nearing optional. After sliding through a row of dresses, I decided on one that barely covered the tops of my thighs, with a very low dip in the back .

Ruslan's words from before Béke drifted back to me, making me smile as I gazed upon the dress.

"Your scars are a signal that you are a fucking survivor, sprite, that you remain unbroken despite them, and that you can hold your own against the most seasoned of warriors. One day, you will tell me the story of each one, and when you're through, we will end the life of every male who inflicted them upon you. You will get the vengeance you deserve, and in the meantime, you will flaunt those scars like the badges of honor they are."

Because I was a survivor – of being chained, whipped, abused, raped, and any manner of horrors people could inflict on one another. I'd gotten the first part of my vengeance that night when Ruslan and I returned to Vasvain and tortured my former captors. The sounds of their screams still echoed in my mind, as delicious now as they were when I'd ripped their balls away from their bodies. Heat flooded my core as more memories from that night surfaced. After we'd killed them all, Ruslan and I had fucked covered in blood, and when we finished, I'd accepted our bond.

During Béke, I had realized I didn't know what I wanted from life. To rule, originally, was Kazimir's idea. After I made my choice of mate, my wants started to shift into fighting for the Félvér. But after waking and realizing what had happened at the end of Béke, and that Kazimir had tried to kill me, my desires had irrevocably shifted.

Sure, I still wanted to free the Félvér.

But now, I also wanted blood. While I may have been the one to fill the land with light, there was no denying the darkness that called to me, especially upon waking from the endless void of it. I wanted to embrace it, to savor it, *use it*. The thought should have frightened me, and yet, somehow, it didn't. It *thrilled* me as the darkness flitted through my magic well and promised to fulfill my deepest desires.

And oh, did I plan on using it to my advantage.

Because what I wanted more than anything was Kazimir dead.

————

LILIANA AND DRAZEN were already waiting for us as we appeared on the street in front of Steel. Blinking, I took in the building with the silvery climbing ivy covering its slate exterior, and the intricate front door carved with swirls and delicate lines depicting a story of love and loss that I'd come to expect from anything Ruslan designed. Liliana squealed and ran over to me, snatching me from Ruslan and linking her arm through mine.

"You look hot as fuck," she commented, looking me up and down.

I laughed. "So do you." And she truly did. Her chocolate brown locks were gently curled and tumbled to her waist, and she wore thick lines of black around her eyes, making the seafoam green color pop. Her dress clung to her every curve, cut out in places to reveal hints of her stomach, and with a corner cut out of the hem, pointing dangerously high.

"Why is it that the two of you always match?" Drazen asked, his voice warm with amusement.

Glancing down at myself, I realized, we truly did. From our dresses to our hairstyles and the way we'd painted our faces, we could have been twins if it weren't for the height, hair, and eye color difference.

Ruslan's smoky grays heated as they perused my form, resting hungrily on the place where the skin of my legs disappeared beneath the black fabric. My core tightened immediately. *This night is about you, sprite. Whatever you want to do, whatever you do or do not feel comfortable with, I will support. If you get nervous or overwhelmed, I will take care of you.*

"I trust you," I replied, offering my mate a small smile.

"Shall we?" Drazen asked, interrupting our mental exchange. He grasped the door handle and pulled it open, waiting for us to enter first. Liliana giggled in response and tugged me forward.

The interior was dim, and if it hadn't been for the dusk outside, my eyes would have taken longer to adjust. At first, the Félvér club seemed empty, but I realized we were only on a landing, and beyond, a set of stairs descended into the earth. Even from here, the beat of the drum reverberated through my body. Drazen descended the stairs first, and Liliana dropped my arm and followed, shooting me an encouraging smile over her shoulder.

Ruslan's large palm found my lower back and rested gently there, thumb stroking softly against the bare skin. "After you, sprite."

My entire body tingled, whether from nerves or excitement, I did not know; perhaps it was a bit of both. When I smoked herbs during Béke, I hadn't anticipated fucking Ruslan in front of the entire tent, and then watching others as they writhed together too. But now that we stood on the precipice of it again, my thighs dampened while my hands shook.

"It's okay to be nervous," Ruslan murmured in my ear, his hot breath fanning across it and making me shiver. "But say the word and we'll leave. No questions, no hesitation. Whatever you need to feel comfortable, sprite."

"It's not that. I just... don't want to be trapped underground," I said, exhaling a shaky breath. His hand found my hip and pulled me into him so that my back was flush against his front.

"When we're down there, you won't be thinking about where we are. The only thing your mind will be able to latch onto is the pleasure I am delivering you. You have me harder than a fucking diamond just standing here, your skin on display and your every curve promising to send me to hell. And I plan on dragging you there with me." He ground his erection into my back to drive home his point.

Our bond flared, and I arched into him, need flooding through my veins. A low rumble emanated from his chest. "You're going to look so fucking good riding my cock, your dress bunched up around your waist and your head thrown back in ecstasy. The Félvér are all going to wish it was them you were riding. And when their future empress falls apart, they're going to hear you scream my name."

"Oh, fuck," I whimpered, my thighs growing slick.

"Are you ready to enter now?" Ruslan purred, his hands drifting over my stomach and up to cup my breasts.

I leaned into him, arching my back as I did so. "Not as much as I am for you to enter me."

A masculine rumble brushed across my ear, sending a shiver down my spine. "Lead the way." His hands left my body, leaving me cold, but with the intensity of his attention at my back, I heated all over again.

Striding forward, I watched my feet as I took the dark steps one at a time, the earthy scent of smoke filling my nostrils the further we went. At the bottom, a gauzy curtain blocked the room from view, but I breezed through it, shoulders back and head held high. With a sashay of my hips, I entered the open space, scanning quickly for any sign of Liliana and Drazen.

Along the walls, small alcoves with similar drapery hid patrons, though the largest at the back of the space had its curtains drawn, and Liliana and Drazen sat inside, already filling glasses with liquor and rifling through bags of herbs. With them, Anton and Slavian and a few of the other Félvér I recognized from Béke lounged against the leather couch rimming the room.

They waved us over, and I picked my way through the tables in the center, noting the states of dress – or undress – of others in the room. Servers wore next to nothing, scraps barely covering breasts and skirts barely covering legs. I felt a bit over-dressed by the time we reached the alcove and slid along the smooth fabric.

"I got you something to drink," Liliana said, sliding me a small glass filled to the brim with a brown liquid.

Lifting it, I sniffed, and smoke with a hint of salt hit my nostrils. "What is it?"

"Whisky," she stated, pinching her own between her fingers and lifting it toward me. "One of my new favorites that the Iron Realm produces. I wanted to share it with you since I know you haven't gotten to try it yet."

I smiled, heart giving a small squeeze. "Cheers!"

We threw back the alcohol together, and it burned from my tongue to my belly, settling there and warming me from the inside out. Not that I needed any more of that, with the lust assaulting my senses and the wetness coating my thighs. Taking a moment to ground myself, I threw up that mental barrier that allowed me to keep everyone else's emotions out, and settled firmly into my own space.

While Liliana and I had been drinking, Ruslan and Drazen had been busy stuffing the herb apparatuses. Ruslan used the tip of his finger to light it, chest expanding as he sucked it down. He handed the herbs to me, still holding his breath. Before I could lift it to my own lips, he grasped my chin in his hand and pulled my lips to his.

"*Open,*" he commanded, and I obeyed, parting my lips and welcoming in his tongue. He breathed the smoke into my mouth, and I inhaled it down, sharing his air and growing dizzy from it. He didn't release my face when I exhaled it back, choosing to remain with our mouths locked and tongues twin-ing. He groaned as I turned to my knees and used my free hand to balance as I straddled him.

His hands found my waist immediately, and he used them to rub me along his length. *"Mmm, I don't think you have anything beneath that dress, do you?"*

"Guess you'll have to find out."

I broke our kiss, staring deep into his iron gray eyes as I brought the herbs to my lips. Without breaking our gaze, he lit and lifted his finger, burning them. Inhaling slowly, I filled my lungs with them, holding for a moment before pursing my lips and blowing a stream straight into his face. His eyes darkened, and a smirk spread as slowly as the smoke dissipating around us. I dragged my lip between my teeth and handed the apparatus back to him.

"So that's how you want to play?" he purred, lifting and inhaling. Beneath me, his cock twitched, and my core tightened in response. He returned my gesture, blowing the smoke into my face in carefully practiced Os. Once the last one drifted past my head, he set the apparatus aside and yanked me closer, forcing my hands onto his broad chest. The short sleeved tunic he wore was loose across his chest, and I immediately slipped my fingers beneath it and traced the tattoos covering his skin. His arms flexed around me, drawing my attention to his rippling biceps and forearms.

My every nerve was alight beneath my mate's touch, and time slowed to a crawl, the entire world dropping away as my focus became where the rough palms would trace next. Dizzy and blissful, I tilted my head back, baring my neck to him. He leaned forward immediately, capturing my back with his hand and licking from the base of my throat up to my ear.

But he didn't stop there.

With a swipe of his hand, he cleared the table in the middle of the space and laid me flat against it. He towered over me, hands braced on either side of my head, and those eyes that had captivated me since I first saw him swirled with a hunger that mirrored my own. I reached for him, grasping his shirt and yanking him down so he was forced to kiss me again.

It wasn't a kiss of love; no, it was a kiss of passion and protection, of claiming and conviction, and I lost myself in it – in him.

By the time we broke away, I panted for air, and with a startling realization, I noticed the other groupings surrounding us. Liliana and Drazen were locked in a similar state as Ruslan and me, twined together, while Anton and Slavian each had a group around them. Anton had his arms thrown wide across the back of the sofa and watched Ruslan and me unabashedly while another male was on his knees before him bobbing his head.

Ruslan stole my attention as his warmth left me, and he knelt before me in a similar fashion, pushing my legs apart. "I was right, sprite. There's nothing here blocking me from you."

I pushed up onto my elbows, watching him as he licked his way up my thigh and toward my dripping center. "Why would I let anything get in the way of us?" I teased, biting my lip.

He growled, nipping the sensitive skin of my inner thigh. "Nothing will ever come between us again."

Before I could respond, his tongue found my slit and licked from bottom to top, sucking my clit into his mouth and tearing a whimper from my throat. "Ruslan," I moaned, rolling my hips against his face. The hair covering his jaw brushed against me in the most delicious way, and I nearly melted as he began to fuck me with his tongue. I threaded my fingers in his hair, nails scratching against his scalp as I directed him lower, needing more of him inside me.

"*Watch*," he spoke in my mind, then sucked on my center, pulling a moan of pleasure from me.

But I did watch, attention drifting to Anton again. The male on his knees still worked him, but another had joined them, and the female Félvér flattened her back against the wall while

Anton lifted his face to her core, licking in a similar fashion as Ruslan did to me.

"Do you like watching her cunt get licked?" Ruslan asked, and my core clenched. He groaned, moving a finger from my thigh to my center and teasing my entrance.

"Yes. Please, I need more," I begged, grinding my hips against his face.

He obliged me by slipping a finger inside and curling it against my walls. "Oh my Goddess," I moaned, louder than I meant to.

That drew the attention of the female I had been watching, and through hooded eyes, she gazed down on Ruslan and me. She sucked one of her own fingers into her mouth, wetting it, and then circled her nipples, groaning as Anton tightened his grip on her thighs.

We locked eyes, both receiving pleasure from the powerful males beneath us, and I couldn't look away as her breaths quickened, lashes fluttering against her cheekbones. With a cry, she came, and our gaze broke as she tipped her head back and rode out her orgasm. My walls fluttered, and I found myself careening toward the edge of release.

"Ruslan," I groaned, tightening my grip on his head.

He slipped another finger inside me, stretching me out, and when his tongue flicked over my clit again, I exploded, arching off the table and crying his name as all I saw was stars. When I finally came down, he had risen, and his shirt was discarded behind him.

Fuck, he was devastatingly handsome, all dark, harsh lines and brooding power that emanated from his pores. There was nothing about him that didn't exude strength and ruthlessness, and as he stripped his belt from his pants, I nearly cried from the depths of my need for him. The outline of his cock was visible in his pants, and I reached for it, wanting to wrap my hand around it and squeeze.

But he caught my hand before I could and tsked. "You're not ready for that yet."

I cocked my head to the side. "I'm not?"

"No," he growled, lifting a discarded apparatus and lifting it to my lips. "You need to suck on this a few more times first."

More wetness gushed from me, coating the table in my arousal. But I leaned forward, allowing Ruslan to light it for me, and inhaled deeply. My head floated among the clouds as I exhaled, filling the alcove with even more smoke. Ruslan dragged from it after me, blowing it out quickly up and away from us. Then he settled back on the couch and dragged my legs from the table and onto the ground in front of him. "As much as I can't wait for you to be my empress, my equal, you look so fucking pretty on your knees in front of me."

Heat exploded within me, and my mouth watered as I gazed up at my emperor, my mate, and my future husband. Squeezing his thighs, I worked my way up to his cock and palmed it, stroking through the fabric. Ruslan caught my wrist and yanked me to his lap, forcing me to spin so his front was pressed against my back. "Spread your legs. Let them see how wet you are for me."

I opened them, the air around my center doing nothing to cool it. The female who had been engaged with Anton stared hungrily at me, and Ruslan's chest vibrated against my back. "Do you want her to watch us?" His tongue traced the shell of my ear, and I shivered, core clenching.

"Yes," I breathed, nerves lighting at the idea.

Ruslan shoved his pants down to his thighs, gripping his shaft and aligning me over him. Ever so slowly, he sank into me, giving the female a show.

"Ruslan," I groaned as he simultaneously stretched me out

and filled me up. Once he was fully settled, he flatted a palm against my back and forced me to lean forward, taking him deeper. "Oh my Goddess," I moaned as he started to move.

He swept my hair over my shoulder, revealing my bare, scarred back with the perfect circle situated between my shoulder blades. "You and I are infinite, Izidora, just like this circle. In this life, in the next life, in all the lives after, we will find each other."

He pistoned into me from below, causing me to cry out at the fullness. "Now, everyone can see your mark. There is no need to hide what we have from the world."

"Us against the world," I whimpered as he thrust up into me again.

"Us against the world," he echoed, yanking me down and grinding my hips into his.

"Fuck," I groaned out, eyes rolling in the back of my head. Reaching down, I found my clit, circling it as the female watched with hungry eyes. The heady combination of the whisky, herbs, and Ruslan was driving me toward another release already.

Ruslan pulled me back against him, changing the angle again, and one hand wrapped around my throat, cutting off a hint of air and heightening my pleasure. His teeth and tongue attacked the bare side of my shoulder, and my pulse fluttered faster under his attention. He dropped his hand away, sucking over that spot, and I nearly exploded. Something between a moan and a whimper escaped my lips, and I circled my hips over him in time with my fingers.

"The sounds you make... the way your walls clench for me... fuck, you are intoxicating." Ruslan's thrusts grew harder as he chased his pleasure.

The female had moved to Anton's cock, her position mirroring my own as she watched Ruslan fuck me. The male on the floor alternated between sucking Anton's balls and sucking the female's clit into his mouth, pulling moans from both of them.

But her attention never left Ruslan and me as she watched us grind together. Wetness gushed down my thighs as I watched the exchange of pleasure across the table, and I groaned in time with her as the male flattened his tongue and licked from Anton's shaft up to her clit repeatedly.

"Make me come," I begged Ruslan, wound so tight I was certain I would snap at any moment.

"What do you say when you want something?" he asked, his tone not at all teasing but filled with wanton tension.

"Please."

"Good girl," he growled, and that was all I needed to fall apart.

"Ruslan!" I screamed, walls clenching his cock like a vice as I came. My hips rocked erratically against his for only a moment before he came too, groaning and burying his face in the crook of my neck as he twitched inside me.

Breathing hard, we pulled away, kissing roughly again as our orgasms subsided. A wave of weariness overtook me as he lifted me off him and pulled the hem of my dress back down. His cum dripped between my thighs, mixing with my own arousal.

Beside us, Liliana and Drazen were joined by Slavian and another female, the four of them swapping positions and partners for their next round of pleasure. Reaching around me, Ruslan poured two more shots of whisky, handing one to me before downing his own. I threw it back, allowing the burn to ground me. It hit me immediately, the alcohol mixing with the herbs until I felt reinvigorated.

More people slipped into our alcove to join the activities, and I sank into Ruslan, reeling from my orgasms and enjoying the moment of blissful unawareness from the world beyond the gauzy curtains.

INTERLUDE

The old Mage worked diligently through the night, long after anyone else would have surrendered to what appeared to be inevitable. His two greatest accomplishments – the new king of the Iron Realm and the king's mate – both needed him, the latter desperately so. All he had ever wanted was to show the world how smart he was, and he could not do that with both of them dead. No one would know of his greatness if they did not survive.

No one would etch his name into the history books, speaking of his ingenuity. His genius. How he had shoved the magic of Mages to new heights, showed off just how powerful their potions, incantations, and runes could be. The Mages might not have had magic inherently gifted to them like the Goddess and Fates chose to do with the Fae, Shifters, Angels, and Demons, but they deserved to be respected in their own right, for their own skill over the forces of the universe.

With a sigh, the old Mage grabbed a bottle of something he'd only briefly experimented with and returned to the side of the ashen female on his table. If his new master's mate died, he would kill himself too, though likely after the Mage himself was flayed and tortured for his failure. The threat of violence from his king kept him working, pouring the liquid between her lips and massaging her throat so it would hit her stomach. He tried everything he knew to repair the heart and spine of the broken female.

Hour after hour passed, and while her body knitted together, her mind was still far away, adrift in a world beyond theirs. Worry crept up his gnarled fingers and along his spine when even the strong salts did not cause her to stir.

The unbridled, fiery hatred that had shone in her eyes, directed at him during each small exchange they'd had, was utterly absent, and the old Mage realized just how much he longed for that look. If she didn't wake...

He shook his head, not even allowing himself to wander down the path of that thought.

His greatest creations were fated for power, for glory, for world-changing impacts. The Goddess was angry enough at him for what he'd done to unbalance her natural order, and he did not want to risk further wrath from her, a moment of petty vengeance taken along with the final breaths of his master's mate. But he did not care to stop his experiments completely, for his ideas were more important than the nature surrounding them. Not that he ever desired to leave his study. The world beyond these four walls and all the books that surrounded him was filled with strife and discomfort.

Here, he knew what to do. Here, he was the smartest in the room. Here, he was God.

Underground, time was merely an illusion, with no way to judge just how long he had been focused on his task. So he continued working, saving his greatest creation, despite the sway in his feet and the tremble in his hands.

———

THE OLD MAGE'S king approached him, flattening his palms on the tome-strewn table in the royal library. The request that slipped from his lips filled the Mage with delight. He'd been banned from continuing his work, but the king was changing his mind. His master's mate had lain slumbering for some time, and the king had thrown all his anger toward the old Mage away like it was sand in the wind. He asked him to make the Félvér even more powerful so the slaughter of the Night Realm would be swift and brutal.

Dark fire burned in those gray eyes the Mage had helped create, tendons popping in his neck as he cracked it from side to side. The king's rage was like nothing he'd ever seen – and he had seen much of it. The motherless child had brimmed with it, lashing out at everything and everyone, until finally he'd unleashed it on his siblings to win the title of heir apparent. The pain he inflicted on himself and others was personal in a way the old Mage would never understand, and as the young male grew into a mature one, he went from laughing him off to trembling beneath his wrath.

He was more than happy to oblige his master, as it gave him the opportunity to continue his life's work.

As he returned down the endless spiral staircase to his lair, he thought through all the things he had wanted to try but had previously not had either the backing or the time for. The king had offered him extra help, though his subjects had to be willing, not forced or coerced like they had been when King Azim ruled.

The old Mage rubbed his withered hands together excitedly as he flipped through pages of an old notebook – one where he'd begun to think and document ways to help Félvér who were unable to shift into their inherited forms.

Long into the night, he poured over his texts, making new notes where necessary and rising only a few times to mix ingredients or search for what he was lacking. Anything he did not have, he noted on a separate parchment to proffer to the finance minister in a bid to fill his order. The pockets of the Iron Realm ran deep, and for this, no expense could be spared.

He would do this for his master because once the king had gained his victories, the Mage's experiments would continue unhindered – at least he hoped.

His greatness, his legacy, were not set in stone yet. There was still time to add more to the tableau of his accomplishments.

II

THE ANNOUNCEMENT

14

IZIDORA

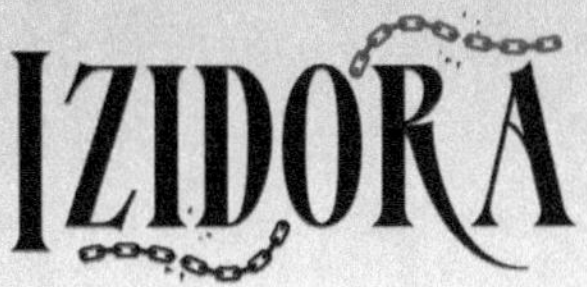

The army spread through the valley that nestled Radence like raindrops on a window. From the roof at Roc Palace, the camp was visible, but it was even more impressive up close. The sheer number of Fae and Félvér encamped in the space should have been impossible, but Drazen and his commanders made it work, somehow.

Though, navigating the camp was like trying to leap from stone to stone in a raging river without getting swept away. A laugh ripped from my throat as Liliana and I ducked just in time to avoid a thick wooden beam, only to pop up in the way of a Fae leading two dark horses toward the stables. We spun to avoid them, colliding and grasping each other for balance. Everyone else seemed to know the steps to this dance, and Liliana and I were unwelcome intruders in it.

I tugged her hand to get her moving again. "Come on, we're already late," I said, grinning. The energy of the camp was invigorating, and I opened my senses to it as we made our way to the central tent where the others waited.

Liliana rolled her eyes. "If it hadn't taken so long to wash the sand out of my hair we would have been here sooner. I'm blaming Drazen."

I snorted, ducking under a bit of rope that acted as a makeshift guardrail for a walkway. "You two weren't even grappling on the ground. It was an *entirely* different show."

Liliana popped up, flicking her wet braid over her shoulder. "You enjoyed it."

Now it was my turn to roll my eyes. "So did every other male there."

She shot me a mischievous smile. "More males for my harem."

We fell into laughter simultaneously, doubling over until a very masculine cough sounded. Straightening, we found Ruslan and Drazen watching us, arms crossed over the broad chests. I took one look at Liliana and burst again, though the males clearly did not find our amusement, well, amusing.

"What have the two of you been up to now?" Ruslan teased, eyes glimmering like smoky diamonds.

"Nothing you should concern yourself with, Russy," Liliana said, patting his chest and shouldering between him and Drazen with a swagger in her step.

I pressed my lips together to smother another giggle that threatened to bubble up.

"Did she just call me *'Russy'*?" my mate asked, incredulous as he glanced over his shoulder at my best friend.

"That she did," Drazen intoned, his eyes glued to her ass as she swayed her hips.

A roar tore through the air, halting Liliana in place. I whipped my head around, searching for the source of the sound and the clanging iron that accompanied it. The two of us caught the direction simultaneously and moved to follow it, shooting each other curious looks. The males tracked closely behind as we closed in on whatever was angry enough to cause such a ruckus.

Surrounding the massive iron bars, a dozen soldiers shouted at one another, racing back and forth with raw meat and whips. Two massive white beasts paced back and forth in the cage, shaking the ground beneath their enormous white paws with their movements.

"Those are Fehérmedve," Ruslan whispered in my ear. "The beasts are legendary for their aggression. They live high and deep in the Agrenak Mountains, and are notoriously difficult to find. Though if you do, you're unlikely to live to tell the tale."

Air fled my lungs as I watched them swipe at the soldiers, baring their teeth and standing on their hind legs before dropping back down. The massive bear-like creatures were as thirsty for blood as I was. "Are you planning on using them in battle?" I asked Ruslan.

A sinister laugh rumbled in his chest. "That is why I had the High Priestess summon them during Béke."

Seeing these creatures charging toward them would be a shock for every Fae standing against us.

"Leave one with me on the battlefield. It's the best protection you can give Izidora," Zuriel said from beside me, nearly making me flinch with his sudden nearness. I hadn't heard my cousin approach, which I supposed was his intent.

"Can you tame it?" I asked him, raising a doubtful brow.

"I have lived for over two thousand years. Beasts do not frighten me," he stated, never tearing his attention from the Fehérmedve. "Have you tried riding them?"

"Ride them?" Ruslan laughed at the absurdity of his suggestion. But his ice blue eyes did not waver, and his lips did not twitch like he had tried to make a joke. "You're serious."

To prove his point, he strolled away from us and through the chaos of the soldiers trying to calm the beasts, flattening a hand against the iron bar. The black eyes of the closest one narrowed on him, and it dropped to all fours, growling low as he approached the Angel. Zuriel didn't flinch as the Fehérmedve swiped at him.

Whispers broke out among the onlookers waiting to see if the beast would eat the Angel. My heart thudded against my ribs as the certainty that Zuriel was about to die filled me. My cousin stood there, stoic and unmoving, like all reason had fled his brain.

But then, the Fehérmedve backed away, sitting on its haunches and blinking. Zuriel slipped between the massive bars, and my jaw dropped open at his boldness. The other Fehérmedve remained at the opposite end of the cage as Zuriel approached its companion. Sliding his hand through the white fur, he *petted* the beast before climbing atop its back and gripping the scruff at the peak of its shoulders to hold himself on.

The Fehérmedve rose to all fours and trundled along the edge of the cage, all the while allowing Zuriel to remain atop its back and *ride it*.

"Tell me I'm not dreaming," Drazen murmured, and I tore my gaze from the absolute madness in front of me to glance around. Dozens more had appeared to watch Zuriel ride the Fehérmedve, and more appeared by the second.

"Nope," Liliana replied, studying the sight. "Zuriel is riding the Fehérmedve."

My cousin dismounted, patted the creature's hide, and easily shimmied through the bars and returned to our little group.

"You've been holding out on me," I chastised him. He knew how much I liked animals, and I pretended to act extra affronted at his secret-keeping.

He shrugged with a wry grin. "You never asked."

"What other useful information do you have in your two-thousand-year memory?" Drazen questioned, earning a half-smile from the Angel.

"There's probably a lot, but you'll have to be more specific if you want me to actually remember it." Zuriel's smile widened, clearly enjoying himself and his secrets.

A threatening rumble emanated from Ruslan's chest. "If any other *useful* war secrets come up during our discussions, please make them known, Zuriel."

He dipped his head in acknowledgement, then swept a hand out in front of him. "Of course. I'll follow you to the war tent."

Ruslan rolled his eyes but strode off in that direction, bringing our entourage with him.

The tent was dark and cool, and I had to blink several times for my eyes to adjust. Our group fanned around the long table, gathering in factions that supported various aspects of our forces.

My mouth thinned when I saw the old Mage. I couldn't deny his helpfulness in both saving my life and helping Ruslan and the other Félvér complete a full shift into their inherited forms. Yet, I didn't trust him, and I didn't plan on befriending him. It was best to keep him at arm's length.

A red metallic cocktail waited for me at the closest end of the table, and Ruslan guided me there, where we stood shoulder to shoulder, ready to command the Iron Realm's forces. Over a month had passed since I'd awoken, and I still wasn't quite strong enough to forego the Demon blood cocktails. At least I wasn't struggling to walk any longer. Now, I was able to spar with Liliana and the others, and I had taken Zuriel's advice about working more with Ruslan, using our mate bond to our advantage. He'd seemed relieved when I suggested it to him, in fact.

He glanced down at me as if he sensed I was thinking about him. I offered him a soft smile, then grabbed the drink. I twisted the lid and sipped while Ruslan called everyone to order.

"With only a few weeks until we need to make an appearance for the Day Realm princess's announcement, I want a status report on all facets of the army. While we are in Zheka, I plan on rallying further soldiers in order to prepare for our assault on the Night Realm. It is time we put the Night Fae in their place once and for all."

The males thumped their chests or the table, sounding their belief in our cause.

"Rares, have you managed to find *anything* to help against Kazimir's binding magic? Ruslan asked, and I turned my attention to the Mage. This point alone had plagued Ruslan's sleepless nights, the guilt of what had happened to me gnawing at him. No matter how many times I tried to reassure him, he couldn't let it go. Because of that, he wanted, almost more than anything, to lock the dark magic away to protect us all.

"Not yet. I will keep working," Rares promised, a tremble in his hands as he braced himself for the inevitable wrath.

To my surprise, Ruslan merely nodded, though his shoulders tensed and a succession of pops filled the silence as he cracked his knuckles. "Drazen," he said through gritted teeth, and his cousin took his cue to enter the discussion. As the males spoke, I flicked my gaze to Liliana, sitting on a bench in the shadows behind the Félvér. She soaked in every word, a slight pinch between her brows as she concentrated.

I should probably do the same.

Refocusing, I spotted carved stone pieces moving about the map of Északi as one of the commanders I didn't know relayed information about new tunnels beneath the Agrenak Mountains. "These will allow us direct entry into the Night Realm, though they are more narrow than previous ones due to the time constraint."

"That's fine, so long as we can converge quickly outside of them," Ruslan said, rapping his fingers against the table.

"With four exit points, it should speed up the process, yes," he replied, straightening.

Anton and Slavian provided further updates regarding the Félvér shifter units and their progress in learning to fight in their fully shifted forms. "It would be helpful if Rares could find a way to extend the life of the potion. Randomly shifting mid-fight and swinging your dick around on the battlefield instead of a sword isn't going to do anything but get you killed," Slavian commented.

Anton snorted. "Speak for yourself. My dick would intimidate anyone who laid eyes on it, no matter the circumstances."

Slavian, Drazen, and Ruslan rolled their eyes while Liliana and I sniggered.

"Let's be realistic," Drazen said, shooting a look at Anton.

He merely shrugged. "I am. I know you don't roll that way, Drazen, but I've caught you looking at Steel before. You have to admit little Anton is a force to be reckoned with."

A laugh burst from Liliana before she slapped a hand over her mouth to silence it.

Ruslan sighed and cracked his neck. "If we can get serious again, we still have much to discuss."

"Fine," Anton huffed, raising his hands in surrender.

Gozzak looked at Xorrek, a question etched into his red eyes. "I wonder if our magic would work with these too?"

"What's your magic?" I asked. I possessed an extensive knowledge of Angel magic, both from the books Ruslan had given me and my lessons with Zuriel. But I realized I'd never looked much into Demon magic despite how many of the blood drinks I'd consumed.

"We both have blood magic, Future Empress," Xorrek stated. "That is how we were able to help you get strong again."

My mouth popped open. "I didn't realize it was from magic. I thought Rares did some weird shit to make it work."

The Demons' lips twisted into wry grins. "Not every Demon has blood magic, but it is one of the more common gifts we possess. Its power varies by the wielder, but in my case, my blood has an enhanced ability to heal. During the Great War, I took a sword to the chest that would have killed any other Demon, and yet the moment I pulled it out of my chest, my veins clotted and muscles knit. I returned to the fray a few minutes later," Xorrek replied, like what he'd experienced was an everyday occurrence.

A newfound appreciation for the two bloomed in my chest. "Thank you for lending me your magic then."

"Anything for the cousin of Zuriel," Gozzak said, and the Angel dipped his head in acknowledgement.

Rares tapped a finger on his chin, considering their suggestion. "I have a few ideas and enough blood at the moment that I shouldn't need another offering from you to test it."

"See it done," Ruslan said. "Now, is there anything else?"

A female I wasn't familiar with raised a few questions about her unit and another about the housing situation. Absently, I dipped into my well of magic and stoked the white fire there. A thought of hatred popped into my mind, and the crystal flared with a wave of pitch black. The heady power rushed through my veins, and I allowed myself to sink into the dark embrace.

"Izidora," Ruslan said with a little force, and I blinked, reverie snapping. He offered me a twisted smile. "Are you ready to go?"

Then I realized most of those present for the meeting had vanished. Heat crept up my chest and dusted my cheeks. Glancing around at my friends, my family, who remained behind, an idea sparked in my head. "Can we all eat together tonight at Ryza?"

"Would that make you happy, sprite?" Ruslan spoke in my mind.

"Yes. I didn't realize what Xorrek and Gozzak were actually doing for me. I want to show them how much I appreciate it."

"Then we shall all dine together."

"I don't see why not," Ruslan commented, glancing around the circle. "In fact, why don't we have a larger gathering? We haven't had a night of celebration since Béke, and I believe we all deserve a small break. You know, the calm before the storm."

Drazen snorted a laugh. "Are you the storm, Ruslan?"

"The fire storm," he pointed out, flicking black flame into his palm. "Alongside the other Dragon shifters, now that Rares has found a potion to assist our transformation."

Images of Ruslan and the other Dragons raining fire on the Night Fae army flashed through my mind, curling my toes with wicked delight. I pushed the images into Ruslan's mind, and he shot me a heated smile.

"Don't tempt me, sprite. You wanted to dine with our friends."

I offered him a lascivious one in return. *"It wouldn't be as fun if it was all pretend. It will be much better after we make it happen."*

"You make a fine point. We cannot marry until we see it through."

"Agreed. Otherwise, what would be the point?" I teased back.

"Are you two speaking mind to mind again?" Liliana groaned. "Every time, it's something sexual. You two are terrible."

A laugh slipped free, and I looped my arm through hers. "Your jealousy is showing."

"Ugh, I don't even care," she giggled back. "But I do care about food. Ruslan, you better have the servants bring the good wine tonight too, or I'll never forgive you."

"Anything for the best friend of my mate and future empress," he drawled, stealing me from her. Amusement flitted through our gathered group, and then we were whisked away by Ruslan's magic, landing in the dining hall at Ryza Citadel moments later. The males divided and conquered the tasks while Liliana and I made ourselves comfortable around a long table, mocking them and earning playful jabs back.

The moment was so peaceful, so light, and exactly what I needed after so many days focused on vengeance. I clung to every drop offered to me, because I knew without a shadow of a doubt that it wouldn't last.

15

ENDRE

The Crystal Fae deserted us at the border of the Day Realm like they couldn't extricate themselves fast enough. How the soldiers hadn't cracked under Kazimir's erratic madness was beyond me. From his taunting about adding their wives to his harem, to trying to befriend them with promises of wealth and positions of power, I was shocked we were still alive. Most days, I was constantly on edge, ready to reach for my magic and sword at a moment's notice. Fates, I was close to cracking, and he was my fucking king. We'd been friends for our entire lives, and with each passing day, I knew the male in front of me less and less. The binding magic was eating away at who he was, and though the loss of Kriztof, Zekari, and Kirigin was acute, the loss of Kazimir was like a slow march to death.

But I couldn't abandon him, or the Night Realm, not when I was the only one still able to break through to him on his worst days. Unfortunately, as we entered the Day Realm, those skills were again necessary.

The white haunches of the Crystal Faes' mounts bunched

and flexed as they galloped in the direction of the lakelands, leaving us on the precipice of the grassy plains.

"Kazimir," I warned as they rode away, "Don't do anything rash. They're leaving now, and we don't have an escort in the Day Realm. We can relax and enjoy the rest of our ride. Maybe we'll even see some of those elusive savannah cats this time."

I really did want to see the predators that lurked among the tall stalks, and since it was only Kazimir, Viktor, and myself traveling through the Day Realm this time, the shy beasts might show themselves.

Kazimir snorted, though not in a condescending way. "You and your animals. We'll relax and stay as quiet as possible so you can hopefully see one."

For the first time in weeks, a grin tugged at the corner of my mouth. "Thanks."

"What did we see last time the Nighthounds went to the Day Realm?" Viktor asked, knowing I would remember.

"Savannah cats, an olyphant, a pack of kutya, and a lot of szarvas," I replied. The olyphants were incredible, though they mostly roamed near the coastal plains, far from Zheka, where we were headed.

The deeper we delved into the Day Realm, the hotter it became. The cool air drifting down from the glaciers was gone, replaced by the brilliant sun beating down and spots of shade that were few and far between. For miles in every direction, there was only grass swaying in the light breeze, and the sound of birds cawing as they flew overhead. Occasionally, the lazy smoke of a fire drifted into the air in the distance, signaling a small village on the plains.

By midday, the three of us had stripped out of our leather chest plates and untucked our tunics, unbuttoning them to allow the weak breeze to cool our overheating skin.

"Fucking Fates, it doesn't ever cool off here does it?" Viktor swore, finally giving up and laying the sweat-soaked fabric across his mount's back. Not that it helped – our horses' hides shone along with our skin.

"Nope," I laughed, tugging off my own shirt and tucking it behind me. Kazimir joined us, grinning like a fool, and suddenly, it felt like when we were children, lighthearted and without a care in the world.

"Pass me the wineskin," Viktor said, holding his hand out for it. Unhooking it from my pack, I tossed it his way, and he squirted the white liquid into his mouth. "At least the Crystal Fae were nice enough to let us have some of their wine."

"And you trust it's not poisoned?" I teased, brushing my wet locks out of my eyes.

"I don't even care at this point as long as it helps me withstand the heat," Viktor commented, tossing the skin at Kazimir.

"The leaves are turning in the Night Realm, and yet here we sweat," Kazimir groused before sipping the wine and tossing the leather back to me. It was still cold despite the air around us, refreshing in its crispness. The Crystal Realm wines were by far the best, with the fertile soil beside their lakes infusing the grapes with the best flavors. I drank down several gulps before passing it along again.

We fell into an easy conversation, the likes of which we hadn't had in months, and ever so slowly, I began to believe that our arrival in Zheka, the capital of the Day Realm, wouldn't bring that much strife.

"Remember when Vadim challenged that Day Fae to a bare knuckle fight?" Viktor snickered, using his shirt to wipe the sweat from his face.

"I do," I said, grinning at the memory. "Both of them were so bloody, you couldn't tell who was winning anymore."

"That's what happens when you're only throwing punches,"

Kazimir commented. "That's why mixing all the styles together is important."

"That fight wasn't about *winning* so much as showing off for a pretty Day Fae female." I rolled my eyes, but a pang of longing for our friend's antics tugged on my middle.

"When it is not with Vadim?" Viktor sighed, though his words were said in jest.

"You're not much better, Viktor," I replied. "When are you going to find someone?"

He shrugged. "Maybe when I have the time. I'm a bit busy, and you stole the only sibling in our friend group."

The thought of Liliana sobered me instantly, and Viktor knew it. "Endre, I'm sorry, I–"

"It's fine, Viktor." But it wasn't fine, and as I gazed over the horizon in the direction of Zheka, I wondered if she would greet me there.

Kazimir remained notably silent, and with a peek out of the corner of my eye, I checked that he was still his normal self, and the madness had not regripped him. Tentatively venturing down the path, I asked him, "So will you marry Taya when we return?"

Holding my breath, I waited for the telltale flash of black in his eyes. But none came. "Maybe if I need a queen eventually, but for now, I don't think it's necessary," was his level-headed response.

"Fair enough," Viktor replied, cutting a look to me that said I needed to drop the subject.

The sun began to dip over the horizon, painting the sky in vibrant hues. It appeared massive as it descended, so much larger than it did when it was directly overhead, and for that reason I was utterly captivated with it, as I had been every time I watched the sun set over the Day Realm. Off to light another part of our world, it crept away until only a sliver remained.

With it, the breeze cooled, finally bringing some relief to our salty skin.

"Should we stop for the night?" I eventually questioned as the first stars winked into existence.

Viktor gestured to a copse of trees up ahead. "We can stop over there."

"Hopefully there's a small stream to refill our waterskins," I said, shaking mine. We were still close enough to the Agrenak Mountains that runoff from the peaks was possible. After dismounting and securing the horses, we delved deeper between the sparse, twining limbs and discovered a stream large enough to bathe in.

Water would be scarcer the closer we ventured to Zheka until we were almost upon the capital city. So we filled every container we had to the brim, then jumped in and washed the dirt and sweat from our skin. The horses were grateful when we led them there to drink too. Cupping our hands, we cleaned their hides, offering them what relief we could before we had to ride into the heat again.

We risked a small fire after clearing brush beside the stream, allowing the horses free reign over the grass they loved to munch. Not bothering with tents, we rolled out blankets and used our bags as pillows as we stared at the stars decorating the black canvas overhead, caressing our magic and refueling us for the ride the following day.

I chewed on the end of a piece of grass and counted them as my eyelids grew heavy, the night cooling quickly and drying my skin.

Viktor cleared his throat, and I opened one eye in his direction. He was propped up on one elbow, looking at Kazimir and me. His sage eyes held a hint of sentimentality that was unusual for our strategic, logical friend. "I know we don't say this often enough, but I think it's important. I love you guys. We're brothers for life, no matter what happens."

Without hesitation, I pulled him in for an embrace, and Kazimir joined us, sharing a moment of affection for one another. "Love you too, Viktor," I said, releasing him.

"Brothers for life," Kazimir echoed, his emerald eyes clearer than they had been in months.

As we resettled ourselves, sleep came easier, and I was whisked away to the land of dreams where Liliana awaited me.

16

RUSLAN

It was Izidora's birthday, and like every year, I had a special event planned to celebrate. Only this year, my mate was finally in my arms, and she would join me as we hiked to my favorite spot in the Agrenak Mountains and watched the sun appear over the horizon.

"Ugh, it's so early," she complained as I pulled her flush against me to wake her.

"Happy birthday, mate," I whispered in her ear, ghosting my hot breath across her neck. Goosebumps broke out across her bare skin, and I nipped at a few along her shoulder before throwing back the blankets and forcing her out of bed.

"It's not even light outside yet," she protested, the words coming out jumbled as she yawned wide.

"I know, but I want to take you somewhere," I responded, kissing her on the forehead and handing her leather pants and a jacket, along with new fur-lined boots, since the ones I'd gifted her when she first arrived in the Iron Realm were irrevocably ruined when we slaughtered her former captors.

"What about–"

"Food?" I smiled. Izidora was always hungry, and I knew

better than to be unprepared. I jogged into the living space and returned with two bags that smelled of vanilla and bacon.

The smile that split her face was worth her earlier grumbles, and fuck if she didn't still make my blood sing with her sparkling eyes. "Okay, fine. Where are we going?"

"You'll see," I promised, leading her by the hand to the spiral stairs that led to the roof. "Hold these." I handed her the bags of food, and she sniffed them longingly as I threw open the hatch.

Taking the bags back from her, I watched her ass as she climbed up the ladder and hoisted herself onto the roof before following her out into the chilly morning air. She shivered, and I wrapped my arms around her, lending my heat to my always chilly mate.

"Now what? Surely you didn't bring me up here before dawn broke to show me something. We've been here before," she teased, entwining her arms with mine.

"Call on your wings. We're going to fly over there," I pointed to a small landing space barely visible across a field of jagged rocks, "and then walk the rest of the way." The rocks were fantastic for protecting the mountain palace I had built for Izidora, but also a pain to cross.

She chewed her lip, eyeing them with trepidation.

"I'll always catch you if you fall," I reminded her, giving her another squeeze before releasing her and stepping back. She needed space to bring her ethereal wings into existence, though I wouldn't mind running my nose through the soft feathers and making Izidora writhe in pleasure from touching the sensitive spots. My Demon-Dragon ones flared behind me, stretching before settling on either side of my shoulders. With one last glance at me, Izidora's white wings appeared, though her teeth still dug into her bottom lip.

Capturing her chin in my hand, I pulled it free. "That's mine to bite."

Her aquamarine eyes blazed with white fire before I released her. Stepping back, I flapped my wings hard and launched myself into the air, hovering as I waited for her to join me. She closed her eyes, lips moving as she spoke affirmations to herself like she did every time she needed a boost, then leaped into the air beside me.

"If you want some light to guide your path, use your magic. But we're going across." Shooting her a reassuring smile, I sailed toward the rocks, barely visible in the pre-dawn light. Taking my suggestion, she threw some white bubble lights into the air, and they chased my mate as she flew forward, remaining within reach of me. Her brow furrowed with determination as we passed over row after row of serrated death. When we landed on a clear patch of rock on the other side, she exhaled, long and slow.

"You didn't even need me, sprite. You are so strong," I praised, and she beamed up at me, relief written all over her face.

"I wish I was more confident with my flying," she admitted, nudging a rock with the tip of her boot.

"You'll get there. You didn't experience it from a young age, so it makes sense that you're nervous now. You won't even need me to fly beside you soon. You'll be leaving me to soar among the peaks by yourself."

The bubble lights danced playfully around us, and I snatched at one in an attempt to catch it.

"And you would want me to do that?" she quipped, raising a teasing brow.

Grasping her shoulders, I crouched down so we were at eye level. I wanted her to see how serious my next words were. "Sprite, I want you to do anything that makes you happy. I'm not going to hold you back from anything. I'm here to empower you, to protect you, and to love you, not to tell you where to go, what to do, or who to be."

"Thank you," she whispered, her voice thick with emotion.

"Come," I said, grabbing her hands. "We need to hurry to get there before the sun rises."

A small path cut through the rock, and we followed it, scaling the mountain through switchbacks and rock scrambles until we neared the clouds. Izidora panted in front of me and stopped to catch her breath more than once. It was a different kind of physical exertion, and one she needed to continue training and conditioning her body. The following day we were set to depart for the Day Realm, and I needed to know she could handle any challenge I threw at her.

"How much farther?" she asked through gasped breaths.

"Not far. We're almost there."

She nodded, the braid down her back whipping around as she gritted her teeth and faced the rocks once more. I grinned to myself and followed her, pride swelling in my chest. If I had to pick one quality about my mate that I loved above all else, it would be her unbreakable will. Nothing and no one would stop her once she set her mind to a task.

"Start climbing to the right," I called, and she shuffled along, scrambling up and over a large boulder. A moment later, I pulled myself up beside her, hearing her delicate gasp as she surveyed the view.

Just below our feet, fluffy clouds hugged the ridge, while at eye level the highest peaks were visible, barely blocking out the light of the sun rising to the east.

"Do you see Vasvain?" I asked her, gesturing to where the sun had just peeked around its apex.

She shielded her eyes as she squinted in the direction I pointed. My Dragon senses were sharper than hers, so while the mountain was clearly visible to me, it might have been a little fuzzy for her. "I think so," she said eventually. "That's where I was hidden all those years?"

"Mmm," I responded, fishing in the bags of food for bacon and handing her a piece. "Every year on your birthday, I came to this spot and watched the sun rise over the mountains. I'd stay up here all day, spending it with you in the only way I could, wondering where my father was keeping you. I guess, somehow, our bond was signaling to me that you were over there, and I wish I had listened to that instinct harder, so I could have protected you from the abuse of King Azim and King Zalan."

A salty tear trickled down her cheek as she stared at me with a love so intense it was nearly painful. All I'd ever wanted was for someone to look at me that way, and all the days I sat here, wondering what it would finally be like to have a mate, could not have prepared me for the depths of devotion I would show this female. My thumb found her cheek, catching the tear and clearing it from her heart-shaped face.

"I love you," she whispered, her normally bright voice reduced to rasps that mirrored my own.

"I love you more," I promised, earning a smile from Izidora. She needed to hear those words as much as I did, if not more.

She was right when she told me being understood and accepted was the most glorious feeling. There were no barriers between us, nothing held back out of fear of judgment. Together, we were raw, emotional, and unguarded, unlike any relationship I'd witnessed before. It worked for us, not only because of our bond, but because of our traumatic pasts.

I pulled her to the ground, settling her in front of me and encasing her in my warmth before handing her a bag of food. We ate in comfortable silence as the light grew around us, clouds whispering past us on a soft breeze that wafted Izidora's rose and plum scent into my nostrils. Since accepting our mating bond, her scent was even stronger and more complex, and I would remember that scent across worlds and lifetimes.

"I have presents for you when we return home," I said once I'd finished my food, dusting the crumbs from my hands off to one side so as not to spill them on my mate.

"Oh?" she replied, craning her neck to look at me and exposing her pretty throat. "Let me guess, I have to wait until we return for you to tell me?"

"Correct," I teased, kissing her bare skin. "But I promise you'll like them."

"I like everything you buy me," she noted with a half-smile.

"Thankfully, you are easy to please," I winked at her, a hint of lust tainting my voice and sending a flush of red across her skin. Grasping her neck with a free hand, I tightened it ever so slightly, cutting off a hint of air. "And I do love pleasing you."

Her dark lashes fluttered against her cheeks, and I pulled her in close, running my free hand across her flat stomach, dipping lower. "Please," she begged, and I continued downward until I cupped her pussy over her pants.

"Like that?" I purred in her ear, sending her shivering.

"Yes," she breathed, rolling her hips against my palm.

I rubbed it against the seam, eliciting a gasp. The scent of her arousal flooded my nostrils, and I inhaled it deeply, my cock hardening against her back. Dropping my hand from her neck, I unfastened her jacket, exposing the thin tunic underneath. Slipping my hand beneath it, I pressed my warm skin against hers and savored the fire that burned between us.

She whimpered as I traced circles across her belly in the direction of her waistband. "Fuck me here, Ruslan."

I needed no further encouragement. I stripped her jacket off, then tore her tunic over her head, leaving her heaving breasts barely contained by the wrap she wore around them. Her pants were next, boots temporality stalling my progress until she was nearly bare before me. "On your hands and knees," I growled, kicking off my own boots and stripping until I was naked behind her.

Her perfectly round ass faced me, her suntanned skin pebbling in the cool morning air, and I took a moment to admire the slope of her back and the muscles rippling across her shoulders as she braced herself against the smooth rock. Stroking myself a few times to the view to relieve the ache in my balls, I drank in our utter aloneness in the mountains that called to my soul. "Touch yourself," I ordered, and she immediately dropped a hand to her center, swirling her tiny fingers over her clit and making herself moan.

"Spread yourself for me," I rasped, watching hungrily as she spread her lips apart and dipped a finger inside. I stroked myself in time with her movements, and she whimpered as her digits slipped deeper.

"I need you."

"Not yet, sprite. Work yourself up for me."

She obeyed, breathy moans escaping her as she ground into her hand. Wetness dripped from her, and it took everything I had to hold back and watch her touch herself without shoving myself into her heat. Her body trembled, and her hips rocked as her pleasure heightened. Closing the distance between us, I trailed a finger along her spine, the ridges of the bone just below the surface of her smooth skin. She shivered at the sensation, releasing a low groan as my hand began rubbing her ass.

"Please, I want you inside me," she begged, looking over her shoulder at me through thick lashes.

"Make yourself come first, and then I'll fuck you into oblivion," I promised, a bead of moisture appearing at the head of my dick as images of us fucking inches from the edge of the rock flooded my mind.

"Okay," she agreed, her fingers beginning to work faster as she brought herself to climax.

Poised behind her, I stroked myself slowly as I waited for the moment she came all over herself. The pulsing pink lips were the first signs of her orgasm, and the reverberating cry she released was the second. She rode her hand through it, and my erection became nearly unbearable as wetness gushed from her.

"Good girl," I growled, pulling her hand away and lining myself at her entrance. In one powerful thrust, I seated myself inside her, and fuck, she was so tight, her walls still fluttering from her release. They gripped me as I began moving within her, and I gritted my teeth as my spine tingled in anticipation. Using one strong hand, I caught her throat and bent her toward me, forcing her spine to arch and take me deeper. "You are going to trust me, and you will not question me. Understood?"

Her pussy clenched around me in the most delicious way. "Understood."

Shuffling us forward, we neared the edge of the rock, and her breath came in shorter gasps that had nothing to do with her lust. "You will overcome your fear of falling today, sprite, and you will do it as you shatter around my cock."

"Oh fuck," she whimpered, trembling against me as I began working circles over her clit with my free hand while the other pinned her in place by her throat. Once she was sufficiently drenched, I slowly released her to the rock, wrapping her long braid around my fist and forcing her head to lift as I fucked her. Izidora's hands were a foot from the edge that careened into nothingness for thousands of feet, and her heartbeat was like a hummingbird's wings at the nearness.

But the thrill was soaking my cock, and I smirked as I slid in and out of her with ease. The slick noises coming from our thighs resounded around the mountain, mixing with Izidora's mewls and my groans of pleasure.

"Are you afraid?" I growled, seating myself fully.

"Yes," she moaned, throwing her head back at the fullness.

"Then I'll have to fuck you harder," I said, releasing her braid and grasping her hips instead.

"Oh!" she exclaimed, cut off as my brutal thrusts shoved her forward, inching toward the edge. The sun crested over the peaks, casting the most brilliant view from our high vantage point. Her gasp was a mix of awe and pleasure, and her pussy tightened around my cock in the most delicious way. She pressed her palms into the rock, forced to still her momentum and push back into me, taking me deeper inside her. "Ruslan, shit, I–"

My grip tightened until she yelped in pain, silencing whatever protest she offered. "You can take it," I told her. "You will survive because you have survived everything else thrown at you. Now come for me."

Those words were her undoing because a breath later, her walls clenched around me, forcing my movements to slow.

"Ruslan!" she screamed, loud enough that the echo of her cry lasted until I roared my release and banished the sound.

"Fuck, Izidora, you take my cock so well." My body twitched as I stilled, sweat dripping down my spine.

My future wife trembled on hands and knees with my dick still inside her, breathing heavy but no longer forcing her way backward and away from the edge. Exiting her was like leaving home, but I pulled her into my arms and carried her a safe distance away, cradling her like she was the most precious gemstone.

"That was..." she started, breathless.

"Exhilarating," I finished for her. She nodded, her aquamarine eyes alight. I smoothed back her hair, tucking it behind her pointed ear, and planted a kiss on her forehead. "I knew you could handle it."

"Deep down, I knew I could too." The shy, sleepy grin that stretched her lips made my heart skip a beat. She was so damn beautiful.

I rocked her in my arms while we came down from our high, until the sun beat heavily on us and the day's tasks called to us.

"Ready to go?" I groaned, loathe to leave this moment of peace we'd carved for ourselves.

"Yep," she said, extricating herself from my embrace and pulling on her clothes.

"I'll move us back to the palace since we are running short on time."

"And whose fault is that?" she teased, her face still slightly flushed from her orgasms.

"Yours." She was fully dressed, and I swept her knees out from under her, earning a squeal as she was trapped in my arms. I chanted the spell to take us home, and the rocks blended together until we stood in our suite. I allowed her to slide to the ground, and she fisted my jacket and pulled me in for a quick kiss before sashaying her way to our closet to change. I watched her the entire time, already hungry for more.

Would I ever tire of my mate?

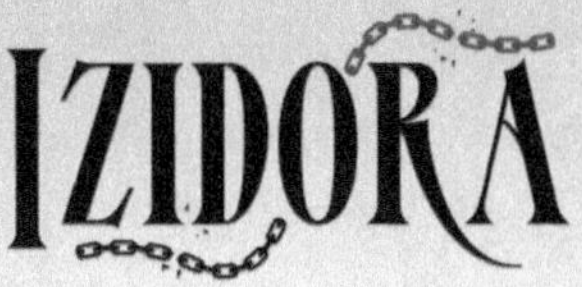IZIDORA

"**P**ut this on," Ruslan said, proffering me a strip of silk fabric when I re-entered our bedroom in clean clothes.

A small smile spread across my lips. "I just changed clothes, surely you don't want to get them dirty again already."

Ruslan huffed a dark laugh that went straight to my core, then stepped forward. Cupping the back of my head, he tipped it up so I could stare deep into his eyes. "Sprite, there's nothing I want more than to spend every moment of every day in bed with you. Hearing you scream my name while you fall apart, those moans you make when I hit just the right spot. Watching you come to life under my fingers." The hardness digging into my stomach made me want to do all of that and more again.

"But we're late for your presents." He brought the blind up and tied it over my eyes. The smooth, cool fabric brushed against my heated cheeks. Hot breath ghosted over my ear a moment later. "And while I am the emperor, and everyone must wait on me, I don't want the food to get cold."

Then, Ruslan whispered the words to move us, and I clutched his broad chest, trusting that wherever he was taking us was going to be incredible. Especially with the promise of more to eat. The flying sensation ceased, and as if to make its point, my stomach rumbled loudly.

Ruslan moved my hands from his torso into his own, and led me forward. I tuned in to my most familiar senses - smell and sound - trying to discern where we were. An interesting mix of musk and leather and sugar hit my nostrils, followed by a hushed whisper.

Stables? Why would Ruslan want to obscure my vision for this?

"Watch your step," he murmured, and I eased a foot forward, finding a small bump in the ground. A few more moments passed before we abruptly turned to the right and a familiar whinny hit my ears.

The silk slipped away, and I blinked a few times as my eyes adjusted to the light.

"Surprise!" everyone yelled, and then I took in the view.

Liliana, Drazen, Zuriel, and a dozen others were gathered around a table arranged in a U formation, and at the center stood Mistik, her dapple gray coat gleaming in the morning sun. A new diamond-studded halter adorned her face, catching the light as she tossed her head as if to say "come here and give me a hug."

I whipped my head to Ruslan, eyes brimming with happy tears. "You put this together for me?"

His answering grin nearly melted me on the spot. "This is your first *real* birthday, sprite. I wanted you to spend it with everyone and everything you love, because you deserve it. Your twenty-second year of life should start off with a bang."

"It already did," I teased in his mind.

"And that was just the first round," he shot back. Then he dropped my hand and placed his on the small of my back. I didn't hesitate to race forward and greet all my friends in turn.

"Happy birthday, Izidora!" Liliana squealed, shoving a box into my hands.

"What is it?" I asked her, admiring the aqua box tied with a white ribbon.

"Open it and see, silly," she admonished.

"I thought we agreed no presents until everyone was seated," Ruslan groused as he came up behind us.

Liliana scoffed. "As if I would wait. I had to get something over you."

"I don't think anything you give Izidora will top what I gave her this morning," he shot back.

"Ugh, your dick does not count as a gift," Liliana scoffed.

I snorted a laugh. "You saw it at Steel, Lil. It definitely is."

Ruslan preened with masculine pride as he shot Liliana a triumphant grin.

With a shake of my head, I pulled at the ends of the ribbon and then wiggled off the lid of the box. Inside were two bracelets, both silver in color with an aquamarine and light green tourmaline framing two letters: I and L.

"They're friendship bracelets!" Liliana exclaimed, impatiently pulling them out and snapping them onto our wrists.

I pulled her in for an embrace immediately. "I love them. Thank you, Lil."

Mistik whinnied again, and I released my friend, turning to my horse. "And don't you look beautiful in your new halter," I cooed, brushing my fingers against her soft fur. She nodded, then jerked me forward, sending me half stumbling into her neck. I wrapped my arms around it and breathed in her scent.

"Just the first in a long list of presents I got you," Ruslan said, amusement lining his voice. "They'll be paraded out as we eat."

Giving my horse one last squeeze, I turned to face him. "Are there more cinnamon rolls?"

He snorted like I'd told a joke. "Would it be your birthday if there wasn't one at least the size of your head?"

"Good point," I quipped, following him around the table to two empty chairs in the very center. A groom led Mistik away, clearing the area for the servants I noticed waiting in the wings, hoisting silver platters on their shoulders.

"She'll be back," Ruslan told me as the first servant stepped forward, revealing a rainbow of fruit. She scooped a handful onto our plates before moving on to Liliana sitting to my right. Zuriel was on her opposite side, along with Xorrek and Gozzak, while Drazen sat beside Ruslan, a buffer between Anton and Slavian. Even Artur, Kriath, and Savaich were in attendance, all toward the end of the table and chatting with a few other Félvér – Natasha, Aliana, and a few other females I knew from the army.

As food continued to pile on plates, Anton leaned down, his eyes dancing as he regarded Ruslan and me. "So how was your hike this morning?"

A warning growl slipped from Ruslan's throat as he stared down the High Lord.

"We had so much fun. The view was... breathtaking," I replied. A laugh burst from Liliana, and I shot her a mischievous grin over my shoulder. Zuriel snorted and shook his head.

"I can imagine the high was... incredible," Anton chuckled, slapping Slavian on the shoulder. The other High Lord rolled his eyes.

"That was the worst joke you've ever come up with, Anton," he sighed.

Before Anton could retort, a rumbling caught all our attention. Cedomir, Ruslan's longtime chef, pushed a cart around the far corner of the stable with great care. He slowed to avoid an uneven bit of stone, then continued on. The smell of vanilla and cinnamon was divine as he neared, and my mouth watered auto-matically.

He came to a halt right in front of us, shooting me a conspiratorial wink before stepping forward and lifting the lid on the cart with a dramatic flourish.

Ruslan hadn't been kidding. The cinnamon roll – or cake – was nearly the size of *me*. Before I'd even had a chance to take in the enormous desert, Ruslan flicked his wrist, igniting twenty-two candles with his black fire.

"Stand up and make a wish before you blow them out," Ruslan said, his smirk stretching from ear to ear.

Rising, I braced my hands on the edge of the table and stood on my tiptoes to get closer to the decadent delight. The smell was even more intoxicating this close. I closed my eyes, preparing to make this wish.

It wasn't hard to come up with what I wanted.

Revenge.

And with that, I blew on the candles, sending them flickering before they winked out completely. Everyone cheered, and then drinks were served, wine flowing easily into my belly as Cedomir sliced the cake and placed a heaping serving in front of me, including extra melted frosting to coat the sides.

"Thank you," I beamed up at him.

"Anything for you, Future Empress," he replied, then moved along, offering pieces to everyone else.

We tucked into our food, and I fell into conversation with Liliana and Zuriel. She had the latest gossip from the citadel, something about three of the servants getting caught in a broom closet in a compromising position.

"Apparently, the first female that walked in just asked if she could join, which only led to more noise, until the head of cleaning found them all and yanked them out of there," Liliana said around a mouthful of eggs.

I stuck my fork into the cinnamon roll cake and moaned as it slid across my tongue. Nothing should be allowed to taste this good. The frosting was the perfect sweetness, the cinnamon and vanilla in perfect harmony, and the core perfectly soft and warm.

My eyes popped open when I heard Zuriel and Liliana laughing. "If I didn't know any better, I'd say you were about to orgasm from Liliana's story," Zuriel teased, a wry grin twisting his lips. "But knowing your fondness for cinnamon rolls, it's entirely plausible that you'd react that way to this cake."

As if to prove his point, he took a large bite of his slice, mimicking me while I tried not to choke on my laughter. Liliana had no such luck and spluttered some half-chewed food onto her plate before shoving the rest down with a long sip of her bubbly wine.

"That's not even the first time that's happened, either," Zuriel continued while Liliana and I tried to calm ourselves. "It seems to be a recurring problem with that portion of the staff. There must be something in their cleaning supplies."

"Zuriel, I didn't know you were such a gossip," I teased, going for a particularly frosting-coated bit of the cake.

Gozzak barked a laugh from down the table. "When Zuriel speaks, I always listen. He somehow knew everyone's business when more Telivér lived beneath Ryza. Maybe that's why he's so quiet. He's gathering information that we don't even realize we're giving."

"But I only shared the juiciest tidbits with you two and Ithuriel," Zuriel replied, not looking at all ashamed.

"Oh, then you have to tell us the most shocking thing you learned. No matter how far back. You do have thousands of years of memory," I teased.

Zuriel's icy blue eyes glittered with amusement. "You two are going to love this one."

"Oh?" Liliana and I said simultaneously.

"Before either of you were born, one of the High Lords had married a Centaur Shifter Félvér, who happened to have a twin brother," Zuriel began, before Xorrek and Gozzak howled with laughter. Zuriel shot them a bemused grin, and my curiosity was piqued. Clearly the two Demons knew of this story.

"As you both know, free use of herbs has been common in the Iron Realm for some time. One night while his wife was out with the other High Ladies, the High Lord partook a little too much. His wife's brother happened to be staying with them at the time, and, according to the rumor, he was the one who encouraged the male to have too much."

Liliana made an oohing sound, rubbing her hands together. "This is going to be good."

I leaned forward, not wanting to miss a word.

"One thing led to another, and the brother shifted into his Centaur form. From which the two had *relations*," Zuriel emphasized.

"Zuriel, you can't leave it that vague, I need details!" Liliana exclaimed, reaching for her drink and knocking the rest of it back.

The Angel chuckled while the Demons barked out laughs. "According to the servant they invited to join them, at first, the High Lord was *riding* the Centaur, if you catch my meaning."

Liliana and I both released a shocked gasp. "No way," I said, hand flattening over my chest.

"Mhmm. And afterward, the Centaur had his way with the High Lord, still in his shifted form," Zuriel added.

"But with which penis?" Liliana pressed.

"What do you mean, which one?" I questioned, brows dipping together.

The four of them burst into laughter again. "Why do you think Konsteon always has that bandana on?" Zuriel asked.

"Because—oh," I said, realization dawning on me. My cheeks flamed, and I giggled away my embarrassment. "So wait, they had a servant join them too?"

"The male took the front while the High Lord took the rear, so to speak," Zuriel said, quirking a brow as he sipped from his liquor.

My mouth popped open into an O. "That is some serious gossip."

"Probably the best I've heard," Liliana added. "So did the wife ever find out?"

Zuriel snorted. "Of course she did. The whole realm knew despite his attempts to pay the servant off."

"So what happened then?" I asked, desperate for more.

My cousin shrugged. "They stayed together. And her brother lived with them for a long time after that, though their staff was... smaller afterward."

Liliana made another suspicious noise. "Do you think the three of them fucked each other?"

"That was the general consensus, yes," Zuriel replied, and both the Demons offered their agreement.

"How scandalous," Liliana commented, though her grin said she was eating this up more than the food on her plate. Honestly, I wanted to know more too. I had so many questions about how all of that played out.

But before I could voice another, Ruslan tapped his knife against his glass, drawing all our attention. He rose, towering over me and everyone else seated around the table. "Now that everyone has had time to eat, let's bring on the presents for my mate."

A few cheers sounded, and Liliana squeezed my arm. "You are going to love them all."

Ruslan winked at me, then released a sharp whistle. A moment later, Mistik reappeared, this time decorated in a set of armor. A piece of metal hugged most of her face, leaving room for her ears and muzzle, with roses etched into its surface, perfectly matching the armor Ruslan had gifted me during Béke. Those overlapping scales that moved so smoothly covered her neck and her sides, while a new saddle strapped over it. The dark leather was smaller than other saddles, but on either side, two sheaths bumped against her as she walked forward, the perfect places for my swords.

"So she is just as protected as you are should you need to ride her into battle, sprite," Ruslan said in my mind. Tears pricked my eyes. He knew exactly how much Mistik meant to me, and to lose her during the war would be yet another reason Kazimir needed to die by my blade.

"Thank you."

Mistik tossed her head, and the groom led her around another corner, only for another horse to appear. She was black like Twilight, though on her nose, a perfect white spot broke up her otherwise flawless color. And then from behind her, three more horses appeared – a black and white stallion with a long, flowing mane and tail, perfectly brushed; a mare whose coat nearly matched the color of my hair with long, lithe legs; and another stallion whose fiery spirit captivated me immediately as he pranced at the end of his lead.

"Once the war is finished and the barracks have been cleared, I am repurposing the stables there to house all your horses," he told me. "You can do with them what you like. Breed them, race them, ride them. All of it is yours."

Leaping from my seat, I hugged him, then raced around and greeted all my new mounts individually. The horses were all gorgeous, and I realized I'd spent too much time with them and not enough with my friends when Ruslan brushed against my mind. *"We have more for you."*

"We?"

"A few others have presents for you too. Liliana was supposed to wait, but we know how that went."

With a sigh, I returned to my seat. Ruslan squeezed my thigh under the table, and I flashed him a sweet smile that I hoped conveyed how happy all of this made me.

Drazen's chair scraped back as he dug behind him and produced his gift. "For some extra protection," he told me as he passed it over Ruslan's head.

I accepted the dark blue box and flicked it open, revealing a dagger small enough to strap to my thigh. "Thank you, Drazen, it's lovely," I said, lifting it from the box and letting it catch the sunlight. The edge looked wickedly pointed and I sliced it through the air, satisfied with the sharp sound it made.

Anton and Slavian gifted me a sack of herbs they swore would make me enjoy my time with Ruslan even more, while the Demons gave me a twin dagger to the one from Drazen. By the time everyone was finished, I had a pile of presents nearly as tall as me – not even counting the horses or Mistik's armor.

The day turned out brilliantly, the sun shining so brightly that it held off the early autumn chill, and between the wine, the love of my friends, and the weather, I was warm, content, *happy* down to my very bones.

By the time the servants returned to clear away our food and drink, the sun was nearly at its apex in the sky, and I was blissfully tipsy. My friends started to disperse, hugging me goodbye and wishing me a happy birthday again, until only Drazen, Liliana, Zuriel, Ruslan, and I remained.

Ruslan stepped away to coordinate the delivery of my gifts to our suite in the citadel, and then Zuriel cleared his throat, jerking his head like he wanted me to follow him. We stepped a little further away, allowing Drazen and Liliana to continue their own conversation undisturbed.

"I have something for you," Zuriel told me, producing a

small cylinder from behind his back. "I didn't want to give it to you in front of everyone else."

My brows dipped together as I studied my cousin. A sadness clung to his eyes despite his attempts to maintain a stoic facade. "What is it?" I asked.

"This belonged to Ithuriel. It is nothing fancy, like the amethyst necklace from Liessa. But he treasured this, and after he died, I treasured it for my memories of him. I think it is time it was yours," he explained slowly, unscrewing the lid. He tipped it to the side, the contents dumping into his hand.

"In Keleti, around the capital, most Angels live in homes built into tall trees. You would love the network of bridges that connect them, so you are forever suspended among the leaves. Unfortunately, many were lost during the great war, including the one where Ithuriel lived with our grandmother. This sliver of wood was all he managed to collect from it." Zuriel uncurled his fingers, revealing a smooth piece of red wood, one end slightly charred.

"He said it was his good luck charm, and that whenever he needed a dose of it, he would roll it between his fingers," Zuriel said, taking my frozen hand and opening it. He placed it there, then covered his palm with mine. "I held it whenever I needed to feel close to him, to remind myself of what he would have said during hard times."

A sob lodged in my throat. "I can't take this from you. He was like a father to you, too."

But Zuriel shook his head. "I have my memories of him. You do not. I will not need it in the future."

"Are you certain?" I pressed. As incredible as it was to be holding something that my true father had once touched, I couldn't take this comfort from my cousin. The pain he hid so well was etched on his face as he nodded. Zuriel hurt, just like I did, just like everyone did, and yet, he bore it all with such grace.

I hoped one day I could be like him. With all the sessions we had been doing, I knew it was possible.

"Thank you, Zuriel," I said, throwing my arms around him and squeezing as hard as I could. "You are my only family, and I don't know what I would do without you."

A wave of sorrow swept over me, so profound that it stole my breath. But as quickly as it came, it disappeared. "You are so strong, Izidora. Ithuriel would be so proud of the female you are becoming. I know I am."

And then, I did cry. Ruslan came to my side, and Zuriel relayed what he'd given me since I was unable to speak. Ruslan pulled me in, rocking me gently from side to side. My ear pressed against his chest, his heart beating steadily in my ear, while his arms muffled everything else around us. In Ruslan's arms, I was always safe, always protected.

"Thank you for everything you do for Izidora, Zuriel," I heard Ruslan say softly. "She loves you very deeply."

"I know," Zuriel replied. "Thank you for taking care of her too, Ruslan. She will need you."

"Never as much as I need her," Ruslan replied, and I felt the depth of his love down our bond. Finally, I was able to drag in a deep breath and rein in my tears. It had been a long day, filled with every possible emotion, and I was exhausted.

Ruslan seemed to sense I was ready to face everyone again, and he relaxed his embrace. I looked up at him, resting the tip of my chin on his chest. "I think I need a nap now. You woke me up too early."

He huffed a laugh, then planted a kiss on my forehead. "Then a nap you shall receive."

Stepping away, I embraced Zuriel one more time. "Thank you. If you ever need to use this again, you know where to find me."

He offered me a soft smile, then secured the wood in its container. "That I do. Sleep well, cousin."

I tucked the precious present against my chest as Ruslan whispered the words to return us to Roc Palace, where I placed my two most treasured items together in the back of our closet. My mother and father were still united, even after death, in their possessions that lived on. I took one long look at the amethyst resting atop the wood, and then I returned to bed, where Ruslan held me until I drifted off into a peaceful slumber.

RUSLAN

A knock sounded on the door to my office, and one of my sentries alerted us to someone requesting an audience. "Enter," I yelled, scratching the last of a set of instructions to the Iron Realm's finance advisor before straightening in my chair. Izidora snapped her book shut and set it on the leather couch beside her.

Liliana swept into the room, steps faltering momentarily when she noticed Izidora. I clocked the movement, curiosity raising one dark brow. She stopped in front of my desk, twisting a paper between her fingers. She opened her mouth to speak, then closed it, repeating the process several times while she struggled to form words. Eventually, she shifted from foot to foot, looking between us, though it was clear she was here to speak with me.

Was it something with Drazen?

"Do you want something to drink?" Izidora asked, probably sensing Liliana's nervousness through her empath abilities. Hopefully, some alcohol would loosen her tongue, though it struck me as odd that the only time she needed that was now.

"Yes, please," she said with a slight shake in her voice as she took a seat in front of me.

On the far side of my desk, a tray with neatly arranged crystal glasses and a hefty etched bottle of amber liquor waited for moments such as these. Grabbing three glasses and the alcohol, I poured a measure in each before handing one to her. Izidora floated her glass to her using tendrils of her white magic.

Liliana threw the drink back with a hiss, not even waiting for the traditional saying of the Iron Realm to pass from my lips. I merely sipped from mine and then rested it against the desk, swirling it as I studied her. Liliana seared her eyes into the paper in her hands, unable to meet either of our gazes. She smoothed the scroll over her leg. "I got this a while ago, but I haven't figured out the right time to say anything."

Her words hung in the air as I waited for her to continue, wondering what that slip of paper held.

Finally, she sighed, then lifted her gaze to meet mine. "Endre sent me this note. He, Viktor, and Kazimir will be in the Day Realm when we arrive."

Her words landed like the fireballs that they were, and my shoulders and jaw tightened immediately. The glass I had been holding shattered, scattering a thousand tiny shards over the table and cutting into my hand. I ignored the metallic scent that filled my nostrils as red coated my vision.

"And you waited until the day before we were supposed to leave to tell me this?" I growled, rising ever so slowly to my feet and towering over the female in front of me. To her credit, she straightened her shoulders and didn't back down. Out of the corner of my eye, I watched Izidora pale.

"We were busy with other things. Plus, you haven't told anyone in the other realms that Izidora is awake yet. It will be a shock to everyone." Liliana defended her actions like the traitor she was.

"Whether she is awake or not is irrelevant. Her protection against that bastard is what matters. Surely you of all people would have thought of that." My words were aimed to wound, but I was pissed and didn't give a fuck.

Liliana's eyes flashed with hurt and then anger. "You don't think I care about that? She's my best friend!"

"She is my mate!" I roared, smashing my fists on the desk and sending more shards spearing into my hands. "And the last time he saw her, she almost died. She spent six months in a void because of him."

The need to slake this rage was all consuming, and I grabbed another glass and threw it against the wall. It shattered with a satisfying crunch, but it barely took the edge off. Izidora hadn't moved, nor was she trying to siphon away my anger. Her eyes were glassy, faraway, and her chest rose and fell at a rapid pace. The urge to race to my mate's side and comfort her warred with the one to wrap my hands around Liliana's shoulders and shake her for her insolence.

"Are you seriously protecting Endre after all of this? After Drazen?" Liliana and I had never explicitly talked about their relationship, but I knew Drazen held deep feelings for her, even if she didn't return them in the same way.

"Drazen knows how I feel about Endre," she replied coolly. "And my brother and parents also live in the Night Realm."

"And all of them are loyal to *him*. Yet here you are, choosing Izidora. So why do you remain loyal to them when you are in *my* realm?" Liliana's eyes brimmed with angry tears, and she crossed her arms over her chest. But I wasn't finished. "We are going to *war*, Liliana. Do I need to start excluding you from our planning meetings? Banning you from training with my soldiers? Should I leave you behind so you don't go running to your *family* with all our secrets, trying to save them?"

In one smooth motion, I was over the desk and towering

over her, shaking with the force of my rage. Slowly, like a predator cornering its prey, I placed an arm on either side of her high-backed chair, caging her in. The light from the windows was snuffed out from my bulk, casting the Night Fae in shadow.

"Where. Do. Your. Loyalties. Lie?" I spit out the words like the venom they were. The fact that I even had to ask that fucking question lit another blaze in my blood.

For the first time, true fear flashed in her eyes, and the smell of it filled my sensitive nostrils. "With Izidora." Her eyes snapped to her *best friend* whose swirl of emotions blasted down our bond, mixing with my own.

Her answer was not good enough for me. Not when she'd lived for free under my roof, drinking my wine, eating my food, wearing clothes and jewels *Drazen* had gifted her. "And?"

"The Északi Empire," she gritted out, fists clenching from where they were bunched up beneath her arms.

"Of which the Night Realm is not a part," I reminded her, turning my back on her and stalking to Izidora. I secured her in my arms, hating how she trembled. That only angered me more. In one rough motion, I switched us so my back was against the couch and Izidora was nestled between my thighs.

"Beg for Izidora's forgiveness," I growled at Liliana.

"She doesn't nee–" Izidora started to say, but my grip on her hip tightened, silencing her.

Liliana's seafoam green eyes filled with guilt as she stared at us, her shield of anger melting as she saw the effect her betrayal had on my mate.

"Is that what was on the note?" she asked in a weak voice.

Liliana nodded.

"Why didn't you tell me then?" Izidora whispered. The shaky breath she dragged in vibrated against my chest, and then I felt that fierceness rising in her, that fire that captivated me sparking to life.

Liliana hung her head. "I don't know."

"You got the note in front of Izidora and didn't tell her?" I clarified, a warning note ringing in my tone.

She nodded again.

"Get. On. Your. Knees." I bit out every word, glaring at Liliana with so much violence that this time, she didn't hesitate to obey.

Sliding from the chair, she prostrated herself on the ground, hair spilling around her as she lifted her gaze. "I'm so sorry, Izidora. Please know that I never meant to hurt you."

Izidora squared her shoulders, leaning ever so slightly out of my hold. I let her go, wanting her to show off her power, what she was capable of. After all, we were the most powerful Félvér in all of Északi, and everyone should quake on their knees in awe of our might.

"I sense your sincerity and regret for not telling us sooner, and I know you've struggled with your feelings for both Endre and Drazen. For those reasons alone I will forgive you. But you hurt me, Liliana. I thought we were better friends than this. I thought we told each other everything." Izidora's voice wavered with her last statement, and twin tears tracked down Liliana's cheeks.

"I know. I'm so sorry. This whole friendship thing is new to me too." She pushed herself to stand, her shoulders slumped.

Izidora rose from the couch and embraced her friend. "Please don't keep something like that from me again."

Liliana gripped her back with an intensity that told me she wouldn't fuck up again. But my rage hadn't abated, and it would take far more time for me to move on from this than Izidora. I stalked back to my desk and righted my chair before settling into it again. Once the two broke apart, I snarled, "You may go now."

"But I thought everything was fine," she protested, glancing between Izidora and me.

"You have repaired your friendship with Izidora, but my trust will take more time to earn back," I snapped, swiping at the shards of glass still decorating the polished wood surface.

Liliana opened her mouth to speak, but I held up a hand to silence her. "Go!" The frayed threads of my self-control were unraveling too quickly for me to stop them. An itch burst along my skin, and through the haze of fury, I spotted black scales sucking in the sunlight.

Izidora raced to my side, placing a hand on my arm and trying to siphon away some of my emotions.

Liliana spun on her heel and stomped to the door, slamming it open with a bang that rattled the books on the shelves. It closed with just as loud of a smack, a roar of fury following it a moment later as I lifted my chair and smashed it against the window.

"Ruslan, everything is okay," Izidora spoke softly, but I ignored her, too infuriated to form a coherent sentence.

Should we even go to the Day Realm if Kazimir and his crew were going to show up like the scorned dogs they were?

"No, it is not," I replied, chest heaving. "I am the emperor, and it is my duty to make an appearance for those who bow to me. But I *cannot* and *will not* risk your life for theirs. Not when Kazimir is fucking insane and might try to kill you again in a fit of jealousy. Especially since no one knows you are awake."

Her aquamarine eyes drank me in, filled with so much love that it made my heart ache. This was the love I had always sought, the love the Goddess had gifted me. And I wasn't going to risk it for anything.

No, we would not be going to the Day Realm.

We would be preparing our soldiers for war and attacking the Night Realm while its monarch was away trying to pretend that he still mattered.

KAZIMIR

The festivities in Zheka were audible from miles away as the Day Realm celebrated the announcement of the little princess. Other than Izidora, who was believed by most to be dead within a few years of her birth and kidnapping, a royal babe had not been born in over a century.

That fact was no longer true, given that Ruslan was King Azim's son. But he was a bastard and usurper, and an illegitimate monarch in my eyes. And a mongrel to top it all off.

Day Fae raced in every direction like golden blurs, already in full celebration despite the fact that their princess would not make an appearance until late evening. After far too long spent on the road, Endre, Viktor, and myself were arriving just in time for the announcement. The Night Crown perched atop my brow, and as the diamonds glittered in the sunlight, attention fell over me exactly as I deserved. I was a fucking monarch on this continent, and it was nice to finally see some of the other Fae acknowledge that.

Whispers behind hands started while we were on the outskirts of the city, and by the time we had ridden halfway into town, a legion of spear-wielding warriors waited to greet us.

Yanking on Fek's reins until he halted, I waited for the Day Realm's soldiers to speak. A blanket of silence fell over the onlookers, and I stole a glance at both of my friends.

"King Kazimir of the Night Realm, please follow us," the male standing front and center said, his deep voice booming out around us. His legion split in half, allowing us to pass through, and once again, we were surrounded by foreign soldiers.

I gritted my teeth but plastered on a smile, nodding to the Fae around me like our armed escort did not bother me in the slightest. We were herded directly toward Aress Keep, the shade of the giant tree in the center casting dappled light on all the buildings surrounding it. But instead of walking through the front entrance, we were directed around to the side and shuffled into a small courtyard where more soldiers waited.

There was no sign of Queen Viktoria or King Consort Geza. Instead, High Lord Domon, who had traveled with us to Béke, waited, arms crossed over his broad chest.

"King Kazimir, High Lords," he dipped his head the barest amount in greeting. The slight didn't go unnoticed. "I'm here to show you to your accommodation. I'm sure you'll want to wash up before the festivities." His dark eyes raked over us, his expression betraying nothing. The golden braided locks of his hair tumbled down his back as he spun on his heel, retreating out of the sun and into the covered walkways of Aress Keep.

Endre, Viktor, and I dismounted, leaving our horses drifting in the courtyard as we hefted our bags and followed the Day Realm's High Lord. We didn't have to travel far before he opened a door, revealing a small room with one adjacent bathroom. He ushered us inside, hovering in the doorway as our bags hit the ground in three successive thumps.

"Unfortunately, this is the only room available. We didn't know you would be coming, and my queen sends her apologies. Please knock on the door when you are ready to leave."

With that, he shut it, and a lock clicked behind him before his footsteps retreated, only to be replaced by two more sets of them.

"Fucking Fates," I swore, balling my hands into fists and punching the nearest wall. Pain laced across my knuckles, but I shoved it away. We'd not even had a chance to speak, and it was clear this would be an uphill battle.

Viktor and Endre whispered furiously behind me, and I spun on them, ready to lash out at something – someone. "What?" I snapped, nails curling into my palms.

Endre glanced at Viktor, raising an eyebrow like he should be the one to speak. Smoothing his hair, Viktor said, "I didn't think we'd have this much issue, but Endre disagrees and says we should have expected nothing less."

"I am a monarch on this continent, and I will be treated as such," I hissed out, and my friends flinched, agreeing with my assessment.

Endre raised both his hands slowly, sweeping one to the side in the direction of our en suite bathroom – if it could be called that. "Why don't you bathe first? It's been a long ride, and maybe Viktor and I can speak with High Lord Domon in the meantime, sort it all out."

Dragging a hand over my face, I nodded. "Fine, see what you can do." I stalked to the miniscule chamber, shutting the door behind me and facing the mirror. Dirt crusted every inch of visible skin, and my scruff had turned into a full beard in the months we'd been on the road. The look suited me, though, making me appear older and more intimidating. Perhaps I'd keep it.

Grumbling, I turned the taps on the bathtub, resigned to bathing rather than showering in the basic space with limited amenities.

More likely a room used for servants and not visiting nobility.

The thought had me clenching my teeth again. How dare they insult me in such a way.

As I sank into the tub, I grabbed a bar of soap and a scrubber from the shelf beside it and began removing layer upon layer of grime accumulated on the dusty roads of the Day Realm. The water was nearly brown by the time I finished, and I let it drain. I hoped the swirling water would suck the Day Realm's monarch's affront down with it.

It didn't.

My mind drifted as I watched fresh water pour into the tub from the curved pipes.

Did Izidora still sleep? Would she be here if she had awoken?

The questions plagued me during my second bath, and it wasn't until the tub drained again that I let them go down with it. It mattered not; she had chosen Ruslan, but she would see she had chosen wrong soon enough.

Endre and Viktor sat on the floor in our shared room by the time I returned, both too dirty to perch on the wicker furniture. In nothing but a towel, I stood before them, crossing my arms over my chest. "What did you accomplish?"

Viktor cut his eyes to me before pushing to his feet. "Nothing. They really are that full, apparently. But the Crystal Realm is here in force – wives, children, extended family of the nobility." He shrugged then walked past me and shut the bathroom door behind him without waiting for me to say anything. Irritation crawled across my shoulders, but I blew out a breath and looked to Endre, who hadn't moved from his position on the floor.

"What about the Iron Realm?"

"The soldiers wouldn't say," he replied, his voice tight. A muscle ticked in his jaw, but I ignored it and rummaged in my bags for fresh clothes. I'd stuffed a set deep into the leather to keep clean for this very day. After all, it was a special one. One by one, I shook out the tunic, pants, undergarments, and vest, then laid them across the bed in hopes that they'd unwrinkle before I needed to wear them.

Since I was at least clean, I selected one of the chairs and propped my feet on a small table while Endre and Viktor took their turns in the bathroom. Running my fingers through my thick beard, I reviewed every aspect of my perfectly hatched plan. As my friends readied themselves to depart, I finally shoved up from my seat and surveyed my clothes.

In a flick of annoyance, I snapped out each garment to force its wrinkles into submission and then shoved the fabric onto my body. Jerking everything into place, I stepped past Endre and Viktor to observe myself in the full-length mirror propped against one wall. My two friends were oblivious to my intentions, and while I had reconsidered this course of action from time to time, the way the other realms had treated me solidified my decision.

They'd all see they fucked with the wrong monarch.

20

DRAZEN

"Ready to go?" Katrina, the Mage assigned to the Day Realm, asked Zuriel, Gozzak, and myself as we stood in Ruslan's office. My cousin vibrated with anger, still beyond pissed at Liliana for withholding information about Kazimir attending the new princess's announcement, and Kazimir for daring to step foot into his empire. Ruslan and Izidora would not be attending, understandably so, so he'd asked Zuriel, Gozzak, and myself to go in his stead.

The Mage had arrived only an hour ago, using the same spell as Ruslan to bend space to her will and speed herself across the continent in record time. She'd headed straight to Rares for a debrief and a restock of potions before arriving in Ruslan's office, ready to move the four of us back to the Day Realm. The last time I traveled such a far distance using this spell, I'd nearly puked all over Ruslan's boots when we landed in the forest outside of Vaenor.

I swallowed down the nerves building in my throat. I wasn't the only one uncomfortable – Gozzak appeared nervous as well, the corners of his eyes tightening. The Demon male raked a hand through his long black hair, then stepped forward and placed his hand on Katrina's outstretched arm. Zuriel did the same, appearing unfazed at the prospect of traveling a distance that took weeks by horse in a fraction of the time.

"See you later, Ruslan," I muttered, my hand joining theirs, and then we were whisked away, the world passing by us in a blur as I gripped Katrina's sleeve like my life depended on it – because it did.

When we finally landed in the Day Realm, it was in an ornate chamber with high, domed ceilings thatched with straw and a stone floor that shone with fresh polish. Immediately, I began sweating and regretting my attire; it was infinitely hotter here than it ever got in the Iron Realm. I'd only ever been to the border of the Day Realm, and Zuriel and Gozzak had never set foot outside the Iron Realm. The three of us were exploring the new land together, and I was grateful to have spent so much time with the Day Fae during Béke so I understood some of the customs.

One of the High Lords that had been in attendance, Soma, waited for us, a wide smile on his face. "Friends, welcome to the Day Realm. So good to see you again." He clasped arms with each of us, echoing the same formal greeting.

Katrina dipped into a slight bow before excusing herself and disappearing through some hanging reeds.

"Where do we go now?" I asked, glancing around. The architecture of the Day Realm contrasted that of the Iron Realm. Where we had sharp edges and dark corners, Aress Keep curled and curved, light and warmth filling every crevice in the building. Doorways lined the walls, spoking in all directions and leading to Goddess knew where.

A booming laugh echoed around the space as High Lord Soma looked the three of us up and down. With a shake of his head and a teeth-flashing grin, he tsked. "Nowhere dressed like that. Come, I will find you some traditional clothing to wear. You will not sweat quite so much in it."

Glancing at my companions, I noticed the deep V of Gozzak's shirt already darkening with sweat, while Zuriel's white tunic was nearly see-through. My own wasn't much better. Shrugging, I followed the male through several covered walkways until we appeared in a similarly decorated chamber with seating for a large number of people, though only a few lounged there. A shallow pool hugged the edge of the space, and some Fae dipped their feet into the water, flicking drops toward one another as they celebrated the day.

Finally, we ducked into a room with racks of colorful clothing much like the ones worn by the Day Fae during Béke. The cloth was lightweight and flowy, and Soma gestured for us to peruse the garments at our leisure. Eventually, I settled on a deep blue set to match my eyes, while Zuriel and Gozzak both opted for golden hues.

"Should we change here?" I asked, glancing around. We were only staying one night, though I wasn't sure where.

"No, no, take what you want and I will show you to your rooms," High Lord Soma responded, gesturing for us to grab our selections.

"I've got what I need," Gozzak commented, and Zuriel dipped his head in agreement.

"Show us the way," I said, throwing the blue fabric over my arm.

Another series of covered walkways took us to a long hallway lined with doors, many propped open, revealing revelers preparing for the announcement. The whole keep was alive with activity, and my carefully honed instincts had me scanning every room, assessing for weak spots or who could be a threat.

At the end of the hall, we crossed paths with King Airre and

Queen Immonen of the Crystal Realm, the latter calling out to us and waving excitedly in our direction. "General Drazen, where is our emperor?"

"I'm afraid he was detained in the Iron Realm," I deflected, not offering more information than necessary. Ruslan was strict with keeping Izidora's status quiet until the right moment – especially since the Night Fae would be in attendance.

"A shame, truly," Queen Immonen replied. "How is Izidora?"

"Nothing to report, unfortunately," I said, dancing around the truth.

"Such a shame. She didn't deserve what Kazimir did to her. We'll have to catch up later once you've had a chance to change," Queen Immonen sighed. The Crystal Fae also wore the traditional dress of the Day Realm, and I was pleasantly surprised that they were interested in learning and adopting the customs of the other realms too.

Guess Ruslan and Izidora really did make an impact on them.

"Yes, of course, Your Highnesses." Chin dipping to chest, I used the cover to glance at High Lord Soma, who waited patiently for our exchange to end. I straightened, catching Zuriel and Gozzak doing the same out of the corner of my eye. "If you'll excuse us, it's rather hot and we were promised these clothes would be better suited for the weather here."

King Airre chuckled, the braids woven into his long, blond hair swinging as he shook his head. "They are much better suited indeed. We'll speak shortly."

High Lord Soma continued to the last three doors in the hall, opening them individually for us. "You all will be here. I'll wait for you to change, then guide you to the main hall. The keep can be quite confusing to navigate."

I clapped the male on the shoulder as I walked past him into my room. "I appreciate it, High Lord Soma. We'll only be a moment."

Closing the door behind me, I made a quick survey. A large bed covered most of the space, though every inch of it was finely decorated. A small sitting area offered me a place to set my clothes while I hurried to an adjacent bathroom to wash. Stripping out of my Iron Realm clothing, I tossed it through the doorway and onto the free couch. The cool water was a welcome relief to the scorching heat, and I cupped my hands, gathering enough to splash my face, then let more trickle down my back and across my muscular chest.

Immediately, my skin felt like it could take a breath, and the sweat that had gathered at the nape of my neck began to dissipate. With one last look in the mirror, I ensured my long hair was properly secured on top of my head, then returned to the bedroom and pulled on the blue linen clothes. By the time I exited the room, Zuriel and Gozzak were already waiting with High Lord Soma. He quickly ushered us along, following the throng of people moving through the keep. I scanned every face for enemies and every wall for potential blockades or escape routes.

Which was rather difficult, given the mass of Fae shuffling like a herd of sheep into a corral. "Looks like we might not have needed an escort after all," I joked, indicating the flow of people.

"Perhaps not," High Lord Soma chuckled. "The Day Fae are very excited to meet the princess. Finally, the line of succession is secure. Though, our king and queen were happy for a healthy babe."

"Of course," I replied, glancing around the crowd in search of the Night Fae. "So tell me, Soma... where are they?"

With the way I dropped my voice, it wasn't hard to guess who I referred to. "High Lord Domon is dealing with them. He drew the short straw." A grin flashed across his dark skin, then he shook his head. "I would not want to be in his position."

"Yeah, you lucked out with us," I laughed. "But they will be in attendance tonight?" I needed clarification because I planned on watching Kazimir like a hawk. Between Zuriel, Gozzak, and myself, he would have a pair of eyes on his every move. We needed to assess his mental state and report back to Ruslan the next day. If we were going to strike the Night Realm, we needed to know what we were working with.

A heavy sigh escaped the big male beside me. "Yes, though not anywhere close to the babe or the other nobles. I'm sure he will not appreciate it."

"I don't expect he will take it well," I agreed grimly, rolling my shoulders. I resisted the urge to crack my knuckles like I was preparing for a fight.

I was, but I didn't want it to be obvious to everyone around us.

The sea of people rounded a corner and disappeared through doors flung so wide I was certain ten could walk abreast into the space. We squeezed through them, stepping into an enormous room with high ceilings that I swore must have been woven with the branches of the giant tree that surrounded the keep. Bubbles of light filled it, golden hues cast across every surface and contrasting with the falling night outside. Much like the Iron Realm, pelts lined the walls and floors, though instead of fluffy fur, these were short-haired and patterned. Tables with long benches lined the hall, creating a communal feel in the vast room as Fae slipped into spots with no apparent order.

"You'll be up there, close to the platform," High Lord Soma commented, pointing toward the opposite end of the hall, where King Airre and Queen Immonen had already settled themselves among their nobles.

Glancing over my shoulder, I nodded to Zuriel and Gozzak, who both scanned the room in search of the Night Fae. There were so many people, it was hard to see through them all, and a muscle ticked in my jaw as they remained hidden. But I plastered on a welcoming smile when we arrived at the table filled with nobility, trying my best to represent Ruslan – the emperor – and his interests.

"There," Gozzak muttered, nudging me with his elbow, and I followed his gaze to a table about fifty paces away, where a glittering crown reflected the light of a thousand golden bubbles. He froze halfway between sitting and standing when our gazes collided like two magic bombs, and the way emerald leeched from his eyes raised the hairs on the back of my neck. They morphed into that same color as they had when I'd dropped from the sky and found his knife in Izidora's chest. Zuriel gripped my arm with more force than I thought him capable and yanked me to the bench beside him.

"I'm just as upset as you are, Drazen, but you cannot lose your cool here," he said flatly. "We will watch him, and we will get our vengeance. But not today."

Blowing out a breath, I nodded, rubbing the back of my neck.

"Don't worry, Drazen, I'll cover him for now," Gozzak said, wisps of shadow climbing his body until his image blurred when he moved. His golden attire allowed him to blend into the crowd as he pushed through it, calling more shadows to cling to his body and cloak his appearance. If it were darker in the room, he'd have disappeared entirely, but with all the bubble lights cast by the attendees, shadows were hard to come by.

Zuriel had already engaged the Crystal Fae in conversation by the time I lost sight of Gozzak, and I tried to focus on what they saide, but to no avail. My body vibrated with the need to fight the male across the room, but his death was not mine – it was Izidora's.

The hush that fell across the hall yanked me from my thoughts and pulled my attention to the stage where the nobles of the Day Realm had gathered, smiling widely.

High Lord Soma stepped forward, and with a tendril of his golden magic wrapping around his throat, he amplified his voice. "Friends, welcome to Zheka for the announcement of the new princess of the Day Realm. I know you are all ready to see the babe, so I won't bore you with long speeches."

"Oh really? Here I thought you were going to give us a philosophy lesson," High Lord Domon teased from behind him, earning the crowd's attention and creating a ripple of laughter.

High Lord Soma took the jest in stride, laughing along with the crowd. "Not this time. Perhaps the next one. You will have to assist me in preparing one, High Lord Domon."

That earned another chuckle, though the sound did not come from me, not when I was already so on edge.

"Anyway, without further delay," he shot a pointed look over his shoulder, "let us introduce you to Princess Gizela, daughter of Queen Viktoria!"

Applause erupted as the queen and her husband appeared from behind the line of nobility carrying the child. Queen Viktoria glowed as she glided forward, the babe tucked into the crook of her arm and swaddled in a deep red wrap. It matched the vibrant dress that floated around her, and King Consort Geza beamed at her with pride. They reached the front of the stage, and the queen adjusted her hold on the child, who woke with a large yawn and stretch.

I wasn't an empath, but even I was overwhelmed with the swell of emotion from those gathered in the hall. Song broke out, the Day Fae falling into tune and creating a lively atmosphere as the monarchs walked the length of the stage, allowing everyone a glimpse of the future queen.

Queen Immonen and King Airre shared an intimate look, no doubt communicating mind to mind like Izidora and Ruslan often did. Taking my opportunity while all were distracted, I searched the crowd for Kazimir, Viktor, and Endre and found them still seated. Kazimir's jaw was locked tight, a muscle feathering beneath his eye. Endre's lips were pressed into a thin line, and Viktor looked between them like he was at a loss for his next action.

Trouble among the Night Fae.

We could work with internal strife, and I made a mental note to mention it to Ruslan. War had not raged in Északi for centuries, so none alive had seen true battle, save for the Angel who sat beside me and the Demon who kept to the shadows to conceal his activities. I glanced at Zuriel then, wondering what he was thinking. Even after all these years of knowing him, I still felt like I didn't know much at all. He and Gozzak were the oldest of the Telivér, followed by Xorrek, and they'd all been captured together. While Gozzak and Xorrek were loudmouthed and brash, Zuriel was quite the opposite. The three had valuable insight to provide in the coming war, and I would accept whatever help they would offer. It would be stupid to disregard anything they had to say.

"Looks like the Night Fae aren't all on the same page," I whispered, dropping my head over my shoulder to better direct my words toward Zuriel. He casually glanced in their direction, his keen eyes missing nothing, then returned them to the stage.

"Undoubtedly. It seems like Endre would rather be anywhere but here."

I agreed with his assessment, sizing up the male Liliana was still hung up on.

"You know Liliana cares for both of you," Zuriel offered willingly, and I blinked rapidly, facing him.

"And how do you know that?" I questioned, brows furrowing.

He shrugged, his face betraying nothing. "You learn to read people after several millennia of life."

"I don't expect her to choose me if he suddenly came

crawling back, begging her forgiveness." I propped an elbow on the table, twisting my hands together before glancing over my shoulder at the Night Fae.

"She doesn't want groveling. She wants–" Zuriel was cut off as High Lord Soma's voice boomed once again, and my heart dipped just a fraction as I reminded myself that I was only temporary in Liliana's life.

"Now that Princess Gizela has been announced to the world, let us feast!"

Golden tendrils of magic carried massive platters of food to the long tables, and we all leaned out of the way as the Day Fae worked together to arrange the food, drink, and plates.

"We'll finish our conversation later," I muttered as Gozzak reappeared and took a seat on the opposite side of Zuriel.

The three of us kept a close eye on the Night Fae, though the Day Fae kept trying to force drinks into our hands. At first, I accepted them, only pretending to drink. But soon, they realized my ploy, and worry about offending them crept across my shoulders. The Crystal Fae celebrated nearly as hard as the Day Fae, and as we were smashed between the nobles of both realms at our table, I knew refusing them was a lost cause.

This was why I never wanted to be king, or an ambassador, or fucking anything political. Just let me fight and not have to play nice.

With a grimace, I knocked back an entire drink, hoping that would appease them. It did not. Instead, more were forced upon us, and I continued stuffing food into my mouth in hopes of offsetting the effects of the liquor.

Queen Viktoria and King Consort Geza sat at the very end of the table, the little princess strung between them, safely cradled in a way they could both watch over her. Eventually, she began to wail, and a female I assumed was a wet nurse fetched her, carrying her away from the party and allowing the new parents the freedom to roam and connect with their people.

Music filled the room after the food cleared, and shortly after, the tables were pushed to the outer edges, making room for dancing and revelry. Standing on the sidelines was entertaining enough for me, and as more alcohol was shoved into my hands, I lost sight of the Night Fae. No one had left the party yet, and I got the sense no one would until the early hours of the morning. Kazimir wouldn't risk disappearing and offending the rulers of the Day Realm – not when he'd traveled all this way to make a point. So I let it go, and surrendered to the jovial crowd, deciding to celebrate the day, and the new life to its fullest.

21

KAZIMIR

Slipping past the guards whose eyes never left us was harder than I'd thought it would be, but I still managed to do so – thanks to a combination of my Night Fae magic and binding magic. The silvery tendrils mixed with the Fates-gifted magic to form a sort of shield around me, rendering me invisible and allowing me to creep through Aress Keep unnoticed.

The wet nurse held the wailing babe close to her chest, cooing to her as they wandered their way back to the royal rooms. On silent feet, I followed, counting the number of Fae nearby and calculating the odds of executing my plan. So far, they were good.

I barely managed to slip inside the door behind the female, trespassing on the little princess's nursery. The crazed grin that broke out across my face would have scared the female had she been able to see me. She sat back into a rocking chair, pulling down her tunic to expose her breast to the babe's mouth, and began a soothing pace while the child suckled. Soon, the little eyes began to drop, and she fell asleep in the nurse's arms. With great care, the nurse rose and carried the babe to a small crib, nestling her among the blankets before dimming the room's lights with a wave of her hand.

Bracing a shoulder against the wall, I leaned, arms crossed, until she settled on a small cot nearby and her breathing evened out. Despite the urge to move, to execute my plan nipping at my skin, I waited a few minutes longer to ensure she'd stay asleep and no one else would arrive. I couldn't fuck it up by being sloppy, not when I was this close.

Five ticked by, then ten, and finally, I unfurled myself from the wall and crossed the room, leering over the crib. The infant slept so peacefully there, I almost felt bad about what I was about to do. But then I remembered the way her parents had scorned me, and how the monarchs of the Crystal Realm hadn't bothered to acknowledge my presence at all.

With a repressed growl, I lifted the little princess and tucked her against my body. She disappeared into my net of invisibility, and I exited the room as quickly as possible, maintaining my magic as I raced through the keep in the direction of our room.

The child remained asleep as I dodged Fae who could not see me, and what seemed like hours later, I finally found the dingy hall where we'd been relegated to a single room. Standing outside our door were Viktor and Endre, thankfully guardless, and when I was nearly upon them, I dropped my magic.

"What the fuck!" Viktor swore when I appeared from nowhere.

"Shh," I hissed, barging through the door to our room and jerking my head for them to follow me.

"Is that–" Endre started before I cut him off.

"Grab your bags. We're leaving." Still holding the princess in one hand, I threw my leather bags over my shoulder and made for the door.

"Hold the fuck up," Endre snarled, stepping into my path. "You are not seriously kidnapping the princess."

"They will ally with us again," I challenged, straightening to my full height and baring my teeth at Endre.

"I think I'm with Endre on this one," Viktor snapped, his sage eyes hardening on me. "That is so many levels of fucked up, Kazimir."

I cocked my head at both of them, the black beast living in my chest screaming to be let out, to punish these detractors. "Then I'll have to execute you both for disobeying a direct order from your king."

"Kazimir, let's be serious," Viktor started, half-stepping in front of the door to block my exit.

A snarl tore from my throat. "I am fucking serious. Get your bags, and get moving before anyone comes looking." My words must have summoned trouble, because shouts broke out down the hall.

Viktor looked between me, Endre, and the half-open door, a war playing out across his face. "Fuck!" He raced to the wall, hefted his and Endre's bags over his shoulders, and then kicked the door wider. "Let's go."

I bolted out first, racing in the direction of where we had left our horses earlier that day. Viktor was behind me a moment later until he noticed Endre wasn't following. "Endre!" he shouted, his voice breaking with a silent plea. Our friend stepped into the hall, his peridot eyes bouncing between us and the noise increasing as it approached. A lone tear slipped down his cheek, but he clenched his fists and raced after us.

I threw out my magic again, rendering us invisible and silencing our heavy breaths and footfalls. Not a word was spoken until we discovered our horses hitched to a post beside the side entrance we'd be shoved through earlier, all still saddled and without food or water. I gritted my teeth at the maltreatment of my steadfast mount, but I was already kidnapping the princess of the Day Realm, so there wasn't much worse I could do to seek revenge against the Day Fae.

Throwing my bags across Fek's back in a hurry, I mounted him and steered him toward the closed gate, Endre and Viktor hot on my heels. "Viktor, blow open the gate!"

A burst of white magic flew forward, splintering the wood and creating enough space for us to slip through. "Stay close," I ordered, focusing on throwing my magic wider to encompass us and our mounts.

We raced through the empty streets of Zheka, most of the Day Fae gathered in Aress Keep or other large halls around the city celebrating. Even if someone had seen us, there wasn't much they could do to stop us as we fled the city.

My heart pounded as hard as Fek's hooves as we flew across the packed dirt streets, and every length we put between us and the keep lifted the worry that my plan would fail from my shoulders.

A hooded figure stepped into the road, facing us and halting our escape a breath before we passed the final row of buildings and crossed the bridge that led into the wider Day Realm.

The magic concealing us bled away, and Desmond, the Mage assigned to the Crystal Realm, stood before us, grinning wickedly. "Desmond, perfect timing. Let's go," I ordered, jerking my head like I wanted him to join me on Fek.

Endre and Viktor pulled up their mounts beside me, Endre's rearing back and neighing as he nearly slid into the Mage.

"Our deal still stands?" he asked, lifting a brow in question, unfazed by Endre's horse's antics.

"You get us back to Vaenor, and we have a deal," I replied coolly, adjusting my grip on the babe.

Without blinking, Desmond approached Fek, reaching his hand out. Gripping it, I hauled him into the saddle behind me. Stretching in both directions, he grabbed hold of Endre and

Viktor, yanking them ever so slightly closer. Then, words swept from him in a language I did not understand, though I knew it was a spell that would move us away from the danger in the Day Realm. That was, after all, why I'd been secretly paying Desmond all these months. As a messenger between the realms of the Északi Empire, he was privy to all sorts of valuable information. Though his price for this stunt was far higher than the gold I'd already offered him.

"What the fuck is happ–" Viktor's voice was torn away as the world blurred around us, and my stomach lurched uncontrollably. The babe did not even wake as we came to a screeching halt before an enormous waterfall just inside the Crystal Realm's border.

I whipped my head around to glare at the Mage. "This is not Vaenor."

Desmond panted behind me, looking paler than the moonlight. "I can only go so far in one day. We'll have to stay here for the night, then tomorrow, after my magic has had time to recharge, we can go again," he countered, slipping from Fek's back.

Weak fucking human Mage.

With a growl, I thudded to the ground beside him, still grasping the child. A moment later, Viktor and Endre dismounted, and Endre immediately reached for the little princess. I let him take her, not wanting to be bothered with the child any more than necessary. He clutched her protectively to his chest, then stabbed a finger into mine. "This is wrong, Kazimir. Of all the stupid shit you could do, you had to do this? What the fuck is wrong with you?"

His messy hair fell in his face, obscuring his peridot eyes, but the hardness in them was unmistakable. He shoved it back anyway, revealing his ticking jaw. The sound that tore from my throat was feral, and black ropes ripped free of their own accord and wrapped around Endre's neck, cutting off his words and air.

My own subject felt as though he had a right to lay a hand on me.

"How dare he..." those three voices twisted and twined in my head.

"Stop, Kazimir! He's just upset." Viktor shoved me hard, breaking the grip of the binding magic and silencing whatever else those voices wanted to say. Blinking, awareness crept back in, first filling my ears with the roaring of the falls, then revealing Endre, bent over and gasping for breath. He backed away from me, draped protectively over the Day Realm's princess. Desmond only watched the scene unfold before him.

"We'll make camp tonight and figure the rest out tomorrow, yeah?" Viktor raised his hands in supplication, and I sighed, raking a hand over my face.

"Fine. Let's find a more hidden spot." I shot Desmond a look that said he was going to help us with camp, and he trudged along behind us until we were hidden in a copse of tall trees. Thankfully, brush clung to the bases, providing us with a bit more shelter and concealment from the nearby road.

Endre wouldn't look at me as he unsaddled the horses with one arm, and I ignored him, not wanting to reward his disrespect. I was his king, and he had to do as I said – even if we had been friends our entire lives.

They would all see soon enough exactly how powerful I was, and they'd bow to me regardless.

22

IZIDORA

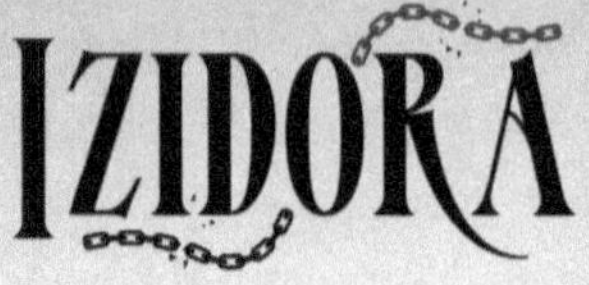

The woods blurred by as I raced on horseback toward my destination. My heart pounded harder than the hooves beating beneath me, barely touching the ground as I egged her on. A black cape billowed behind me, snapping in the wind and occasionally snagging on a branch. From what I raced away, I wasn't sure. All I knew was the all consuming need to fly fast and far. My horse stumbled, nearly pitching me from its back, and I instinctively clutched the package I carried against my chest. We recovered, and I breathed a sigh of relief as the trees broke apart ahead, revealing the night sky and a thousand stars glittering down on me. The new moon graced the sky, and as I slowed my mount to a walk, I looked up at her, wondering why the Goddess and the Fates felt the need to war through the Fae rather than taking up their issues with each other. Behind me, other horses slowed, their riders as breathless as me. All wore deep hoods that shielded their faces, and as I glanced down at my arms, I only saw black fabric, except for—

"Ruslan, Izidora, you need to come to the citadel immediately," Liliana shouted, her voice laced with panic. Both of us bolted upright in bed immediately, whipping toward the open bedroom door where Liliana stood, her hair a mess and wings still out. They fluffed themselves nervously as her seafoam green eyes tightened with worry. A singular glove graced her wringing hands – the iron-proof one that allowed her to open the hatch to Roc Palace.

"What's going on?" Ruslan was the first to speak, clearing his throat around his sleep-thickened voice.

Not a speck of light broke through the heavy window coverings, and the hearths in the rooms crackled ominously as we waited for an explanation. It was either very late or very early, which meant that whatever news my best friend carried was not good.

"Princess Gizela has been kidnapped."

All the air fled my lungs as those five words hit me like a punch to the gut. I clutched my chest, my heart nearly beating out of it to meet my hand as I tried to draw a breath. My lungs would not inflate, and panic clawed its way up my throat as my own trauma was triggered.

Not her, too...

"Sprite," Ruslan cried as our bond flooded with fear. His strong, bare arms wrapped around me instantly, cradling me against his chest as I tried to stem the tears that threatened to overflow.

"We'll be there in a moment," he growled at Liliana, who disappeared into the sitting area.

"You are safe, here with me in our bed. Tell me five things you can see," he encouraged, using a soothing tone as he tried to break through the panic.

"Your... tattoos," I gasped. "Fire, clothes, books, my hair."

"Good, how about what you can feel?"

"Warmth... skin... fur... bed. I smell wood and smoke and roses. I hear your heartbeat."

Ruslan smoothed my hair down my back, rubbing circles there as he encouraged me to breathe. Finally, I was able to draw a deep, serrated breath, and I swiped at the tears that had fallen down my cheeks.

"We need to deal with this. Are you up for it?" Ruslan asked, attention raking over my face, searching for any sign that I might need more from him.

Steeling myself against my trauma, I nodded. "We take care of our people."

"That's my sprite," Ruslan praised, pressing a kiss to my forehead before releasing me and sliding out of the bed and into a pair of loose pants laying on the floor. He tossed me my own clothes that had been scattered about, and I dressed quickly, joining him and Liliana in the living space.

The two of them were still tense around each other, but he gripped her arm all the same and moved us to Ryza Citadel. Rares, Artur, and several others were already in Ruslan's office by the time we arrived, all in various states of night dress.

Ruslan dropped Liliana's arm but held mine as he tugged me to the chair behind his desk, sitting me in it while he braced his arms on the back of it, the two of us holding power positions in the room. "Someone tell me what the fuck happened."

Rares spoke up, wringing his withered hands. "Princess Gizela was kidnapped during the festivities, and the Night Fae are the prime suspects. There was no trace of them by the time the princess was discovered missing, and a gate where their horses were tethered was blown open. Drazen traced their prints to the edge of Zheka, but they disappeared before they even reached the bridge. Vanished, like they were never there."

I chewed my lip as I listened to the recounting of events, and Ruslan's hand tightened on the chair, making it rock ever so slightly backward. "How did you find out?"

"Katrina appeared to me," Rares said. "I immediately sought out Artur and Liliana so we could meet."

Ruslan nodded, then cracked his neck from side to side, filling the room with pop after pop. "Where is Desmond?"

"We haven't tried contacting him," Rares noted.

"Try right now," Ruslan gritted out, and I didn't have to use our bond to follow his train of thought. There were few full blooded Mages on the continent, and only Mages, or those with Mage blood like Ruslan, held the power to move through space without leaving a trace.

Rares muttered a spell, his form shimmering slightly as he spoke into the air at someone we could not see. "Can you please fetch Desmond?" A pause. "What do you mean he isn't around?" Another. "And he didn't attend the announcement with the king and queen?"

Ruslan shook behind me, the wood creaking beneath his fingers as his rage rose. Instinctively, I pushed soothing emotions toward him, hoping to calm the storm brewing within.

"Okay, thanks for letting me know." Rares re-formed, pinching the bridge of his nose before facing his master. "Desmond has disappeared. Left everything behind. Hasn't been seen in days."

"Fuck!" Ruslan roared, and I leaped from the chair, immediately snatching his arm and siphoning away his emotion, trying to calm him down. He cracked his knuckles, disregarding me completely as he turned on the old Mage. "How could you let this happen, Rares? I thought you had the Mages under control. How did you not see the signs of his treason?"

My mind worked over the problem at hand as Rares and Ruslan hurled violent words at each other. The Night Fae knew about the announcement, which meant that Desmond must have passed along the information. And then, he helped them escape Zheka with the little princess in tow.

What else had he revealed?

"Hey!" I shouted over the males, trying to get their attention.

"What else did Desmond know that could hurt us? He's clearly been working with the Night Fae for a while."

Artur paled, glancing at Rares, and I interpreted that knew at least a few important pieces of information that should not fall into the enemies' hands.

Blowing out a loaded breath, Ruslan braced his hands on the desk, lifting his head in a menacing way to glare at his advisors and Liliana. "We were planning on launching an assault on the Night Realm while he was away, but now that it appears he has already returned, we need to change tactics. Priority number one is getting Princess Gizela home to the Day Realm, as soon as possible. Artur, put together a rapid strike team to assault Este Castle. Rares, contact Katrina and tell her to move Drazen, Zuriel, and Gozzak back as soon as she is able. Liliana, I want you working with Artur on mapping ways in and out of the castle until Drazen is back. I don't give a fuck that your brother and family are still there, if you want to remain in the Iron Realm, you will give us every fucking detail you can remember. And don't say there's only one way in or out, because I know about the underground tunnels. Are we clear?"

Liliana lifted her chin and squared her shoulders under the vehemence of my mate's words. I looked between them, waiting for her to agree to his terms. I was still a little upset with her for keeping information about Kazimir attending the announcement to herself, but not nearly as upset as Ruslan still was. Finally she said, "Give me parchment and ink and I'll tell you where every hidden tunnel is."

Tension I didn't realize I was holding bled from my shoulders as she agreed to reveal everything she knew. Lilana's jaw ticked, hinting at the fury that she held about the actions of her brethren.

"I want to be part of the strike team," I said forcefully. My magic was fucking powerful and useful, and more than anything

I *needed* to do this. For me as much as Princess Gizela. Liliana dipped her head in agreement, crossing her arms over her chest.

Ruslan spun on me, forcing my heart to skip a beat as emotion flooded our bond. "I can't risk it, sprite. Please understand. The battlefield is one thing, but entering Este Castle is another."

I quirked a brow at him, popping my hands on my hips. "So you're not going either?"

"I didn't say that," he said, a warning in his tone.

"Where you go, I go. Period. You are my emperor, my future husband, but most importantly, my mate. We are better, faster, stronger when we are together."

"I can't go through the pain of almost losing you again. First the burnout, then Kazimir..."

"I'm not letting another babe be kept from her rightful home because of some fucked up male who thinks he knows better than everyone else. I am strong, I am powerful, and I am pissed the fuck off. They should fear my wrath."

A wicked smirk crossed his face, and his iron gray eyes flashed with black fire. *"Damn right they should."*

"Rares," Ruslan barked, not bothering to look at the Mage. "Prepare extra Demon blood drinks for the road. I want to ensure we're fully stocked."

"Do you want a shifting potion too?" he questioned, pulling a notebook from his robes and beginning to scribble.

"Yes, as many as Artur says we'll need for the team." He finally faced his advisors again. "Make no mistake, our first attack will not be our last. After we've secured the princess, we march on the Night Realm."

23

ENDRE

Desmond managed to land us on the northern route slightly south of Vaenor before his magic stuttered out. Princess Gizela woke again with an ear-shattering wail, and I tucked her closer to my body, gently swaying from side to side in an attempt to soothe her. All night, she'd cried, and only just before dawn had she finally exhausted herself to the point of sleep.

I sliced Kazimir with a sharp, sidelong glance. He didn't even notice.

To trust him with the princess's care would be an absolute mistake. I had to get her away from him and to safety immediately.

My decision wasn't even difficult. "I am going to ride ahead to the castle. You guys check in with Vadim."

Without waiting for a response, I dug my heels into my horse's side and galloped away.

The streets of Vaenor blurred by as I dodged Fae moving about their days. With my hood up, I looked like any other hurried rider. At the gates of Este Castle, though, I was forced to slow and reveal myself. The sentries standing at attention recognized me immediately, and by the mix of raised and furrowed eyebrows, I knew my appearance was highly unexpected.

The leader shouted for the gate to open, and with a groan, the newly reinforced metal gate swung inward. With only a sliver to allow me passage, I pushed forward and trotted to the stables. Normally, I'd speak with the grooms and check over my mount, but when Princess Gizela wailed again, I merely tossed off the reins and strode straight for the front doors.

They loomed open, looking like the maw of a beast waiting to swallow me whole.

Temporary darkness engulfed me as I entered, eyes adjusting away from the bright light outside. My hurried footsteps refused to drown out the blood raging in my ears as I pounded the carpet runner toward the High House Wing. Este Castle was silent, almost tomb-like, and I wondered for a fleeting moment if they could sense the return of their king, or if everyone was so exhausted from the months we'd been back that they needed extra respite while he was away.

Princess Gizela fussed again, and I shifted her to a more comfortable position. She hadn't eaten since we left the Day Realm, and I needed my mother's help to care for the tiny infant. I rounded the last corner and nearly sprinted to House Zadik's apartments. Shouldering open the door, I found my parents seated on the plush red couches that centered our living area.

"Endre, what–" My mother jumped to her feet, a concerned expression breaking across her face.

"Mother, I need a wet nurse, immediately." My tone left no room for argument. She swept her eyes over me once and bolted from the room.

Must look as crazy as I feel.

Fury still boiled my blood, so I didn't care that she was already gone. In fact, I welcomed her hurried action. At least *someone* else saw this madness and wanted to act. These new feelings about my friends ate at every memory, and I didn't know what to do with them all.

"Who is that?" My father's voice was flat and hard as he approached.

"Princess Gizela of the Day Realm," I gritted out, throwing back my cloak to reveal her face.

My father's head whipped up, eyes wide. "How?"

"There's a lot I haven't told you," I admitted, preparing myself for the disappointed sighs that would likely ensue.

"Let's take care of the babe first, then talk." He squeezed my arm, then walked past me to the open door, glancing up and down the hall before closing it softly and leaning against the wall beside it. I shifted from foot to foot as we waited for my mother to return, anxious to get the princess out of my arms and into those of someone who could care for her.

What seemed like an eternity later, my mother rapped on the door, whispering, "It's me."

My father opened it, allowing her entry, followed by a young female wearing the attire of a kitchen maid.

"We can trust her," she assured me, no doubt reading my pinched expression.

With a wary perusal, I offered her the babe, who woke with the shuffling and immediately began to wail. Her cries were so anguished that they nearly split my ears. The female accepted her from me with a confident nod, then walked past me to a chair in the far corner to nurse.

"Okay, son, tell me what in the worlds is going on," my father said, leading me toward the center of the room and guiding me to sit on a couch.

I buried my face in my hands, adrenaline sizzling out of my blood now that we were finally somewhere safe. After a few shaky breaths, I smoothed back my hair and locked gazes with my parents who sat across from me, holding hands as they clung to each other for support.

"Izidora rejected Kazimir... and then he tried to kill her. That's why we left the Iron Realm in such a hurry. We're forbidden from entering it again unless we have a death wish."

A gasp slipped from my mother, and she covered her mouth to stem any further sound.

My father opened his own mouth to speak, but I held up a hand to silence the questions that were poised to flow. "I'm not finished. Kazimir has binding magic now. At first, we thought it would help defeat the Iron Realm and save Izidora, but when we arrived and found her perfectly happy there, it started to break him. He was desperate to win her back. Eventually, it became apparent that she would not choose him, and that's why we voted to make him king of the Night Realm. It wasn't until after that, that he started to become more erratic and paranoid." I clenched and unclenched my fists, fighting the burning in my eyes as disappointment with my own actions settled in my chest. "On our return journey, we decided on the lies we'd tell to cover up subverting the law and keep him in power. The others all believed he would get over it with time, especially after Taya showed up. But this," I gestured toward the babe in the corner, "just proves that I was right all along."

My parents shared a long look before my father released the expected drawn out breath laced with disappointment. But to my surprise, he did not chastise me. "Son, thank you for telling me all of this. I'm not sure what we can do at this point." He paused, looking down at his open palms before lifting his head again. "I suspected something was off when you all returned, but I had no idea just how far things had fallen. I served King Zalan for decades during his madness, and I can serve Kazimir just the same. We will not let the realm fall to ruin."

Blinking, I stared at him, nails digging into my palms and

straightening in my seat. "That's it? You'll just serve him like you did King Zalan?"

"Endre, honey," my mother tried to soothe me, reaching across the table that divided us, but I jerked away.

"No, don't try to placate me like you did for all those years serving a different mad king. You know this is wrong." Turmoil settled across my shoulders, and I dragged a breath in through my nostrils, trying to calm myself.

"We do, but our hands are tied. Unless I can convince the other High Houses to depose him – which, given Kaztar's infatuation with Kazimir, I think is highly unlikely – then the best action we can take is to steer the realm in a direction that benefits the people at large," my father tried and failed to justify his logic to me.

"Unbelievable," I swore, nearly knocking over the table as I snapped to my feet. Without another word, I spun on my heel and stalked toward my room.

"Endre, where are you going?" My mother's footsteps chased me, the light patter so antithetical to my dark mood.

"I need some space," I gritted out, slamming the door to my bedroom in her face.

"Give him time," I heard my father say, his voice muffled by the wood between us. My mother sighed and retreated, and I stomped toward my bathroom, turning the taps on the shower and stripping out of my clothes. Bracing my hands on the counter, I stared at myself in the mirror, questioning the male I had been and the male I wanted to become. With a hard shove, I forced myself to stand beneath the cold water and embrace the pain.

It was the least I could do when the male I served caused so much of it. I hated to admit that my father was right. What could we fucking do about the situation we found ourselves in? Why hadn't I seen this coming? Why hadn't I done more to stop *any* of this?

I smashed my fist into the tile, cracking it and splitting the skin across my knuckles. A hiss slipped through my gritted teeth as the cuts stung in the spray of water and blood dripped onto the ground. Each speck of ruby diluted and disappeared, much like I wanted to do from this fucking realm and from the idiotic choices I'd made since we'd rescued Izidora from that cave.

24

KAZIMIR

A knock on my bedroom door allowed me to tear my face away from Taya's. "Come in," I called, shoving her off my lap. Her gold eyes flashed with hurt before she straightened her clothing and perched on the edge of the arm of my chair like an ornament. Crossing her arms over her chest, she pushed up her ample cleavage, only accentuated by the deep dip in the dress she wore.

Desmond entered, carrying with him a velvet pouch that offered a sharp rattle when he walked. "Ah, Desmond, good to see you. Please have a seat."

The Mage glanced around the ornate space, finally selecting a low couch across from me. "So, what do you need the crystals for?"

He proffered the bag to me, and I accepted it, drawing open the cinched center and spilling the gems into my open palm. Amethysts, quartzes, opals, and topazes glinted in the light from the crystal chandelier overhead. Glancing at the female still clinging to me, I growled, "Leave us."

With a pout, she stomped off. The door slammed with enough force that the painting of myself commissioned on my coronation day rebounded against the stone wall. The crown, intentionally skewed on my head, grew even more crooked as it resettled at an angle against the wall. Rolling my eyes, I returned my attention to the task at hand. I'd make it up to her later, but she couldn't know about the magic all the anointed kings and queens of Északi possessed.

"The stones assist with channeling the power I must wield to make you Fae," I stated, arranging the stones on the table between us after evaluating each for its purity. Satisfied with the collection, I went to my desk and lifted the hidden bottom of a drawer to retrieve the paper I needed. The High Priestess had handed it to me in secret the day after she placed the Night Crown on my head, and the moment I read it, I knew the Fates had provided me yet another gift. It hadn't taken much to sway Desmond to assist me, not when his humanness crippled his strength and lifespan.

"Now, remove your clothes," I instructed, skimming the words written in a flowing script. It looked ancient, and I wondered just how long this parchment had existed, how many royal hands had looked upon these words and used them. If the history I remembered from childhood lessons served me, at least a dozen kings had cause to wield such power for their political gains. My ancestral line included.

The Mage did as instructed, not bothering to cover himself as he reclined on the couch. Examining the array of the crystals, I ensured their proper order, then, one by one, placed them along his body according to the instructions written by some long-ago monarch.

"Can you make that bigger while you're at it?" he joked as I placed a few near his dick.

"Don't think it works like that," I grinned devilishly. "If you can survive the pain of the procedure, you're welcome to join me in my harem tonight."

He snorted, closing his eyes and tucking his hands behind his head as I finished placing the stones. With one last sweep from paper to his body, I confirmed everything was in place, then stole a cushion from behind him and tossed it to the ground. Kneeling, I placed my fingers on either side of his head, and I tapped into my magic. The source of moonlight and black binds in my chest swirled as I called it to my palms and out into the world. Silver dipped into a dark gray as my magic caressed Desmond's body, testing before trapping itself in the crystals. Once every stone had been filled, they began to glow, and the scent of burning flesh filled the air.

Beneath my palms, muscles ticked in Desmond's face, but no sound slipped from his throat. Pushing more power out of me, I willed it to begin the transformation, and after a few moments, bubbles popped out of his boiling skin as his body rearranged itself from its basest form. A pained sound escaped him then, and I pushed harder, wanting to ensure the transformation from the Mage's human form to a Fae one succeeded.

I sensed the change happening just before the stones exploded, sending shards scattering throughout the room. With a yell, Desmond jerked off the couch, his skin seeming to rip apart and sew itself back together at the same time as he writhed on his hands and knees on the carpet beside the couch. His ears grew a slight point, and his thin frame thickened with new muscle. When he lifted his gaze, his once dull eyes were sharper, and as one last wave of transformation swept from the base of his spine to his head, he choked out a cough.

Then, ever so slowly, he raised his gaze to mine, revealing a devious smirk. New power lurked within him, and as his creator, I sensed it, almost like an extension of my own.

I offered him my hand, but he ignored it, pushing to his feet with the ease of a Fae. He flexed and admired his new body, testing it with a few jumps and squats before he finally returned his attention to me. "I think I might take you up on your offer. I want to see how much better this body fucks."

"Grab your clothes and I'll show you the way," I instructed. He wasted no time pulling on his pants, but left his chest bare as we slipped from my room and strolled to the stairs that spiraled up into the rooms where my females waited for us.

The space was dark and sultry and smelled of sex. Already, several played with one another, warming up for a night that would leave everyone sweating and satisfied. After all, they did miss me while I was gone.

Taya was splayed over a soft, circular bed in the center of the space, her emerald green robe hanging loose and exposing one soft breast, nipple already hard as she waited for me. Lazily, she traced swirls over her skin, and my cock hardened as I drank in her spread legs and wet pussy.

In another corner, my least favorites touched and teased, and I snapped my fingers twice to garner their attention. Once they'd sat upright and ensured their eyes were firmly on me, I told them, "Please ensure our friend here enjoys himself tonight."

The four grinned, and one crooked a finger in Desmond's direction and beckoned him forward. With a wink, I left him for the bed with Taya. It dipped beneath my weight as I crawled onto it, and then I hovered over the gold-eyed female, brushing the silk aside to reveal her other breast.

"My King," she purred, threading her fingers through my hair and guiding me to her nipple. I suckled it, grazing my teeth before flicking it with my tongue. She moaned, nails digging into my scalp, and I obliged her again, biting it just enough to hurt. With a pop, I released her, yanking my shirt overhead and tossing it to the side. The others made their way to us, crawling on their hands and knees just the way I liked before waiting patiently for my permission to join us on the bed.

"Come," I said, releasing them from their positions on the floor. They set to work removing the rest of my clothes, caressing my skin as it was bared with tongues and wet lips. Once I was naked, I edged back against the headboard, allowing them to touch me and each other as I watched.

Taya was the first to sink onto my hardness, moaning with pleasure as I stretched her out. Her pussy clenched around my cock as one of the others bent her head to lick at her clit, while a third licked my balls from behind. The groan that escaped me was primal as the two of us were serviced, and Taya leaned back, bracing herself against a fourth to give the female licking her better access. I lifted the hair of the one closest to me so I could watch the action, directing her head closer to the redhead's slit.

"Ride my face, baby," I ordered, and she spun her hips to face me, allowing me access to her pussy while she pulled Taya in for a kiss. The females fondled each other's breasts, both moaning as my tongue and dick pleasured them. The other two entertained me with movements of their own, grinding their hips together beside me and putting on a show of their pleasure.

Before dawn rose the following day, I was going to fill each of their bellies with my cum. Taya's walls clenched around me, and I growled into the pussy of the female riding my face. "That's it, Taya, milk my cock."

She cried my name, her hips stuttering as I exploded inside her. With a groan, I tossed the female off my face, then gripped Taya's hips and flipped her over. My dick was still throbbing inside her, and I speared deeper, wanting to fill her so deep that she'd fall pregnant that very night. Pulling out slowly, I flattened a palm on her belly and forced her to remain still. Then I swiped my fingers through the wetness seeping out of her and shoved my seed back inside. "Stay there."

Her eyes tracked me as I moved to the two females pleasuring each other. Separating them, I pushed one to her hands and knees, and the other to her back. Entering the first from behind, I forced her face into the cunt of the other. She moaned as I slid my length inside her, then dropped her head and let her cries fill the pussy in front of her. Licking and sucking the other female's lips sent more wetness gushing over my dick. Their cries mixed and matched as I quickened my pace, and I wasn't sure who was getting the most pleasure.

The fifth rode Taya's face, who, as instructed, remained where I left her, and by the time I came again, the whole room smelled like sex. Humidity hung in the air, and with the back of my arm, I wiped the sweat from my face. Desmond, like me, was surrounded by females, though he hadn't broken in his body nearly as much as I would have if I'd just become Fae. Instead, he reclined like a fucking king and let the females lick and suck all over his body. He shot me a wink and then flipped one of them with his newfound speed and strength, entering her and causing her to cry out with the force of his assault.

One by one, I filled each of my whores with cum, grinning to myself with each successive blow. The Night Realm would rule this continent, and my line of succession would ensure that once I crushed the so-called empire, it would remain in Vaszoly hands until long after my death.

THE NEXT DAY, I swept through the halls of Este Castle, my subjects offering me sweeping bows as their king passed them. My council awaited me, brimming with anticipation – or trepidation. Either was likely, given I preferred to keep them on their toes. The wood-paneled room hushed as I entered it and took my seat in the carved chair at the head of the rectangular table. To think, not even a year prior, we'd sat around this very table and plotted to keep the throne from High Lords Valintin and Luzak.

Now, there were two fewer seats in the front of the room.

Clearing my throat, I called my council to order. All eyes were on me, including Endre's *ungrateful* ones, as I rapped my signet ring against the polished mahogany. The proposal I planned to present would bring glory to the Night Realm, and they would get on board with it after they listened to my explanation. The heirs leaned casually against the walls, while their fathers, plus Kaztar and High Lord Jaku Volak, waited patiently, hands folded on the table in front of them. A smattering of new advisors settled in their seats toward the back of the table – Desmond being one of them.

"My Lords," I started, rising from my seat and allowing my chair to scrape against the ground dramatically. "By now you would have heard of our newest guest's arrival. Princess Gizela will remain in the Night Realm until I receive the respect I deserve from the other monarchs on the continent. I hate to use a babe as a bargaining chip, but we are under threat from all sides."

I paused, waiting for the words to sink in among my counselors. No one moved a muscle, hanging on my every word. I let the tension build for a moment longer before revealing the next part of my plan.

"The army will march on the Crystal Realm in a show of force. They will know that we are not afraid of them and that we have the might to take them on. The looming threat of invasion will no longer control us; instead, we will show that it is I who is in control of the situation."

The room remained silent for a beat, though I knew from experience it wasn't because anyone disagreed. They were merely processing my words and kicking themselves for not proposing it first.

Kaztar was the first to speak – my loyal friend. "Brilliant, My King. After hearing of how you were disrespected during your trek through their realm, it makes sense that we strike there first. But how will we march thousands and thousands of soldiers there without their knowledge?"

Desmond smiled widely, leaning forward and bracing his elbows on the warm wood in front of him. "If I may interrupt, I have a plan for that."

I indicated he should continue with a dip of my chin, then resettled into my chair, crossing an ankle over a knee.

"As a Mage, I have a spell that allows me to move great distances in short periods of time. Now that my abilities have been... enhanced, I believe I will be able to move more people further distances. However, thousands may be a stretch. That is why I request that anyone in the army with strong magical abilities be sent to me for testing. The spell itself is not complicated, but its execution takes finesse. I believe there are at least a few in the Night Realm who may possess the ability to channel such magic."

The High Lords listened intently, and High Lord Nikolai Arzeni, Vadim's father, rubbed his jaw as he thought. "Desmond, how long would it take to assess someone for this talent?"

The corners of the Mage's mouth twitched up. "I could assess a large group within a few hours."

Nikolai looked to his son, the head of my army. "Vadim, can you pull those you think might be able to wield such magic today?"

"Yes, father. Desmond, if you will meet me at the barracks outside the city walls, I will have them ready for you to assess." With that, he pushed off the wall and slipped through the double doors hiding the meeting from the rest of Este Castle. Viktor and Endre watched him go with guarded expressions I could not place.

"Now," I returned my attention to those remaining, "I'd like to leave as soon as possible. I have no doubt a retaliation is coming, and we need to be the ones to strike first."

Viktor's father, High Lord Erik Adimik, cleared his throat, drawing my attention. "We should leave a small regiment to guard Este Castle. I doubt they'll bring the full force of their army into the Night Realm though the Agrenak Mountains, and if they try to enter through the Crystal Realm, it would take months for them to reach us."

I rested my temple on my closed fist. "Agreed, Erik. Viktor, any other thoughts?"

His gaze lifted from the ground to meet my eyes. "Nothing from me."

"Do we have healers ready to go?" I asked High Lord Tibor Zadik, Endre's father.

"They can be ready to leave today if necessary," he replied in a cool tone that made me raise a brow.

Uncrossing my legs, I leaned forward ever so slowly, my gaze never leaving his. "Do you have an opinion you'd like to share with the group?"

Behind him, Endre's lips flattened into a thin line. But his father replied, "I worry about the optics. The residents of Vaenor have grown used to the army's presence, and their sudden departure might cause some concern."

"Vaenor is the most protected city in the Night Realm due to its location. A small regiment is more than enough," I snapped. Even then, the crashing of the ocean's angry waves against the sheer cliffs surrounding Este Castle was audible. "The last Vaszoly king ensured that the walls around Vaenor were erected. The castle can hold the people of the city if need be. There is no need to worry about optics."

Endre and Erik's expressions did not change, but I was finished with their protests.

"Good, you are dismissed. Begin preparations to depart. I will supervise Desmond's activities for the day." Chairs scraped back as my advisors filed from the room, but I remained seated, running a hand over my face when I was finally alone. The beast raged inside me, excited and hungry for blood, and I blew out a tense breath in an attempt to calm it.

Not quite yet, but soon. So soon.

I hoped Desmond was right about Fae being able to wield the magic necessary to move through space and time. After all, Ruslan could. The ability to move an army like that would make or break our war efforts, and if there was a way to work around limitations like speed, I was going to snatch the opportunity.

Once I'd stewed thoroughly on my plans, I departed the council room and wound my way through the castle. The Night Crown that rested atop my brow was askew, but I didn't straighten it as I walked because it gave me an air of ease that my people needed to see. When I broke into the sunshine outside the castle, I couldn't help but be reminded of the autumn days spent riding the Northern Route from the Agrenak Mountains with Izidora by my side.

I was her fucking savior, and she'd rejected me for the male that imprisoned her. She should have accepted *our* bond, and I would not rest until she knew that was the biggest mistake of her life. I'd show her exactly the price for choosing Ruslan.

Starting with burning the Crystal Realm to the ground.

25

RUSLAN

It took an entire fucking week to gather the small force that would penetrate the Night Realm and recapture Princess Gizela. Time that clawed at my waking hours, and Izidora's too. Her lower lip was cracked and raw from how she'd chewed it day after day, and down our bond, her fear for the tiny princess was like a dagger constantly digging between my ribs. The mate in me wanted nothing more than to wrap her in my arms and siphon away her pain, to soothe her as Kazimir, once again, forced her to relive her trauma.

As everyone gathered in the war tent, my attention drifted to her, standing firm and strong by my side. Her chestnut hair was braided back, armor secured in place, and twin swords strapped to her back. Chin high, she faced our friends and did not waver in the face of what we were about to do.

My fucking sprite.

Drazen, Zuriel, and Gozzak ducked through the flaps and *finally* joined us. Katrina slipped in behind them and shuffled through the crowded space toward Rares, whispering something in his ear. The three had remained in the Day Realm to do what Drazen called "damage control" while Katrina recovered. The added benefit of having them there was that we were able to soothe Queen Viktoria and King Consort Geza through complete transparency into our plans to rescue their daughter from the clutches of the fucking insane king of the Night Realm.

Spread on the table like preparations for a bloody banquet was a carefully drawn map of Este Castle, pinned down in all four corners by large, unpolished rocks. Liliana had worked diligently with Artur to map all the ways in and out of the castle as well as all hidden passages that cut through the walls. She'd guessed at a few rooms where the little princess might be held, marking them with fat red Xs.

"Everyone knows their assignment once we arrive?" I asked, bracing my arms on the table and studying the drawing one last time.

"Liliana, Drazen, Savich, and I will take the Royal Wing," my mate said, her arms crossed over her chest as she peered down with me.

"Gozzak, Xorrek, Kriath, and I will search the spires," Zuriel confirmed, his icy blue eyes flashing with determination. He'd revealed yesterday that he could speak with Izidora mind-to-mind, much like we could down our bond. Communication between the three groups thus fell on my mate, and she leaped at the opportunity to ensure everyone would make it in and out safely.

"Artur, Anton, Slavian, and I will search the lower levels," I stated, leveling a serious look at the two High Lords. Normally, they were trouble, but ever since Béke, the two had straightened out, for the most part. When they heard of Princess Gizela's kidnapping, both had volunteered immediately. "Once we find the princess, relay the message to Izidora so we can extricate ourselves from the halls of Este Castle. We will meet in the woods outside the city."

Rares handed out potions, Demon blood to the females

and Slavian, and the disgustingly thick shifting potion to Drazen, Artur, and me. Anton, Kriath, and Savich could perform a full shift, thank fuck, into an Eagle and Bear, respectively.

"Everyone ready?" I said, the severity in my tone leaving no room for joking and teasing. We had no idea what was waiting for us at Este Castle – an army, traps, Kazimir with his binding magic. Stealth was of the utmost importance.

I would not let him hurt Izidora again.

One by one, we filed out of the tent and into the autumn night. A shiver wracked Izidora's petite frame until the group clustered around us, close enough that it would be easier for me to move us all to the woods in the Night Realm.

Gripping Drazen by the arm, I tugged him closer and growled in his ear, "If anything happens to her, you will answer for it."

My cousin's blue eyes were hard and his jaw set in a firm line. "Nothing will happen to her. If anything, they should be afraid of her."

We glanced sidelong at my mate. Her posture was tense, focused, and she nearly vibrated with fury. We could scent it too – sharp, potent, and deadly. Drazen was right; Izidora was not to be fucked with, and it made me all the prouder of how far she had come.

"Everyone grab onto me," I ordered, holding out my arms. Nearly a dozen hands took positions across my body. Closing my eyes, I sucked in a breath, allowing the black fire in my chest to flare to life as I uttered the words to move us through space and time.

The world blurred by as my chanting continued, sweat breaking out across my brow as mountains bled into trees and rivers, until finally, the briny smell of the ocean assaulted my nostrils. I ceased the flow of magic, and we landed in the middle of a clearing, surrounded by tall, knotted trees with thick boughs that twisted toward the sky.

I swiped at the salt on my face. While the others stepped back, Izidora raced forward, wrapping her arms around my waist. "I love you. Stay safe."

The heady scent of roses filled my nostrils as I dragged in a deep breath, burying my face in her hair. I imprinted the feel of her in my arms on my memory as every fiber of my being begged me to keep her by my side. "I love you. You are strong. You are powerful. If anyone tries to hurt you and you don't kill them, I will."

Using her long braid as leverage, I yanked her head back and captured her mouth in a bruising, desperate kiss. The feel of her soft lips against mine as I pressed further into her wasn't enough – I needed more, needed her to understand the intensity of my love for her. Not caring about our audience, I swept my tongue against hers and crushed her against me. A whimper slipped into my mouth as she clutched at me, seeking purchase where there was none against my slick armor. With a groan, I finally released her, both of us breathless. Our gazes collided, and those aquamarine eyes that had captivated me since the moment I saw her in the ballroom at Este Castle blazed with white fire.

When she stepped away, she was framed in a white halo by the rays of the moon peeking through the trees, and truly, she looked like an Angel. Without breaking eye contact, she threw back her drink, not even shuddering at the metallic taste.

While she might have looked like an Angel, I knew she'd unleash her darkness tonight. And I was fucking thrilled for it. A wicked smirk lifted the corners of my mouth as she drew the twin swords etched with long-stemmed roses from her back.

Finally tearing myself from her, I surveyed the three gathered groups. "We meet back here," I reminded them.

"See you on the other side." Drazen clapped me on the

shoulder, then led my mate through the trees and out of my line of sight. Watching her walk away was like my soul being ripped in two and my heart being slashed by the Fehérmedve's giant claws.

We waited until Zuriel's group departed before hanging a right and sneaking through the woods. I'd taken the most dangerous section – the one where there were sure to be more guards and Fae lingering about late into the night. A breeze rustled the trees as we crept along, carrying with it sounds of clanging metal and boisterous voices. I snapped up my closed fist to halt our progress as the scent of smoke filled my nostrils. Creeping forward, I crouched behind a tree, then peered around it.

Row upon row of long buildings filled a clearing just outside the city walls, while around them were stores of food, horses, and stashes of weapons. Judging by the size, this encampment could hold tens of thousands. A few piles of construction materials caught my eye when a group of soldiers moved away from them.

Fuck, this was a new addition.

Gritting my teeth against my rising frustration, I took stock of the layout, trying to memorize what I could and assess any danger from my vantage point. While the camp was enormous, only a few hundred milled about the buildings and fires.

Where were the rest?

They hadn't seen us and appeared to laze about rather than prepare for an attack. With no time to waste, I hurried back to Artur, Anton, and Slavian. In a low voice, I relayed what I had seen. Then, with grim faces and sharper eyes, we continued our trek.

Once we reached the bridge leading into the city, we threw up the hoods of our cloaks, trying to blend in among those coming and going from Vaenor. No guards patrolled the city walls – likely because of the fucking army stationed outside it – and we quickly slipped inside among a group of merchants. Within a few minutes, we found the alley Liliana had marked.

This area of Vaenor was dark, dingy, and not a place where people asked questions.

The house on the end looked like it had been abandoned long ago, though a heavy lock still remained on the door. With a glance in either direction, I brought black fire to my palms, melting the metal and then using my earth magic to bend and break it so that it fell away. Wordlessly, we entered the space, knives drawn and ready for a surprise attack.

None came.

Instead, dust-covered furniture sagged over the dirt floor, and the thick glass window panes let in the barest amount of light from the moon. In the center, a threadbare rug skewed haphazardly. I kicked it aside and revealed the trap door that led into the tunnels.

Artur gripped the metal handle and hefted the heavy wood with a creak and a groan. Slavian stood by the window, peering through the grime to ensure no one had followed us or was coming to investigate the sound. With a stiff nod, he cleared our entrance. Dropping down, I landed with a heavy thud, followed by Anton and Artur. At last, Slavian joined us, not bothering to close the door behind him. We didn't expect anyone to discover the entrance – not if no one had for decades before. I had to hand it to King Zalan; his paranoia was certainly assisting us as we invaded his former castle.

The passage was dark and damp, and Artur offered his green fire to guide the way.

"Everything okay?" I asked Izidora down our bond, needing her reassurance.

"So far so good. Just entered the passage into the castle."

I left her alone then, wanting her to focus on what was in

front of her rather than be distracted by me. I'd done everything in my power to prepare her; it was time for me to trust that it was enough. My stomach still ached at the thought.

The dirt gave way to stone as we entered the castle grounds, and I began counting the passages popping up along either side of us. The one we searched for was nothing more than a sliver about twenty from the first one. Apparently, all the others dead-ended, in an attempt to trap any unwanted intruders.

Artur stopped short, then retraced his steps, running a palm along the rough wall until it disappeared. "Here."

Banishing his fire, he turned to the side and shimmied his way between the wedges. Anton followed, cursing low as his armor scraped against the rock. I nearly cursed myself at the tight squeeze, wondering how King Zalan ever thought he might fit through these.

What felt like an eternity later, we fell into an open chamber with a spoke of passages leading in all directions. "The one directly across," Artur muttered, keeping his voice low. He beelined to it, disappearing into the darkness, and Slavian, Anton, and I followed, casting motes of fire to guide us. It wasn't long before we reached the first turn, then the second, until we came to a fork. The left hand path led to our destination – the kitchens.

Lights extinguished, darkness surrounded us as we drew our weapons and prepared to breach the castle. I pressed my shoulder into the stone, feeling it give beneath me. With a groan, it opened slightly, but not enough to allow us entry. Switching positions, I pressed my hands against the edges to push it to the side.

Bags of root vegetables and barrels of spices greeted us, not a soul in sight. But I didn't lower my guard as Artur and I crept forward, scanning every crevice for a Fae that might give us away. Anton and Slavian picked their way carefully behind us, pausing when we reached the door that led into the main kitchen. This was the spot we were most likely to encounter someone, and I readied my blade to slice and sever.

Flipping the pommel in my hand, I opened the door, revealing two young females sitting at a table and peeling vegetables. A scream tore from their lips at the sight of us, and I wasted no time spilling their blood over their work. They weren't to blame for their mad king or the kidnapping of Princess Gizela, but protecting both the babe and my mate were my top priority and I couldn't risk alerting anyone – namely Kazimir – to our presence.

"Let's hope no one heard that," Anton muttered, clearing the room along with Slavian.

"Up the stairs," I ordered, jerking my head to the steps that led to the bowels of the castle.

On silent feet, we ascended, sneaking off the first landing and venturing in the direction of the servants' nursery. The sound of crying children was notably absent, and all who lived on this level seemed to be deeply asleep. No one opened their door to investigate the screams of the late-night kitchen maids.

At the end of the hall, a door was slightly ajar, and with as much gentleness as I could muster, I eased it open, hoping to find the little princess there. The room was empty, but as I flared my nostrils, I caught the scent of milk. The princess had been there, but judging by the empty crib and basic cot, it had been some time.

"She's not here," I informed Izidora.

"Liliana says to go up a few levels and search. Zuriel hasn't found her either."

I motioned for the others to follow, and we returned to the staircase, winding up to the next level and exiting in a similar manner. More doors stood wide, revealing barren rooms with no sign of life. The hairs on the back of my neck rose as we neared the end of the hall, and with a spared glance behind me, the others seemed just as tense as me.

Tightening my grip on my sword, I glided forward on silent feet, tuning into my heightened hearing to assist me. A single closed door drew my attention, especially the repeated swishing sound that drifted from behind it. Pausing, I listened for a moment before grasping the handle and twisting. With one swift movement, I threw it open, revealing five leather-clad soldiers waiting with wild grins. Three in the back had arrows notched and aimed directly at us.

"Down!" I shouted, hitting the floor with enough force to rattle it. An arrow whizzed over my head a heartbeat later. I treated my drop like a push up and launched myself back to my feet, charging forward and not stopping to see if Artur, Anton, and Slavian were okay. My blade clashed with the closest soldier, and with a mighty shove, I overpowered him and used his momentum to knock the arrow-wielder behind him off balance.

He blasted me with silver magic in return, causing me to stumble too, but I caught his waiting blade with the metal cuff on my wrist, allowing it to dent my armor but save my skin. I needed every ounce of my magic to ferry us back to the Iron Realm, so I gritted my teeth and swung at him, using my strength to force his back to the wall.

Beside me, Slavian and Anton battled, the former kicking a Night Fae in the stomach, sending him flying backward with a forceful grunt as all the air fled his lungs. Fire heated my backside as Artur cooked two in their armor, their screams piercing the air before gurgling into silence.

Only the one in front of me remained, and the tip of my blade was pointed at his throat. "Where are the others?" I growled, finding sick satisfaction in the way the male trembled.

"I don't know what you're talking about," he protested, and

for his lie I pressed my blade into his throat – not enough to kill, but enough to draw blood.

"Let's try a different question. How many others are there in the castle tonight?"

His throat bobbed, causing more metallic ruby to run down his neck. "Only a few. We were in here gambling when we heard the screams from below. Figured the intruders would find us eventually."

"A likely story," I grinned maniacally, causing the male's eyes to widen. Vacillating between severity and levity was its own kind of thrill, especially with how thoroughly it frightened my prey before I slaughtered them like the weaklings they were. "Where are the others?"

The male whimpered as the tip dug deeper into his skin. "Other parts of the castle."

I sighed and pinched the bridge of my nose with my free hand. "You're making this difficult. Why don't you want to please me?"

Utter confusion crossed his frantic expression, and I relished in the mental pain I was inflicting. "What?" he managed to stutter after a moment.

"Beg for your life." My tone was like ice, spearing into him as hard as my blade.

He released a whimper that satisfied the parts of me that got off on others' pain. "Is that a no?"

A lone tear slipped down his cheek, and the scent of piss filled the air. I glanced at Artur, who merely shrugged. In one swift motion, I removed the male's head from his body, allowing it to fall at my feet with a satisfying thump.

"There are soldiers in the castle," I relayed to Izidora.

"We know," was her strained reply.

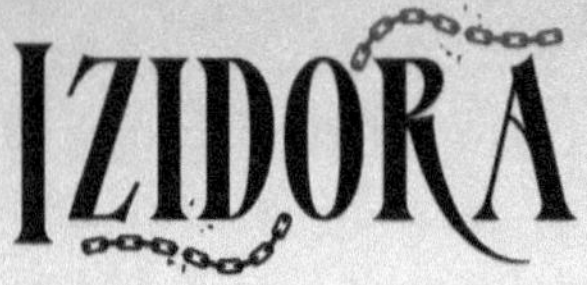 IZIDORA

Being in the tunnels brought back distant memories of the mere days I'd spent in the Night Realm before Ruslan came for me. Bubble lights floated around us, provided by myself and Liliana, as we walked behind the walls, using the same passages to navigate the Royal Wing as we had when we snuck from my room to the High House Wing. A pang of longing swept through me as I recalled how much fun I'd had with my friends, and how all of that had been lost when Kazimir went insane and the remaining Nighthounds chose him over Liliana and me.

Were they all in Este Castle, totally unaware of who moved behind their walls?

"Only a bit further," Liliana whispered, her voice barely traveling down the line and reaching Savich and me.

The cramped space was triggering a medley of physical sensations, from my heart galloping against my ribs to nausea churning in my gut.

What if Kazimir caught us and chained me again?

Panic clawed its way up my throat, and I forced myself to inhale and imagine myself flying on Ruslan's back through the

Agrenak Mountains. Wide, open space. Endless air. Puffy white clouds…

We broke into the hub of the spoke, and I sucked in a serrated breath, trying to regain control over my emotions. But I was struggling – with the narrow, oppressive spaces, the threat of facing the Night Fae, everything that Kazimir *had fucking done*. Liliana grabbed my hand and squeezed, offering her silent support. It only slightly tempered the images of that knife sailing toward my chest, and the clanking of chains filled my ears.

My best friend took charge of my body as I grappled with my mind and forced me to step into the next passage behind her. I did not release her hand as we navigated the final steps toward my old rooms.

We dead-ended at the door that led into them, and Drazen squared up with it, preparing to open it. Savich also took his place in front of us, while Liliana notched an arrow into her bow and aimed it toward the door. The iron arrow tipped in poison would paralyze its target with only a graze against the skin.

The passage was too narrow for me to draw my swords again, so I called on my magic instead. Opening up to that well of white fire wrapped protectively around a spear of dark crystal and moonlight, I pulled my power to the surface of my skin, ready to unleash my light or manipulate my foes. The scrape of rock against stone was the signal that Drazen had begun to open the door, and shouts rang out in the distance.

Fuck.

"Prepare yourselves," Drazen hissed, then with a mighty shove, flung the door to the side, revealing my old bedroom and a stream of soldiers bursting through the door beyond.

Liliana's arrow shot straight over Drazen's head and landed in the exposed neck of one in the front, sending him to his knees and those following him stumbling over his dying body. In a flash,

Drazen shot forward and engaged them in combat, Savich hot on his heels. The big males fought brutally, while Liliana moved off to the side and emptied her quiver. The door was a chokepoint that halted their progress and helped us pick them off.

But then I remembered the closet.

Whipping to the side, I raced in its direction moments before the door slammed open and a line of soldiers forced their way into the room. Fire coated my twin blades as I pulled them from their straps on my back, and the first soldier had the audacity to laugh as I sank into my fighting stance and held my blades high. He towered over me, but he did not scare me.

I was an insidious bloom, and it was time to show him my thorns.

In a flurry he could not follow, I sliced him to ribbons, the wickedly sharp blades Ruslan had gifted to me cutting through his leather armor like butter. The eyes of the soldiers behind him widened a fraction as he fell at my feet, and by the warmth coating my face, I had no doubt that I wore his blood. The third in line was too busy watching his fallen friend to see the arrow flying in his direction, and the iron tip tore through his neck, coming out the other side and catching a companion in the shoulder. They both dropped, leaving the second for me to kill.

"There are soldiers in the castle," Ruslan relayed to me.

"We know," I shot back, wanting to return to my prey.

I smiled a vicious, triumphant smile that showed this male how I would savor his blood coating my blade. He raised a hand to throw magic at me, but my shield was rock solid and faster than him. The moonlight shattered against my shield like it was nothing more than a delicate glass, and as I dropped it, I used my flame-coated blades to hack off his hand, then spear him through the stomach. His jaw dropped as he clutched his wound, burning his hands, and as he fell, I yanked my blade free. The pleasure of watching the life dim from his eyes was divine.

Gone was my trepidation about returning to this place. Power thrummed in my veins, and I imbibed every dark drop.

The room was silent, save for the pounding of my heart, and when I glanced up from my fallen foes, Drazen and Savich looked on with pride swimming in their eyes. Liliana held her bow in one hand and saluted me with the other, earning a laugh from me.

But then, a tiny wail broke the silence.

I leaped over the dead bodies and raced through the closet that still held all the dresses I never got to wear. There, in the living area, was a young female clutching a baby to her chest, frozen in shock and fear.

Drazen and Savich barreled through the other door, and the female was immediately surrounded as the four of us crept toward her. Liliana slipped to my right, trying to circle out of the female's field of vision. I shot my best friend a questioning look, needing to know if she knew the nursemaid.

A subtle shake of her head told me she didn't.

"Give us the child," Drazen commanded, holding his blade in one hand and extending the other.

The Night Fae female shook her head, still unable to speak. The little princess cried in her arms, wailing louder as tension filled the room.

"Give us the child, and no harm will come to you," Drazen promised, his tone more like a caress and less like a command.

I winced as the child's screams reached a piercing crescendo. Whatever soldiers remained on patrol would no doubt hear and rush toward the sound.

"Zuriel, we found her. In my old rooms in the Royal Wing."

"We've got her. Take the potions," I relayed to Ruslan, then

returned my attention to the female Drazen and Savich were backing into a corner.

Heavy footsteps grew louder, and I glanced toward the door. "Liliana lock it," I whispered in a rush. Kazimir had once taught me how to do so, but having not practiced it since, I didn't trust myself to do it. Moonlight ripped from her palms and sealed the area around the door. Her brow furrowed as she focused, and I was so busy watching her that the first bang against it startled me.

Gripping my weapons, I tore my attention back to the female caretaker.

"You have nowhere to run. You are surrounded. This is your last chance to hand over the babe, or we will have to kill you." Drazen took a step closer, his expression utterly serious. He meant every word – I knew it, Liliana knew it, and the Night Fae female knew it.

She looked between the four of us, her gaze lingering the longest on Liliana and me. A lone tear slipped from her green eyes, and she gingerly extricated the babe from her hold and held her in Drazen's direction. The moment he had hold of Princess Gizela, Savich's blade sliced through the air, ending the female's life. I didn't take as much satisfaction in her death as those of the males.

"We need to get going," I shouted as the banging on the entry door grew more forceful and shouts rang out in the hall outside. "Take the potion, Drazen."

Handing the baby to me, he dug for the vial in his cloak and lifted it to his lips. She still screamed, and my ears continued to bleed as I held her. Tapping into my magic, I attempted to soothe her, offering her happy, healing emotions and siphoning away the panicked ones. She calmed quickly in my arms, and I breathed a sigh of relief when the only sounds assaulting my ears were from the angry guards at the door.

It was poetic, really, that I was the one to rescue her when I had been the first kidnapped princess.

Without another moment of hesitation, I led us back to the tunnels, throwing bubbles of light into the air as we entered the darkness.

"We're on our way," I mind-spoke to both Ruslan and Zuriel.

Drazen closed the door behind us, and with renewed purpose, I focused all my energy on getting out and stoking the fire in my chest, should I need to call on my magic again for another fight – especially if Kazimir were to make an unwanted appearance. Given that we trudged behind the walls of the Royal Wing, it was likely he was only rooms away.

Our footsteps were hurried as we retraced our path, nearly missing the sliver in the rock that led to the getaway tunnels. Fortunately, I was small enough that I could shimmy sideways while still holding the princess, but when we burst into the wide, rocky tunnel, I was grateful for the space once again.

"We're in the clearing. No sign of Ruslan yet," Zuriel notified me, and worry knotted my belly. I hadn't heard from him since he told me there were soldiers in the castle.

"Ruslan?" I whisper-shouted down our bond, just in case he needed to focus. What if my persistence got him killed?

Silence.

We rushed along, and my heart rate ratched up with each step.

"Drazen, Ruslan isn't answering me." I tried to keep the panic from my voice and failed.

The male skidded to a stop in front of me. His usual nonchalance vanished like smoke in the wind. "When was the last time you spoke with him?"

"When he told me there were soldiers in the castle," I replied, voice shaking. My arms trembled around the little princess, and I fought to keep my emotions from bleeding into her and waking her again.

"Fuck," Drazen swore, and Savich released a string of colorful curses before turning as if to return to the castle to save my mate.

"Where do you think you're going? We have to stick to the plan," Drazen hissed, stopping his soldier in his tracks.

A convulsion rippled through Drazen, and the three of us said, "Oh, shit."

"Drazen, you need to get above ground. Now." The big, burly Félvér grasped him by the arm and began half-running, half-dragging his general toward the hint of moonlight that filtered through the door we'd left open to find our way back.

Indecision rooted me in place, my heart torn between the dark tunnel we'd fled and the males scampering toward the cliff-side. Liliana tugged my arm again, tearing me back to reality. "You heard Drazen. We have to stick to the plan."

I sent another nudge down our bond, hoping to get something, anything back. Still, he did not respond. But I could still *feel* him, which was enough incentive for me to move my feet and chase after Drazen and Savich. By the time we spilled into the briny night air, Drazen was stripping out of his clothes and blue scales were rippling across his body.

"Run!" I shouted, taking off in the direction of the woods and our remaining party.

Drazen's shift was happening too fast – Ruslan was supposed to move us further away from Vaenor before their Dragon forms took over so we could fly the remaining distance home and conserve magic energy.

"Ruslan, we need to get out of here, now!" I shouted down our bond, and finally, I got some acknowledgement.

"Tell Drazen we'll meet him in the skies," he growled, and a

moment later, a roar shook the ground beneath my feet, nearly pitching me sideways mid-stride.

Even in the darkness of the night, my mate's Dragon form was visible in the skies, sucking in every bit of star and moonlight. Beside him, a deep green Dragon carrying two riders flew toward us. Drazen's wingbeats dusted the ground as he lifted off, Savich barely hanging on as he climbed.

Calling my wings to me, I took a running leap and soared into the night, flying hard and fast away from Vaenor. Liliana was right by my side, bow in hand and ready to fire at any pursuers.

Ruslan banked to the left, and I tracked his movements, brow furrowed.

What was he doing? Where was he going?

Then I saw them.

Hundreds of soldiers raced from rows of long buildings outside the city walls.

Those weren't there the last time I left Vaenor.

Some gripped bows and arrows, and swirls of moonlight swept around others as they gathered to face the intruders – us. Ruslan opened his mighty maw and released a stream of black fire over the buildings, all of them igniting immediately and filling the sky with acrid smoke. More shouts rang out as the city woke from its slumber, and from my vantage point, lights popped into existence as far as the eye could see.

If Kazimir was in Este Castle, there was no doubt he was awake and watching the giant Dragon destroying his army's camp.

Ruslan released another stream of fire before banking sharply and flying in our direction.

"Land on my back, sprite," he instructed, and I halted my forward motion to time my landing.

I snapped my wings shut as he dipped beneath me, falling perfectly between his large black spines. Gripping his sides with my legs, I fashioned my cloak around me in such a way that the baby sleeping against my chest was secure and I could rest my arms.

Zuriel, Gozzak, and Xorrek were already waiting in the air above our meeting spot when we reached them, quickly spreading themselves out over the Dragons' backs while Kriath soared through the night in his massive Eagle form.

Zuriel placed his hands on my shoulders, giving them a light squeeze. "You did it, cousin," he shouted over the wind.

"I did for her what was never done for me," I replied, grip tightening ever so slightly on Princess Gizela.

His icy blue eyes were sad, and for once, he let me feel the depth of his emotions. Closing my eyes, I welcomed the sympathy and validation, because I was fucking proud of myself for standing up for the powerless and doing whatever it took to protect her, despite the panic that had gripped me while I faced it.

"If I had known, I would have done the same for you," Ruslan repeated the sentiment that had always filled me with a sense of safety and certainty. Somehow, after all this time, he still felt responsible for what had happened to me, despite him not having a hand in it.

"I know."

We flew through the night, stopping when the potions began to wear off for the Dragons. Midway through the wall of mountains that separated the Night and Iron Realms, we landed on a large, icy plateau. As the sun broke over the horizon, I carried Princess Gizela to a large boulder perched on the edge, settling in with her as we welcomed the new day.

"Your mother is going to be so happy to see you," I told her, my throat working around the lump settling there. Little tufts of golden hair caught the rising light, contrasting against her silky, pristine skin.

Thank the Goddess she was unharmed – at least physically.

So many feelings bubbled up in me, and rather than shove them away, I allowed myself to feel the depths of them all. I had to, if I wanted to be free.

Grief, for my mother dying as I was ripped from her arms, then lost to the world for twenty-one years. Anger, at Kazimir for daring to do something so fucked up after how long he'd searched for me and all his claims of loving me. Pride, at holding my own in a fight and delivering vengeance to those who dared try to harm an innocent babe.

Ruslan interrupted the wildfire of emotions burning through me as he settled on the rock to watch the sun rise in solidarity.

"Don't ever ignore me like that again," I snapped, dulling the edge of my pain on him.

"I was a bit busy trying to get away from the dozens of guards that found us in the middle of the castle," he replied, but there was no bite or admonishment in his tone, as if he knew my emotions were an inferno that needed an outlet.

"I thought I lost you," I whispered, voice cracking like the wall I tried keeping my emotions behind.

"Not a great feeling is it?" he quipped, and I ripped my gaze toward him.

"Fuck you," I hissed, jaw clenching over the words.

His smoky eyes shone with amusement. "You will, later." His hand wrapped around my throat, thumb tracing my jawline and making my heart flutter. "You and I will burn together while we relish our victory. I plan on making you come until you forget your fear and all you know is my name."

His words went straight to my core, heating it and my blood in the best way.

"I always want your fire, sprite. Seeing you sad kills me." He dropped his hand from my neck to my braid, yanking my head back. Ruslan's lips touched mine with a tenderness that I only expected when we were utterly alone. "Mate, future wife and empress. You are the air I need to breathe. I love you. I will never leave you."

When I opened my eyes again, the sun hit the smoky center of Ruslan's eyes, lighting them up in a way that showed me his soul. "I love you, mate. Us against the world."

A small cry interrupted our moment, and I sent soothing emotions to the princess.

"Can we go home now? My arms are getting tired," I laughed, the sound of it everything I needed to release the turbulent emotions swirling within me.

"Let's grab the others, and I'll move us as far as I can," he promised, helping me to my feet and off the boulder.

We huddled around Ruslan like we had before, speeding off in the direction of Radence, with one victory of many under our belts.

If only I didn't have this nagging feeling that we were missing something.

INTERLUDE

The scaffolding stood like an ominous storm in the center of the square in front of Este Castle, where, only months before, the body of the former king had been burned and sent to the Goddess. That day, others would die, but as traitors, they were not permitted to burn and return to the mother of all nature. No, once they were dead, their bodies would be tossed into the raging ocean whose anger would pummel them into the sharp rocks until they were nothing more than ragged sinew.

The nobility sat on risers with their backs facing the castle so that no one missed the view of the consequences of betraying the Night Crown.

A hushed crowd of Night Fae lined the streets around Este Castle, waiting to catch a glimpse of the morbid display. It had been some time since there was a public execution of this scale.

Two noble families had gone against the new king, and he needed to appear strong to his subjects.

"Houses Valintin and Luzak, please step forward," the king commanded, standing off to the side of the scaffolding with his hands clasped behind his back. A glittering crown of twisted black metal and diamonds adorned his head, glinting in the midday sun. The rest of his attire was that of a warrior's, as if he needed to remind his people that he was also a renowned fighter and would deliver death sentences himself.

Six Fae stepped forward.

The two High Lords held their heads high, peering over the crowd gathered in front of them with the same disdain they'd given their new king prior to his departure. Their wives and children looked like they'd barely slept or eaten since the news of their deaths had been delivered. The two males did not even bother to beg for their families' lives.

"Tomaz Valintin and Vaklav Luzak, you have both been accused of treason and found guilty. For your crimes you will be put to death, along with your families, banishing the last of your bloodline from the Night Realm." The king read their sentence with a barely contained smile, though the nobles seated behind him shifted in their seats, many clenching their hands around their clothes or pressing their lips into a thin line.

"Alekzi Valintin, you are also accused of assaulting a female and have been found guilty. For that crime, you will also have your hands and genitals removed prior to death."

A whimper escaped the young male as the king rolled up his parchment and stuck it in his pocket. With a nod of assent, two of his guards grabbed Alekzi and dragged him forward. He kicked and screamed the entire way, and it took another set of guards to hold him still enough to deliver the first part of his sentence.

His parents watched on, their heads held in place by a soldier so they could not look away as he was finally executed. They were dragged forward next, bodies and heads now piling up at the king's feet. The king spared no one, even a few distant relations who'd scarcely spent time in Vaenor around the other nobility. The only sound filling the capital city was the whoosh of his blade as he brought justice down over and over again, until House Luzak also was no more.

"Let this be a lesson to any who dare cross King Kazimir Vaszoly. The price for your betrayal will be death." With a pointed look at the nobles seated flush with the castle's walls, he wiped his blade on the back of Tomaz Valintin's tunic and returned to its interior, where his harem awaited his arrival, and his cock throbbed with its need for release.

III

THE AMBUSH

27

ENDRE

Much to my dismay, Desmond managed to find over two dozen soldiers who could perform the moving spell. I, unfortunately, was one of them.

Clenching my teeth around the words, I cast a net of thought around me, willing those assigned to my group to join me as we crossed distances in a blur. In three days, we'd managed to move tens of thousands of soldiers, horses, and equipment to the border, and with each successive spell, my apprehension grew.

I didn't want to destroy the Crystal Realm.

But I had no choice, not when Kazimir was watching my every move. I felt like an island in the middle of the sea, alone in my thoughts and feelings and adrift in my purpose.

Sweat soaked my hair as we reached the day's stopping point, and without a word to my group, I stalked away. My knees banged the ground beside the large lake, and I dipped my hands into its cool waters, bringing them to my face and splashing it as I tried to calm myself. Over and over and over, I repeated the process, trying to cleanse myself of whatever it was that wanted me to abandon my friends.

"Can I join you?"

I whipped around to find Vadim standing there, a hand stroking his long beard as he examined me. His long hair was tied into a knot on the top of his head, though after a day's worth of travel it was almost as messy as my hair. Wet drops from the black strands landed on my face as I nodded, then returned to the bright blue waters of the lake.

I sat back on my haunches, resting my elbows on my knees, and just stared into the distance.

Vadim settled beside me, heaving a long breath before rubbing a hand over the back of his neck. "I'm worried about you, brother."

Without bothering to look at him, I asked, "Why?"

"You've always been the quiet, sensitive one, but I don't think I've heard you speak more than a handful of words in the past few days." He picked up a rock and tossed it into the lake, the smooth stone skipping across the surface before sinking somewhere in the distance.

"And?"

"And my point exactly. You want to be anywhere but here. Is it Liliana? Or something else?"

The irony of Vadim trying to talk about my feelings for his sister wasn't lost on me. "I do miss her. I was hoping to see her in the Day Realm…" I trailed off, hoping he'd believe my lie about my sullen mood and not that I didn't want to slaughter the Crystal Fae.

"But she wasn't there."

Vadim selected another rock and loosed it across the water. I watched it hop and sink before responding.

"Yep. And we left in a hurry."

Please go away.

"Why weren't they there, do you think?" he questioned, and I didn't need to ask who he meant by 'they.'

"By my guess, Izidora likely still sleeps, and neither of them wanted to leave her side." I shrugged, toeing a few rocks until I found one I wanted. Grabbing it, I hurled it across the lake, where it landed with a plunk.

"Which means we are doing the right thing by preemptively attacking now. Ruslan's focus will be divided, and we'll have an easier victory, with less bloodshed." Vadim's reassurance fell flat for me, because, like everyone else, he only came up with logic that suited our current situation rather than the other way around.

And no one seemed to remember the prophecy either.

The words repeated themselves automatically in my mind, just like every time I thought about it these days.

"The ones that are part of all will be born under a full moon
Her white light will fill the land
But her mates darkness will rise
Kings will fall
Rivers will run with blood
There is a choice
Follow the light
Descend into the dark
The harrowing pass decides it all"

There were no harrowing passes in the Crystal Realm – only lakes and giant willow trees, glaciers and towering pines, and sand and ocean toward the coast. This campaign was pointless. What were we destroying, really? Vineyards? The Crystal Fae were the most peaceful. They didn't want war. They wanted to sip wine and lounge lakeside.

I said nothing, and eventually Vadim sighed and rose to his feet. "There's always room around our fire for you, Endre."

He hesitated for only a moment before walking away. I

chucked another rock into the water, wishing I could take my anger out on something other than these rocks and this lake.

———

Dawn broke over the horizon, and my horse shifted nervously beneath me. Tension bled through all our mounts, as if they knew that many of them would die this day. The soldiers on foot around me held their breath, waiting for the sword or axe to fall and end their lives. I'd never been to battle before. Fates, none of us had. The last ones in Északi took place before my parents were born.

And yet, here I sat, atop my mount, waiting for the signal to begin wielding my axe and magic to kill, to maim, to destroy.

Across the open plain, the Crystal Fae wore stoic, stern expressions, hands gripping spears and archers shielding magic wielders behind them. On both sides, large bodies of water provided all the material they needed to work with for anything they couldn't conjure we had a few tricks of our own to deal with their elemental magic.

Kazimir rode his dark horse down the front line of Night Fae soldiers, shouting orders and words of encouragement, all the while allowing black to creep into his eyes and blot out the emerald color that was as familiar as my own peridot.

We were only miles from Vlisa, the capital of the Crystal Realm, and yet I did not see King Airre doing the same for his soldiers.

Did he think he would win so handily that riding out to battle was unnecessary?

"...show them how powerful the Night Realm is and that we are not so easily banished! We are not swayed by pretty words and pretty gifts. We are fierce, vicious, and independent. We are the true Fae of this continent!" Kazimir finished, eliciting a resounding roar from the infantry.

Returning to the rear of the guard, he plucked a stag's horn from Vadim's outstretched hand and lifted it to his lips. The trumpeting call was more akin to a death knell as it rang out across the land, signaling the start to a war that would bring Északi to its knees.

Gritting my teeth, I dug my heels into my mount's sides, driving him forward among the rest of the cavalry. Kaztar and I raced along, shouting orders for our males to break off in various directions and clash with the Crystal Realm's soldiers from an advantageous position.

The sun was momentarily blotted out as a thousand black wings beat together, our archery unit better suited for their task from the sky. A volley of arrows from the Crystal Fae attempted to take them down, but in perfectly rehearsed unison, a silvery shield encompassed them, sending the arrows bouncing off and down onto the field below. Their returning fire was rapid and precise, cutting down nearly half of the Crystal Realm's archers on the first attempt.

The skies had their advantages.

The magic wielders behind the Crystal Fae quickly brought water from the lakes and created an icy barrier for them, tiny holes appearing in the shield just in time to fire an arrow before closing over again. Night Fae plummeted from the sky as they traded back and forth, some with enough force to crack the ice and reveal a warrior hiding beneath. They were shot down without hesitation.

Kaztar and I peeled off in different directions, trying to surround the foot soldiers and herd them into a group so our infantry had an easier time picking them off. But they were either clever or prepared by a seer, and any time we began pushing one way or another, they'd cut across, move forward, or move backward.

The sun rose higher in the sky.

I passed Viktor locked in battle with three Crystal Fae, his heavy strikes making him slower than the lithe bodies surrounding him. One circled out of his periphery, and without thinking, I yanked on my mount's reins and kicked him in Viktor's direction. Drawing a dagger from a sheath strapped to my thigh, I grasped the blade and threw it end over end toward the Fae whose blade was arcing toward Viktor's shoulder.

It sank into the space between the Fae's shoulder and neck, dropping him and slowing the momentum of his strike. The blade glanced off Viktor's shoulder guard, and he whipped his head around after he dispatched the other two.

"You're welcome," I said. We locked eyes, acknowledging that I'd just saved his life, before I spurred my horse on. He returned to the fray, cutting his way toward his father who fought a few lengths away.

Mine was in the very back of the company and out of the battle, thankfully, managing the healers we'd brought with us.

Another pass around the foot soldiers brought me back to Kaztar, whose horse had a large gash in its side and was struggling to walk. His blade dripped blood, but he looked otherwise unharmed. "You okay?" I shouted over the clang of blades.

"Yeah, but my horse is not," he called, angling the injured animal toward me.

I leaped from my mount and rushed to Kaztar. Placing my hands on the sweaty hide, I willed the gash to close, and tendrils of silver magic swept from my palms across the horse's skin, knitting the flesh back together. The stallion tossed his tangled mane, letting me know he was good enough to continue the battle.

"Thanks, Endre," Kaztar said. "Domi would have killed me if I came home without him."

I snorted, since his wife would have undoubtedly followed through on it. "She loves her horses more than you."

"That she does," he grinned, scanning the area behind me for threats. "Watch—"

But the rush of footsteps had already reached my ears before Kaztar spoke, and I whirled around, axe already swinging. It sank deep into the chest of an approaching Crystal Fae. He clutched at the wound and fell to the ground, spluttering blood with a wet cough. Another swing of my axe delivered the swift death he deserved instead of the slow, painful one he would have experienced from a wound like that.

All shadows disappeared from the battlefield as the sun peaked in the sky.

"Let's end this," I told Kaztar, striding away and throwing a leg over my mount's back.

We took off in a gallop to assess the battlefield, scanning for opportunities to break apart their lines. The archers had been dealt with, the icy shield only protecting the magic wielders who took turns shooting the flying archers from the sky with spears of ice. They had started to understand the tactics of their opponents, and one by one, flew to the back of the line to exchange their bows for swords and drop to the ground to battle with magic and sword against the barrier and those behind it.

"Over there!" I shouted to Kaztar, pointing toward where Vadim and Viktor were fighting with their fathers in the center of the field, bodies piling up around them as they danced with their swords.

We turned in unison and cut our way through the fight toward them.

"I thought you'd never show up!" Vadim shouted with a laugh as he cut a deep slice into a Crystal Fae's leg.

"Need a break?" I replied, throwing another dagger into an oncoming soldier.

"Fuck no," Vadim shot back, kicking the legs out from beneath one opponent and sending him flying into another.

"Haven't you heard? The great warrior Vadim can fight for days on end with no breaks, no water, no food. In fact, he needs no food to survive," Kaztar teased, slicing into an opponent who was running by with his blade.

Erik snorted and wiped the sweat from his face with the back of his hand, taking a momentary break from the chaos around us with the addition of my blade and Kaztar's. "Us old males on the other hand–"

High Lord Adimik never got to finish what he was saying. Blood dribbled out of the sides of his mouth as he looked down at his chest, where an icy spear protruded, the tip pointed in my direction. My mouth dropped in shock, and Viktor released a furious cry. "Father!"

"Viktor watch out!" I screamed, throwing up a shield over both of them just as another icy spear flew in our direction.

"Fuck! To our left!" Vadim shouted, silvery magic bursting from him just in time to block three successive ice shards.

"Hold it!" I ordered, joining my magic with his and forming a barrier around as many as we could manage. The icy assault persisted, banging like a drum and forcing us to pour more power into maintaining our safe position.

Viktor dropped to his knees in front of his father, holding him by his shoulders and repeating, "It's going to be okay."

But Erik's eyes were already growing distant, and a river of red dripped from both corners of his mouth.

"Endre! Help me," Viktor begged, but I knew there wasn't enough healing magic in the world to save him, especially not on a battlefield where we were under attack.

"There's nothing we can do," I whispered, but my voice still sounded like screaming through the cacophony of battle.

"No, no, no," he cried, cradling his dying father against his chest.

"Son, tell your mother I love her... when you see her. It was... my honor to battle beside you," he wheezed, using the last of his air to convey his feelings for his family. Then, he slackened, going utterly limp in his son's arms. Hot, angry tears tracked through the blood and sweat on my face, leaving two lines of grief.

We'd already lost so many.

"I can't hold for much longer," Vadim rasped, his hands shaking as he held the connection to the magic fueling the shield.

From my position atop my horse, I looked between Viktor, Vadim and his father, Kaztar, and the battle around us. "Viktor, take my horse and your father's body to the back. We'll hold the line."

With a numbness that only comes from loss, he ripped the ice from his father's chest and heaved him into his arms. I hit the ground with a thud, then held my mount steady as he draped Erik across. Viktor's sage green eyes were nearly as empty as his father's as he took the reins from me and turned the horse in the opposite direction. He said nothing as he departed, as heartbroken as I'd ever seen him.

"Ready?" I finally said to Vadim and Kaztar, gripping my axe in one hand and a jagged dagger in the other.

Vadim managed to nod before dropping the silver shield from around us. It was like popping a soapy bubble, and the cacophony of sound assaulted us as quickly as shards of ice flying from desperate Crystal Fae. They were losing, badly, and they knew it.

The sun began its daily descent.

The four of us held the front line, succeeding in pushing back the Crystal Fae until they were nearly even with the edge of the lake. Though, it was no longer the bright blue hue the Crystal Realm was known for; no, it was a deep scarlet, only broken by the bodies floating lifelessly along its surface.

Vadim roared, channeling his rage into his blade and slicing down three opponents in quick succession. High Lord Nikolai, Vadim's father, fueled himself similarly, and by the way he clenched his jaw, I knew he was just as upset as the rest of us. But there was no time to mourn on the battlefield – that was only available in the aftermath. With renewed vigor, we pushed forward, fighting to make sure that those who died on our side did not die in vain.

A gust of wind blasted across the battlefield, carrying on it the words 'retreat.'

The Crystal Fae did not hesitate to race away as their leader gave them permission to escape their certain deaths.

The four of us stood and watched them flee, instructing our soldiers not to follow. They'd fought well and earned the reprieve. Besides, we needed to regroup and decide what our next steps would be. Exhaustion filled every part of me as adrenaline fled my veins, and my limbs were nearly impossible to move as I trudged back to our base camp.

Kaztar, Vadim, Nikolai, and myself were covered in blood, and I had no idea how much of it was mine. There was no use trying to rinse in the lakes either – not with their current color.

Barrels had already been cracked to celebrate our victory by the time I reached the healer's tent. My father worked furiously over his patients, barking orders at assistants, shouting for clean bandages, wisps of silver assisting him for a more serious case. I stood for only a moment at the entrance before deciding to let him work and speak to him later.

The sun neared the horizon.

In the war tent, Kazimir, who looked cleaner than anyone else in our camp, Viktor, Vadim, Desmond, and several others were bent over a map of the Crystal Realm.

"We should chase them down, finish the job, then take Vlisa," Vadim was saying, gesturing to locations on the map that were out of my field of vision.

I wasn't going to be party to this.

Backing away slowly, I tried to slip away unnoticed. But Kaztar had already seen me and offered a victorious smile, and Kazimir beckoned me forward. "You were brilliant, Endre. Great job out there."

"Thanks," I muttered, busying myself looking elsewhere so he didn't see the mixed emotions in my eyes.

They continued their discussion while I trudged forward and took a spot between Viktor and Vadim. "I agree, Vadim," Viktor said, rubbing the side of his dirty face while he thought. "Now is not the time to let them come up with another plan. We must strike while we have the advantage. We should wait until nightfall, when our magic will be at its strongest. It will help refuel us as we raid Vlisa."

"How many did we lose?" I asked, seeing as no one else seemed to care.

"Not even a tenth of the army. Most are still chomping at the bit to continue the fight," Vadim grinned wolfishly, as though the father of one of his closest friends hadn't just fucking *died*.

We all coped with grief in different ways.

I tuned them out as they continued to debate how to proceed, nodding at the appropriate times. I wanted nothing more than to find my tent and collapse onto my bedroll, but it appeared that was not an option. What I could do was find something to eat, so I excused myself and went in search of a fire that would have a cook or two providing hot meals for the soldiers.

After accepting a steaming bowl of stew and some bread, I scarfed down the food, hungrier than I thought. I returned for a second helping before deciding I'd had enough if I didn't want it all to come up in a few hours' time. Fighting was much easier on an empty stomach – especially with what Kazimir was asking me to do.

———

WE RODE into Vlisa with a trail of fire and blood in our wake. The Night Realm's soldiers tossed torches into buildings along every outlying town between our camp and the capital of the Crystal Realm, and villagers who joined up with the retreating army were slaughtered alongside them. Those who fled were allowed to race away, because our target was Blire Palace, where King Airre and Queen Immonen were no doubt watching our advance. Their palace was beautiful, with a strategic advantage of being able to see for miles in every direction, but that night, the only thing visible was red.

The crystal palace reflected the color of the water, and the once ethereal structure looked more like an omen as we approached it. Residents of Vlisa had already taken refuge – either outside the city or in their homes. I cared not, so long as they weren't in our path. The streets were barren, save for the remaining Crystal Fae soldiers, who took one look at the advancing army and retreated to the palace courtyard.

Kazimir split the line of the Night Realm's army as he rode to the gates. "Surrender and no more harm will befall you!"

King Airre appeared behind a dozen rows of soldiers, his white hair disheveled as if he had been pulling at it while he watched us destroy his realm. "You will pay for this!"

"From where I sit, it looks like I have already won. Who will make me pay for this? You?" Kazimir tipped his head back and laughed, an obnoxious, grating sound designed to intimidate but only serving to irritate me.

The king of the Crystal Realm punched the side of his palace, before turning to converse with someone out of view. "Fine. We surrender. On one condition."

"Name it," Kazimir shouted with a wave of his hand.

A stone settled in my stomach because I knew what King Airre would ask for, and had no doubt that Kazimir would not hold to his promise.

"I want my mate to live."

And there it was.

"Done," Kazimir replied. "Open the gates."

They swung inward noiselessly, and Kazimir guided his mount through them, followed by the rest of his nobles. The sea of Crystal Fae parted for him, quickly cornered and surrounded by our own soldiers.

Kazimir dismounted, handing the reins to Kaztar, and King Airre stepped from within the doors of his palace and into the night. He threw up a smattering of floating lights, the rest of the Night Fae adding to them so the space around us was nearly as bright as day. No one wanted to miss what happened next, and it made me sick.

Slowly, the rest of the Crystal Realm's male nobles trickled out, mothers clutching children to their chests as if they could protect them from what was about to happen. Blire's inner halls were lined with witnesses, and I only hoped that some could find away to escape this place and tell someone, fucking anyone, what had happened.

King Airre knelt on the ground, lifting his ceremonial sword and dipping his head in deference to Kazimir. Then, he spoke the official words of surrender.

Air caught in my throat as I watched the scene unfold in slow motion.

Kazimir accepted the blade, and in one smooth motion, drew it and sliced through the neck of the king of the Crystal Realm. A shriek like nothing of this world shattered the shock around us, and Queen Immonen burst from within the palace, helpless as her mate's head hit the ground. She fell at his side, a sob wrenching free as she grabbed at his falling body.

She never managed to close her hands around his tunic. Her long, platinum hair fluttered to the ground, mixing with her husband's as the mates joined each other in death.

Bile rose in my throat, and it took all my focus to breathe slowly through my nostrils and keep the contents of my stomach down.

Beside me, Vadim and Viktor were stone-faced, not even flinching as two Fae we'd spent considerable time with were mercilessly slaughtered. Only Kaztar had the decency to glance away from the scene and gather himself.

The Crystal Realm's nobles stood in utter shock, blinking and unable to speak as the blood of their monarchs pooled at their feat. Kazimir cast them a dismissive glance before addressing his army.

"We have won a great victory on this day. The Crystal Realm is ours!" A roar rose up from the soldiers, riding the high of their victory. Then, he turned to the Crystal Realm's forces. "Anyone who will pledge loyalty to me here and now will keep their lives. Otherwise, you will be executed."

A fucking tyrant.

The thought crossed my mind before I even realized it, and in that moment, I knew that staying in the Night Realm was no longer an option for me. I had to get out, I had to find Liliana, and I had to save the rest of my friends from Kazimir's madness.

28

IZIDORA

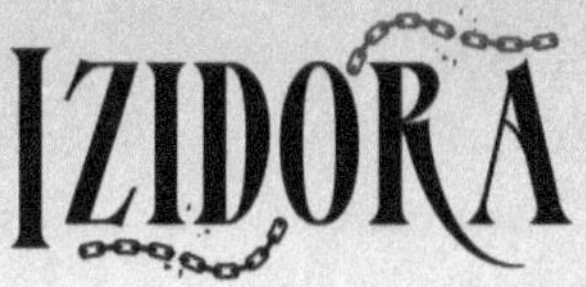

Rares was waiting for us in the courtyard of Ryza Citadel, alternating between wringing his gnarled hands and smoothing his gray hair down and away from his face. Around him, people buzzed with an anxiety that scraped against my empath magic, and I gritted my teeth, focusing on creating a barrier around my mind that would block the oncoming feelings assaulting it.

"What is it, Rares?" Ruslan snapped as we approached, and the low hum of conversation slipped away as Fae and Félvér alike stopped to listen to the conversation.

In my arms, Princess Gizela wailed, and my already fraying nerves nearly broke as I had to use more magic to calm the babe. As if Liliana could sense my waning patience, she lifted her from my arms, catching my eye as she walked into the citadel and hopefully toward someone who could give Gizela the care she needed.

Anton, Slavian, and Kriath jogged to catch up with Liliana. Guarding the princess was as important a duty as listening to whatever news Rares would relay to us, and the High Lords knew we'd tell them regardless.

"Desmond appeared to me earlier, looking for you," he began, his throat bobbing roughly as he swallowed.

"Desmond?" Ruslan growled, his fists balling before he cracked each knuckle slowly, sinisterly, as if he were imagining popping each vertebra in the traitorous Mage's neck. "What did he want?"

Rares glanced at me, then Drazen and Artur, and finally back to his emperor. Sucking in a sharp breath, he said, "The Crystal Realm has fallen."

My mouth popped open involuntarily, and the world around me swayed as I leaned into Ruslan.

I knew war was coming, but...

The reality hit me like a tidal wave crashing against the shore, sweeping aside everything I thought I knew about how this war was going to unfold and replacing it with the desires of the oncoming storm.

"And what of King Airre and Queen Immonen?" My voice was thin and strained as I tried to process what the old Mage's words meant.

He dropped his head, then shook it. Zuriel stiffened perceptibly beside me, and the shock must have shaken him to his core for his body to betray his carefully guarded emotions.

On my other side, my mate's rising fury was like that of a wildfire, and anything in his path would be consumed without mercy. "How?" was his clipped question, posed to the Mage whose countenance paled beyond its usual pallor.

"When Desmond appeared... he was holding their severed heads as proof."

Bile rose in my throat, and I gagged on the words.

"Fuck!" Ruslan shouted, grabbing the nearest object and throwing it into the stone side of the citadel, causing the barrel to shatter and wood to splinter and shower down on the bales of hay stacked there.

The males surrounding me swore curses and oaths that were so forceful and creative they raised my brows to my hairline.

Drazen was the first to break away through the mayhem and start planning. "Let's take this inside. We need to gather the leaders of our forces and decide our next move."

"Someone needs to return the princess to her parents, too," Ruslan snarled, wrapping me under his arm and hauling us inside the citadel. "Send whoever you can spare, Rares. And tell them to relay the news of the Crystal Realm *in person* to Queen Viktoria and King Consort Geza. They'll need to ready their army as well."

His grip trembled with rage, but I did not fight him, sensing that he needed some semblance of control at the moment so he didn't lose his shit in front of the entire Iron Realm. I didn't think I could have moved my feet if I was propelled by my own will regardless. I still couldn't process the fact that Kazimir and the Night Fae had marched on Vlisa and killed King Airre and Queen Immonen.

Tears burned my eyes as I remembered the Crystal Realm's queen – her lithe frame, incredible intuition, talent for prophecy, and wisdom that had helped me during the days I was lost in my choice of light and dark.

The choice I made was the right one.

Certainty settled in my bones, more strong and sure than ever before. My mate's dark hair was a mess from fighting and flying, so similar to my own emotions in that moment. We understood each other, intuitively giving each other what we needed without having to ask for it.

In their last moments, were the mated monarchs afraid? Or did they know that no matter where they were, in this lifetime or the next, they'd find each other?

Because fear suddenly gripped me in a way I'd never experienced, sinking its claws deep into my belly and digging in. If

Kazimir could march so easily into the Crystal Realm as we snuck into his realm, what else was he capable of?

And how the fuck did he get an entire army there so quickly?

We had underestimated him, and we were paying the price for it.

Had kidnapping the little princess been a trap for us all along?

My head spun with these questions, and the halls of Ryza flew by, not registered by my anxious mind. It wasn't until we stood in Ruslan's office and he plopped me on a plush couch that I realized where I was.

"Bring us food and water immediately," he snapped to one of the females standing guard outside his office.

She saluted him and rushed off in the direction of the kitchens. Drazen, Artur, and Zuriel had followed us to the wood-paneled study, and only Zuriel had the decency to glance at his dirty, bloody clothes and then around him before finding a seat on the elegant furniture. Even if we wanted to wash, I didn't think any of us could bear the guilt of doing so knowing that the people of the Crystal Realm likely suffered every moment of the Night Realm's army occupation.

Drazen immediately went to the shelf where Ruslan kept his drinks, tossing glasses toward each of us and then circling around with a bottle of amber liquor and pouring a measure into each of our glasses.

My hand shook as I lifted it to my lips.

"Drink it all. It will help," he murmured before moving on.

I wasted no time knocking back the alcohol, relishing the burn as it passed my mouth and entered my throat, finally settling in my belly.

Silence reigned until Rares returned, drawing all our attention simultaneously. Behind him was Liliana, her seafoam green eyes shining with anger.

"Yrene has taken Princess Gizela back to the Day Realm and will return as soon as she is able," Rares informed us before gesturing to Drazen to pass him the bottle.

I'd never seen the old Mage drink, and my brows shot up my forehead as he pulled straight from the bottle. Clearly, we were all rattled by the news.

Behind them, a few servants appeared, carrying plates of food from the kitchen and placing them on free surfaces around the room before disappearing and closing the office door behind them.

Ruslan returned to the high-backed chair behind his desk from his place at the window. A rough exhale preceded his knuckles tightening over the back of it. "It's time to use the tunnels beneath the Agrenak Mountains. We can be in the Crystal Realm in two days' time. We'll head them off before they can enter the Day Realm."

"But they got to the Crystal Realm in a week's time. Who is to say they won't be in the Day Realm by then? And moreso, how did they manage that? Desmond couldn't have moved a force like that on his own." The strength in my voice shocked me as I interjected, and everyone's attention landed squarely on me.

"She's right," Drazen said, tipping the last of his drink into his mouth. "And since Kazimir is a fucking maniac, he probably thinks he can race right into the Day Realm unencumbered since there was no one to protect the Crystal Realm."

Artur nodded slowly, though Zuriel only reclined backward and crossed one ankle over his knee before reaching for a bunch of grapes and eating them off the vine.

"Something to add, cousin?" I asked him pointedly, since he was the only one of us who had seen war before in his two millennia of life and was somehow acting so cavalier about the conversation.

"Both yours and Drazen's assessments are correct," he

confirmed. "But Kazimir also answers to a council, and I suspect that they might proceed with more caution, given the... violence of his previous actions."

Ruslan studied the Angel for a moment, head cocked slightly to the side. "We have enough forces to split between the two realms – hedge our bets. There are two exits not too far from one another that we can use as well, so if the army needs to rejoin quickly, it can."

Liliana piled two plates with food, bringing one to me and perching on the arm of the couch. Balancing the plate in my lap, I gathered soft bread, meat, and cheese into a neat little pile and popped the whole thing into my mouth, chewing slowly and savoring the smoky flavors.

"What about Kazimir's binding magic? That still poses a huge risk. We don't know how much he is capable of at once, or if it will rip the flying Félvér from the skies despite the potion powering us." The crease in Drazen's brow told me just how much the prospect of meeting Kazimir in battle with the dark, dangerous magic in play bothered him.

My mate focused on the old Mage who was tasked with finding a solution. "Rares, have you figured out anything to stop us from losing access to our magic should he use it on us?"

He shook his head. "Fates-gifted magic is volatile, unstable, and damn near impossible to recreate. I'm sorry, but I've done all I can."

Ruslan's knuckles went white on the back of the chair, and he dipped his head, hiding from the others what I could so clearly feel down our bond – fear. He didn't want me on that battlefield without a solution to work around the magic that had rendered me powerless and blocked my magic from manipulating Kazimir's emotions.

But I had gotten so much stronger over the past few months.

The idea came to me out of nowhere, and I sucked in a sharp breath, kicking myself for not realizing it before.

"We won't have to worry about Kazimir's binding magic," I said, setting my plate aside and sitting up straighter, confidence filling me. "I am an empath. If I can keep him calm from a distance, he won't have access to it. When he was here during Béke, I walked him back from the edge of it several times."

"Absolutely not," Ruslan snarled, his head whipping up and smoky eyes boring into mine. The black fire simmering there no longer scared me like it used to, but it heated my low belly all the same.

"I will protect her," Zuriel swore, his expression hardening with determination. "Leave a small regiment with me just off the main battlefield, and once we get an eye on his position, Izidora can concentrate while we guard her."

"My range has gotten a lot better," I assured my mate, who looked not at all convinced of our plan.

"Your range will never be far enough for my comfort," he spoke mind to mind.

"Give me a choice in all this," I snapped back.

"I would die without you, Izidora."

"I know, but you've empowered me. I can hold my own thanks to you."

"No. Your inner fire is the one you should thank. I only showed you the way to release it."

"Then let me use it. Let me show them just how powerful I am and just how much they underestimated me."

Ruslan's hands pinkened as blood returned to them, and he blew out a long, hot breath. The glare he leveled on my cousin promised violence. "We will fight together, me in my Dragon form, and you on the ground. If anything happens to her..."

"You'll kill me. Slowly. I know," Zuriel retorted, rolling his eyes.

Liliana snickered from her perch on the rolled arm of the couch, and I winked at her from my position below.

"One last thing, Rares." Drazen glanced at Artur and Ruslan, then continued. "When we took the potion, it worked a lot faster than expected. We were racing from Este Castle, and our timing was off. Why?"

Rares tapped his chin, then opened his notebook and flipped furiously through the pages, a finger tracing different lines of scrawled text. Without looking up he asked, "You were under duress?"

"We'd just fought off a bunch of armed Night Fae, so yeah," Drazen deadpanned, reaching for an apple and biting into it with a satisfying crunch.

Rares produced a pen from nowhere, then began writing in the nearest blank space, leaving us all hanging.

Ruslan growled a warning, drawing the Mage's attention. "I think I just figured out how to make the shifting ability permanent."

"Really?" The hope in Ruslan's voice was undeniable.

"Adrenaline. That's what kickstarted the potion and caused it to work faster. I believe if I give you the potion, then inject an artificial adrenaline substance I created, followed by an incanta-tion, I might be able to give you the ability to go back and forth. I'll need to try it on a smaller Félvér Shifter first."

"Drazen, Artur, nominate someone," Ruslan snapped, yanking open a drawer and pulling out a clean sheet of paper. Artur offered up a name, and Ruslan wrote it down along with a quick note, signing it with a flourish at the bottom. He offered the paper to Rares. "Go. Now. Report back immediately. We don't have time to waste."

The old Mage vibrated with excitement as he accepted the paper and disappeared from the room.

"Someone wants to turn into a big, bad Dragon whenever they want, huh?" I teased my mate.

"Now that we've gotten all that sorted out, can we please go bathe?" Liliana complained.

I snickered around my mouthful of food until Ruslan leveled his gaze on us. "The two of you may go. We still have much to discuss."

Swallowing down the last of my food, I grabbed my plate and rose from my position on the couch, heading for the door with my best friend and delicious snacks in hand.

Ruslan's heated regard swept over me as we left the room.

"To answer your question, yes, I do want to be a Dragon whenever I want. I love when you ride me, mate, and I promise you'll be screaming to ride me tonight whether I am a Dragon or a God among mortals."

My thighs dampened as images of me riding him filtered through my mind, my chestnut hair spilling over my breasts and my head thrown back in ecstasy.

"Guess we can't get married until that happens, then."

His soft chuckle echoed in my mind as I left him and the other males to plan.

LILIANA

Was Endre all right?

I couldn't keep thoughts of him from my mind, not after what I'd learned about the Crystal Realm. I only felt slightly guilty that I thought of him before my father and brother. If the Night Realm was truly marching on the empire, none of them would have stayed behind in Vaenor.

A knot settled in my stomach, making the food I balanced on my plate as Izidora and I traversed the winding halls of Ryza look like shit.

"To the apartment?" I asked, if only to break the silence and shatter my worried thoughts.

"Mhmm," Izidora responded around her food, scattering a few crumbs from her mouth as she did so, then chuckling to herself for making a mess. My mouth twitched up as I tried to smile, but the nausea churning in my belly made it hard to feel the levity of the moment.

She swallowed down her food, then popped a fat purple grape into her mouth. "Thinking of Endre?"

"Ugh, how did you know?" I whined, rolling my eyes. Sometimes having an empath for a best friend was a good thing, other times, not so much.

She shrugged, picking up a bunch of grapes and dangling them above her mouth. "You usually only worry about one thing."

"It's because I'm so confident in all my abilities," I attempted to tease, flicking my braid over my shoulder, but the words were as hollow as I felt.

"I'm serious, Liliana," she said, slowing her gait so she could meet my gaze.

"I know," I replied, blowing an errant strand of hair out of my face.

"Tell me how you feel," she encouraged, and as we trudged up the stairs that spiraled to the top of the spire where our apartments were, I sorted through the complex web.

"I know I sound like a parrot, always repeating myself, but I want him to choose me. To choose the right side of this war. We are going to win, and I don't want him to get killed because he chose to stay loyal to Kazimir."

The double doors at the end of the hall were a welcome sight, promising a hot shower to wash away my worries and the blood splattered over me.

"Say it as many times as you need to. That's how you feel, and there's nothing wrong with that." Izidora nodded to the sentry stationed outside the apartment doors as he opened it, allowing us entry into the luxurious space.

We placed our leftover food on an end table, then traipsed to the enormous bathroom. Well, it wasn't the biggest one Ruslan had – the one at Roc was much bigger and much nicer, and I had gotten spoiled using it while Izidora slept through the seasons.

My birthday had come and gone during that time, and the males had done their best to celebrate with me, but while

Izidora had lain in the bed on the other side of the doors to the living area, it wasn't the same.

Who knew thoughts of Endre would make me so sentimental?

"You can shower first," Izidora offered, hopping up on the marble counter and kicking off her boots.

"You sure?" I asked, crossing to the knobs and turning them regardless of her answer.

She grinned back at me. "As long as you don't take all the hot water."

I shrugged, peeling off my clothes. "I make no promises."

"That's fine, if we run out, you can go ask Drazen to heat it with his Dragon fire," she teased, bringing a laugh from somewhere in my chest.

The water was warm and inviting when I stepped into the glass box. Fog gathered and rolled out of the top, sticking to the glass on its journey. "You know when he breathes the hottest fire, right?"

"When you're on your knees?"

Laughter bubbled up from us in unison, and I dunked my head beneath the artificial rain pouring from the ceiling. My hair was instantly soaked, the chocolate brown darkening even more and clinging to my body. Reaching for soap, I rubbed it over my body, lathering away sweat and blood that wasn't mine. "We make a good team," I called out as a tiny ruby river swept away from my feet.

"That we do. We should have a kill count on the battlefield. Make it a competition," Izidora replied, and I rolled my eyes even though she couldn't see me.

"You're almost as bad as Ruslan," I teased.

"Well, we're mated so I think that means we just become more alike as we grow closer," she quipped.

I swiped at the steam coating the glass so I could see her sitting outside the shower. She faced the mirror, slowly unplaiting her hair. We locked eyes, and something like hurt shone in her aquamarine orbs.

"You want vengeance that badly?"

"It's more than that. I want them to see my power and fear me." She chewed her lip and lifted a coarse brush to the ends of her hair. "I am so fucking tired of these males thinking they can scare me or walk all over me. I want it to be the other way around for a change."

Sighing, I nodded and retreated. I understood exactly where she was coming from. It was hard being a female in the Night Realm, especially a pretty one. There, I was treated more like property or an asset, especially in the eyes of the court. Vadim had tried to provide me with a semblance of control over my life through fighting, but in the end, I knew King Zalan would marry me off to whomever was in his favor when the time was right.

Thank the Goddess that never happened.

In the Iron Realm, I felt like I had far more autonomy and opportunity, and not just because my best friend happened to be the future empress.

When I was finally clean, I didn't bother shutting off the water. Instead, I reached for a towel and wrapped it around myself. "It's all yours."

Izidora hopped off the counter and left a trail of bloody clothes in her wake as she entered the shower. I took her spot on the counter and used a large-toothed comb to brush out my long locks as she washed.

"I don't want to end up like Immonen."

Izidora's confession drifted toward me on a cloud of steam, but there was no airiness to her words.

A muscle feathered in my jaw as I clenched it around the tears that burned my eyes. "She didn't deserve that."

"No she didn't." Izidora's voice was as hard as the marble upon which I sat.

"What about Domi?" I asked, fisting an especially tangled spot in my hair and working the brush over it.

The crashing of the water lessened as Izidora stepped beneath it. "I hope she's not suffering. She saw what we saw during Béke."

"But Kaztar practically worships the ground Kazimir walks on." A disgusted noise slipped from my throat, and Izidora made a similar one.

"If Ruslan ever made such a grave error of judgment, I wouldn't bow to his desires," she swore.

Izidora was fire incarnate, and Ruslan knew better than to play with a flame he could not control. If she said she didn't like something, he wouldn't hesitate to eradicate it from this earth – that's how much he loved her.

"That's because Ruslan is pussy-whipped and will do whatever you say," I snickered.

"Don't let him hear you say that. You know he wants people to think he's ruthless and unhinged." The water ceased flowing, and my best friend emerged from the fog. Water dripped from the ends of her long hair and pattered against the floor as she approached me.

"He is unhinged. Especially when it comes to you," I grinned at her in the mirror before gesturing for her to sit on the counter and spin around so I could brush out her hair. "So, what are we going to do until night falls?"

"Sleep until tomorrow," she laughed. "We've been up for nearly two days straight."

Acknowledging how long it had been since we'd slept sent a wave of exhaustion through me, tugging at my eyelids and pulling my jaw open in a wide yawn. "Let the males deal with the battle plans. We deserve our beauty sleep."

"Exactly," she said, sighing as I raked the comb across her scalp.

Izidora was the friend I'd always wanted, and I knew I was the friend she'd always needed. We crawled into bed together, wrapped in fluffy robes, not caring that Ruslan would probably shove us to the side when he was ready to sleep. It wasn't long until the lazy afternoon sun lulled me into a deep slumber, and despite the worries that plagued me about Endre, I allowed myself to rest and recover.

We were on the right side of the war, and by the time it was over Északi would be united and at peace

30

KAZIMIR

"They're likely to split their forces between the Crystal and Day Realms, not knowing if and when we will move on," Viktor assessed, bending over the enormous map splayed out over a table in the war tent.

Bubble lights floated in the canopy overhead, allowing us to meet despite the darkness beyond.

"If that is what they plan to do, then their forces will spill out of the mountains here and here," Desmond said, bringing two carved markers to the base of the Agrenak Mountains, one in the Crystal Realm, another in the Day Realm. They weren't far apart, which meant our attack would have to be brutal and swift.

"What if they decide to invade the Night Realm instead of meeting us here?" Endre questioned, earning a sharp look from me.

"They won't. We hit them where it hurts, and Ruslan is the type of male to meet us head on. He's cocky and thinks his mixed bloods will give him an advantage," Viktor quipped, eyes never leaving the map and the pieces placed on it.

"They do give him an advantage," Vadim pointed out.

"Not if we attack at night while we are strongest," Viktor argued. With the loss of Viktor's father, we were not weaker in strategy. Viktor was sharper than ever, willing to take more risks, and thirsty for blood – everything I needed to win this war and put this so-called empire to rest.

"And if they don't split their forces?" I asked, just to be sure.

A good king examined every angle.

A fire crackled and popped in the corner of the tent as a breeze fluttered beneath the flaps. "Then they're likely to go to the Day Realm and approach from there," Viktor confirmed.

"Vadim, set up a patrol near the exit Desmond marked. We want to know when there is activity there," I commanded, and he nodded, confirming his orders.

After doling out tasks for the rest of the group, I dismissed them, wanting to get some rest before the battle began. It was only a matter of time before they would appear, and I wanted to be fully prepared for the *exciting* reunion we would have.

Settling in my luxurious cot, I threaded my fingers behind my head and stared up at the dark canvas ceiling, falling into my favorite daydreams. The binding magic thrashed in my chest as I imagined the deaths of Ruslan, Drazen, and the rest of the mixed bloods that they'd worked so hard to create.

I no longer daydreamed of Izidora falling in love with me; no, the daydreams I had of her were filled with locks and chains and legs spread wide, waiting for me to take the pleasure I wanted. I didn't need her love, because she would be mine regardless. Mine to play with, to carry my heirs, to support my claim to the Night Throne.

All. Mine.

———

A HORSE RACED through the busy camp, dodging fires and tents and Fae milling about. As he drew closer, I recognized the rider as one of the scouts sent on a patrol earlier that evening toward the mountains. A wild excitement glinted in his eye as he pulled up short. "We can hear activity behind the rocks," he pronounced, his horse's sides heaving from the effort of returning with fortuitous news.

A wicked grin spread across my face, and I looked at the sky, where the first stars winked into existence. Vadim dismissed him with orders to pass the message along to others throughout the camp. Word spread like wildfire, and soldiers shoved to their feet, rushing to their assigned spots for further instruction. I remained in front of the largest fire, hands clasped behind my back while I watched my army prepare for battle.

Only black leather armor adorned the bodies of my soldiers, helping us blend into the night as we prepared to ambush the army of the Iron Realm. Orders were shouted from group to group, and they peeled off in different directions, creating layers and waves for our attack. Pleased with the progress, I threaded my way through thousands of tents until I found Fek. My steadfast stallion pranced in place, anxious to get moving as he sensed the urgency and anticipation in the air.

I offered him a lump of sugar, and he munched it greedily before tossing his mane as if he were asking me if I was going to get on. Bracing my foot in the stirrup, I threw my leg across his broad back, ensuring that my sword was secure, and steered him in the direction of the spot where the battle would take place.

In the distance, Endre and Kaztar rushed off to different flanks as we surrounded the base of the mountain. But I rode straight up the middle, wanting to see the look on their faces when we overpowered their forces.

Unfortunately, the flat plains of the Day Realm didn't

provide me with an exceptional view, though we were lucky that some of the only thick copses of trees happened to be near this exit from the mountains. I chose the highest point I could and halted Fek, glancing overhead as the moon rose higher, greeting her children and blessing us with victory.

And then, we waited.

The rumblings behind the mountain grew louder, and I tried my best to gauge their numbers by the increasing volume. They didn't bother to smother their sounds, as if they couldn't possibly expect anyone to be nearby, waiting for them to pop out from their secret tunnels.

Their arrogance ended tonight.

Silence waited beyond, the well-trained soldiers of the Night Realm more than prepared to ambush them. None were stupid enough to give away our position, not when their lives depended on it.

The first sign of Iron Realm soldiers' emergence was a loud scraping of stone.

Slowly and with a grinding that caused my ears to flinch, an opening appeared in the rock, large enough for ten males to pass abreast. A horde appeared with bundles in their arms and weapons stowed at their hips, sauntering into the Day Realm without a care in the world. They dispersed, tossing their goods aside before turning back for another trip in and out of the tunnel.

Cloaked in darkness, we waited for more to appear.

Calling upon the black and silver ropes swirling in my chest, I rendered my stallion and I invisible so I could creep closer, unseen and unheard. Within half an hour, thousands had emerged and busied themselves with making camp. A crazed smile spread across my face as they continued to move about in ignorance.

I scanned those remaining in the tunnels for any signs of my true targets – Izidora, Ruslan, and those damned mixed bloods that would surely give us trouble. No familiar faces beckoned me to draw my blade and end this conflict before it truly started.

Gritting my teeth as my vision flashed black, I spurred Fek closer, needing to peer even deeper inside the rock. Finally, I recognized a few among the crowd, but none that I would draw satisfaction from binding and forcing to watch as I slaughtered their army. As if my thoughts had summoned it, that dark beast inside me snarled, furious that we'd been snubbed by those who dared question my power.

If they weren't here, we'd fucking draw them here.

Yanking on Fek's reins, I steered him in the direction of Vadim and his father, who waited among the infantry to give the signal to attack. Dropping my protective covering, I slid from my mount's back and padded toward him.

"We need to attack now," I whispered.

Vadim's evergreen eyes scanned what was in front of him before responding. "We need to wait a little longer. Their full force isn't here."

"Nor is it going to be. There's no sign of Ruslan here."

High Lord Arzeni swore under his breath.

"That's a good thing," Vadim argued, shooting a look at his father. "It means we'll be able to crush this part of his army and decimate their numbers. All the more reason to wait."

Viktor crept into our little circle, crouching low and bending his head to join our hushed conversation. "If we can find a way to block the tunnel from closing, we can attack now."

A breeze swept across the plains, and we all stiffened, holding our breath. Then, a shout of alarm rang out in the budding camp, and the scraping of blades filled the battlefield.

"Fucking Fates, we need to go now," I snapped, already turning back for my mount.

"Goddess damn it," Vadim swore, then popped up and shouted, "Charge!"

The roar of three hundred thousand Night Fae filled the night sky as they descended over the Iron Realm's army.

31

DRAZEN

Another cartful of Iron Fae ground to a halt in front of me. "Half of you add your supplies into the cave," I instructed, pointing to a carved opening in the rock across from us. "The other half, grab your tents and join the others in making camp outside." The company offered me a salute before their commander divided them up. All around me, soldiers performed their duties with ease, taking what little time we had left before the real battles would begin. Unfortunately, we were stuck in the Day Realm until Ruslan called for us.

As the general of the Iron Realm's army, I wanted to be where the action was, carrying out battle plans I'd so painstakingly put together after reading countless histories from the greatest generals Ravasz had ever seen – including a book by the Deathcaller himself. Instead, I was stuck in the back of the tunnels, coordinating the new arrivals and trying to organize for the moment we were needed.

The next cart rolled forward. I opened my mouth to speak, but my voice was drowned out by a tidal wave of sound. Every head whipped toward the maw of the mountain, and I cursed the torches that lined the hall and prevented me from peering into the night.

The rage-filled battle cry was unmistakable, especially as a horn cut through the receding wave of it.

Fuck me.

Our calculations had been partially wrong. Kazimir did barge into the Day Realm, thinking he could conquer it as handily as he had the Crystal Realm.

Only we wouldn't be lying in wait for him; he had lain in wait for us.

We were being ambushed.

A dozen orders sprang from my throat as I tried to organize before everything slipped into chaos. "You! Send word to Artur and the others who went to the Crystal Realm that we need reinforcements. *Now.*" The Iron Fae I'd pointed at immediately hopped into one of the carts still half-filled with supplies and sped off in the direction of the artery that linked up with all other tracks beneath the Agrenak Mountains.

"Commanders, organize your units!"

"Shift if you can, drink the potion if you need it!"

"Build a wall of fire and earth around our perimeter!"

"Ready the arrows and whips and tip them in toxins!"

Around me, every warrior sprang into action. A group of Félvér females shifted into large birds and screeched as they flew through the tunnel and out into the open, shifting again and relaying my orders to those outside my shouting range.

Screams erupted before a fire could illuminate the night. Cursing, I yanked a glass bottle of shifting potion from a nearby cart and chugged the thick liquid down. "Once I breathe my Dragon fire over them, everything will catch. I need you to ensure the entire Day Realm doesn't burn while we cook the Night Fae alive. Organize a unit to fly over the lines and build a wall around us to prevent its spread," I commanded one of the winged Félvér leaders.

"Yes, sir," he replied before racing away to corral his unit. I trusted him to carry out my orders, and with the itching already spreading across my skin, I knew I needed to get outside, fast.

I sprinted and shouted orders along the way, doing everything I could for those under my command before I could no longer communicate with them. The shock of the ambush had worn off, and training began kicking in all around. The flow of people out of the tunnel was hindered by its narrow opening, but the screams from beyond had everyone charging through and not lingering. Pride swelled in my chest as none of my soldiers balked at the challenge before us.

By the time I reached the exit, the Day Realm truly looked like the day, with large fires spearing into the sky and blasts of silver knocking infantry about. Behind me, two deep voices called my name, and I spun and stripped off my armor simultaneously as they caught up.

Xorrek and Gozzak, the two Demons who had volunteered to lead, careened to a stop, their red-rimmed eyes wild with excitement, followed by High Lords Anton and Slavian, the two Félvér bachelors who sought violence and pleasure like it was their job.

"Before you go mute, what do you want us to do?" Slavian asked.

My sword clattered to the ground, along with the plates covering my arms. "They've probably surrounded us on all sides. Hold the line as much as possible and try to get everyone back inside without letting the Night Fae in." I was naked from the waist up by the time I finished speaking, and already, lapis lazuli scales coated my skin.

"Can I trust you to lead while I'm in the sky?" I asked, kicking off my boots.

Why had we split our forces like this?

"Absolutely. We've sat in on enough meetings that we know what to do," Xorrek replied, drawing two axes from his back.

"Besides, we fought in the Great War," Gozzak said, flashing his white teeth, highlighting his sharpened canines, while Anton did the same, his eyes glowing golden as his Wolf prepared to take over.

The shift ripped through me before I could respond. My Dragon form was so massive, I knocked the Demons back. They recovered quickly, calling on their membranous black wings and shooting into the sky, offering me a salute before they flew into the midst of the chaos, leaving Anton and Slavian to bark orders on the ground. I was airborne and roaring a heartbeat later, not wanting to crush my own people beneath my massive talons.

With sharpened eyes, I scanned the battlefield. At the very back stood a dark horse that nearly blended into the night, and alongside it, two far too familiar faces – Kazimir and Desmond. Cursing the Goddess, the Fates, and the Night Fae, I flew toward them, ensuring I had their full attention as I sliced through the air, flaunting my massive Dragon form.

Desmond, at least, had the good sense of choking when he saw me. Kazimir, on the other hand, betrayed no emotion.

I could kill them both and end this war before it even began.

A snarl tore through me, and I opened my jaw to blast them with blue fire. But as the burn built in my throat, Desmond latched on to Kazimir, and they disappeared from existence.

Fuck!

I blasted the space they had occupied anyway, unleashing some of my rage and making a point should they still be watching me. Banking, I changed course for the edges of the battlefield.

A group of Félvér and Iron Fae worked diligently on the wall of earth, but a winged legion of Night Fae fought with them, and the Félvér were falling faster than the wall was rising. A roar blasted in their direction as I tried to disrupt the focus of those with black feathered wings. Green eyes widened and filled with terror, and if my Dragon form could smile, it would have as I barreled toward them.

I snapped my jaws around a group of three and ripped them from the sky before slicing another with my talons and sending him tumbling, wingless, toward the earth. All attention landed heavily on me, and blasts of white energy magic pelted my scales, followed by a few arrows and jabs from swords.

My scales were tough, but each impact was painful, and I released a menacing hiss once an arrow pierced the membrane of my wing. The male was dead before he had time to draw a new arrow from his quiver. Another's scream was cut short when I crushed him between my sharp teeth.

The wall rose higher with the Night Fae distracted, and I fought fiercely despite my growing injuries. They needed to finish it, and quickly, because once they did, the Night Fae would be cooked alive. But these injuries were uncharted territory, and fear speared through me as a sword sliced deep into my side. Another roar ripped from my throat, and I thrashed my tail in the sky, knocking more winged fuckers from it.

Would the potion wear off if I was bleeding too much?

As soon as the thought crossed my mind, I felt it.

Shit, shit, shit.

With a furious bellow, I ripped apart a handful of Night Fae, cast one last look at the wall, then banked toward the main area of battle, hoping I could at least get one solid blast in before I was reduced to a Félvér once more.

The hot, dry wind of the Day Realm accosted me as it blew across the plains, bending the stalks of tall grass even more than the hundreds of thousands of feet trampling it.

We were far outnumbered.

How did they have so many?

The number that spread across the plains had to be double the force I'd brought with me, if not double our entire army. My gut twisted, and I shoved my fears to the side.

Another Dragon, a smaller female with red scales, rose to meet me, and I gnashed my teeth in hopes she would understand what I wanted to do. We were running out of time – and soldiers. Her maw opened, and ruby embers built in her throat. I did the same, allowing the blast to build there before unleashing it on the thousands of Night Fae fighting their way toward my lesser force.

Heat licked across the ground, blue and red dancing together as we aimed to create as much chaos as we could. The howls of those caught on the fringes of our streams were not nearly as satisfying as I wanted them to be. Hurriedly, I counted our army's numbers, praying to the Goddess, to the Fates even, that we hadn't lost as many as I feared.

We had.

With a growl, I jerked my head at the female, urging her to continue, while I flapped furiously toward the exit of the tunnel where my armor, hopefully, waited for me to return. The empire's army had been decimated so significantly in such a short amount of time that piles of Iron Fae and Félvér bodies nearly blocked the entrance to the tunnel. Night Fae had overwhelmed our forces on the outside, and the ones on the inside couldn't get out in time to defend their brothers and sisters in arms.

Spotting Gozzak and Xorrek drenched in hot blood and fighting off three Night Fae each, I lost my focus and crashed into the ground, fully male once again. Leaping over the dead and dying, I found my clothes and pulled them on without taking my eye off the fray.

"Fall back!" I shouted, hoping my voice would carry across

the carnage. Digging deep into my well of magic, I lifted my hands and formed a ring of blue fire around the mountain's entrance, hoping to buy my soldiers enough time to slip through them and return to the tunnels.

"Above!" Xorrek shouted, flinging an axe at a descending Night Fae.

I pushed my magic to its limits, increasing the height of the fire to deter any easy entrance behind it. The red Dragon appeared moments later, lending her fire to the forces trying to fly over my wall. She lasted only a minute before she was peppered with so many arrows she crashed to the ground.

A group of piercing cries ripped the air, and the females who had been working on the wall raced toward the opening of the cave. I allowed the blue fire to dip just enough to aid in their entrance, but as they blew by me, I counted their numbers and gritted my teeth over the additional loss.

"Gozzak! How many left?" I shouted, my arms trembling as I approached burnout.

"Only a few more!" He flapped his wings furiously to remain aloft, still shooting arrows at the approaching Night Fae. He managed to force them back long enough for a group of Iron Fae to burst through the blue flames.

They spluttered and dimmed, breaking apart in sections, and I knew I couldn't hold it much longer. "Close the door!" I commanded the last few Iron Fae to race by me, and when the scraping of stone sounded in my ears, I nearly cried out with relief. Sweat poured off of me like rain in a thunderstorm, and every shaky step I took backward was hindered by the dead.

"Get inside!" Xorrek yelled, still hovering a breath above what was left of my blue flames.

"We go together," I said through clenched teeth.

"You don't get to sacrifice yourself to save us. We go now," Gozzak replied, diving down and catching me under the arms.

The blue flames sputtered out, and the Demons hefted me between them and raced to the narrowing opening.

Hundreds of my soldiers still fought beyond the rock, and I watched every last one of them until the door closed behind us and cut them off permanently.

They would die out there, and there was nothing I could do to save them.

So I shook off the Demons and stood with my quivering palms braced against the rock and listened to their screams, until there was only silence on the other side.

My first battle as general, and I'd fucking lost.

The only saving grace was that the majority of our forces, the most valuable and well-trained, had gone to the Crystal Realm. But now we knew where the Night Fae were, and how many filled their ranks.

We already knew Desmond was working with them, but the tunnels? How long had he creeped over Rares's shoulder, learning everything he could and everything he shouldn't? How often had he broken into the Mage's private chambers and plucked further knowledge from the trove with which King Azim had entrusted Rares? With Desmond on their side and the unknown of how many more secrets he possessed, and the sheer number of males on that battlefield, fear gripped my chest, constricting until black spots danced in my vision.

Because one thing was certain.

We were fucked.

32

IZIDORA

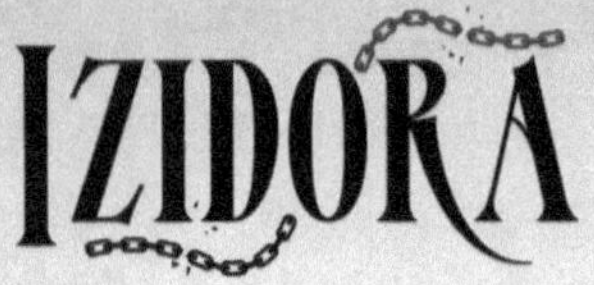

Stepping into the Crystal Realm was like stepping into an entirely new world. I barely managed not to trip over myself as I exited the gaping maw of the mountain, jaw hanging open. In every direction, waterfalls spilled over cliff edges, roaring into my ears and misting the world around them. The tips of my swords dropped as I beheld a massive glacier, its icy fingers digging into the dirt at our feet and climbing behind us into the towering peaks in the distance.

The bond between Ruslan and me hummed contentedly as I opened up my feelings of wonder to him, and he opened up his feelings of love to me. "It's so beautiful," I gasped, breathless.

"Look over there," my mate replied, directing my attention with the tip of his finger. In the distance, a massive lake spread across the land, reflecting thousands of stars off its glassy surface. From this angle, I couldn't tell where the night sky began and where the water ended.

"Incredible," I breathed, taking a cautious step forward, off the worn path and out of the way of the soldiers pushing out of the cavern behind us.

"Not as incredible as you, sprite," Ruslan murmured, wrapping his arms around me from behind and forcing my swords down at my sides. "It's safe to relax and take in the view."

We gently swayed from side to side as I did just that.

Below, our soldiers readied camp for us, fires popping into existence and dotting the rolling green landscape. After being in near darkness as we traversed the tracks beneath the Agrenak Mountains, I was more than ready to sleep in the open with the winking lights of the stars to soothe me.

"Do you think they are nearby?" I asked eventually, after scanning every inch of the beautiful landscape sprawling over the horizon.

"I don't know. I can't see any troop movement or telltale fires from up here." Ruslan tensed behind me. "I don't see any fires, actually, besides ours. There are cities all along the lakes, but none of them are lit."

My brows dipped as I tried to discern the shape of buildings along the lakes, but my search yielded nothing.

"Does that mean…" I trailed off as bile rose in my throat.

"That Kazimir burned them to the ground? Likely." Ruslan's tone was as icy as the glacier gripping the stone above us. "Vlisa is at the other end of that lake."

"And if it's dark, that means they aren't there."

Liliana popped through the tunnel and joined us in our examination of the Crystal Realm. The corners of her eyes tightened, and she played with the ends of her hair before flinging it out of her way and crossing her arms. It had been harder than she wanted to admit to part from Drazen, but she refused to leave my side given that this was the most likely place to fight the Night Fae.

Or so we thought.

I chewed on my lip, thinking. "What if it's a trap? What if they want us to think that they've moved on so we let our guard down, and then they spring out of nowhere?"

"I think the trap was set elsewhere," Liliana whispered, and Ruslan's arms tightened reflexively around me before he dropped them away.

"Stay here," he instructed, his smoky eyes swirling with worry as he jogged through the crowd of people exiting the mountains.

Sheathing my swords, I wrapped an arm around Liliana and tugged her close. With a sigh, she rested her head on my shoulder, a few escaped tendrils of her chocolate brown locks tickling my nose.

"Drazen and Endre will be all right," I reassured her.

"I know," she said, but her words rang hollow.

I resisted the urge to shift from foot to foot as we waited for Ruslan to return. When he did, he didn't bring relief with him. A giant bird soared overhead, buffeting us with the wind from his massive brown wings. Kriath flew straight across the lake, headed to Vlisa. Zuriel joined us at the edge of the cliff, and the four of us waited in silence for our Félvér friend.

The soldiers continued to build the necessities of a war camp below us, unaware of what transpired above. By the time Kriath returned, nearly an entire city had popped up. Midair, the Eagle shifted into a male, and Kriath landed lightly in front of us. While his body remained bare, his face did not. A grim and haunted expression greeted us, only accentuated by the breaking dawn. I sucked in a breath when he lifted his head to look his emperor in the eye.

"They're dead. Every last one of them. Bodies lining the streets of every city..." He squeezed his eyes shut as if he could banish the images that would forever be burned into his mind. "Most of the cities along the lake are nothing more than ashes."

Liliana gasped and covered her mouth. Tears pricked my eyes, and my fingernails bit into my palms. Rares had said the Crystal Realm had fallen, but I hadn't realized the extent of

Kazimir's atrocities. The male who'd rescued me from the cave wouldn't have killed hundreds of thousands of innocents.

But the male I thought I knew had never existed.

Kazimir had never wanted me to truly become my own person. He wanted to save me and force me to depend on him. Kazimir was, and always had been, a monster. Only now, he allowed the black to seep through instead of coating it in colorful lies and manipulations.

Ruslan punched the side of the mountain with so much force that the rock cracked and splintered from the point of impact. "I will kill that motherfucker."

Shouts rang out from the people still within the mountain, yanking our attention toward them instead of the Félvér who had flown over what remained of the Crystal Realm.

"Find the emperor!" someone exclaimed, and I instinctively stepped forward as his worry slapped against my mental barrier.

The crazed look in Ruslan's eyes did not lesson as he stomped inside, and I chased after him, Liliana and Zuriel hot on my heels, the crowd parting for us as we searched for the speaker. We found him sweat-soaked in a half-empty cart at the edge of the tracks surrounded by a handful of other soldiers offering him food and water.

"My Emperor," he panted, lowering the metal canteen he had been sipping from. "There has been an attack in the Day Realm. We were ambushed and overwhelmed. General Drazen sent me here to request assistance."

Before the messenger had even finished speaking, I snatched Ruslan's hand and sent calming emotions into him. He needed to keep a level head, especially with the number of people gathered around us. Ruslan may not admit to it, but he cared deeply for Drazen and the others we'd sent with him to the Day Realm. Losing Drazen especially would slice open his deepest wounds of being utterly alone and abandoned that had only begun to close after I'd accepted our mate bond.

"Fetch Rares," I instructed the nearest soldier, splitting my focus between my magic and my logic. Ruslan's anger raged against the soothing emotions I pushed his way, and the muscles twitching in his jaw told me he was losing the fight to maintain his calm.

The old Mage joined us, and I relayed the news. "How do we get there quickly to help them?" I asked Rares, still pushing emotions toward Ruslan. I didn't have the time and energy to siphon from him, not with a battle looming ahead of us.

"The Mages can join together to move a large number of our forces to the tunnels closer to Drazen's location," he offered. "But it won't be everyone at once, and we will have to leave supplies and nonessentials behind."

"Does the tunnel there create a bottleneck like the one here?" Liliana blurted out, her head whipping around, clearly mulling over something.

"Yes, why?" Ruslan responded.

"They were waiting for us just outside of the entrance," the messenger added before tipping his head back and draining the last of the water.

Ruslan cracked his neck, then shook his hand loose and popped his knuckles one by one. "Contact Queen Viktoria and tell her we need the Day Realm's army, and in a hurry. Then move the best fighters to a place close to the tunnel exit in the Day Realm. We need to be far enough away that we don't pop into existence in the middle of the Night Realm's army, but close enough that we can move quickly to join the battle."

He blew out a frustrated breath, rolling his shoulders and scanning those around him. "We'll leave a group behind to pack up and load the supplies. Rares, return here once you've moved as many as you can and oversee the supplies returning to the meeting place below Vasvain." Ruslan's instructions were rapid fire and ruthless, and those around us listening in to the conversation were quick to relay messages.

Within minutes, every retinue had set to work repacking everything that they'd spent hours arranging. Not a single one grumbled. Everyone knew what was at stake.

Rares left in search of the other Mages, and two lines quickly formed in the exit of the tunnel – one of soldiers streaming in with supplies in hand, and another streaming out, armed with potions and weapons of all types.

My hands trembled as we melted into the flow of people, only breaking away once we'd reached the plush green grass some distance from the mountains. Units were re-forming around their commanders, strapping on armor, sharpening weapons, tucking vials of potion into hidden pouches.

The rising sun shone off the metal armor covering the Iron Realm's army, casting a false gleam over a land filled with death. The first group to depart braced their hands on one another's shoulders and dipped their heads, closing ranks to make the Mage's job easier. She returned moments later to fetch another group, and the process repeated over and over as thousands of people were moved the distance necessary to catch up with the other part of our army.

Fear skittered down my spine as Ruslan instructed us to draw closer to him, and I held my breath as we were whisked away from the Crystal Realm and into the Day Realm.

Right into the middle of a bloody battle.

33

ENDRE

The first wave of the Iron Realm's army was slaughtered with the same mercy Kazimir had shown the Crystal Realm – none. He'd even left the bodies where they were, and carrion birds circled the entire day, picking apart the dead until nothing but rotting meat and bones remained in between plates of armor. It made me sick.

I sat atop the earthen wall the Iron Fae had managed to build, staring out over the Day Realm, plotting the best way to escape this madness. Behind me, Fae celebrated our victory and danced around large fires, not caring that they'd barely slept in days and dawn was moments away. I supposed this wall provided a semblance of security, though I doubted any of the soldiers put any thought into that.

My waterskin offered nothing to me when I lifted it to my lips, and I tossed it away, watching it skitter across the top of the packed dirt and disappear over the edge. Sighing at my own stupidity, I floated to the ground to fetch it.

The earth swayed beneath my feet as I hit the ground, giving me pause. Brushing my hair away from my face, I glanced around, finding nothing in the near-darkness. Shaking my head,

I stepped toward my errantly discarded waterskin, stooping to lift it from amid the bent grass. The ground shuddered again as I grasped it in my hand.

I snapped my head up as the first whispers of sun entered the sky.

The waterskin plopped back into the grass as I beheld the beasts approaching me.

Giant olyphants outfitted for war approached, their metal-covered tusks dusting over the ground as they lumbered forward. At their feet, legions of Day Fae armed with long spears marched in perfect unison. And amongst them, leashed kutya strained against their masters, barking and growling and foaming at the mouth as they scented the blood awaiting them.

Oh, fuck.

Snapping my wings out, I leaped into the sky and raced toward the war tent. Viktor and Vadim hardly left it, preferring to sleep on cots there, and I had to tell them – to warn them. Not because I wanted the Night Realm to conquer Északi, but because I wanted my friends to *live*.

As I soared over the camp, I screamed at the Fae still reveling to sober up and find their weapons. They ignored me, too caught up in their own egos to fathom that we could possibly be under attack. We'd had the Iron Realm's forces cornered in the mountains for nearly two days. They hadn't left because sounds of life still rang out from behind the rock.

Barreling into the war tent, I found my friends dozing. "Wake the fuck up! The Day Fae are here."

Vadim blinked awake, his evergreen eyes still addled with sleep. "What?"

"The Day Realm's army marches on us," I hissed, kicking Viktor a little too roughly with my dirty boot.

"What?" he groaned, turning to his other side.

"For such a smart male you sure are fucking stupid sometimes," I told him. "Get up because we're going to have a fight on our hands. They have olyphants."

The mention of the massive animals woke him up, and he bolted upright, snatching his sword at the same time.

Vadim was already strapping daggers all over his body. "I didn't realize they'd trained some for war."

"Why couldn't they have told us that when we were allies?" Viktor released something between a moan and a groan as he strapped his weapon to his waist.

"Where is Kazimir?" I snapped.

"Here," a voice sounded behind me, and a light breeze entered the tent alongside the king of the Night Realm.

At least his eyes were clear and emerald green.

"The Day Realm's army approaches from the south," I warned, and Kazimir raked a hand over his face, eyes coming up darker.

Fuck.

"We can fly over the olyphants and take them down that way," Viktor grumbled, looking as exhausted as my soul felt. Dark circles ringed his eyes, and even the dirt and sweat coating his skin couldn't hide the pallor.

Gritting my teeth, I bit back a retort about harming the magnificent creatures because it would fall on deaf ears. Since losing his father, Viktor had become even more invested in this war, and Vadim wouldn't stand against both Viktor and Kazimir. Regardless of everyone else, Kaztar was a lost cause.

After tying up his long hair, Vadim unscrewed the top of a waterskin and poured some into his cupped palm. Splashing it across his face, he shook himself off like a dog. "All right, let's fucking go. We don't have time to waste. Kazimir, can you alert Desmond? We might need his help if we start getting trampled."

"We need to keep some of our forces by the mountain, too," Viktor reminded us. "If the Iron Realm hears signs of battle beyond, they may join the fray and we'll be fucked on both sides."

"My father can command that unit. I'll lead the charge toward the Day Realm," Vadim said grimly.

"Don't forget the Dragons," Kazimir snapped, the air shifting around him as he allowed the binding magic to rise within him. Bile rose in my throat, and I ripped my gaze away before any of my friends witnessed my disgust for our king.

"Goddess damn it, it's too early for all this shit," Viktor swore, punching the tent canvas out of the way as he stalked from the tent.

Every one of our nerves were frayed from days of fighting with not enough sleep. My magic was dangerously low, and with another attack on the horizon, I knew I would be tapped out sooner rather than later. Vadim's thoughts must have mirrored mine because we exchanged a hard look and left Kazimir behind as we raced off to manage our respective parts of the army.

Kaztar was asleep in his tent, and quickly roused once I relayed instructions.

Our horses were tethered not far from our tent, and I saddled them while he shouted at the males under our command to ready themselves. By the time we were ready to depart, the ground beneath our feet shook with the force of the beasts approaching. Risking a few precious seconds to determine their location, I shot into the sky, black wings making me an easy target against the bright blue.

The olyphants had reached the earthen wall and were making quick work of breaking it down. Already, one had smashed through it, opening a path for spear-wielding warriors to stream through.

Snapping my wings shut, I landed harshly on the muddy

ground, bracing my fist against it to regain my balance. "We need to move as a unit, and now."

"How many?" Kaztar asked.

"They just broke through the wall. We weren't prepared for an attack, and you know it." I was *tired* of hiding my feelings about this situation. No one listened to me, and we were fucked because of it.

I should go join the Day Fae and be done with it.

He clenched his jaw around the truth and nodded. Kaztar's horse reared as he dug his heels in, urging his mount forward. Stomping my boot in the stirrup, I threw myself over my stallion's back, landing rougher than my mount deserved. He wasn't the source of my anger and it wasn't fair for me to take any out on him. Still, I snapped the reins and shouted at Fae to part for us as we raced off to join the rest of the cavalry.

The infantry had organized faster than anticipated, and thousands took to the skies in the distance, looking like a murder of crows as they soared high and fast. Our horses ate up the ground beneath them, until we flew as one in a race to defend against the Day Fae.

It wasn't until we got closer that I noticed the olyphants weren't only outfitted with metal armor.

From hidden pockets in that armor, arrows flew through the air, piercing the wings of the oncoming Night Fae. The screams started fast and increased as they plummeted from the skies, some using their magic to bounce off a shield against the ground, while others, likely as exhausted as we were, smacked against it with a sickening crunch.

As the ones behind them landed and drew their swords, the Day Fae released the kutya, snarling and foaming at the mouth as they raced across the plains. They were fast, legs moving in a blur of gold, and some cut toward the charging horses. The first leaped and caught a throat in its jaws, ripping and bringing the horse down to the ground. When the rider pitched forward, the kutya snarled and pounced on him too. A few skittish horses reared as more approached, bucking their riders and nearly trampling them as the kutya nipped and ripped at their flanks and heels.

I barely managed to avoid the rider falling in front of me. Digging my heels into my horse's sides and crouching low on his neck, I urged him to jump over the piling bodies. His haunches bunched and then we were airborne. On our descent, a kutya leaped for us, fur around his maw stained with blood. Liliana's face flashed through my mind, and on instinct, I blasted the beast away with my silvery magic. The whimper that caught in its chest hurt me, but I pushed the feelings away as my survival instincts kicked in.

A trumpet from the closest olyphant assaulted my ears and stole my attention, and a second wild, furry beast took its opportunity to strike, aiming for my horse's flank. With a harsh yank on the reins, I turned him, trying to save his life. But I managed to put myself in harm's way instead, and the sharp teeth dug into my thigh.

"Fuck!" I swore, smacking the flat of my axe over its head and forcing it to open its jaws. With a yelp, it released me and fell to the ground.

Hot, ruby liquid poured from the wound, quickly coating my leg. The world spun, and I clamped my hands over my thigh, willing the burst vessels to knit and close before I passed out from blood loss. Wearily, I dug inside and found my magic well stuttering, the silvery moonlight barely wisps of gray.

I'd have to heal what I could and leave the rest for later.

Gripping the saddle blanket, I stripped a piece of cloth from it and tied it over the tattered meat of my thigh with a pointless hope that it would stave off infection. Once it was properly secured, I rejoined my unit in racing toward the lowered spears and sharp tusks of the olyphants.

"You good?" Kaztar shouted over the pounding of hooves and screams of dying soldiers.

"Good enough," I gritted out. My thigh throbbed through the lie.

He nodded, standing in his saddle and crying out orders to split and avoid the spears and tusks by approaching from the side. Half our unit banked left, Kaztar leading them, and the other half followed me as we angled away in the other direction. The Day Fae paused, looking between the two groups, and the moment was all we needed to find an opening in their defenses.

"Charge!" I screamed, bracing myself for the losses that would ensue.

The two groups came together like a cacophonous crescendo, where screams of the dying Fae and animals clashed with the snarls and trumpets of the triumphant. The trampled, burnt grass absorbed what blood it could, until too much had been spilled and it slicked the ground instead.

The sun rose higher in the sky, giving the Day Fae everything they needed to use their magic, while the Night Fae suffered with the meager drops that remained of ours.

And still, we kept fighting.

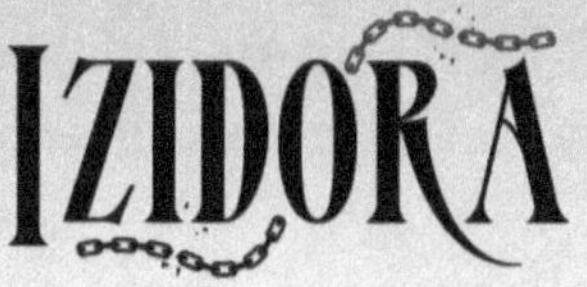 IZIDORA

Fear slammed into me like a tidal wave, tumbling me around and around until I didn't know which way was up and which way was down. Air solidified in my throat as I struggled to breathe, struggled to think of *anything* other than unending, unyielding pain. With a cry, I clutched my head as my knees slammed into the ground. Tears streamed down my face as more screams rent the air.

There was so much death.

I felt it so acutely, like a knife stabbing me between the ribs. Like a slice through my stomach. Like an arrow through the shoulder.

The shock of arriving lengths away from the bloody battle-field froze me in place, and the reality of what had been set in motion when I made my choice was laid bare for me to see.

Ruslan wrapped me in a protective embrace immediately, and Zuriel stepped in front of us, creating a semi-shield with his body. "Put up your mental barrier, now!" my cousin barked at me, and Ruslan squeezed me tighter, reassuring me that I was safe so I could focus on building up the wall around my mind.

Stone by stone, I reinforced that wall until the screams did not pierce my soul and the pounding of fear was only my own instead of that of the entire battlefield in front of us.

Already, the Iron Realm's army sprang into action, joining ranks with what appeared to be the Day Fae's army. "What are those?" I gasped out, eyes landing on massive gray beasts outfitted with gleaming golden armor.

"Olyphants. Don't get tangled up beneath their feet or they'll crush you," Ruslan warned, his arms tightening a fraction before releasing me.

"How are they already here?" Liliana blurted out, her sword glinting in the sunlight as she drew it from its sheath.

A massive red horse barrelled toward us, and Ruslan stepped protectively in front of me, drawing black fire to his palms. White flames licked up my arms as I readied myself to fight, not wanting to be left out of the action. But as the rider closed in on us, I noticed a familiar bulky form with a wide, warm smile.

"King Consort Geza!" I called out as he pulled up in front of us.

"Nice to see you awake and vibrant as ever, Izidora," he grinned back. "Thank you again for your assistance in returning our daughter."

Tears pricked my eyes, and I swallowed around the lump in my throat. "She didn't deserve to suffer as I did."

"And because of you, she did not," Geza replied, dipping his head.

"You did not tell me you had moved the Day Realm's army north," Ruslan growled, but there was no animosity in his tone. If anything, a hint of gratitude peeked through.

"After you rescued Gizela and told us we needed to prepare the army, we decided to get a head start," the large male shrugged. "You can't blame a father for wanting to take vengeance for his daughter."

A pang of sadness traveled through me at his words. My true father, Ithuriel, never got that opportunity, and my supposed father, King Zalan, was the one who had colluded with King Azim to chain me in a cave and abuse me.

Ruslan squeezed my hand, our flames joining together and blending into a smoky gray - the color of his eyes.

"I am glad you are here, King Consort Geza. Let's crush the Night Fae once and for all," my mate swore.

"I am more than ready," he snarled, refocusing his attention on the battle. "Stay whole." With those parting words, he clucked his tongue, spinning his mount and racing toward a group of olyphants. His golden braids bounced off his back as he crouched low on his horse's neck, and he truly looked like a fast-moving sun as he rejoined the fray.

Already, Artur and the other leaders shouted orders to their units, and one by one, the Félvér gulped down the shifting potion or called on their other forms, ready to wage war against the oncoming Night Fae. Black dots flew through the blue sky above, and below, horses whinnied and reared as what looked like massive, feral dogs raced in their direction. One launched itself at a dark bay mare, locking its jaws around her neck and tearing.

"Kutya," Liliana whispered, following my gaze.

The horse and rider fell, and the ones behind them barely managed to dodge their bodies before being attacked by more kutya. The male blasted it with a wave of silver before his attention turned to a second kutya using the opening to strike. The dog-like creature sank its teeth into the male's leg, tearing a howl of pain from his chest.

Liliana and I sucked in a simultaneous breath when he drew an axe and smacked the beast. Because that wasn't any random axe-wielding Night Fae.

It was Endre.

Liliana froze, not even blinking as Endre's leg bled a ruby river. Fingers curling inward, she appeared to be on the verge of moving, but ripped her gaze away and returned her attention to me.

"Do you want to–" I started, but she cut me off.

"Endre made his decision, and it wasn't me. Drazen, however, is barricaded in the mountain, possibly injured, and we are here to aid him," she snapped, teeth digging into her bottom lip. She glanced at the sky, and I offered her a moment of privacy to collect herself.

Ruslan too was watching the battle, and I addressed him now that my own emotions were under control. "Where is Drazen? We have more than enough soldiers fighting here to end the Night Realm if we all band together. We've got them surrounded."

He nodded. "We do, especially with the Day Fae and their beasts. Take my hand," he snapped, and Zuriel, Liliana, and I did as instructed. Moments later, we were whisked across the battlefield and into the mountain, where the energy was frantic and the sound of battle was still audible. I reinforced my barrier, just in case.

"Oh thank fuck," Drazen said from behind us, and I whipped around, meeting the eyes of the Dragon Shifter. Blood spattered his armor as if a painter had tossed a brush in his direction repeatedly, but he looked otherwise unharmed. Liliana released Ruslan and raced to Drazen. She threw her arms around his neck, and he lifted her in the air, arms tightening protectively around her.

The sight warmed my heart in a way I hadn't realized I needed. War was upon us, and the reality was so much worse than I could have ever imagined. The ones we loved most were in danger, and a life after the war wasn't promised. Amid the chaos of battle, anything could happen. I squeezed Ruslan's hand, seeking more comfort from him.

I couldn't lose him; it would be the death of me too.

"I'm so glad you're okay," Drazen murmured in Liliana's ear before setting her feet on the floor again.

"I'm glad you're okay too. I thought I was going to be sick when I heard that you'd been ambushed here." She looked up at him with love shining in her eyes, and I felt like an intruder on what should have been an intimate moment. But I couldn't tear myself away, not when this was the light I needed to remind me what we were fighting for. Vengeance was one thing, but safety, security, and love was a higher, more important purpose than that.

A rumbling laugh sounded in his chest. "Is the prettiest female in the Északi Empire admitting to having feelings for me?"

Liliana gave him a playful smack as she pushed out of his arms. "Don't get any crazy ideas, Drazen."

A warning growl from Ruslan shattered the moment and forced our attention back to the matter at hand. "The Day Fae have arrived, along with a good portion of the rest of the Iron Realm's army. Can you fight?"

Drazen dipped his chin. "If you can provide cover for us to exit."

"Consider it done. I'll have the Dragons shift and fly here. Wait for my signal to open the mountain," Ruslan instructed, clapping Drazen on the shoulder. The males exchanged more than words with that look and that touch.

Liliana returned to my side, and we allowed the two a moment for themselves. I elbowed my best friend in the side, and she shot me a warning look. A smile pulled at my lips, but I didn't voice the tease I had planned. Instead, I said, "We need to find a place for me to work my magic."

"First, we need to find Kazimir," Zuriel emphasized, tucking strands of white hair behind his ears. He was all seriousness, not a hint of emotion playing across his sharp features.

Liliana scoffed. "He'll be at the back of the army, pretending like he's a big, tough male, but not actually helping them fight."

"A true leader fights alongside his soldiers," Ruslan interrupted, pulling me into his arms. The intensity of his emotion melted into me despite my mental barrier, and I allowed it, soaking up every bit of himself he offered me. My mate, my one true love, my soul. His love was all I needed in this world. Together we were unstoppable, and we'd been training together for this very reason.

"Or her soldiers," I corrected him, earning a small chuckle.

"Or her soldiers," he echoed, our exchange lifting a hint of fear from my stomach.

"Win this battle for us, and I'll marry you," he teased mind-to-mind.

"Why would I marry you if I win the battle? You should be begging to marry me. Falling to your knees and pleading for me to give you a drop of my attention," I quipped back.

"Then I suppose we have a competition on our hands. Whoever kills more Night Fae will have to beg the other to accept a new marriage proposal."

I spun in his arms, and he grasped the back of my neck and forced me to peer deep into his eyes. "Deal," I whispered, a smile blooming on my face. Ruslan kissed it away, then released me. Our friends – our family – watched on with a mosaic of expressions, ranging from exasperated to feigned disgust to starry eyed jealousy.

"If we can move along now," Liliana said, rolling her eyes and pretending to gag. Ruslan beckoned her forward.

Zuriel placed his hand on Ruslan's shoulder, and Liliana did the same, waiting for him to whisk us back to the battlefield.

Drazen watched Liliana go, his eyes holding an emotion as deep as the ocean-blue that colored them. As we disappeared, I vowed that we'd win this war – by whatever means necessary – so my best friend too could find the happiness and love she deserved.

35

RUSLAN

Anarchy was the only way to describe the battlefield when we returned to it. Lines were shattered, Fae from all realms scattered and fighting in disparate groups. The massive olyphants had spread further afield, stomping all beneath their feet. Arrows rained down, both from the backs of the beasts and the skies above them. Howls of pain melded with roars of rage amid the sharp clash of swords.

Izidora remained wrapped protectively in my arms until I was certain we were far enough away that a spear wouldn't fly out of nowhere. "Zuriel, Liliana, keep my mate safe until I return. I need to coordinate the Dragons," I growled, looking over the plains in search of Artur and the others in charge of the Félvér units.

Izidora stepped out of my embrace, a white fire burning behind her aquamarine eyes that made me so fucking proud to call her my mate, my wife, my future empress. "We fight together. I'm strong on my own, but I'm stronger when I'm with you. Hurry back."

I crumpled over her words and the strength of her conviction in them. "Yes we are," I replied, tucking an errant lock of chestnut hair behind her ear. "If I find Kazimir, I will call for you."

A wicked grin crossed her heart-shaped face. "His death is mine."

Grasping Izidora's hand, I brought it to my lips and kissed the back of it. The large ruby ring I'd bought for her during Béke still adorned her finger, even now. The sight made me smirk, and I paused for a moment, drinking in my mate's glorious form one last time. "I love you, Izidora. Until my dying breath and through whatever awaits me beyond this life."

"I love you, Ruslan. My broken emperor. Us against the world." She slipped her hand from mine and stood on her tiptoes to stroke my cheek. I leaned into her touch, turning my face and kissing her open palm.

I knew I lingered too long with her, but fuck, I couldn't tear myself away when our immediate vicinity was filled with war.

I couldn't lose her.

I couldn't leave her alone.

We would win the day, win the continent, and once the dust settled, we'd live a peaceful life, wrapped up in each other without fear of being ripped apart.

Sucking in a sharp breath, I broke away, racing across the open plains in the direction of Artur and the others. Unsheathing my sword was a necessity fifty paces in as Night Fae dropped like violent raindrops from the skies and attacked the Félvér. Together, they fought like one large beast, and pride swelled in my chest as I slashed my way to my brethren.

Finally, I found myself within shouting distance. "I need twenty Dragons! Take your potions. We need to cover the tunnel."

They immediately slipped backward through the ranks, others stepping up to cover them as they tipped the foul liquid back and stripped out of their armor. Konsteon, the Centaur

Shifter, piled everyone's clothes in a fabric sling for safekeeping and then shifted into his half man, half horse form. I slung the wrap over his back so he could safeguard them until the potions wore off. He was easier to find among the masses, which made jumping back into the fray less of a hassle.

"Thank you," I told him as I tossed my own armor in among the mix, keeping my sword handy until my skin began to itch uncontrollably.

He merely nodded and notched an arrow, tracking a Night Fae attempting to breach our line via the skies.

"Cover me!" I shouted, sprinting toward the back of the company where an open field waited. Footsteps pounded the grass behind me, and a roar tore from the first Félvér to shift. Mine took over a moment later, my black Dragon form freed from within the confines of my chest.

I was airborne in two flaps of my mighty wings, and in a few more, I soared high above the battlefield, blotting out the sun on tens of thousands of soldiers. The darkness I brought to the skirmish wasn't metaphorical. I would yank the entrails from the Night Fae with my sharp talons and toss them over the ones who were still temporarily breathing, laughing as they waited to die.

The other Dragons settled into a V behind me as we raced toward the mountain. Almost immediately, more Night Fae shot into the sky, many bearing bows and arrows aimed directly toward my vulnerable wings. A stream of smoke fled from my nostrils, burning my throat as I threatened to unleash more onto the soldiers lining up for their deaths. As the first took aim, a small, golden Dragon to my right opened her maw and cooked him alive. Others dodged the flames, dipping out of the wave of heat and right into the path of other Dragons waiting their turn to roast. Bursts of colorful fire filled the skies, knocking the Night Fae out of existence and sending them crashing onto the field below.

The ones who survived quickly removed themselves from our path – not like that would save them in the end.

From my vantage point, I assessed the battle.

The Day Fae's numbers were significantly less than those of the Night Fae, but the olyphants and kutya were making a dent in their line. Spears of dark golden warriors aimed true over and over again as their giant beasts continued to clear the path. The Night Fae's attention was divided between them and the Iron Realm's army, the Iron Fae units using swords and magic to batter the forces, while the Félvér units fought fiercely with every weapon in their arsenal.

Once we freed Drazen and the rest of our army, we'd have the Night Fae surrounded on three sides with almost no hope of escape.

Where was Kazimir?

I sharpened my focus to an encampment set away from the battlefield, finding healers and wounded soldiers en masse.

But no sign of their king.

Probably using that fucking power he possessed to render himself invisible, just like he'd done when he kidnapped Izidora.

The mountain was fast approaching, and I slowed, pulling up and executing a twisting maneuver so we faced the battle-field. Below us, a large company of Night Fae waited just beyond the exit of the tunnel, preventing Drazen from joining the battle. Opening my maw, embers burned in my throat as I prepared to free the fire from my belly.

The fear widening their eyes was delicious.

I savored every moment as all around me, the Félvér released their power in unison. A rainbow of colored Dragon fire swept over them, the shrieks of ten thousand dying males ringing in the air for only a moment before they turned to ash.

Once every last one had been roasted, I realized my mistake. That kaleidoscope of colorful fire licked between the trees and swept into the grasses beyond. The Day Realm's plains were notoriously dry, especially after the long summer we'd had. And now, despite the garnet liquid soaking them, they were catching.

With a crazed roar, I flapped backward, crashing into the side of the mountain to let Drazen know it was safe to open the door. After all, there was no one left in the charred clearing at the base of the mountain. And nothing would be left if I didn't control the wildfire I'd created.

It consumed every blade of wispy grass and turned every tree to dust, racing faster than any horse in every direction.

Heavy stones ground open, and Iron Fae spilled onto the burnt earth. Drazen was at the head of them, followed by Xorrek and Gozzak, and finally, Anton and Slavian. The five took one look at the destruction in front of them and then snapped their attention to me.

Fuck, I wished I could speak to them, to tell them what needed to be done to rectify the situation. But Drazen shouted for any Félvér who could wield water to race to the fires, while others worked on putting them out with dirt, and still more tried to suck the fires back and hold them away from the delicate landscape until they could be extinguished.

I didn't have to do everything myself; Drazen was more than capable of handling the situation I'd created. After all, he'd been fixing my mistakes for years. So I gnashed my teeth at the Dragons still hovering in the air, urging them to follow me to the battlefield. We'd have to fight with teeth and claws instead of fire.

The successive thuds of the Dragons landing on the third side of the battle were like omens of what lay ahead as the Night Fae were forced to split their attention yet again. Izidora flashed me a sadistic smile as I dug my claws into the earth beside her, unleashing a roar over everyone in her periphery.

Her aquamarine eyes somehow both brightened and darkened, and she returned her attention to the fray with renewed vigor. *"Like we've been practicing?"* she spoke down our bond, raising her twin swords.

"Exactly like that," I rumbled back, swiping a group of Night Fae with my talons. Izidora raced forward, stabbing and slicing in quick succession as they were off-balanced and knocked to the ground.

"Again!" she called, launching herself off the chest of one dead male and ducking under the strike of a still-living one.

I did as my mate bid and smacked a second group around, allowing her to finish them off. *"I'm counting all of these for me, you know,"* she teased.

"Absolutely not, they count for both of us," I argued. To prove my point, I snapped out and ripped a soldier in two with my sharp teeth. Then I turned my massive head toward her and dropped the broken body at her feet. *"That is one for me."*

She scoffed, then slipped under my belly and emerged from my talons just in time to stop one from thrusting his sword into my ankle. *"That counts as two since I saved your scales."*

"You can't make up the rules as you go along," I stated, swinging my tail like a club and sending a group flying. They landed with a satisfying crunch against some of their fellow soldiers.

"We didn't agree on them before, so naturally I have to do it now," she pointed out, charging forward and taking out another male. I huffed, and a plume of smoke fled my nostrils. I didn't protest further, enjoying our little game and the threads of lust it wove between us as we battled for our numbers. In my Dragon form, I could protect her, provide her with enough cover to rack up the kills she desired.

But in the end, I'd show her why I was the emperor, and after the battle, she'd ride me until all she saw was stars.

36

ENDRE

I wasn't sure whose blood I was covered in anymore. The kutya bite still stung, and I could barely grip my saddle as my muscle tissue weakened. The sun beat down upon us as if it had a personal vendetta against the war waging beneath it. For the late fall day, it was hot as fuck.

My waterskin had run dry an hour before, but there was no time to return to the back of the line to refill it. Our attention was split as we fended off attackers on two sides, and as twenty-one Dragons quaked the ground beneath me, I knew we were fucked. Behind them, a violent inferno blazed, racing toward the battlefield while the Iron Fae we'd beaten back into the tunnels two nights prior streamed out of it, trying to rein in the blaze.

"Kaztar!" I called out, searching for my fellow horseback rider.

He was nowhere in sight. I shoved my heels against the stirrups, trying to get a better angle. "Fuck!" I swore when pain lanced through my thigh, and I collapsed down before I'd managed to see anything. Still, I kept searching, trying to find someone, anyone, and figure out what the fuck to do next.

A flash of long hair caught my attention, and I returned to

the spot I'd ghosted over a moment before. Liliana fought fiercely in the midst of the Iron Realm's army, sticking close to the Dragons. Even across the battlefield, she took my breath away. Her seafoam green eyes danced with determination, and her teeth were gritted behind every strike. Light scaled armor hugged her figure, and my heart sank for a moment as I realized just how firmly she'd settled into the Iron Realm if she'd shucked the traditional fighting leathers of the Night Realm.

It was a way of declaring her loyalty without having to speak.

Without thinking, I kicked my horse in her direction, the Night Realm's army parting for me as I pushed to that front. Shoving the reins up my mount's neck, I lowered myself in the saddle, giving him his head so he could race even faster. His hooves pounded into the churned earth, flying over discarded weapons and bodies of the fallen, dodging those still locked in struggles.

None of it held my attention like the female in front of me. As I closed the distance between us, she whipped her head to the side, and our gaze collided like two exploding stars. Liliana halted in her tracks, and Izidora swept from behind her, slicing deep into the shoulder of one of the soldiers under Vadim's command. Izidora said something to her – likely that the blow could have killed her – and Liliana broke our trance. She wasted no time in rejoining Izidora and Zuriel, fighting side by side with them as they advanced through her brother's forces.

Shaking my head, I returned my awareness to my surroundings just in time to see a sharp talon slicing through the air above me.

Oh, shit.

With no time to do anything other than react, I threw myself from my horse and rolled over my shoulder to lessen the impact. A heartbeat later, the Dragon's foot smashed into the ground, the sharp edge of his claw sinking into the horse's hide. He released an anguished whinny before careening to a stop on his side, dead.

The giant beast didn't cease his movements. Backstepping, I tried to get out of the Dragon's way, but his focus was firmly on me. With a black so dark it seemed to suck in the light around it, I could only assume it was Ruslan. I raised my hands in surrender, dropping to my knees and praying to the Goddess that I wasn't about to get roasted.

With a mighty swipe of his claws, he cleared the area around me of Night Fae. Liliana rushed forward, Izidora reaching for her hand and missing before chasing after her. The growl that rumbled in his chest made me glad I was already close to the ground.

"Ruslan will allow you to say goodbye," Izidora panted when they skidded to a stop in front of me.

"Good to see you awake, Izidora," I said with a sad smile. "You didn't deserve that. Just like you didn't deserve anything else that happened to you. I'm glad you finally found your happiness."

Izidora's eyes grew glassy, but with limited time, I wanted my sweetest words to go to the female I'd loved for longer than I cared to admit. Liliana's chest heaved as she stood parallel with her best friend, and a tear tracked down her cheek as she stared down at me.

The sun shifted, spilling its rays into her seafoam green eyes and making them even brighter than they already were. She looked so beautiful, despite the flecks of blood that adorned her face and the wild way her hair hung, covered in sweat. She could have crawled out of a mud pit, and I'd still think she was the most gorgeous Fae to ever exist. Clearing my throat and swiping my hair out of my face, I admitted everything. "Liliana, I'm so sorry I didn't stay. You were right about everything. I'm a dumbass for choosing him over you. He's insane, and you are –

were – the best thing to ever happen to me. I'll die happy knowing that I got to have you for a little while at least."

My chest constricted, and I itched to reach out and pull her to me for one final kiss before I departed this world and never saw her stunning smile or the sultry sway of her hips again.

With a choked sob, she fell into me anyway, nearly knocking me over as my thigh screamed in protest. I was covered in blood, filthy, and so very wrong in my decisions, and yet here she was, giving me everything she had in the very last moments of my life. I clasped her to me, one arm circling her waist and the other grabbing the back of her neck. I hesitated only a moment before crashing her lips against mine.

Even among this hell, she tasted like heaven – sweet berries and fragrant flowers with a hint of peppery spice. The smell of her, the taste of her, would linger until my last breath. Our tongues twined as I deepened our kiss, and I savored every inch where we touched. Something wet brushed across my cheek, but I didn't stop until both of us needed air. When we surfaced, twin rivers were carved into her dirty face, and I knew mine was a mirror to hers.

"I love you, Liliana. I'm sorry." My voice broke over the words I should have said months ago – years ago. Pushing her hips away was the hardest thing I had ever done.

"I love you, Endre." Her words were a whisper, but I heard them clearly over the din of battle around us.

"Wait!" Izidora screeched, stepping between her mate and me. His dark eyes narrowed on her, and when he lowered his head to her level, I had to clench my teeth to keep my jaw from falling open. "He can be useful to us."

Izidora braced her hands on her hips as they had a silent conversation. I held my breath, glancing from Liliana to them and back, hoping, praying, that Izidora could convince him. Because I would betray every secret the Night Realm had.

Kazimir needed to be stopped, and I had information that could help.

Izidora's Angel cousin stepped into my periphery, scrutinizing me with his cold, ice blue eyes. "He won't betray us," Zuriel pronounced, causing Izidora and Ruslan to rip their attention to him.

"Ruslan wants to know if you can guarantee that," Izidora relayed with an arched brow.

Zuriel straightened to his full height and nodded. "I can. I just read his mind."

With those words, my jaw did drop open – as did everyone else's.

37

KAZIMIR

Cloaked in my magic, Desmond and I watched the battle unfold, set back from the main action. I kept a close eye on Endre, Viktor, Kaztar, and Vadim, gauging just how handily we were winning. We outnumbered their forces, especially after our crushing victory during the ambush. The Dragons wouldn't make a difference, of that I was certain.

Endre raced off into the fray, cutting a line straight to the front toward the edge closest to the Dragons.

Good, he was finally getting on board with our plan instead of balking the entire way.

But a flash of chestnut beneath one of the massive black beasts caught my eye, and a swell of heat crept up my neck. I clenched my reins and squinted, needing a sharper look.

Izidora.

Covered in dirt and blood, sporting the armor she'd worn during Béke, she battled against the Night Fae – her fucking people – with that mongrel bastard by her side.

She was fucking awake?

A muscle feathered so strongly in my jaw I forced myself to

open my mouth and suck in a deep breath. The binding magic thrashed in my chest, surging against the grip I held over it to maintain our surreptitious position.

Take her take her take her take her...

A growl rumbled in my chest, and I dropped my hold over it before it consumed me. I needed to maintain a clear head and lead this army. Fek leaped forward as if he would race to her location, and I yanked on the leather, tucking his chin so hard into his neck he halted immediately.

Vadim raced toward me, half-carrying his limping father, and shattered my view of the female who had rejected me. High Lord Nikolai clutched his side, barely holding together a deep wound across his abdomen. "Kazimir," Vadim panted, "we're getting wrecked out there. We need to fall back. Everyone's magic is tapped out and the Iron Realm just got reinforcements."

"Their reinforcements are nothing," I dismissed, scanning the battlefield for her once again.

"My King, I must agree with my son," High Lord Nikolai wheezed, recalling my attention. His bearded face was pale, and more ruby gushed between his fingers.

"Let me get you to the healer's tent, father," Vadmin insisted, hiking Nikolai up higher on his shoulder.

I wanted them gone so I could find her again. "Return to me once you've dropped Nikolai off," I ordered. Vadim nodded and continued on to the frenzied tents at the rear where both Night and Crystal Fae healers tended to the wounded – though the latter with much more reluctance that would have to be beaten out of them.

Beneath me, Fek shifted from foot to foot as if he wanted to join the fray. But I ruled the Night Realm, which meant that my life was more valuable than those of my soldiers, and I had no heirs – yet. No, we could not whet our appetites for blood today.

Even if all I wanted was to capture Izidora and return to the Night Realm with her, install her by my side as it always should have been.

When Vadim returned, he glinted with more daggers than I could count. Standing before me, he attempted to redo his hair so that it no longer fell in every direction. "I have nothing left, Kazimir. Neither does Viktor – if he's still out there. I left him to return here once my father was injured."

An olyphant trumpeted in the distance, rearing back before stomping down with enough force to shake the ground even at this distance. A dozen soldiers were crushed beneath its feet, and the ones who managed to avoid the strike were thrown backward, then speared into the ground by the Day Fae who ringed the gray beast.

"My King, now that we know the true force of the other realms, would it not be wise to fall back and regroup? I am certain I can find a way to defeat the olyphants and the shifted ones if given some time and resources," Desmond said, straightening and puffing out his chest.

"I will not be made a fool of – not again," I snapped, raking a hand over my face. "We keep pushing."

Why did the people who served me not understand this?

I was growing weary of having to explain how these things needed to go.

A blast of heat from the wildfire started by those damn Dragons swept over us, the strong breeze carrying embers to the few pieces of grass that hadn't been churned into mud.

"We also don't want to get swept up in that," Vadim said pointedly, following my attention to the multicolored fire battling against a host of Iron Fae. At least Ruslan was failing in that regard too, and had been forced to split his forces to clean up his mess. Pathetic.

"My King, no one would blame you for saving your soldiers

from an uncontrollable fire set by the so-called emperor of the continent. He is their savior?" Desmond scoffed. "No, he is their executioner."

"Their executioner..." I murmured, considering his proposal as I took a broad survey of the battlefield.

If I pulled back due to the fire, I would look like a benevolent king who cared about his people, and appearances were everything. With a sigh, I acquiesced. "Give the order to fall back. We'll move to Vlisa as quickly as we can and regroup from there."

My army was nowhere safer from an inferno than beside a lake, after all.

Vadim wasted no time in racing back to the fray, shouting orders as he went. Desmond and I turned our horses toward the healers' tents, readying for our swift departure. A group of three Night Fae with the ability to use the Mage spells gathered in the center of the camp, linking arms to amplify their power. The words whispered out of them, and they flung their net of magic over us and all the injured, then whisked us deep into the Crystal Realm.

The long, aqua lake greeted us, and the crystal palace that had once been the beating heart of the capital reflected on its glassy surface. I left the healers to their work as I surveyed the haggard groups popping into existence as they retreated from the Day Realm.

The flow of Night Fae slowed to a crawl before finally ceasing altogether. Scanning them, I finally found some of my commanders – Vadim, Viktor, and Kaztar. They dismissed anyone who'd been in their groups, Vadim pulling a few aside and giving them hushed instructions. Once the soldiers seemed to settle in, the three grouped and strode toward me.

"Where is Endre?" I hissed. He wasn't among the riders leading their horses to the edge of the lake to drink, nor was he among the healers with his father. In fact, there was no sign of his messy hair and terrible attitude.

The three of them shared a look before Viktor opened his mouth to speak.

"He defected."

INTERLUDE

Nights during the winter in the Iron Realm were long and dark, and the chill was impossible to chase from the room, even with two roaring hearths. A couple lounged beside one atop a fur rug, with blankets draped over their reclined bodies. Sparks escaped the confines of the stone fireplaces, dancing between them. The female swirled a glass of burgundy wine slowly, her seafoam green eyes trained on the male across from her. Reaching out ever so slowly, he brushed a lock of chocolate hair away from her face, revealing a pointed ear as he tucked it away.

"You can't fall in love with me," she told him, taking a sip from her wine to cover the slight shake in her hands.

The male flexed his arms before bracing them on the floor behind him and crossing one leg over the other. "It's just sex," he said with a nonchalant air, cocking his head to the side and studying her. His own long locks were tied up away from his face, though a few strands slipped free with the movement.

Setting her glass to the side, the female swept the blanket off her body, then turned to her knees and examined the male in turn. Ever so slowly, she lowered her hands to the floor, scrunching her fingers in the thick fur rug. With a sensual sway to her hips, she crawled to him, climbing over his legs and straddling him.

"Just sex," she emphasized, tracing a finger along his strong jaw.

He lifted a hand from the floor and twisted it around her long, loose hair. "I can give you what you need, Liliana." He used his leverage to yank her head back and bare her throat.

"And what's that, Drazen?" she purred, her tongue flicking out and wetting her lips.

His blue eyes darkened as he studied her fluttering pulse. "Domination."

The sweet scent of her arousal filled his nose, and he inhaled deeply as he ran it along her neck and up to her ear. She gasped a moan, rolling her hips over his growing hardness.

In one smooth motion, he flipped her on her back, pressing her into the soft rug with the weight of his body. He nipped at the crook of her shoulder, drawing goosebumps to her skin. Her lashes fluttered against her high cheekbones as she arched off the floor.

A hand immediately found her throat and pushed her into the ground, causing her eyes to fly open. They were nearly black with lust, and the male's nostrils flared at the sight. "You only move when I tell you to. Understood?"

"Yes," she whispered around his hand.

"Good girl."

Shifting his weight ever so slightly to allow her some air, he trailed his other hand down her ribcage and found her peaked nipples. She remained still beneath him, waiting to see what he would do next. Her heart thudded with anticipation and excitement, while her thighs grew damp with the promise in his eyes.

The male captured one bud and rolled it between thumb and forefinger. After a sharp tug, he growled, "You're going to get on your knees and take out my cock. I want to see tears streaming from your face as you gag on it."

Then, he released her, leaving her bereft of his touch as he rose to tower over her. Without tearing her gaze from him, she did as she was bid, quickly tying back her hair before slipping his loose pants down his hips, allowing his hardness to spring free.

"Oh fuck," she whimpered at the sight of it.

The male grinned devilishly, threading his fingers in her hair and guiding her toward his groin. "Welcome to the world of Dragon dicks, little vixen."

IV

THE APPROACH

38

Izidora

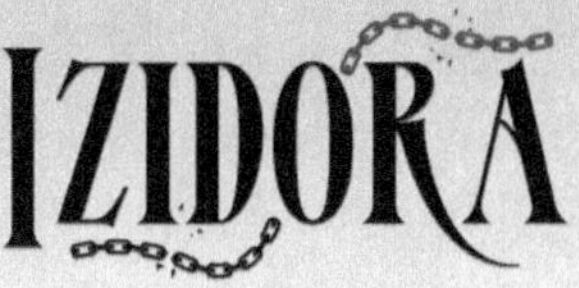

"We need to free some Crystal Fae to help us," I argued, crossing my arms over my chest and glaring at Drazen across the strategy table.

"Izidora is right," Liliana and Endre came to my defense at the same time, exchanging one of many awkward looks that had occurred since he'd defected from the Night Realm. The tension hanging between the three of them was enough to set my teeth on edge, and after a week of it, I was about ready to force Zuriel to read all their minds to pronounce their true feelings for all to hear.

The Angel perched on a stool in the corner of the gray canvas war tent, unnaturally still as arguments about how to put out the fire raged on. I still couldn't believe he could read minds and told absolutely no one until the moment Endre was on his knees before Ruslan, waiting to be burnt alive.

Was that how we'd been able to communicate all this time? Or did we truly have a mind to mind connection like I shared with Ruslan?

Every one of us in this tent was soot-soaked, exhausted, and thirsty. Dragon fire was apparently very difficult to snuff out, and even with the might of the Iron and Day Realms' armies, we were barely holding back the blaze.

"If we shift into our Dragon forms, we can go to a coastal town and pick up volunteers and be back within half a day. If the Night Fae are still in Vlisa, they won't even know we were there." Ruslan rose from his chair and stalked out of the tent, ending the conversation.

I spun on my heel and followed him. "I'm coming with you."

I nearly slipped in the mud as he came to a startling halt and captured my mouth with his for a quick kiss. "Of course you are. We might need your magic to convince the Crystal Fae to help."

Grinning, we rested our foreheads against one another. "Thanks for having my back in there."

"Us against the world," he hummed. Ruslan kissed my forehead, then tugged me along behind him as we wound our way to Rares's tent, where the old Mage worked round the clock churning out potions and making shifting permanent for the Félvér who could only partially shift or lacked the ability entirely.

Rares barely acknowledged us as we entered his space, too focused on working with a patient. The female shifted into a Wolf, howling at the absent moon, before shifting back, her golden eyes shining.

"Thank you," she choked out, eyes shining as she swung her regard first to Rares, then Ruslan.

Down our bond, I felt Ruslan's pride and happiness for her, but his expression remained impassive as she dipped into a bow and departed the tent with a bounce in her step.

"My turn," Ruslan growled his command, his tone sending a shiver down my spine and heating my low belly. We'd been so busy with everything else, we hadn't been intimate in weeks, and my body ached for his in a way that nearly drove me to orgasm from his raspy voice alone.

His nostrils flared, and he winked at me, his smoky grays holding a promise for later.

"At least I know you can handle the pain," Rares grumbled, handing Ruslan a potion before running a sharp needle over a bright white flame.

I chewed my lip as my mate swallowed the drink, then ripped his shirt overhead, baring his tattooed torso. The ones trailing down his fingers flexed as he prepared himself for the injection. Without thinking, I grabbed one of his fingers, stroking the back of it soothingly.

"I'm here, and you're safe with me." His nervousness made sense – after all, Rares had injected him with Goddess-knew how many concoctions as a child, all against his will.

"Love you, sprite."

"Love you, Ruslan."

He flinched when the needle slipped into the boulder of muscle at his shoulder, and I pushed soothing emotions into him. Ruslan subtly shook his head, and I relented, allowing him to feel the pain and process his feelings.

Rares chanted an incantation over Ruslan – one that had been the background music for the past week while we remained in the war camp – as he worked his magic to provide Ruslan the permanent ability to shift into a Dragon. Back and forth on the opposite side of the tent, I paced, waiting for the process to complete. My eye caught on the perfect circle between my mate's shoulder blades, the one that marked us for each other and told the world we'd been permanently claimed. Heat bloomed in my low belly as the bond that tied us together hummed contentedly. I stroked it absently, drawing goosebumps to Ruslan's skin.

Those goosebumps turned to scales.

"You need to get out of the tent, now. I don't want you shredding it to pieces when you shift," Rares instructed, stepping back and ceasing his incantations.

Ruslan stripped off the rest of his clothes and burst through the canvas within moments. I followed him into the hot midday air, watching as he raced toward a nearby space that had been cleared for this purpose. Black scales rippled across his legs as he put distance between himself and the war camp. Skidding to a stop, I held my breath as wings popped from his back, and with a mighty roar, his massive black Dragon form forced its way into the world.

In three flaps, he was airborne and soaring toward the sea, in the opposite direction of the raging wildfire. The sun did not shine off his scales; his scales sucked in all the light, and it was as breathtaking as it was terrifying.

"Out of my way," Drazen yelled, and I whipped around, side-stepping just enough for the male to race by me, lapis lazuli scales already taken over his entire body. Liliana jogged behind him, stopping to join me as Drazen's shift tore through him.

"They'll be able to shift back now, right?" Liliana asked, a hint of worry in her tone.

"Should be," I replied, hoping it were true.

What if Ruslan became stuck like this?

"Then you'd have to figure out how to take a much, much bigger dick," came his reply to a thought I hadn't realized I'd shared.

Smothering a blush and a smile, I tracked his movement through the sky. He pulled up sharply, flapping his strong wings to carry him higher, higher. Until he stopped altogether and let himself fall, tumbling head over tail toward the earth.

"Ruslan!" I screamed down our bond, terrified that something had happened to him.

But a manic laugh echoed back and I realized he was *flaunting* his new abilities. Where terror gripped my chest in its claws, exhilaration expanded his as he tested his limits. Wings snapped out mere moments before he would have plummeted into the ocean, and then he shifted to the side, sending a spray of salty water flying as he dipped a talon into the endless blue. Drazen backflipped and joined him in skimming the glittering water, releasing a roar when Ruslan dipped again and sent a wave sailing in his direction.

The two rose again as they neared land, putting plenty of space between them and the burnt earth where the Day and Iron Realms' armies camped. Their wingbeats buffeted those beneath them as they prepared to land in the open field. When Ruslan was about ten feet above the ground, his wings tucked close to his body before disappearing entirely, and then my mate returned to himself, rolling over his shoulder to take the impact of the landing. Excitement bubbled up inside me as I raced toward him. Disregarding his dirty state, he caught and lifted me into the air, spinning us as he shared his unbridled joy.

"I can shift whenever," he grinned, sounding like a child who'd been given the present he'd always desired.

"You can shift whenever," I echoed, tossing my braid over my shoulder and wrapping my legs around his waist. He hugged me, forcing all the air from my lungs along with a laugh. He was elated, and other than the moment and day after I'd accepted our bond. I'd never seen him so happy. His joy imbued me with more power as I drank from it.

Ruslan hardened, and with our current position, it didn't take much for him to grind against my center. A groan escaped me before I could smother it. It had been far too long, and I wanted nothing more than to rip my clothes off and let him take me right there on the churned earth. Nudity had become as common as drinking water in our army's encampment, and with how loose the Iron Realm already was with sexuality, I didn't think anyone would care. Though they would *definitely* watch – which only made more heat pool between my thighs.

"We have to clean up our mess here, sprite, but when we return home... I am going to fuck you so hard you won't be able to walk for a week," he purred, his words making my core clench.

"Then we'd better be on our way to the Crystal Realm," I bantered, unhooking my legs and sliding down his body.

———

WE FLEW over the ocean in the direction of a larger village near the coast, close to the Day Realm's border. From Ruslan's back, the dark, navy waters were endless in every direction, aweing me as the sun glittered across its surface.

"How far are the other continents?"

"A few weeks sailing by ship. Would you like to visit them some-day, mate?"

"I would love that, after I've finished exploring our continent."

"I will take you wherever you want to go. All I want is for you to be happy."

"I know."

We lapsed into silence again, and I let the steady beat of his wings lull me into a hazy slumber as the sun warmed me against the wind.

"Sprite?"

I jerked upright, not realizing I'd dozed off. Blinking, I real-ized we'd traveled quite far while I slumbered. Dozens of ships rocked back and forth in the ocean below us, some with sails furled and others without any to be seen. The water was no longer a deep blue, but rather a bright aqua, and from above, the clarity of it offered unfettered views of intricate rock formations and large fish gathering around them.

"I thought you said this wasn't a busy port?"

"It's not supposed to be."

My brows furrowed as I examined the boats and what waited on the approaching shore.

"Relay the message to land in the field beyond." Ruslan swung his mighty head in the direction of a grassy clearing between the closest lake and the town.

I shouted his orders over the wind, and several Dragons back, Liliana and Zuriel did the same. The group flew low enough that when the townspeople pointed and shouted overhead, their cries reached my ears. Some Crystal Fae raced into their homes, while others rushed away from them and splashed into the bay's waters.

The Dragons landed in quick succession, and I slid from my mate's back before he shifted into his Fae form. Unhooking my backpack, I handed it to him, then sighed as he dressed. Losing sight of his muscular form was always a disappointment. He smirked, then bent me backward for a kiss before tucking me into his side and leading the way into the town.

At the gates, a group of withered, sun-hardened males waited with fishing spears and hooks in hand. "What do you want?" the boldest yelled, brandishing a wicked looking trident.

"I am Emperor Ruslan of the Északi Empire, and I am here to free you from the oppressive Night Realm. It is time the Crystal Realm returned to the Empire." The utter command in his voice would have been terrifying if I wasn't intimately familiar with the softness hidden beneath his sharp exterior.

The male scoffed. "You all call yourselves emperors and kings, but you never care for the everyday people. All you nobles care about is swinging your cocks and trying to make yours look bigger than the others."

Ruslan was on him in a second, lifting him into the air by his throat. His trident clattered to the ground, and his companions took a cautious step back. The smirk that crossed Ruslan's face was wicked and promised violence. "My cock *is* the biggest, and if you didn't see it the first time, I am happy to fly overhead again." He released his grip on the Crystal Fae male and let him fall to the ground in a coughing heap. "Now, I am here trying to liberate you and give you all the wonderful inventions the Iron Realm has produced to make your lives easier. All I ask in return is that some of you return with me and help put out a fire."

Another male stepped forward, wary but intrigued. "In the Iron Realm?"

"Day Realm," Ruslan admitted, cracking his neck from side to side.

"I'll go, but only if I can make my home in the Iron Realm."

"And why would you want to do that?" he purred, circling the male with a predatory gaze.

"Because it beats trying to make a home among the Shifters or the Mages," he shrugged, trying to appear nonchalant, but the hook trembled in his hand.

"Why would you go to another continent?" I asked, my curiosity dragging me forward.

"The war," he said, glancing between my mate and me. "Thousands are fleeing the continent for safe haven. The Night Fae came through not too long ago with conscription orders. None of us want to fight." He glanced behind him at the disorganized band of males wielding fishers' weapons.

"We must end this," Ruslan growled into my mind.

"Agreed," I shot back, clenching my fists. Fucking Kazimir.

Did he have to force his pain on everyone else because he wasn't male enough to deal with it on his own?

"You will find safe haven in the Iron Realm," Ruslan promised the male, then raised his voice so the rest of the crowd could hear what he had to say. "Any who come with us to fight the fire will have ample opportunity to start a new life along what little shoreline the Iron Realm has to offer. We could use skilled fishers like yourselves."

Murmurs swept through the crowd, and even beyond them, to the Fae whose heads barely poked out from doorways and windows in the village beyond.

The trident-wielding Fae looked upon his brethren with a sneer. "Will you really bow to this arrogant prick?"

"Watch how you speak about your emperor," I snapped, striding forward.

He turned his disrespectful regard on me. "What are you going to do about it, little bitch? You couldn't hurt a fly."

Tipping my head back, I released a bone-chilling laugh. I let the sound linger in the air for an uncomfortable moment before I snapped my gaze forward again, spearing the male with a sinister look. "I am your future empress, Izidora Valynor, and I have survived more than you can imagine in that tiny brain of yours." I took a menacing step toward him, but he did not flinch. He continued to sneer down at me, which only set my teeth further on edge.

Fucking arrogant males.

"You see, everyone looks at me and sees a tiny, powerless female. They try to take advantage of that. But what they don't know is that I am *tired* of males thinking less of me than I am," I continued, cocking my head to the side and offering him a saccharine smile. The dark crystal flared to life in my chest, and I pulled on the intoxicating emotions to imbue myself with more power. Ruslan smothered a smirk, his eyes swirling with smoke and lust as he drank in the sight of me taking this old male on.

White flames flooded my palms as I closed the distance between us again until we were only a step apart. While I may have been forced to look up at him, it wasn't because he deserved it in any way; no, my height prevented me from bearing over him in intimidation like Ruslan would have done.

But I didn't need that to make him respect me. There was more than one way to force a male to bow before me. The

Crystal Fae squared his shoulders and continued to look down his nose at me. Big fucking mistake. "Do you consider yourself to be a brave male?"

"I am a brave male. I fight for my family," he stated with conviction.

"Brave enough to withstand torture for them?" I purred, fire crackling in my palms as I pushed more magic into them.

"Of course," he said, but his swallow gave away his nervousness.

I cocked my head to the side, studying him as I slipped my way past his mental barriers with unsurprising ease. Then, I called further on those dark emotions filling the crystal in my chest, using what Zuriel and I had been practicing on the male. At first, I only offered him morsels of pain – the ache of a rib, cramp of a foot, spasm of the back. It wasn't long before the first grunt slipped past his lips.

Pathetic.

The sound wasn't nearly as satisfying as I wanted it to be. So, I provided him more. His face contorted, and with a gasp, he fell to his knees. "What are you doing to me, witch?" he gritted out, clutching his chest.

"I thought you were brave?" I teased, circling him as he cried out.

Behind him, the other Crystal Fae subtly stepped back.

"Agh!" he screamed as the first imaginary whip landed across his back. The scars on my own stung, my penance for delivering this pain. But this sensation had been my life for many years, and with the rage burning inside me, I was immune to its sharp call. I was stronger, braver, *better* than he would ever be. I was an insidious bloom, beautiful and deadly and powerful beyond measure.

No male would disrespect me without consequences.

"Let me know when you'd like to yield," I purred, crossing

my arms over my chest. The torture I delivered was exhilarating coupled with the complete domination of this male. No wonder Ruslan loved to mix pleasure and pain – it was almost addicting, feeling this utter power and control over another.

Two more lashes broke him. A pity, really, as I was having so much fun. I let a third imaginary one land before I pinched off the flow of pain, ready to release it again at a moment's notice.

"I yield, I yield!" he shrieked, falling to his hands and knees, panting and sweating.

Dropping to a crouch beside him, I ensured that he knew exactly what my face looked like when I granted mercy. He needed to remember that it was by my will alone that the pain stopped. The way his blue eyes flinched with my proximity, I knew the message had been delivered. Keeping my attention on him, I said loud enough for all to hear, "I endured hundreds of whip lashes across my back and have the scars to prove it. If that is not enough to inspire your loyalty and respect, then I don't know what is."

Straightening, I scanned the hushed crowd of Crystal Fae and let them see the resilience fused to the core of my being. "We don't have time to waste. If you want a new home and a better life, you'll come with us. Now."

I spun on my heel and stalked back toward the clearing where two dozen Dragons crouched and waited for riders.

"There's my sprite," Ruslan boasted down our bond.

When I faced the town once more, an entire crowd of people walked behind my mate.

"Did I really convince that many to join us?"

"You did. No matter where you are in Északi, power and strength is respected. You, Izidora, have it, without question."

Ruslan stripped and shifted, and I stuffed his clothing into the backpack before crawling up his hide and settling between his spikes. No one else rode him, as a further example of how far the two of us were set apart from other Fae. Ruslan and I were the most powerful in all of Északi, and those who weren't already familiar with us would do well to remember that.

Once everyone had found a Dragon to ride, I told Ruslan to take to the skies, and we soared back to the Day Realm with a small victory won and another on the way.

39

RUSLAN

Far away from the wildfire, the Dragons landed one by one, ensuring the wind from our wings didn't anger the flames further. Kneeling, the others assisted the Crystal Fae in sliding from their backs. They all raced toward the blaze without hesitation, relieving tension in my chest I hadn't realized was there.

"It will be okay," Izidora said as she handed me my clothes.

"Thanks to you, it will." It was true – it had been her idea to go for them, and she was the one who convinced them to come. Pride flared inside me as I gazed into my mate's aquamarine eyes.

How did I get so lucky?

"Come, I need you all to myself," I said, holding out my hand to her.

My mate accepted it willingly and without hesitation – so unlike a year before when I'd first brought her to the Iron Realm. The blaze died with the light of the sun as we trekked through the mud and haphazardly arranged tents, freeing up soldiers to tackle other tasks that had gone undone as we worked to contain it.

The Night Fae had disappeared in the blink of an eye, their tails tucked between their legs like the dogs they were as we squeezed them on three sides. It mattered not that they retreated; regrouping would allow us to slaughter them the next time we met in battle. Their little ambush failed in the end, though our army suffered heavy losses that wouldn't go unnoticed.

Their army was far larger than I ever dreamed it could be.

We needed to return to the Iron Realm as soon as possible. Before Izidora and I reached our tent, King Consort Geza stopped us. "Thank you for staying to protect the Day Realm. I will not hold the fire against you, My Emperor."

I cocked my head and studied the Day Fae king. "I am grateful for your assistance, Geza, but do not think you will ever be able to hold anything against me."

A wide grin spread across his dark skin, flashing his white teeth. His eyes crinkled with amusement at the corners. "No, I don't suppose I will ever be able to, not after you and Izidora risked your lives to return Gizela to us."

He proffered his bare forearm, and I clasped it, allowing a smirk to play across my face. "I take my duties seriously. Which means, I need to return to the Iron Realm and prepare for the next battle once the fire is out. I trust you can continue to clean up from there?"

"Indeed," he replied, his deep baritone booming over the camp. "Please let us know if there is anything we can do in the future." Our greeting broke, and he dipped his head respectfully to Izidora and me before continuing on his way.

We entered our tent – one of the few that had the luxury of a padded cot – and my mate sank onto a pile of stuffed bags that acted as a makeshift chair, pulling off her boots and armor piece by piece. "I am exhausted," she complained, rubbing her eyes with the heels of her palms.

I crouched behind her, massaging her tense shoulders. "When we return home, you can sleep as long as you need to recover. No training, no pressure, no duties. You deserve rest, sprite."

A blissful sigh escaped her lips, and she leaned into me, groaning as I worked over a particularly tense spot. "But I want you with me."

I kissed the top of her head, inhaling her rosy scent like it was my own personal drug. "Once this war is over, we'll go away somewhere, just the two of us, and you can have every part of me you want all to yourself."

"After we're married," she teased, a soft laugh escaping her.

I couldn't help the grin that spread across my face, but I let her win this one. She deserved it after the performance in the Crystal Realm. Her body loosened as I continued to work. Then, I scooped her up and carried her to the soft pallet in the center of the space. Her arms looped around my neck, holding onto me as desperately as I held onto her. Gently, I placed her gently among the blankets, tucking them up to her chin. Her eyelids were heavy, drooping, and I knew she wouldn't be awake much longer.

"Rest. I'll be back shortly," I murmured, kissing her lips, then her forehead.

"Where are you going?" she half-whispered, half-yawned, doing a little shake and then snuggling deeper into the pile.

"To speak to Drazen and ensure the fire is truly out." I straightened slowly, and she nodded into sleep, her breath deepening almost immediately. I lingered longer than I should have before drifting outside and under the stars.

As I searched for my general, I found myself at the fringes of the camp, near the animals. Endre was there, slipping between piles of stored goods. Silently, I followed him, wondering where he was going and what he was doing.

I didn't trust the motherfucker not to turn on us. He'd shown his loyalty when he'd left in a hurry with Kazimir after he tried to kill my mate. And, as much as I hated it, I was pissed at him for hurting Liliana too. The female had grown on me, and she and Izidora were nearly as inseparable as we were.

But I'd never tell her that.

Endre grasped a ladder, hefting it under his shoulder and picking his way carefully so as not to knock anything over as he traversed the supplies. He seemed not to notice me, but I still stuck to the shadows and lightened my steps. When he broke through the stacks of boxes, I lingered behind the one at the end, watching as he approached a weary-looking olyphant.

The massive gray beast was still soaked in blood, his flappy ears drooping on either side of his head. One mighty tusk was chipped and broken. With great care, Endre braced the ladder's feet on the ground, then leaned the top two rungs against the olyphant's hide. The beast sighed but made no other protest. Gingerly, he ascended the rungs, and I narrowed my eyes when he stopped about three-fourths of the way up. Silver light danced beneath his fingers, and ruby returned to ashen skin. The olyphant made a contented noise, shifting his weight around as his shoulder wound closed.

"There, all better now," Endre murmured to him, rubbing soothing circles over the freshly healed wound.

He descended the ladder with as much care as he'd climbed up it, constantly checking on the olyphant to ensure he wasn't hurting it.

"He's been doing that every night, you know," a voice said from behind me. I glanced over my shoulder. Liliana stepped closer, her eyes fixed beyond me.

"Has he?" I said skeptically, lifting a brow.

"Yeah. He really likes animals. Even healed some of the kutya, even though one nearly ripped his leg off." She shrugged, pretending like she didn't care. We both knew that was a lie, but I didn't comment on it.

"I don't trust him," I stated flatly.

"I know you don't," she replied. "But you trust me, right?"

"I do – for now. That is always subject to change," I warned, my voice threaded with a hint of violence.

Silence stretched between us as Endre turned his attention to another wounded creature.

"Drazen is with the other Dragons," she finally said with a weary sigh.

I nodded, taking one last look at the two Night Fae in our midst before striding off. Liliana remained there, watching, and I wondered what she would do when we returned to the Iron Realm with two males desperately in love with her.

40

KAZIMIR

"Bring the traitor to me," I commanded the sentries stationed outside the council room in Este Castle. The leather-clad males did not hesitate as they raced off in search of him. Bracing myself against the doorframe, I surveyed the comings and goings down the stone-lined halls of my home. I watched as servants scurried about, taking care of their assigned tasks, while nobles and rich merchants from Vaenor traipsed the halls, all pausing to bow to their king.

The females dipped into obscenely low curtseys, allowing me a view of their cleavage in their low-cut dresses. None of these high born could keep up with my appetite, and not a single spark of interest flickered in me as they batted their lashes and continued on their way. At the thought of my whores sucking and fucking it later, however, my cock twitched.

Murmurs drifted from those gathered in the council room, but I ignored them. Their opinions no longer mattered. My seat on the Night Throne allowed me final say in all matters – including this one.

Especially this one.

Feminine shrieks filled the halls, followed by the sharp

sound of a drawn sword. The voices were indistinct, but I could tell the argument was heated nonetheless. Crossing my arms across my chest, I waited for my guards to handle the situation. A sharp slap and rough thump silenced the cries, and my kingsguard dragged a limp High Lord Tibor Zadik down the hall.

"High Lady Renata put up a fight. We had to knock her out, my king," the first one said.

With a sigh, I stepped aside, running a hand over my face. Of course she protested her husband's – Endre's father's – arrest. The males tossed Tibor into an open chair, propping him up when he started to slide. "It appears you also had to knock Tibor out," I stated flatly. "I cannot read his charges while he is unconscious."

"Apologies, My King. He fought us too, especially after we knocked out his wife." The males sketched twin bows and disappeared from the council room, shutting the door softly behind them.

Around the large wood table sat the remaining High Lords of the Night Realm – Kaztar, Viktor, Jaku, and Nikolai, Vadim's father. Vadim leaned against the wall along with Jaku's heir, both stone-faced and arms crossed over their chests. Desmond perked up at the sight of the slumped, disgraced former High Lord.

"I have some smelling salts that will wake him," the Mage offered.

"By all means," I barked, sweeping out a hand to indicate that he should continue, before settling into my high-backed chair at the head of the table.

From his robes, he revealed a vial containing small pink rocks. Crouching beside Tibor, he uncorked the top, waving it beneath his nose. I drummed my fingers along the table, waiting for him to return to wakefulness.

With a series of rapid blinks, he came to, straightening when he realized where he was. "My King, I–"

"Save it, Tibor," I snapped, my patience thinner than the silk robes Taya wore.

His teeth clacked shut, and eyes that reminded me so much of my traitorous friend filled with profound sadness. I continued to drum my fingers, the rap, rap, rap sound of them echoing around the silent room. Ever so slowly, my pace slowed, dragging out the tension building like a rolling thunderstorm.

Finally, the tapping stopped altogether. Dragging my hand off the table, I settled both in my lap and leveled my serious gaze on the traitor. "Tibor Zadik, your son has committed treason against the Night Crown, and as all family members of traitors must be killed alongside the true one, you are sentenced to die, along with your wife, Renata Zadik."

To his credit, he did not flinch. But the sigh he released almost broke through the wall of hate and pain I'd built around myself.

Almost.

"You are like a son to me, Kazimir. Always have been, always will be, until my dying breath. I'm so sorry your grief has broken you so. You never deserved to be left behind by your father, and Renata and I tried our best to make up for his absence. Cazius's death was a true tragedy, and your mate rejecting you, another. If my death will ease your pain, then so be it."

He squared his shoulders and lifted his chin, not bothering to sneak a glance at his former peers and ask them to intervene.

"I will take your son's life too, once I slaughter the Iron Realm and all its supporters. Traitorous blood will not continue to multiply in the Night Realm," I gritted out. The scraping of my chair against the stone floor was the only sound in the deafening silence as I rose to my feet and towered over everyone seated at the council table. "Not now, not ever." I shot a pointed look at each of my High Lords in turn, and then at their respective heirs.

No one blinked.

Not even Tibor.

"Do you have nothing to say in your son's defense, Tibor?" I asked, rounding the table and sitting on a hip on the smooth surface beside him. The position allowed me to sneer down at him, but the former High Lord didn't alter his defiant posture.

"Endre is where he belongs," he stated with conviction.

The back of my hand cracked against Tibor's cheekbone as black flashed over my eyes. The binding magic reared to life inside me, and two thick coils of rope burst from my hands, wrapping themselves around his wrists, then up his arms, like two sinister snakes.

A muscle feathered in his jaw, and his nostrils flared as he sucked down air, but he did not scream or cry out. I flicked two more cords toward his legs, securing them to the chair and rendering him fully immobile. The binding magic begged to be unleashed, but I yanked it back into compliance before a rope could leap from my hands and wind around his throat.

His death needed to be public for all to see.

"Your sentence will be carried out at dusk tomorrow," I snarled, shoving his chair further away from the table and bracing my hands over his bound arms. "Until then, you will be under guard in your apartments, along with your wife. If you try to escape, your death will be slow and torturous."

Straightening, I sneered at the four remaining High Lords and their heirs. "You are all dismissed."

Silently, they rose and filed from the room, leaving Tibor and myself alone. My hands curled into fists as he continued to look at me with those pity-filled eyes. I was his fucking king – he wasn't allowed to make me feel like I was in the wrong when his blood was traitorous.

With a curse, I dragged myself away from him and stalked from the room. The doors banged against the wall, nearly muffling my order to have him returned to his apartment.

The people in the halls of Este Castle parted in a silent wave, hurriedly acknowledging my presence as I passed them. I needed to bury myself in something wet and warm and forget all about the people who continued to betray me. I would not lose control over the Night Realm, not when so many other things had been snatched from me.

Taya waited for me in my chambers, sprawled across my bed in a satin robe. Her red hair fanned out over a pillow, and as I threw my sword to the ground, she straightened, the green fabric pooling around her waist and baring her breasts. "I've missed you today, My King. Where have you been?"

"Shut the fuck up and suck my cock," I growled, yanking her head forward and down. My knees hit the edge of the bed, and she fumbled with the fastenings of my pants before shoving them down my hips. Her golden eyes flicked up to me as she wet her lips, then she lowered her head and wrapped them around me.

Her nose hit my stomach on the first stroke, and she gagged, sucking my cock deeper before releasing it with a heady moan. Bunching up the silky green fabric on her back, I ripped it away, leaving her naked in the cold room. She shivered but did not complain as she licked the underside of my shaft. A pointed nail scraped the center of my balls, and I groaned, grasping the back of her head and forcing her lower on my dick.

She sucked in a breath when I allowed her to come up for air, sniffling and blinking away tears. "Did I say you could stop?"

"No," she whimpered, her eyes flaming as I grasped her chin.

"And you're still not pregnant," I tsked. "You disappoint me."

I slapped her, then shoved her toward my hardness. "Keep going, and maybe you'll earn my seed."

"Please, My King, I want it," she pouted before opening wide and taking me again, quickening her pace.

I flexed my glutes, enjoying the show she put on for me. When my balls tightened, I fisted her hair and yanked her head away. Then, I shoved her backward. "Spread those pretty legs for me."

Braced on her elbows, she dropped her knees to the side and bared her core to me. I shoved my pants off before ripping my shirt overhead and climbing onto the bed with her. It dipped beneath my weight, and I grasped both her ankles and forced her legs further apart. In one harsh thrust, I buried myself inside her, groaning as her walls clenched me.

"That's it, milk my cock, baby." Digging my hands into her hips, I slammed into her over and over again, chasing my release.

"Oh, fuck, Kaz–"

I growled a warning.

"My King. My hero. I belong only to you."

"That's right," I gritted out, thrusts becoming erratic. "Say it again."

"I belong to you," she panted, body writhing beneath me.

With a grunt, my cock spurted out ropes of hot liquid, coating her inner walls, and she sucked in a breath, rolling her hips against mine as she begged for every last drop. After the final twitch of my dick, I slipped out of her and off the bed, stalking to the bathroom to wash up. Taya knew better than to move, and no protest filtered over the sound of rushing water as I spun the knobs for the shower.

The hot water wasn't enough to banish the crazed thoughts from my mind, and every swipe of soap against my body was another idea painting my mind, masterpieces coming to life where I ruled all of Északi and Ruslan was dead.

Ruslan was weak for allowing the other monarchs to keep their positions.

When I was finished, there would be no one left alive to challenge my claim.

41

RUSLAN

The first snow of the year dusted across my shoulders as I exited Ryza Citadel, seeking out my mate. We were due to meet with Queen Viktoria this afternoon to discuss the refugees fleeing both the Night and Crystal Realms. The Crystal Fae we'd brought back with us to the Iron Realm had settled along the coast, but with fewer houses and less space to offer refugees, the Iron Realm was not a long-term replacement for their homes. The Day Realm was vast, but the majority was farmland and the crops they produced were essential to the war effort.

Not that we'd be marching anywhere soon with winter descending on the Iron Realm. Unless the Night Fae decided to go on the offensive again in the Day Realm, the army was staying put for the winter. I cracked my knuckles one by one as I made the trek to the stables. Északi was divided in two, with the Night Realm's hold over the Crystal Realm, and I was displeased with the current arrangement.

At the first sign of fresh green grass, we'd march again and reclaim what we had lost.

In the stables, I found Izidora brushing the long, gray mane of her favorite mare, Mistik. Fluffy white flakes landed on the horse's mane and in Izidora's dark chestnut hair. I paused for a moment and drank in the view, feeling like an intruder on the moment of solace my mate sought. Whenever she wasn't training or with me, she was here, among her favorite animals.

"Once the war is over, I'll build you a separate stable by Roc Palace where you can keep a hundred horses if you'd like," I said loudly as I approached, not wanting to startle her.

She shot me an appreciative smile over her shoulder, then returned her attention to her horse. "You know I can feel you coming."

"I know, but I still don't want to scare you," I murmured, wrapping my arms around her from behind and kissing the top of her head.

"Only everyone else," she quipped, leaning into my embrace.

My hot breath fanned over her ear as I bent closer. "Exactly."

Izidora shivered, but not from the cold. "Are we going all the way to the Day Realm?"

"Queen Viktoria is coming here, actually. Katrina just sent word," I replied, giving her some space to work, but my hands lingered on her hips.

"When?" she asked, working the last knot out of Mistik's mane.

"Soon. I came to fetch you." A blast of flurries swept through the stables, and Mistik snorted steam into the frigid air, eliciting a laugh from Izidora. The sound was sweeter than any decadent dessert my chefs could bake, and when it slipped from her lips, it made me weak at the knees.

"It is getting cold," she admitted, spinning to face me. Flakes coated her dark lashes as she tipped her head back, and I brushed a few stray hairs from her face.

"Then I'd better get you inside to warm you up," I grinned.

"Let me put Mistik away, and then you can get me some hot chocolate," she quipped, ducking under my arm and grabbing Mistik's lead.

"Have you earned it?" I bantered, watching her hips sway as she walked away.

"Do I have to?" she retorted, stealing a smirk from me.

The mare's stall was still open, and she didn't need much coaxing to return to it, given a bundle of hay and a warm blanket awaited her there. Izidora settled the cover across her horse's body, securing the straps under her belly and around her chest to ensure it remained in place. Then, she proffered Mistik a handful of treats. As the horse munched sugar cubes, Izidora planted a soft kiss on her velvety nose.

The encounter warmed my heart. I loved seeing Izidora happy, and after the stress of Princess Gizela's kidnapping, the battle, and putting out the fires in the Day Realm, she was finally starting to relax again. She approached, then wrapped her small arms around my waist, sighing into my chest. I held her there, stroking her back, until she released me.

We didn't always need words with how familiar we were with one another. We were one soul in two bodies, and nothing would ever change that. I draped an arm around her shoulders and kept her close to my side as we walked back to the citadel, protecting her from the bitter wind bringing fluffy white flakes to the Iron Realm.

My sprite was always cold, and I was her Dragon, here to offer my heat.

Down the hall from my office on the first floor of the citadel, the servants had readied a formal meeting area, complete with a roaring hearth and soft furs draped over iron-gray couches arranged in a semicircle. When we arrived, the last one was arranging a wintry centerpiece on the table in the center, and once he had finished I sent him away with our refreshment requests.

Pulling Izidora into my lap, I caged her in with my body, giving her the warmth she needed. Her hands were like ice, and I kissed each finger in turn before tucking them around my backside. She relaxed into me, resting her head on my shoulder, and my own muscles unwound as we settled there, listening to the crackling fire.

When we were like this, nothing else in the world mattered.

The servant cleared his throat, breaking our silent comfort. I had half a mind to snarl at him, but Izidora shot me a teasing, warning look and sat up, graciously accepting a steaming mug. The scent of peppermint and chocolate wafted in my direction, and she moaned when she sipped the gooey liquid. "Cedomir has outdone himself yet again."

My chef had taken it upon himself to concoct many new recipes for my mate to try once he learned of her affection for sweets – one that we shared, much to the dismay of my muscled physique. I plucked the drink from her small hands, earning a noise of protest, and allowed the hot liquid to wash over my tongue.

"It is decadent," I commented, smirking as I handed the mug back to Izidora.

"And it's all mine," she teased, turning away from me and guarding the drink.

A chuckle rumbled in my chest at her playfulness, and I snuck my hands beneath her jacket and tunic to rub her low back while we waited for Queen Viktoria's arrival.

It wasn't long before a sentry heralded her entrance.

The queen of the Day Realm swept into the room with a shiver, her lips spreading into a wide grin when she saw us. "Emperor, future Empress, you look cozy," she commented. Her colorful attire fluttered behind her as she approached, the fabric much too thin for the blustering day in the Iron Realm.

"Queen Viktoria, you look lovely," my mate said, rising from her perch on my lap to greet the female. They exchanged kisses on both cheeks before squeezing each other's hands and settling down. "Can I offer you something warm to drink?"

The queen sniffed the air, looking pointedly at Izidora's discarded mug. "That smells delightful. I will have one of those. Emperor, I will not say that I have missed the Iron Realm's cold in the past year."

I snapped my fingers, and a servant rushed off to fetch more hot chocolate. "At least we won't be bracing ourselves for the Night Realm's bitter ocean winds during Béke this year."

She snorted, shaking her head. "Béke is a relic of the past, it seems."

Izidora chewed her lip, settling beside me and resting her palm on my thigh. "We must find a way to help those who are currently suffering." My mate had the kindest of hearts. It was the suffering of others that concerned her more than anything, for she understood the depths of depravity Fae could inflict on one another.

"I quite agree," Queen Viktoria started. "However, the refugees from the Crystal and Night Realms arrive at our border in droves. It appears the demand for ships and passage to the other continents outstrips the supply and availability of them."

"You are receiving refugees from the Night Realm as well?" I asked, leaning forward and bracing my elbows on my knees.

"Indeed. From what Geza has told me, they all speak of the impossibility of getting on ships in Vaenor. Apparently there is a retinue at the docks blocking all passage from anyone new to the sailing profession. If you are not already on a list, you are not allowed to pass."

The servant returned with more mugs, and the queen

accepted one, wrapping her long fingers around it to warm them.

"Anything else?"

"They complain about conscription. Lately, most have been fleeing it. Since Kazimir returned to Vaenor, he has sent out another wave of requests. Boys barely old enough to call themselves males have been drafted." She shook her head all the way down to her chest, releasing a heavy sigh.

"Their army was enormous. Even with the dent the olyphants and Dragons made in it, we're still outnumbered," Izidora commented with a frown.

"We were also out-strategized," I added, resting my hand over her palm and giving it a reassuring squeeze. "If it weren't for the arrival of the Day Fae, we might have suffered another huge loss."

Queen Viktoria sipped from her hot drink, giving a little dance of delight at the flavors. "It is too hot in the Day Realm for such treats, but for this, I could return to the Iron Realm again."

We shared a laugh as her comment eased some of the tension we all felt about the current state of the continent.

"But in all seriousness, we were happy to have arrived in time to assist. Now, we must discuss how to handle these refugees, because there is not enough housing in the Day Realm for them."

"Nor is there in the Iron Realm," I sighed, pinching the bridge of my nose. "We need more miners, and I assume you need more farmers?"

"We had to pull many farmers to fight," Queen Viktoria confirmed.

"As did we from the mines." I mulled over our options, then continued. "We could set up an apprentice program with those who are left manning our industries. Their pay would be increased if they could also house their apprentices. And those who are stationed in barracks could have their pay increased if they opened their homes to the refugees as well. Their families will be able to join in the war effort from afar."

Another sip of minty chocolate passed over the queen's lips as she considered. "Can you provide this extra pay, My Emperor?"

"If you need it, I shall provide," I said. This war needed to be won, no matter the cost. The Iron Realm had enough in reserves to spend at this pace for a few years more before reassessment would need to occur.

"I shall give my High Lords the task of coordinating with their local leaders." Finishing the last of her drink, Queen Viktoria placed the mug on the polished wood table between us.

"Do you have anything else to add, mate?" I prodded, wanting Izidora to participate in the discussion. She often only spoke when she had a solid point to make. She was still hesitant about her future role as empress, since she'd grown up away from all of the politics and ruling, but I knew she had nothing to fear. Her kindness, her empathy, her compassion were more valuable than all the hours my father spent beating the rule of law into me.

That was yet another way in which we were better together.

The Fae of Északi would be better for our union once the war was finished.

"Nothing that I can think of. Your solution seems fair and balanced," she assured me with a soft smile.

With another snap of my fingers, a servant brought me paper, and I scribbled out instructions for the Royal Treasurer. "Send us the amount you need once you have an estimate, Queen Viktoria."

The queen of the Day Realm rose from her chair, smoothing the vibrant fabric of her dress. "Thank you for the hot chocolate, and your time. We'll be in contact."

42

IZIDORA

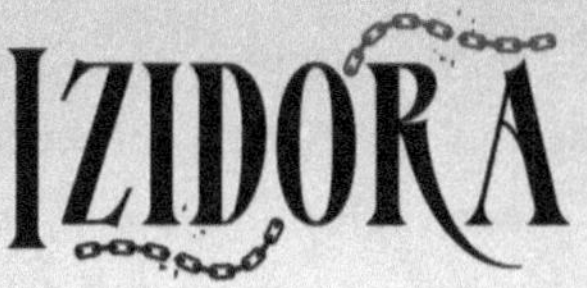

Ruslan and I both stood, offering polite goodbyes and watching as Queen Viktoria swept from the room with as much grace as she'd entered. Once the doors closed behind her, a tired sigh escaped me, forced from the pressure of my past decisions compressing my chest. "I don't want anyone else to be hurt because of my choices."

Spinning me to face him, Ruslan crouched down so we were eye level. "None of this is your fault."

"Isn't it?" I asked, eyes prickling and guilt gnawing at my belly. "Would you have kidnapped Princess Gizela, slaughtered King Airre and Queen Immonen, and caused one crisis after another had I rejected our bond?"

"No," he murmured, brushing a thumb over my cheek. "I would probably have ended my own life. But you should not have had to endure Kazimir to save the rest of the continent. You deserve happiness. You have suffered enough."

Hot tears spilled over, tracing a trail down my cheek. "But if by choosing him, I could have saved tens of thousands of lives, wouldn't that have been worth the pain of being by his side?"

"Fuck that," he growled, yanking me into him and holding

the jagged pieces of me together. "He would have suffocated you, smothered your inner fire, and you would be a shell of who you are. Your spirit is what makes you the most incredible female in all of Északi, and the first time I saw it, I knew I had to set it free. Kazimir did not – does not – see you that way. You were his project, his damsel in distress. Saving and owning you was his goal. Empowering you was not."

His words were a balm to my shattered soul. A sob wracked my frame, and I twisted my hands in the fabric of his jacket, letting my anguish escape. He held me as tightly as I needed – tighter, even – to give me the safety to fall apart. Finally, my cries turned to hiccups, and then to ragged breaths. Pushing out of his embrace, I wiped my runny nose on my sleeve, releasing a tiny, pained laugh. "I am a mess."

"Then we'd better get home so I can clean you up," he purred, whispering the spell to move us to Roc Palace. When we settled, it was not in our suite. Thick steam filled the underground grotto, sinking into my lungs and cleansing them. I inhaled the herbal scent that clung to it, allowing it to open my nose and mind. Lights flickered on, though they were still faint, revealing the tranquil space where no one would hear or disturb us.

Ruslan stepped closer, deft fingers working over the fastenings on my jacket and sliding it off my shoulders. Then, he slipped his hands beneath my tunic and skimmed them up my ribs. My breath hitched as he removed it, baring my skin to the heated air

Immediately, my nipples pressed against the scraps of lace binding my breasts. Steam coated my skin, giving it a sheen of sensuality, and I ran my hands up Ruslan's broad chest, savoring the hard muscles that pressed back into them. He captured one and brought it to his face, rubbing his beard against it before kissing my palm.

Then, he released it and found his way to my hips, gripping them and lifting me. I wrapped my legs around his waist, feeling his hardness dig into my center. He flexed his hips and pressed in, pulling a moan from deep in my throat. "Your wanton sounds get me so hard, sprite."

I ground against him, needing the distraction from my guilty conscience.

As if he sensed my neediness, he murmured, "Let me make you feel good. Let me take care of you."

"Please," I whimpered as a finger traced my nipple, then twisted the straps holding my breasts and ripped them away. The steam caressed my bare torso, the tantalizing sensation only heightening my pleasure.

Ruslan took his warmth with him as he released me to the ground, but I did not protest as he discarded his clothes, throwing them in a heap along with mine. I hooked my thumbs in my pants and slid them down my thighs, facing him as I kicked them off.

Ruslan was like a god with his chiseled physique on full display and his massive dick pointing straight at me. I raked my gaze across every inch of him, appreciating the fine lines of his muscles and swirls of his tattoos. His biceps flexed as he swept a hand across his head, slicking back his hair. He took his time exploring me, and I widened my legs so he could see my glistening center. The growl that rumbled from him when he scented my arousal sent heat straight there, dampening my thighs further.

"You are so fucking exquisite, Izidora," he purred, taking two steps toward me.

I remained motionless as he circled me, a predator assessing his prey. The darkness in me called to the darkness in him, and I wanted pain with my pleasure. He came to a stop behind me, and a shiver skittered down my spine as he closed the remaining distance between us. A featherlight touch traced each vertebrae, stopping to circle the mate mark between my shoulder blades. When his fingers found my hips, he dug them in, forcing me to feel his full length pressing against my back.

Fuck, I needed more.

I raised my arms, threading my hands in his hair and yanking his head to my bared shoulder. He nipped there before sucking the skin into his mouth. "Oh," I gasped out, loving the sting of his teeth.

A hand slid through the moisture coating my skin, smoothing across my low belly until it found the apex of my thighs. I was already throbbing, ready for my mate's touch. The pad of his finger tapped against it, causing me to arch into him. "More," I pleaded.

"How much more?" he purred, tracing his nose along the sensitive parts of my neck and blowing his hot words across my ear.

"All of it," I begged, grinding against his hand.

He tsked, then stepped away. "I'm going to have you nice and slow, Izidora. There is no rush to return to the world beyond these walls. Nothing matters until I'm thoroughly finished fucking you."

Ruslan's words, along with the heat in his smoky gray eyes, had my knees weakening. Lifting my hand, he directed me toward the steaming water, guiding me down to sit on the rocky edge of the pool. The stone bit into my ass and thighs, but I didn't care as he knelt in the water and brought his face to my core.

Low blue lights flickered around us, casting shadows across the walls, but the ones within the water highlighted every muscle on my mate. His shoulders bunched and flexed as he planted the first kiss on my inner thigh, spreading them wide to give himself access to me.

"Your pussy is weeping for me." Another kiss, this time on the other side. The desire to rub my legs together to relieve the ache there was overwhelming. His thumbs kneaded the tense muscles there, allowing me to open further for him. He didn't stop as he flicked his tongue over my clit.

"Yes," I hissed when he sucked it into his mouth.

My head fell back, hair creating a cascade of chestnut that brushed my fingers and the wet ground beneath my palms. The sharp poke of the rock into them only heightened my pleasure as Ruslan worked his tongue over me. Dipping lower, it entered my core, lapping at my wetness like it alone would quench his thirst.

"Ruslan," I panted, rolling my hips toward his mouth, wanting, needing more.

His massaging fingers crept higher until his thumbs brushed the outer edges of my slit. I moaned, the sound a beg for him to slip one inside me. He obliged, but with only the tip, then flattened his tongue and raked it across my clit. "Fuck!" I swore, sweat forming on my brow as my body heated from the inside out.

He smirked against me, sinking his finger to the second knuckle. "If you want more, take it."

"Is that a challenge?" I asked, my voice breathy and filled with lust.

"I told you the first time we met that I like it when they fight back. Force your pleasure out of me, mate." His eyes were molten, and I wasted no time grinding against his hand and mouth, forcing his finger deeper and his scruff brushing against my thighs. I rode his hand like I would ride Mistik, and he growled, adding a finger and spreading me wider.

"You're still so fucking tight. I have to loosen you up before you can take me."

"I want you to split me in two. Make me feel alive, Ruslan."

He curled his fingers against my inner walls, finding that spot that would send me into sweet oblivion. He attacked my clit next, causing me to cry out. I rode his face just as hard as he shoved back into me, and all I could feel was pleasure and pain, the combination intoxicating and sending me careening to the edge. With a scream, I fell apart over his fingers, my walls clenching them and holding them in place as they continued to stroke me.

"That's it, come for me," he growled, face still firmly between my thighs.

My chest heaved as he wrung every last drop of pleasure from me, and when I finally came down from the high, he slipped his fingers out and rose, drops of hot spring water mapping the carved muscles of his torso. His cock was painfully erect and beaded at the tip. I reached for him, nearly dragging him forward and lining him with my throbbing center.

A hand wrapped around my throat, forcing me to look up at him. "Two more."

With a whimper, I nodded against his hand. He crashed his lips against mine, sucking the bottom one into his mouth and sinking his teeth in it. My cry was cut short as he shoved himself in, grunting and groaning as my pussy wrapped around him. Still sensitive from my orgasm, the sensation was almost too much, but all care disappeared when he began to move.

Ruslan's tongue swept around my mouth, forcing me to taste myself. I moaned, grasping at his back for purchase and digging my nails into his slick skin. His free hand flattened across my lower back, pinning me in place as he pounded into me. The water sloshed around our legs, adding to the slick noises coming from between our thighs.

His length filled me so completely, it was impossible to be more joined together. The feeling was *divine*, and I never wanted to go without this, without him. Fuck Kazimir and fuck my brain for trying to convince me I should have given this up to save lives. Ruslan was my true mate, the person who understood me, who saw every raw piece of me and still wanted more.

Who didn't flinch when I woke and found this new darkness swirling inside me. In fact, he'd stepped aside and told me to show him more.

"I love you," I groaned out, breaking our kiss and gasping for air around his hand.

"I love you more, sprite," he panted, eyes wild with lust. "You and I belong together. Nowhere else but here. Don't ever let yourself think otherwise again."

"Okay," I whimpered, his words drawing pleasure from the deep part of me where our bond wound its way around my soul. We dropped whatever barriers we'd erected around our minds, and the intensity of his love for me filled me just as thoroughly as his dick. I was brimming with it, and that only sent more pleasure tingling through every nerve.

He dragged himself out, so fucking slowly, and my mouth dropped into an O as he brushed against that sensitive part of me. Pausing there, he rocked against it and tightened his grip on my neck, making the room spin. Sweat poured off me, and with a cry, my second orgasm tore through me.

"Good girl," he praised, switching the hand on my neck to the back of my head. My lashes were still fluttering against my cheeks as I came down from my high, and he did not hesitate to intensify our connection. A whimper escaped me as he slipped his other hand lower and pressed against my ass. He traced a lazy circle over the hole, making my core clench. "Give me one more orgasm, and then I want to come on those pretty breasts of yours."

Biting my lower lip, I nodded. He teased me again, dragging his cock out to the tip before slowly sinking all the way in. Working my other hole with the same slowness, he opened me up and slipped the first knuckle inside me. The fullness was exactly what I needed, and I melted into his hold, so much pleasure built up in my body that I had no energy to spend holding myself upright.

"Fuck, fuck," I chanted, my mind blanking of everything but the sensations he was giving me. The thrusts became faster, his finger slipping deeper, and I cried, whimpered, and moaned, begging him to bring me over the edge one last time. His cock thickened inside me, pressing against my walls, and I broke, his name ripping from my throat.

With a growl, he pulled out, jerking himself before coating my belly and breasts in his hot cum. We panted together, coming down in unison. Wrapping his arms around me, he lifted me from the edge and into the pool, kissing me thoroughly as he settled us into the water. My body was relaxed in a way I hadn't known I needed, and I allowed myself to drift with him, appreciating the moment of solitude with my mate.

Silence reigned for a few more moments before he murmured, "The choices you made are finished now. There's no use in dwelling on what could have been. It's a lesson I learned long ago, when I was forced to come to terms with killing my siblings for the title of heir apparent."

Picking my head up, I gazed into the smoky swirls of his eyes. "But choices have consequences, ones you can't even know until after they're happening."

"And if you let yourself fall into the trap of endless what-ifs, you'll never move forward," Ruslan said. "And for us, sprite, continuing forward ensures we stay sane."

With that sentiment, I couldn't agree more. Prior to my rescue, I had no autonomy – not really. Since then, though, it had been one difficult decision after another, and I was starting to realize the full weight of their outcomes.

"Is this what ruling is? Being faced with impossible choices, or ones where there's no right answer?" I asked him.

"That is what life is. Whether you are an empress or a miner, a chef or a fieldworker, no one is gifted with the foresight to know which decision is good and which is bad. Fuck, even the seers can only provide a glimpse into an uncertain future," Ruslan replied, heaving out a sigh.

My heart twinged as I was reminded of Immonen and the visions that had plagued her during Béke.

I couldn't believe she was dead.

"Our choices affect those visions. The Fates like to toy with us all, to push us in whatever direction pleases them or causes chaos. The Goddess merely provides us with a crumb of knowledge to guide us."

A heaviness settled across Ruslan, and without a second thought, I pushed soothing emotions into him. He rarely shared just how much this war, taking care of all these people, burdened him, as he continued to give me space to heal.

But we were a team, and we always worked better together.

Water rippled lightly against my ears as he pulled me in tighter, holding me like I was his most precious gemstone. "I am so glad you chose me."

A knot tightened my throat. "Me too," I said around it, digging my nails into his strong back as I squeezed him with all my strength. "You are my everything, Ruslan."

"And you are mine, Izidora."

43

VADIM

In the middle of the night, the halls of Este Castle were eerily quiet. Viktor, Kaztar, Domi, and I tiptoed from the High House Wing down a passage toward a nondescript alcove. Memories of chasing Liliana and Izidora down this hall flicked through my mind, and a pang of longing and guilt settled low in my stomach.

This was for my sister.

The room where the young noble Fae gathered in secret was the only place I could think of where we wouldn't be overheard by ears attuned to hints of treason in hopes of climbing the social ladder and securing a spot on the king's council.

The runners lining the halls muffled our footsteps, and I breathed a sigh of relief when we arrived at the hidden door without incident. Viktor scanned our surroundings while I opened the door, ushering Kaztar and his wife inside. With one last glance, Viktor stepped backward, melting into the narrow passage with us. The door closed with a soft snick, and we threw up bubble lights to guide our way.

Silently, we trekked to the room where tables, chairs, and sofas sat haphazardly. The secret getaway from the terror that had reigned in these halls for far too long was thankfully empty. For the first time in months, my shoulders fell away from my ears and I felt as if I could breathe in the privacy and shelter this room provided. Casting more light around us, we pulled back chairs and faced each other across a worn wood table.

I rubbed my beard absentmindedly, trying to figure out how I wanted to express my concerns. Before I could speak, Kaztar turned to his wife, all semblance of cool collectedness disappearing like he'd removed a mask during a ball. "Domi, I want you to return home and stay there until I come to get you. It's not safe for you here any longer."

Domi scoffed, crossing her arms over her chest. "I am not leaving you."

"Please, Domi," Kaztar pleaded, sinking to his knees and bracing his hands and forehead on her thighs. "I wouldn't be able to live with myself if something happened to you," he said, lifting his head and showing her the deep lines that anguish carved into his expression.

Her eyes were harder than steel as she glared at Viktor and myself, before returning to her husband. "If you had listened to me in the Iron Realm, none of this would have happened."

"I know. I'm sorry," Kaztar's voice broke over the words, and his hair fell in front of his face as he dipped his head into his wife's lap again.

Viktor and I sat in awkward silence during their exchange. Air stilled in my lungs as I waited to hear what she would say.

"What if something happened to you? Do you think I would be able to live with myself if something happened to you after I ran home like a scared little child?" she finally snapped, her anger still sharp as a knife.

"But–"

"But even if I did return home, we have no guards for the

estate any longer. They've all been conscripted." She ripped her ire in my direction.

I held up my hands in supplication. "If you wish to return home, I will send them with you. Kazimir won't notice their absence." It was true, and I was willing to lie about our numbers to protect Domi. Kazimir was too busy fucking his whores half the time to remember the might of his army, and at this point, I didn't have much to lose. It was only a matter of time before my head rolled off the scaffolding and my body was tossed into the angry sea.

"Are you sure?" Kaztar asked, picking his head up and searching my face for any deception.

I blew out a breath, deciding it was time to share my worries. "I am certain. When do you think Kazimir is going to remember that Liliana refused to return with us? By all accounts, she was here when Ruslan, Izidora, and those other Dragons rescued Princess Gizela too. It's only a matter of time before my father, mother, and I end up like House Zadik." Voicing that statement settled a stone in my gut and made my blood run cold. Sure, I'd acknowledged it was a possibility in the back of my mind. But to speak the words aloud, to those who were closest to me, made them far too real.

Viktor visibly flinched beside me. Tibor and Renata were like parents to us, just as much as Kazimir, and losing them was fucking hard. Kazimir forcing us to watch their execution was what finally changed my mind about the whole situation. Thankfully, Viktor saw the truth about our friend after that, too. Or, former friend. He wasn't the same male we'd known even a year prior.

"We won't let that happen," Kaztar swore, but I shook my head.

Slicking both palms over my hair, I sighed. "You can't

promise that, not without risking House Rass." I tried and failed to keep the hopelessness from my tone.

"He's right," Domi pointed out, crossing her arms over her chest.

Viktor drummed his fingers against the table, thinking. "Kazimir won't notice their absence, not with how many new recruits are coming in from the countryside. Take them, stay safe, and if we need to flee, we will at least have a place to go."

"I can spare ten thousand. Can you house them?" I asked Domi.

She uncrossed her arms, rubbing her palms against her thighs before nodding. "I can find places for them."

"Good. You should leave under cover of darkness. The new moon is in a few days. That will be the best time to go," I said.

"We'll need to send some of those who can do the spell Desmond taught them," Kaztar insisted.

"That's how they'll have to leave regardless," I replied. "We can't have reports making their way to Kazimir about thousands of soldiers marching through the woods in the Night Realm away from the capital."

Desmond's magic trick was handy, I had to admit, even if the Mage was whispering maddening thoughts in Kazimir's ear. Ever since he'd arrived, Kazimir had gotten so much worse. It was as if the Fates planted him in our path, trying to steer the outcome they wanted rather than the one the council fought for.

Sighing, Domi finally acquiesced. "Fine. But I want to be kept in the loop. I won't stay there if I don't know what's going on."

Kaztar lifted her hands and kissed the backs of them tenderly. "I promise I will write to you daily, my love."

We lapsed into silence, so used to holding our tongues that

none of us knew what to say next, or even how to express the feelings we'd buried deep in the recesses of our minds.

Finally, I shattered it with a shocking statement. "We have to stop Kazimir. He can't be allowed to rule any longer."

Viktor nodded grimly. "He called me to the harem room earlier. He wants to march on the Iron Realm, through the Zherzha Pass. I say we let him."

"Fuck," I swore, locking my fingers on the back of my neck and looking up at the ceiling while I gathered myself. "We're all going to die there."

"Not if we encourage him to fight on the front lines. He's gone mad enough that with the right appeal, we can make it happen. Someone in the Iron Realm will finish him off," Viktor argued.

At least I wasn't the only one who'd thought through this plan.

"And you want to bet your life on it?" I snapped, unconvinced. There were causes worth sacrificing my life for – I'd once believed finding Izidora was one of them. This campaign against the other realms at the behest of Kazimir, though? Not how I wanted to die. Not something I wanted to die for.

"What other options do we have?" Viktor mumbled, turning his palms over and studying them. The dejection in his tone summarized exactly how I felt, and more stones settled in my gut as I looked at my last remaining friend.

He was right.

Our options were limited.

And in order to be free, we'd have to try to escape certain death.

———

A BITTER WIND ghosted over us, blowing our dark cloaks back as we slipped into the night. Domi yanked her hood higher, preventing the air from sweeping it over her head and revealing her long hair. Vaenor was nearly silent this late at night, and the lamps along the streets were dimly lit, allowing for the stars to breathe and be seen.

It was the perfect night for a surreptitious escape.

Our footsteps hardly made a sound against the cobbled paths, and the swish of our cloaks against them was quickly silenced as we buried ourselves deeper inside them. We ducked down a back alley littered with trash and discarded items, leaping over still puddles that reflected the stars above. Finally, after switchtracking several times to ensure we weren't followed, we found one of the many cracks in the city walls and shoved through.

No travelers crossed our paths as we entered the forest, though the fires burning beside the barracks beyond were like a beacon. The woods were even silent around us, providing us with much needed cover should someone in a position of power within the ranks discover four hooded figures creeping through the night, and decide to whisper of them to their king.

I'd done too good a job at convincing them of our cause, and their loyalty remained firmly with Kazimir.

The day before, I'd pulled aside a small, trustworthy unit, instructing them to be ready to depart at the late hour under the new moon. They were a haphazard mix of skilled warriors and village watch, most from House Rass's region toward the Crystal Realm. Those who left their families behind there were more than happy to accompany Domi to her home.

A dark figure strode toward us, picking his way through the trees with careful precision. Thousands of soldiers slipping away in the night would not go unnoticed, and noise was a sure way to draw attention in our direction. In the day, their absence could be easily explained away.

We stopped short of each other, slipping off our hoods to

reveal our identities. Noiselessly, the captain jerked his head, indicating the direction in which Domi's guards waited. We followed him a short distance, where spread through the trees, groups of leather-clad soldiers clutched their meager possessions and waited for their comrades to spirit them away in the night.

Viktor and I hung back, speaking in low voices with the captain while Domi and Kaztar said their goodbyes. A sniffle caught my attention, then a long, pained sigh. Out of the corner of my eye, I watched them embrace passionately, and then Domi backed away, her hand lingering in Kaztar's until it was no longer possible for them to stay connected.

With a sharp salute, the captain left us, herding Domi toward a group of fierce-looking males. Her eyes never left Kaztar, even as they winked out of sight.

The High Lord threw up his hood, his head hanging as we began the trek back to Este Castle.

Probably barely seeing the ground beneath his feet.

His love for Domi was admirable, and as much as I appreciated that, the bachelor life was for me.

But what of Liliana?

My sister and Endre had grown close in their time together as we traversed Északi, and now, they were reunited in the Iron Realm.

Would my friend marry her? Would she even want that? Would I ever see her again?

Those were the thoughts that plagued my mind as we crept down the streets of Vaenor. My mother and father were absolutely distraught, to this day, over her year-long absence.

At least I still had my father.

Glancing sidelong at Viktor, pity rose from within me. We'd lost his father on the battlefield in the Crystal Realm, a freak accident that had hardened him in his duty to take down the Északi Empire.

But now?

We were both more than ready to betray our lifelong friend, the one we'd spent countless nights just like these with, out in the open, under the stars, huddled around a fire to keep warm as we searched for Izidora. That male was long gone, and sometimes I wondered if I ever really knew him in the first place.

Was it the binding magic that drove him into madness?

Or was the obsession with Izidora always there, and we'd swept it aside because of our constant duty?

I'd never have answers to these questions, and with a heavy sigh, I accepted that there was nothing I could have done in the past to change the present. But the future? That I still had control over.

The three of us parted ways before we reached the castle, not wanting to be seen together as we re-entered. A little-known servant's entrance provided me entry, and I hoped I'd remained unseen. When the High House Wing came into view, I breathed a sigh of relief.

My mother and father didn't even wake during my absence, and I thanked the Goddess for her assistance as I crawled back into my lukewarm bed. Tucking my hands beneath my head, I stared up at the ceiling, mind swirling with possibilities and plans to do what had to be done, until finally, my eyes grew heavy and I could keep them open no longer. And when I slept, I dreamed of my sister and a life where she was safe and happy.

44

IZIDORA

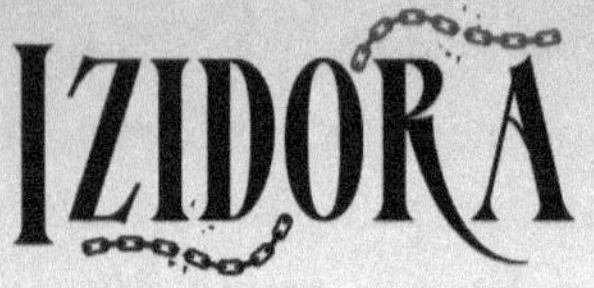

The bitter cold of the depths of winter in the Iron Realm drove me and Zuriel to train indoors, in the arena beneath Ryza Citadel. The familiar walls greeted us as we lit the tall chandeliers where my cousin had first taught me to fly. We faced each other, magic swirling around our swords. It had been too long since I'd completely depleted myself, and I itched for a serious spar.

"You're not going to read my mind to defeat me, are you, cousin?" I teased, stepping cautiously to the side and trying to bait him into striking.

A sly grin crinkled the corners of his icy blue eyes. "Where would the fun be in that?"

"Winning?" I quipped, feinting a strike and flinging magic from the end of my blade.

With a grace and ease I could only dream of, he sidestepped the ball of white energy and fired back with one of his own. It dissipated over my shield like smoke in the wind, and I used the opportunity to ready my swords for a strike. Lunging forward, I popped the protective bubble of my own making, only to meet air when I swung.

Snapping my head up, I barely managed to roll and dodge Zuriel as he dropped down from above. "You have more than magic and swords at your disposal, Izidora. Use them."

Calling on my wings, I tucked them tight against my back so they wouldn't interfere or leave me vulnerable while still getting accustomed to fighting with their weight. We ducked, dodged, and struck out at one another in a flurry of activity before I disengaged, panting.

Pretending I was studying him for an opening, I snaked my magic toward Zuriel's mind, slipping inside it and pushing heavy, sluggish emotions on him. He blinked slowly, his movements growing lazy, before he snapped back to awareness and shoved me from his mind.

We'd practiced the magic often enough since I'd awoken that it was as easy as breathing, and the signals that I was delving through his mind were easily detected. But secretly besting him through my empath magic wasn't my intention.

Having him mentally off-balance allowed me to strike with less chance that I'd get caught with an errant blow as I tried to close the distance between us. A combination Ruslan had taught me recently came to mind first, and as Zuriel offered up the intended slash, I slipped under it, then pivoted on the ball of my foot and landed a hard kick across his abdomen.

He grinned, whipping to the side and forcing me backward with a series of rapid, light strikes. I tried to hold my ground, but his momentum carried him forward, and my hurried parries did nothing. Sucking in a breath, I cleared my mind and forced a wall of white magic outward, the impact stopping his advance and allowing me to dance away and regroup.

"Very good," he praised, rolling his shoulders and lifting his sword.

His next attack was so fast I nearly missed it, and on pure instinct I shot into the air, tucking my legs and allowing him to pass beneath me. I landed heavily, bracing myself against the mat before throwing another blast in his direction, trying to knock him to the side. He blocked it, sending the magic right back to me. A ring of white fire burst around me, protecting me from further attack while I righted myself.

Panting, I lifted my swords, the gems encrusted in the hilt glittering beneath the thousand tiny lights overhead. "Who would guess that only a few months ago I could barely walk the length of this room?"

Zuriel shrugged, holding a teasing smile to his lips. "You've worked hard to recover. You've never let anything stop you, cousin. I didn't expect you to stay weak for long."

A laugh slipped out and I found myself grinning widely. Warmth blossomed in my chest as I realized once again I'd proven to myself and others that I was not a victim of my circumstances, and I would do whatever it took to overcome them. "I am a survivor. Always have been, always will be. People can underestimate the beautiful bloom, but my thorns are sharp and I have no qualms about stabbing people with them."

As if to prove my point, I danced around Zuriel, throwing my sword out lazily as a distraction before following it up with a kick to his calf. The Angel returned one to my ribs, knocking me off balance, and I stumbled backward, scrambling to lift my sword. But Zuriel was fast and had thousands of years of fighting experience, and it wasn't long before my back was against the wall and the tip of his sword pointed at my throat.

"I yield," I said, but there was no bitterness to my tone. I couldn't expect to truly win against such a skilled fighter when I had scarcely a year of training on my own. Everything Zuriel did was meticulously planned, and what he allowed me to do was a test of how I would react to whatever Kazimir decided to throw my way. My deepest held desire was to slice into Kazimir's skin and watch his lifeblood coat my blade, and Zuriel knew that as well as anyone, if not more.

He relaxed his arm, then tossed his sword onto the mat some feet away. "I want to work on one other thing with you." He gestured for me to follow him.

"Okay," I responded, placing my swords beside his and walking to the center.

Zuriel's white feathered wings flared wide and lifted him off the ground. He hovered in the air above me, and I had to crane my neck to look up at him. "Use your magic to pull me from the sky," he instructed, inching higher.

I quirked a brow, then tapped into the crystal wrapped in white fire and moonlight, allowing the crystal to flare with blackest of black colors – a necessary step to controlling another's movements. Not one that I hesitated to do any longer. The heady thrill of the dark power thrummed in my veins, and I closed my eyes momentarily, savoring it, surrendering to its call.

Then, I snapped my eyes open, a wicked smile spreading across my face. I spilled more blackness into the crystal, then attacked. Willing Zuriel to return to the earth by imagining a tether around his ankles, sweat rolled down my temples. He only continued to rise. I pushed more magic into my will, gritting my teeth. His ascent slowed, then ground to a halt. But his feet remained firmly in the air.

"Why isn't it working?" I huffed, dropping my hold and using my sleeve to wipe at my face.

"Because I am resisting you. Kazimir's binding magic might see you coming and fight with yours, like it did before. You need to be prepared for that." Zuriel flapped once, twice, sending a breeze across my heated face.

"Right. I'll try again," I said, steeling my spine and readying for another attack. Images of Kazimir choking me in the stables of Ryza flitted through my mind.

If I beat him then, I can beat him again.

I tried not to let my mind wander to our last encounter, where I'd failed to save myself.

Never again.

That was why I called on the darkness again, willingly entering it and offering it loving caresses. Sucking in a breath, I released the air slowly, focusing on my magic. More dark emotions rose, until I brimmed with fury, and rage, so raw and powerful that I thought I might explode if I didn't release them.

My attention snapped to Zuriel, and I unleashed everything I'd stored at him, willing him to crash into the ground. He dipped, nearly halfway, before righting himself. "Better. Add more fuel to your power."

I allowed my hatred of Kazimir to fill me, the heat starting in my toes and traveling to the top of my head. My muscles tensed as they flooded with adrenaline, and I forced myself to focus on channeling that into what I wanted my magic to do. With a scream, I threw everything at the Angel, and he plummeted to the soft mats, landing with an echoing smack.

He dusted himself off, then leveled a serious gaze on me. "Remember what you did just then. Keep it close for the future. You will need it," he said cryptically, and once again, I felt like he knew something I did not.

With his mind reading abilities, I was certain he knew *many* things no one else did.

I can't believe he kept this a secret for so long...

"I think that's enough for today," he stated, interrupting my thoughts.

I kicked myself as I remembered Ruslan reminding me to come to the war council meeting today. "Yeah, we've got to get to the war room," I commented, retrieving my swords and sheathing them in their pretty scabbards.

We made the trek up the spiraling stairs, away from Rares's

chaotic workshop that bustled with Félvér day and night as they assisted in making potions or tending to the herbs needed to make them. The halls of Ryza were busier than usual with the cold driving more indoors, but we managed to arrive at the new war room just in time for the meeting.

Zuriel and I slipped inside, joining Ruslan, Drazen, Liliana, and the others around the massive table covered in maps and battle plans. A few more trickled in behind us, and I took my place at Ruslan's side. Once everyone was gathered, he began.

"We were surprised and out-strategized before. Let's make sure that doesn't happen again. While I don't think the Night Fae will move until winter is over, we can't be certain. The time to plan is now."

"How are we supposed to plan when Kazimir is insane?" Drazen grumbled, surveying a map of the Night Realm.

"His madness does present a problem. It makes him unpredictable," Ruslan commented.

"But he has Viktor to help with his military strategy," Liliana piped up. "He's the best strategist the Night Realm has ever seen, and Kazimir knows that – trusts him with that. He's unlikely to go against what Viktor says."

Ruslan turned his attention to my best friend. "And what would Viktor do?"

Endre's input would have been valuable to this question.

But Ruslan still didn't trust him – rightfully so.

Liliana's brows dipped as she thought. "Trying to enter the Iron Realm directly is a mistake – everyone knows that. We have the advantage here, with the high peaks, especially with the threat of avalanches as the snow falls thicker every day." She paused, running her fingers absently over the paper in front of her. "Viktor would either wait out the winter or return to the Day Realm for a second assault. Try to draw us out because they cannot penetrate the Iron Realm."

"So you think we should send reinforcements to the Day Realm?" Drazen asked her.

Zuriel interrupted before Liliana could reply. "What about how they moved away so quickly during the last battle? Desmond could not have done that alone."

"Zuriel has a point," Rares said from somewhere I couldn't see. I hadn't realized the old Mage had even entered the room. "Desmond always thought that Mage magic wasn't tied to blood since it is potions and spoken spells. But I didn't have the time to study it with my other priorities. He must have figured out a way to teach the Night Fae."

A threatening rumble reverberated in the room as Ruslan braced his hands on the table and glared at his Mage. "Do you mean to tell me that all this time, we had another option than the tunnels or relying on the handful of Mage Félvér to move about quickly?"

"Well, technically it's possible, yes. Magic is everywhere in this world, though each magical race can only pull on certain strings of it," Rares's voice grew small as Ruslan's commanding presence expanded. Pressing my lips together, I smothered a smirk as the old Mage quaked beneath my mate's wrath.

"You've finished giving the permanent ability to shift to those who need it?" Ruslan questioned, and Rares nodded. "Good. This is your new priority. If you can't figure out how to contain Kazimir's binding magic, figure out how to get my people the fuck away from him."

The room was poised with tension on the verge of breaking, so I sent soothing emotions in all directions, doing my part in shifting the conversation back to more productive topics.

"So, when and where should we station our troops?" I asked.

"If we're going off Viktor's strategy, the Day Realm," Liliana declared, tapping the map with her finger.

"And why aren't we going on the offensive?" Drazen challenged. "We could use the advantage of the Iron Realm – the impenetrable mountains – to enter the Night Realm and slaughter them during the winter when they won't expect us to come."

"If Desmond has taught them how to move through space, what's to stop them from bypassing them altogether?" Zuriel added.

Fuck, he had a point.

My heart beat a staccato rhythm, breath catching in my chest at the idea of Kazimir popping into existence in front of me when I least expected it.

"I won't let that happen to you," Ruslan spoke mind-to-mind.

"But what if it does?"

Panic clawed up my throat as unbidden images of that possibility played out in my head.

Ruslan knew better than to placate me. *"Then we will fight him off. You are powerful enough to destroy him with a single thought. Just because he caught you off guard last time doesn't mean he will again. You've been training so hard, and I have no doubt that you will end his miserable existence the next time we meet him on the battlefield."*

Side arguments had broken out while we conversed mentally, and Ruslan growled a sharp command to silence the room. "The forces will remain in the Iron Realm until we know what the Night Fae's next move will be. Going on the offensive could lead us right into a trap. It's better to be ready to react than to make the wrong move."

"But that's what happened last time, and we were ambushed," Drazen argued, looking to his commanders for support. They nodded their agreement.

I tuned out the volley of new arguments, not knowing enough about battle tactics or strategy to add much else. These males were all educated in the art of war, though only Zuriel,

Xorrek, and Gozzak had real battle experience. Liliana remained intently focused, and I wondered where she had left Endre. Ruslan had tasked her with ensuring Endre remained within the lines Ruslan had carved with his acceptance into the Iron Realm. Catching her eye, I jerked my thumb over my shoulder, hoping she understood I wanted to talk when the council concluded. She nodded, then returned her attention to a heated argument between Drazen, Zuriel, and Ruslan.

"… and spies will hopefully give us more insight into their plans," Drazen finished.

"Fine," Ruslan agreed. "Rares, while you're figuring out how to allow non-Mages to use spells to move, give some thought to how our spies can communicate more effectively, like we do with Katrina now."

"Yes, My Emperor," he responded immediately, admonished and ego bruised.

He probably didn't like that Desmond figured out something instead of him.

After an update on our numbers and training, we were dismissed, some choosing to linger in smaller groups to discuss specifics, while others hurried from the room, on to their next task. I hooked my arm through Liliana's and we entered the quieter halls of the citadel. I waved at Ruslan over my shoulder, letting him know we'd talk later.

"Where is Endre?" I asked my friend as we strolled toward the tower that held our apartments.

"In my room," she grumbled, glancing over her shoulder to see if Drazen was following. He and Ruslan watched us disappear into the spiral stairwell, and our bond saddened with the distance. Once we were out of earshot of the Dragons, she whispered, "I haven't gotten off since we've been back. I'm so horny I could die."

I snorted a laugh, squeezing her arm in reassurance. "You won't die from lack of sex. What's stopping you?"

"Babysitting Endre. How am I supposed to sneak off with Drazen if I have to constantly keep an eye on him?"

"Don't you want Endre?" I questioned.

"It's complicated. As much as he said on the battlefield, my heart still hurts. I don't want this to be some sort of trick, you know? We fuck, I say something I shouldn't, he runs back to Kazimir."

Using my empath magic, I felt the depth of her confusion, mistrust, and hurt. But mixed in with it was love and lust, and with the mix of emotions swirling inside her, I couldn't blame her for keeping both males at arm's length.

"Ruslan doesn't trust him either."

"I know. Which only makes me feel guilty about not trusting him too. I mean, I do to some extent. I just can't let myself be vulnerable like that with him. Not now." Her words faded from existence, leaving the stairwell silent except for the light pad of our feet against the stone.

I understood her sentiment. Not when war was out there and there was no certainty of who would be left standing at the end of it.

We reached the landing that held our apartments, and I guided her into the one Ruslan and I kept at the citadel. The sentries nodded to us as we slipped past, and a fire was already roaring in the hearth.

Snagging my favorite blanket from the pile beside the fire, I wrapped it around myself and settled on the closest couch, snuggling into its warmth. I leaned my temple against the back of it, waiting for Liliana to settle across from me.

"I know I said this last year, but we need to escape this dreadful cold and spend time on the beaches of the Day Realm,"

Liliana laughed, tucking her feet up under her after kicking off her boots.

"If we win this war, next year we will," I promised, grinning widely. I wanted to explore the far flung parts of the continent more than anything, but other priorities pressed in from all sides, nearly making me explode with anxiety.

Not wanting to allow Liliana to change the subject from what I knew she really needed to talk about, I pressed on from my earlier line of questioning. "What do you want from them?"

Liliana tipped her head to the side, mirroring my position. "I've said this a dozen times, but I want to be chosen. For me. Because they see who I am deep down and love every bit of me, like Ruslan does for you. But," she released a heavy sigh, "I *also* want a male that can force me to submit to them. I'm strong, I'm a fighter, and I'm wild. I don't want someone to tame me. I want them to show me they're powerful enough for me to trust they'll take care of me."

"That makes sense," I reassured her. "Why not tell both of them that?"

She shrugged beneath her blanket. "Because I just want them to do it, you know?"

"If I've learned anything since being out of chains, it's that I have to say exactly what I want and how I feel if I want my needs met. Ruslan does a good job of anticipating them now that we're bonded and he knows me, but unless you suddenly become mated to one of them, you're going to have to use your words." I sneaked a foot out from beneath the blanket and nudged her leg playfully.

Liliana grinned in response. "Well when you put it that way, it seems so easy."

"When it comes to emotions, it's always easier said than done. Trust me, I'm an empath," I snickered.

She rolled her eyes in response. "Okay, fine. I'll talk to them. But I'm going to practice on you a few times first."

Clearing my throat, I deepened my voice to mimic those of the males. "Oh, Liliana, all I want to do is force you to your knees and make you suck my cock." I barely finished the words before we both doubled over in hysterics.

My abdomen was sore by the time I came up gasping for air, tears blurring the form of my friend across from me. We both swiped at our eyes, coming down from the moment.

"Fuck, I needed a laugh like that," she said.

"Me too. It's been too tense and too stressful around here." I scooted across the couch and hugged her tightly, swaying as she wrapped her arms around me in return.

"But everything will be okay, in the end." She gave me a tight squeeze and broke our embrace.

"In the end," I sighed, returning to my corner and wrapping the fur tightly around my shoulders. The logs in the fire popped and crackled as a large one burned out completely, sending a hint of smoke into the air.

With how fickle the Fates and the Goddess were, I sincerely hoped it wasn't an omen of what was to come. Liliana and I sat in silence, staring at it, until she finally decided she couldn't wait any longer to return to Endre. I bid her goodbye, but remained wrapped up in my thoughts, wondering when and how this war would end.

Would the pain all be worth it in the end?

45

LILIANA

Drazen and Endre sat awkwardly on the couch across from me. Since we'd returned to the Iron Realm, I'd avoided both of them like the plague, but I couldn't avoid them any longer, not when Drazen's expression grew guarded every time our gazes collided and Endre followed me like a lost puppy around the citadel.

To be fair, Ruslan insisted that I constantly watch Endre since he didn't trust the male – which made avoiding this conversation very difficult.

But Izidora was right, and I really needed to have it with them.

Sighing, I flicked my hair over my shoulder and rounded the chair to sit. First, I crossed my legs, then thinking better of it, uncrossed them. Blue and green eyes studied me while I tried and failed to get comfortable. Eventually, I gave up and blurted out my confession. "I've been sleeping with Drazen, and I don't want to stop."

Endre looked stricken, and he attempted to mask his face but failed.

"But," I held up a hand to stop him from spiraling, "I don't want to *only* sleep with Drazen."

The half-Dragon's mouth twitched before his usual impassivity returned.

Swallowing, I did as my best friend suggested and asked for what I wanted. "I want you both to dominate me. Share me. Make me your whore."

My heart pounded as I made my request, hoping they'd say yes. As much as I hadn't wanted to grow fond of Drazen, our time together had turned into more than just sex. If I was being honest with myself, the Iron Realm felt more like home than the Night Realm ever had. I loved the Iron Realm's carefree sexuality, and it wasn't something I wanted to give up, even if it wasn't the norm in the Night Realm.

During Béke, Endre had shared me with others at Steel, though he wasn't ecstatic about it at first. But when he saw how much pleasure the attention brought me, he was all for it. Endre was the type of male who put my happiness above his own, and until he'd left with Kazimir, I thought we might truly be something. That choice shattered my heart in a way that Drazen had unwittingly put back together, and holding Endre at arm's length since we'd been reunited was my way of coping with the reopening of that wound.

It was Drazen who spoke first, his ocean blue eyes glittering with amusement. "I think our little vixen needs more than one male to tame her."

Endre looked between the two of us, a war of emotions playing out over his face. I wrung my hands nervously, aching for the response I so desperately craved.

"I should have chosen you before. I won't make that mistake twice," Endre finally said, his voice strong and filled with conviction. His peridot eyes locked with my blurring ones, and I saw the truth of his words through those windows into his soul.

He was choosing me. They both were.

"How is this going to work?" he asked, glancing between Drazen and me.

The worst part over, I rose, closing the distance between them. I held out a hand to each one, and they took them. "Well... we can make ground rules. Like, we can only play when we're all here, or we all keep separate rooms."

"I'm vetoing the first one," Drazen commented, stroking his thumb across my knuckles.

"Agreed," Endre said, using his free hand to brush his hair away from his eyes. "No offense, Drazen, but I'm not into males."

"None taken," he responded with a wry grin. "I'm not either." He stood, towering over me and forcing me to crane my neck back to look at him. "But I do want to make our little vixen scream our names as she comes around both of our cocks tonight."

Endre rose to Drazen's challenge, and the two males loomed over me, sporting sultry, sinister grins. "We can share my bed tonight," I said breathlessly as Endre pulled me forward and Drazen crowded me from behind.

My nipples hardened against the scraps of lace that covered them, and through my thin tunic, they brushed against Endre's muscular chest. Drazen's hands came to my shoulders, sweeping my hair over one and baring the crook of my neck. His fingers trailed against my exposed skin, drawing a shiver from deep within me. My thighs clenched involuntarily as Endre lifted the hem of my shirt and brushed his hands across my bare belly. A low moan escaped me as they drifted toward the laces of my pants.

"Endre, relieve her of her shirt," Drazen ordered, stepping back and allowing Endre to strip me.

With the slowness of a male savoring his last meal, Endre's hands skimmed beneath my shirt, raising the fabric inch by tantalizing inch. I lifted my arms overhead, allowing him to pull it off, and he discarded it without taking his hungry eyes off me. My chest rose and fell rapidly, and my skin was alight under the heat of his gaze.

Endre cupped my covered breasts, lifting them and squeezing them roughly before hooking his fingers beneath the lace and tugging. He only pulled it enough to reveal my hardened nipples, and I sucked in a sharp breath as he pinched each one in turn. Drazen's hands returned to my back, and the males worked the delicate scraps over my head, leaving my torso bare for them.

Even the roaring fire in the hearth couldn't stop the shiver that shook my spine.

"So beautiful," Endre murmured, his hands returning to lift my heavy breasts, massaging them with his rough, calloused hands.

Behind me, Drazen bent his head, hot breath ghosting across my skin. "On your knees," he commanded in my ear, sending another wave of tingles down my back. Hands on my shoulders, he guided me to the thick fur rug beneath our feet before wrapping my hair around his fist. "Now, I want you to take out Endre's cock and get it nice and hard."

He allowed me enough movement to lift my head up, and Endre blazed with desire, the firelight reflected in his darkened eyes. Obediently, I reached out, skimming my hands over his covered abdomen before my fingers caught on the fastenings of his pants. He was already erect, and when I finally worked his pants lower, his cock sprang free, dripping for my touch.

With a firm hand, Drazen guided me forward, and I parted my lips, sucking Endre into my mouth. He hardened further as Drazen kept pushing my head forward until my nose touched Endre's belly. Drazen held me there as I struggled to breathe, and Endre groaned, low and longing in his throat. Tears pricked my eyes moments before Drazen guided my head back, the sharp tug on my scalp delivering an extra measure of pain.

Gasping, I released him, a string of spit still connecting us. "Good girl," Drazen praised, releasing his grip on my hair. "Now suck him deep into your pretty throat. Show him how much you missed him."

My core throbbed at his praise and his next command. Through dark lashes, I looked up at the male I had ached for and watched as his eyes rolled to the back of his head as I sucked him down. I fisted his base, using tongue and hand to pleasure him. His attention never left me, a riot of emotion flowing through him as I perched on my knees with his dick in my mouth.

He stroked the side of my face as I opened my throat for him. "Such a good little whore." Sweet, sensitive Endre had a secret side filled with filthy words and commands that made me want to balk and obey simultaneously. The first time he'd uttered those words to me, I'd almost orgasmed on the spot. Hearing them again made me want – need – to be touched, because if I didn't have their hands on me soon, I would combust.

I made an indiscriminate, needy noise around him, earning a shove on my head from Drazen. "You'll take him until we say otherwise, and only then will we give you pleasure."

Whimpering, I continued to suck, the salty taste of Endre filling my mouth. He stroked my face, whispering praise, and with each subsequent one, I wanted to work him faster, harder. I was desperate for more, skin on fire with the need to be touched. My focus was wholly on Endre and getting him off, so much so that I didn't realize Drazen had stripped behind me.

His hardness dug into my back as he crowded me, joining me on the floor. His big thighs wrapped around mine, while his arm snaked around my waist, pinning me in place. With his free hand, he traced a path around my navel, finally dipping it toward the waistband of my pants. "Did I say you could stop?" he growled in my ear, and enough awareness returned to me that I recognized my lips had stilled around Endre's cock. "I can smell how aroused you are, little vixen."

Endre ceased his gentle movements against my face and gave it a sharp slap. Then he flexed his hips, burying himself deeper. "You heard Drazen. Keep going."

Every nerve was alight as I licked the underside of his shaft. Despite the three of us being alone, without an audience, I'd never had hotter sex in my life. Together, these males were giving me every bit of domination I desired, and with the way wetness gushed down my thighs, I knew I was going to come quickly when they finally touched me.

If this was considered inappropriate in the Night Realm, then those prudes had no idea what they were missing.

Drazen's hand forced its way into the tight fabric of my pants, and when his fingers brushed my clit, I nearly cried with relief. The noise I made around Endre's cock had him swearing, and his hand went from my face to the back of my head, controlling my movements. "You're going to swallow every drop of me," he said, his eyes blazing with lust. Through blurred vision, I nodded around him, and that earned a stroke along my slit from Drazen.

I moaned again, and Endre's cock thickened and throbbed in my mouth, letting me know he was close. Drazen slipped a finger inside, groaning himself. "You're so wet already, Liliana. Does getting called filthy names and forced on your knees turn you on?"

I couldn't respond, not when Endre controlled the movements of my head and stole my breath as he forced my nose to his belly. Drazen's finger dipped in and out of my core and my attention was torn between my pleasure and Endre's. Flaring my nostrils, I managed a sip of air moments before Endre groaned, "I'm going to come."

Hot spurts of liquid shot down my throat, and Drazen curled his finger against my inner walls while the heel of his hand ground into my clit, drawing a moan from me as I swallowed.

"That's our good girl," Drazen praised, slipping a second finger in.

Finally, I opened my mouth, jaw aching as Endre slipped out. I panted, the room spinning as Drazen curled his fingers inside me and pressed down on that delicious spot. Quickly, Endre stripped out of his clothes, then joined us on the fur, his hands tracing swirls in my skin and over my breasts and nipples. Hooking his arms beneath my armpits, he forced me to my feet, knees aching in protest. Drazen wasted no time in stripping my pants off and tossing them to the side.

The three of us were all naked, and I didn't even have a chance to admire their muscular forms before Endre threw me over his shoulder and marched me to my bedroom. With delicious power, he tossed me on the bed, causing it to bounce, before he and Drazen forced it to dip with their weight.

Perched on my elbows, I raked my gaze over the bodies of the males before me. Drazen was massive, with bulky muscle and a heavy cock to match. His body was a testament to his strength, and the tattoos marking his arms gave him a dangerous vibe. Endre, on the other hand, was leaner, but by no means less muscular, with broad shoulders and a trim waist that dipped straight toward his still-hard dick. Only one tattoo marked his chest, right over his heart – his family's emblem, a wolf howling at the moon.

"What do you think, Endre? Does she deserve to come?" Drazen asked as if I weren't even in the room.

"I definitely do," I retorted, my legs dropping open invitingly.

Drazen smacked my center, drawing a gasp from me. "Little vixens don't get to decide when their pleasure is delivered. They have to earn it by being good."

Playing along, Endre tsked. "I think she needs another lesson first. Get on your hands and knees."

Pouting, I did as I was told, flipping over. Endre gripped my jaw, forcing my mouth to open. "No." That one word, said with so much force, made my center *weep* with pleasure. "Crawl to Drazen," he commanded.

The half-Dragon boasted a smirk as I slinked toward him. When I was close enough, he guided my lips over to the head of his dick. The bed moaned as Endre worked his way behind me, smacking my ass hard when he rounded my backside. I yelped, then took Drazen in my mouth, hoping that by being obedient, Endre would swirl his fingers around my clit.

I was rewarded when Drazen groaned.

"That's it, Liliana, take all of him. I know your jaw is nice and loose now," Endre said, dipping a finger in before removing it completely. I whimpered, working Drazen faster in hopes Endre would touch me again.

"I think we should fill her belly and her pussy with our cum. Don't you, Endre?" Drazen asked, ignoring me while I sucked on him like my pleasure depended on it – because it did.

Endre's fingers trailed lazily up and down my slit, avoiding the bundle of nerves at the apex of my thighs. Sweat started to form along my spine, and drool dripped from the corners of my mouth as I struggled to keep Drazen in it.

"I think so. Has she got you hard enough yet?" Endre answered, pausing mid-stroke and hovering a breath from my clit.

A moan of protest vibrated from my throat, and Endre pinched it between his fingers, causing me to cry out and suck

Drazen deeper into my throat. "Fuck," he swore, his gaze locked on where he disappeared into my mouth. "Definitely."

Endre grabbed me by the hips and dragged me off Drazen, then flipped me on my back so my legs were spread and waiting for the Dragon. Drazen fisted his cock, then crawled toward me, lining his shaft with my entrance. The tip hovered there, swiping through my wetness and circling over my clit. "Drazen, please," I breathed, rolling my hips forward in an attempt to get more.

"Beg him more," Endre instructed, slapping my breast.

"Please, I need you inside me. I need you to make me come," I begged, and Drazen stilled at my entrance, cocking his head to the side with a sly grin.

"Mmm, little vixen, I love to hear you desperate for it. Tell me how bad you want my big dick."

"So, so bad. Please give it to me. Having it in my mouth wasn't enough." My chest rose and fell rapidly, heart racing wildly as Drazen pushed against me.

He was so thick, I cried out when he entered, and without waiting for me to adjust to his size, he seated himself fully. "Fuck, your cunt feels even better than your mouth." He began to move, sliding against my walls and stretching me in the most delicious way. A few strands of black hair escaped their tie, falling in his face and sticking to it as he sweated along with Endre and me.

"You take him so well, Liliana. Look at him sliding in and out of you," Endre said, wedging his body beneath mine and forcing me to look down at where Drazen and I connected. He deepened that angle, and I moaned, feeling even fuller. Endre kneaded my breasts, pinching both nipples between his fingers at the same time and sending zaps of pain straight to my core.

"I spilled down your throat, and Drazen is going to fill that sweet pussy of yours with his cum. Do you want that?" Endre asked, his voice deepening with lust.

"Yes," I whimpered, clenching around Drazen and drawing a curse from him. Endre hefted me higher, banding an arm around my waist to support me while his other hand found my clit and began circling it.

He brought his fingers to my lips, forcing them into my mouth. "Suck on them. Get them nice and wet for me so we can make you come for us."

I did, taking them deep and gagging while I locked eyes with Drazen. His nostrils flared, jaw flexing at the sight. Endre returned his sopping fingers to my core, and I allowed my head to drop back as he pressed in just the right way to set my legs trembling. Drazen grabbed my hips and hoisted them, and I was almost suspended between them, Drazen fucking me with his length and Endre's fingers working me into a frenzy.

"Oh, fuck, please," I started to babble, words incoherent as they drove me deeper and deeper into pleasure.

"She's getting close," Drazen noted, a hint of strain to his voice.

My pussy *throbbed* as the two males hit the right rhythm. "Don't stop, please, don't stop."

"We won't, not until you come for us," Endre swore, his erection digging into my back again.

"Oh Goddess, I'm–" My words were cut off as my orgasm tore through me, whole body jerking but trapped between them.

"Yes, that's it, take me, little vixen," Drazen growled, pumping his hips faster. Endre dropped his hand away, allowing Drazen to deepen the angle and drag out my release. Our skin slapped together, filling the room along with my cries until all the light faded from my vision and Drazen's sex-touseled hair filled it. With a groan, he finished too, dick twitching inside me and spilling his cum, just like they promised.

Breathless, the three of us lay there, intertwined and sweating. Eventually, Drazen pulled out of me, and Endre jogged to the bathroom to fetch towels to clean ourselves with. In the middle of my bed, I nestled between them, heartbeat steadily slowing, though my pussy was not at all ready to slow down, not with the two naked, muscular males on either side of me.

"So will we all sleep here?" I asked, not wanting the moment to end.

"Yes," Drazen and Endre said simultaneously, and I pressed my lips together to suppress a giggle.

"Thank the Goddess. I'm too tired to move," I sighed. Drazen rolled me onto my side, kissing me deeply, before Endre did the same, twisting me to face him and hooking my leg over his hip. His hardness dug into my stomach, and my core weeped at the feeling.

Drazen closed in behind me until I was sandwiched between them. "Are you sure about that? We could take you like this, right here." A spitting sound preceded the brushing of his fingers against my ass.

I whimpered. "I might have energy for more."

Endre gripped himself and notched his head at my entrance. "You are our little whore. You will take both our dicks at the same time because we told you to, not because you want to."

Fuck me, that mouth.

Without waiting, he slid inside, groaning as he was enveloped in my heat. "I missed this feeling, being buried inside you."

"She feels good, doesn't she," Drazen agreed, swiping from the wetness gushing out of me and adding it to the mix at my asshole. His finger slipped in with ease, my ass already stretched out from our more recent encounters. I moaned, head dropping back to Drazen's broad chest. His teeth dug into my shoulder, and not to be left out, Endre wrapped his fingers around my neck and kissed me. Our tongues danced and twined while Drazen worked another finger in, then a third, until I was panting and writhing against his hand and Endre's length.

"Relax," Drazen whispered in my ear, tongue tracing a path down to my neck. His hardness nudged against me, and Endre released my mouth, allowing me to breathe. Drazen pushed in slowly, giving me time to adjust this time, and *fuck*, I'd never feel so much pleasure at once. Endre hiked my leg higher, opening me more for Drazen, and once he was moving comfortably, Drazen's hands dug into my hips to steady me.

Endre kissed me again, and the two males took turns pumping in and out, fucking me together. My eyes rolled back in my head and I moaned, breaking away from Endre to relish the pure pleasure the two of them delivered. They might have been using me as their little whore, but I was *so fucking okay* with it.

Their paces quickened, and I whimpered, "Oh my Goddess."

My clit throbbed with the need to be touched, and somehow, I worked a hand between Endre and me to find it. The moment I brushed the pad of my finger across it, my inner muscles clenched. Every nerve in my body vibrated with pleasure, lightning bolts shooting through me until there was nothing but the feeling of the males pressed against me and inside me. "Oh, fuck, Endre, Drazen," I swore, the world spinning around me.

"Are you going to come for us like a good little whore?" Drazen growled, nipping my shoulder again.

"Yes," I panted, fingers working furiously as I chased my release.

"Tell me what you are," he commanded.

I gasped, hips jerking. "Your good little whore."

"And do you like being filled with two cocks?" Endre said, a hand gripping my face and forcing my eyes back open.

"Yes, so very much." I was sinking into pleasure so deep, I wasn't sure I'd ever be able to come up for air.

"Thank us for giving you our cocks," Drazen ordered, and I knew I was nearing the bottom.

"Thank you for–" A cry ripped from my throat, and pleasure crashed through me like a tidal wave, sweeping away all reason, all time, all thought.

"That's it, come for us," Endre groaned, his dick pulsing inside me. Drazen's did too, and from the sheer force of my own orgasm, I had them drowning in pleasure with me.

"Fuck, little vixen," Drazen swore at the same time as Endre said, "Fuck, Liliana."

We came together, shaking and moaning until every last drop was wrung from each of us. Throbbing was the only sensation I could comprehend for several minutes. When awareness crept back in, my chest was still heaving from the force of my orgasm. "That was…" I trailed off, unable to form words.

"Incredible?" I pictured the smug expression Drazen wore perfectly just from the tone of his voice.

"Yeah," I breathed, and he backed out of me, allowing me to flop on my back.

Endre exited me too, reaching over the side of the bed for the towels on the floor. "Good thing these are already here."

He tossed one at Drazen, then knelt between my legs with another, cleaning me thoroughly. Both of them kissed me in turn again, though this time, there was no lingering want. My eyes were heavy, and I allowed the males to shift me around until they got comfortable and covered us with the blankets. With a sigh, I turned on my side, curling into a ball with my back touching Drazen and a hand draped across Endre's chest.

A heartbeat moment later, I drifted off to sleep with a soft smile tugging up the corners of my lips.

46

RUSLAN

Drazen and I braved the blistering cold to survey the day's training. It was as if the Fates decided to fuck with us this winter, bringing in bitter winds from the mountains and snow that needed to constantly be cleared. Fires were fueled by magic day and night to warm the area, and as we passed one, a blissful moment banished the misery of the weather. Thankfully, tents had been converted into stone buildings before the harsh season set in, though they were crude and lacked the normal comforts of a true home. They stretched all the way to the base of the mountains in the distance, housing the tens of thousands brought together to defend the Iron Realm

Smoke curled from chimneys, the sign that our army was settled in for the winter.

We'd lost too many in that first battle against the Night Realm.

The sun broke through the clouds overhead, scattering light across the mountains surrounding us. A flash of scales caught my eye, and I followed the flight of six Dragons through the peaks, patrolling the Iron Realm's borders. Once they'd passed us by, I commented, "We should fly with them. I'm itching to shift."

Drazen met my mischievous grin with one of his own. "Rares should have thought this up years ago if he wanted to stay on your good side."

"He should have," I replied, striding into the officers' quarters and rushing to shut the door behind us. It was quiet as we walked the length of it, waiting until we neared the end that opened into a clearing before stripping out of our clothes. We stowed them in an empty corner, then braced ourselves for the ball-shrinking greeting that awaited us. Calling on the well of black fire slumbering in my chest, I stoked it into an inferno and raced out the door. In three steps, my scales scattered over my skin, and in another three, wings burst from my back. The shift tore through me, and I flapped wildly, shooting straight toward the clouds.

A roar filled the air as I burst through them, echoing around the valley that nestled Radence in its protective embrace. I loved flying before, but soaring among the peaks in my massive Dragon form was incomparable. Drazen bellowed a response, finding me in the air, and I swiped my tail at him. Smoke trailed from his nostrils, and he gnashed his teeth at me. Undeterred, I dove at him, forcing him to flare his wings and slow his momentum. The air I left in my wake buffeted him, and he chased me once he'd regained his bearings.

We rolled through the sky and twisted through the peaks of the Agrenak Mountains until we caught up with the other Dragons, joining them in dipping through the clouds and surveying the snowy landscape beneath us. Lazy smoke drifted from the small villages tucked into valleys, and the din of metal striking rock reached my sensitive hearing from the mines within the mountains. With my keen eyesight, I spotted little white bundles of fur trekking through the snow, the rare hares with thick, warm fur that lined the cloak and boots I had gifted to Izidora upon arriving in the Iron Realm.

We drifted toward the coast, the mountains growing shorter as we neared the ocean. The briny air hit my nostrils before the deep blue water entered my vision. Among the multitude of dark haired Fae below us, blondes slipped about, the refugees from the Crystal Realm finding solace in the small fishing village. Many looked up and waved to us as we flew overhead.

Banking again, we turned toward the border with the Night Realm, flying closer to the rolling hills than the sharp peaks as we scanned for attackers. More small villages lined this side of the border than the one with the Day Realm, the mountains beginning to soften as they exited my kingdom. In the distance, they bustled less than they used to, a testament to just how many Night Fae Kazimir had conscripted into his army.

Dipping lower, I left the cover of the clouds for better visibility as we neared the Zherzha Pass, the only true path between the Night and Iron Realms. The ice and snow was thick in the harrowing pass, and precariously perched boulders threatened to tumble down and crush anyone attempting to traverse the rocky path below.

Turning nearly sideways, I skimmed between two narrow peaks, challenging my agility and flying prowess. Behind me, the other Dragons banked and flipped, slipping between them without breaking formation. Once the challenging course was complete, I slowed, allowing the wind to carry me forward.

Drazen released a strangled sound, jerking me from the peaceful moment. His massive lapis lazuli Dragon form entered my field of vision, and he jerked his long neck toward the rolling hills to our left. I followed his direction, trying to discover what had him in a panic.

My wings nearly seized when the clouds parted, casting light on the landscape beyond.

Hundreds of thousands of Night Fae, dressed in matching leather armor, landed across the hilltops, some popping into existence, while others tucked their black feathered wings away and strode forward, bundles in their arms.

They hadn't seen us yet.

Quickly and noiselessly, I aimed upward, leading the Dragons into the clouds and high enough that the air grew thin. Drazen was right beside me, trying to communicate as best we could when our speech was limited.

But there was no mistaking what we'd seen.

They weren't waiting for the snow to thaw before launching their next campaign.

No, the Night Realm was preparing to attack the Iron Realm, through the Zherzha pass.

***

INTERLUDE

The Angel female fell to her knees, bruising them against the hard floor. Her eyes turned milky white, and she froze, head tipped toward the ceiling, palms braced against her thighs. The male raced to a nearby desk, snatching parchment and ink to record the female's words. She trembled from head to toe, orbs of her eyes roaming over something beyond this world. When she finally opened her mouth to speak, a rough, unearthly voice pronounced a prophecy that raised the hairs on his arms.

"The ones that are part of all will be born under a full moon
Her white light will fill the land
But her mates darkness will rise
Kings will fall
Rivers will run with blood
There is a choice
Follow the light
Descend into the dark
The harrowing pass decides it all"

In an elegant script, he wrote his wife's words, intent on his duty. Her voice dropped away, filling the room with silence, but she remained locked in the vision. His heart galloped in his chest, pounding against his ribcage when she remained motionless for another minute without speaking. The ink dripped over the edge of the parchment as he sat poised and waiting for more words.

She had been silent for too long, he thought.

Carefully, he set his work aside, then crawled toward her, easing her from her kneeling position and into his arms. He stroked between her brows and caressed her soft, pink lips, hoping to give her enough sensation to guide her back to the land of the living.

Minutes passed, and with each subsequent one, his breath flowed less and less. Panic sent a shiver down his spine, settling low in his belly. He was about to call for help when she began to stir. She blinked rapidly, her eyes returning to the deep, crystalline blue he had fallen in love with. She sucked in a jagged breath, bolting upright, only to be gently stopped by the male holding her.

In a panic, she attempted to rise again, but he only tightened his arms around her, smoothing her hair while he made soothing noises. Tears slipped down her face, one by one, as she let her grief overwhelm her. She felt like she was drowning, and the wetness dripping on her chest and into her ears didn't help the sensation.

"What did you see?" he asked, melodic voice tentative and curious.

Through sobs, she managed to say, "War."

"My love, war is already around us." He scooted backward, still holding her, until he braced himself on the wooden chest that sat at the foot of their bed.

She shook her head forcefully. "My vision was not of a war here, in Keleti, but in Északi, thousands of years from now."

"Then why has it upset you so? You know better than anyone that the Fates like to toy and play with the outcome of our lives. The Goddess gifts you these visions for insight into possibilities," he reminded her.

"Because I *saw* you," she whimpered, turning to her knees to face her husband. Her waist-length white hair cascaded over her shoulders as she reached up to cup his face. "You wrote down the prophecy, yes?"

He nodded warily, his icy blue eyes holding true fear in them.

"Please, can you retrieve it?" she pleaded, dropping her hands and scooting back.

He rose, crossing quickly to where he had discarded it. Returning to her side, he snaked an arm around her waist and hoisted her to her feet. Once she was secured at his side, he guided her to their bed. It sank as they settled on the edge, and he handed her the parchment.

She scanned the page, lips forming silently over the words. "This isn't about Keleti," she murmured, fingers dusting across the page.

The male rubbed his palms over his thighs, anxiously waiting for his wife to reveal the secrets the Goddess had gifted to her. She'd already said as much, so there had to be more.

"You will play a role in making this come to pass. For it *will* come to pass," she insisted. "Zuriel, your cousin is the one with the white light. She will change the course of history in Északi – in our world."

"How is that possible?" he asked, brows dipping together.

"I feel it in my bones. It will be millennia from now, but all the same, it will happen. And you *must* be there when it does." A sudden wave of bone-deep weariness swept through her, and she leaned her head on his shoulder, taking what comfort she could from her husband.

"But if the bringer of the white light is my cousin, that means she will be Ithuriel's daughter. And how will we end up in Észa-ki?" The concern in his lyrical voice grew as he processed his wife's words.

"You cannot tell him," she pressed, lifting her head from his shoulder and turning his face to her.

The Angel shook his head out of her hold. "I can't keep this from him."

"I know he is like a father to you, but you must. You cannot tell anyone about this, otherwise what needs to come to pass will change. You must ensure the war happens." Her voice reached a feverish pitch as she grew frantic, trembling from head to toe.

Wrapping her in a loving embrace, he tried to calm her. He knew she hadn't told him the whole truth, and if he was going to keep this secret, he wanted to know every bit of it. "I promise to keep this to myself, if you tell me everything."

The sigh she released sent rocks plummeting into his gut, and the words she spoke after caused him to bleed a river of tears. Their shared grief did not relent, not when the following day, the Angel king's officers came knocking, and the pair were forced to join the war against the Demons after all.

V

THE ASSAULT

47

IZIDORA

Liliana, Zuriel, and I were training when Drazen and Ruslan burst through the door, both half-dressed with crazed looks in their eyes. Zuriel halted his advance and spun to defend me before the bang of the door against the wall had ceased echoing around the room. He relaxed when he realized that our intruders were only Ruslan and Drazen. But the agitated energy that surrounded them nipped at my shoulders, especially as my mate rushed over and swept me into his arms. My twin swords clattered against the ground as I dropped them so as not to injure Ruslan. The ferocity with which he squeezed me stole my breath, like he couldn't hold me close enough.

"What's wrong? You're scaring me," I whimpered, my voice muffled by his strong chest. Through our bond, I sensed his terror and rage, mixing together in a deadly cocktail.

"The Night Fae approach our border," he gritted out, fingers flexing at my backside.

Liliana sucked in a breath, a sharp and poignant contrast to the one that was lodged in my throat.

Kazimir dared attack my home?

Rage blossomed in my chest, banishing the knot of panic,

and I welcomed the burning bloom, allowing it to fill me completely. The darkness inside me whipped through the crystal in time with the fire that surrounded it. I was more than ready to end Kazimir's pathetic life and exact my vengeance.

It was time for me to show the continent who would rule them after the rivers ran ruby and the Night Fae surrendered to us.

"How far?" I asked, my voice threaded with steel.

"They're in the foothills now. With their new magic, they could easily move into the Iron Realm at any time." Ruslan released me, his smoky gray eyes holding me steady as a million unspoken words passed between us.

"Then we'd better dress for war," I stated, squaring my shoulders and lifting my chin.

A wicked smirk spread across my mate's face. "There's my sprite."

The five of us raced up to our apartments, Drazen and Ruslan shouting orders as we wove through the halls of Ryza Citadel. The buzz of activity was akin to that of a beehive, with anxious energy filling the air immediately. I threw up a mental shield, not wanting to absorb the emotion when I needed – *wanted* – to allow the blackness to swallow me whole and fuel the rage that would lead to my twin blades dripping blood.

As we reached the top of the spire that held our rooms, Liliana skidded to a stop. "What about Endre?" she asked, glancing from Drazen, to Ruslan, to Zuriel, and back. Already, she was braiding back her hair, readying to fight.

"Bring him with us," Drazen said decisively. "Let him fight alongside us, and if he doesn't, we'll roast him alive."

My brows arched at the vehemence in his words, but I said nothing. After all, these males screamed violence, and the tension building around us left no time for niceties. She dipped her chin once, then hurried down the hall, Zuriel hot on her heels.

"Where is your armor?" I asked the two Dragon Félvér.

There were no sentries at our door, and Ruslan pushed inside. "On the couch. I moved us here, thinking that's where you'd be. We left it behind to find you."

"We need to move quickly and plan our attack," Drazen reminded me, hurriedly donning his armor.

Ruslan followed me into our bedroom, where the iron gray suit he'd gifted me was arranged neatly over a mannequin. I was already mostly dressed for battle, but the few plates that covered my shoulders and chest were difficult to put on by myself. Quickly, I strapped metal cuffs over my wrists and forearms, then slid on the lightweight, scaled metal armor over my legs and torso, the links bending and flexing with me. Finally, Ruslan fastened the thicker metal plates, still light enough for me to fly, but with more protection than what was underneath.

Ruslan handed me a pair of leather gloves, too. "It will be cold where we are going and I don't want your hands to freeze when you need them the most."

I *ached* for him, his thoughtfulness, his love. "Thank you," I whispered, accepting them. Flexing my fingers, I prepared to pull them on, only for my attention to snag on the large ruby ring I still wore – the one Ruslan had gifted me as a replacement for the one he'd enchanted more than a year ago. I pulled on the right glove, slipping the ring onto a finger there, before securing the left and returning the ring to its rightful place. Let the Night Fae see it as a reminder of who my fucking mate was, should they decide to challenge me.

Fuck, so much had happened in the time since I'd left the cave, the prison of the first twenty-one years of my existence.

Dragging in a serrated breath, I walked to the mirror. A spark of shock swept through me as I beheld the *warrior* reflected back at me. Her long, chestnut hair was plaited tight against her scalp, the braids sitting on top and woven intricately down her back. The dark gray armor gleamed in the light, hugging her curves and rippling down her body as she shifted from side to side. In her aquamarine eyes, there was a fierceness that was breathtaking, made all the more so by the hint of anxiety that lingered.

But she – I – was so fucking strong, and I would not let my fear rule me. I wasn't a victim, and I would *never* let anyone make me a victim again. If we lost this war, I'd ensure that I went down with a fight and took as many motherfuckers with me as I could.

The insidious bloom would reveal herself before the battle was over.

Ruslan stepped up behind me, his massive frame dwarfing mine as we locked eyes in the mirror. He too wore dark gray armor in a similar style to mine, though where roses were hammered into the finer parts of my armor, Dragons were hammered into his. Metal gloves covered his hands, and he ran them back through his dark hair, his eyes hungry as he perused my form.

"You are so fucking sexy, sprite. I can't wait to slaughter the Night Fae with you."

I grinned back at him. "So you'll prove you're worthy of marrying me?"

"When it's all over, I'm going to fuck you covered in their blood. And then, you will marry *me*," he growled, then kissed the top of my head in a tender move that contrasted the violence in his tone. He wrapped his arms around me from behind, inhaling deeply as we stole one last moment together.

"I love you, Ruslan."

"I love you, Izidora. Until my dying breath, and after."

Voices drifted beneath the doors of our room, breaking our

moment and forcing us to face what waited in the Agrenak Mountains. With a low groan, Ruslan unwrapped me, but he did not release my hand as we strode into our living space, where Liliana, Endre, Drazen, and Zuriel were all dressed for battle.

Endre had donned pieces of metal armor over his leathers, a symbol of his loyalty that wasn't lost on me. His peridot eyes shone with a hardness that surprised me for the sensitive male, and he dipped his chin at me, acknowledging his future empress with deference.

Stepping forward, I looped my arm through my mate's, and the others closed in around us, easing Ruslan's magical burden. With a lurch, we landed in the war room at the barracks, where the officers were already arguing and soldiers raced in and out, requesting orders and rushing off to relay them.

The chaos ceased the moment their emperor arrived. Ruslan stood at his full height, his presence commanding obedience and loyalty in a way that made my core clench. He launched into battle plans, deciding that we had to attack first and control the field. The Night Fae could pop into existence beside us, and we needed to keep the fighting out of the Iron Realm.

Drazen, Artur, and the others agreed readily, and given they hadn't seen the Dragons flying overhead, we had an element of surprise. The sun was dipping lower in the sky, and I chewed my lip as I glanced repeatedly out the window. If we were going to attack, we'd need to do it soon, before we slipped into darkness.

"The Night Fae's magic is stronger at night, shouldn't we wait until tomorrow?" I said, my voice wavering slightly.

"No. We need to attack now." Ruslan's tone was firm, and I narrowed my eyes at him.

"Trust me," he spoke mind-to-mind.

Without missing a beat, he continued, "We're vastly outnumbered, so we need to be smart." His voice dripped with ferocity, and I returned my attention to the room, scanning the faces of every last person gathered around the war table. Each held a grimness that came with the seriousness of battle, and only a few allowed the hint of fear that tasted like a bitter potion to show on their faces.

Rares entered the room, breathless as he shuffled forward. "The Mages and others who possess the talent are ready to move you, My Emperor."

"Good. Any last questions?" Ruslan braced his metal-covered hand on the table and leveled a serious look at each attendee.

"No, My Emperor," they said in unison.

Ruslan waved a hand, dismissing the group.

Then he turned to me, a darkness shining in his eyes that made my blood sing and my own darkness rise to the surface. "We stay together out there." In one step, he closed the distance between us, a haunted expression emerging. "I've trained you well. Zuriel has trained you well. Drazen has trained you well. But I would die without you, Izidora, and I need you by my side as we fight. The Night Fae have proven they have hidden tricks, and I don't trust them for a moment not to pull some other shit. I'm not arrogant enough to think we will win this without a lot of bloodshed, given their numbers against ours."

He cupped the back of my head, supporting it as I gazed up at him. "But we have secret weapons too," I whispered around the knot in my throat. "You've prepared well for this."

"We do," he murmured, his thumb caressing my cheek. "Give me your strength, and I will give you mine."

"Us against the world," I said, hands crawling up his armor until I stood on tiptoes and yanked his head down.

The moment our lips locked, the world fell away, and he consumed me like a wildfire. The kiss was desperate, filled with love, lust, and longing, the ache down our bond insatiable as we faced what was surely our end. We'd been playing defense this whole war, and as my body trembled against my mate's, I wasn't sure if it was from desire or genuine fear that we might lose.

Breathless, we broke apart, staring deep into one another's souls and accepting that the prophecy that predicted we would change the world was about to come to pass.

———

THE FOOTHILLS of the Agrenak Mountains provided cover for both our army and the Night Realm's, unfortunately. Legion by legion, we moved across the border, re-entering what I had thought was my home, once upon a time. I chewed my lip as I surveyed the landscape, looking for each of my friends.

Zuriel and Ruslan were with me, leading an elite unit of Félvér, and at our back a massive white bear-like creature – a Fehérmedve – paced restlessly back and forth. My cousin went to the beast, threading a hand through his snow-white fur, and he calmed, gazing forward at the hill that barred us from view.

In the distance, Liliana, Drazen, and Endre directed foot soldiers toward what would be our front line.

Anton and Slavian were somewhere in the distance with more Félvér, and Xorrek and Gozzak, the two Demons whose blood had made such a difference in this war – and in my recovery. I couldn't stress about all of my friends and family now, and as much as it pained me to do so, I locked my worry away in the far recesses of my mind.

Our army was scattered between the last sharp peak and the hills in front of us, preparing to circle and strike from every angle, splitting the Night Fae's attention.

Kriath dove toward us in his massive Eagle form, shifting at the last moment and landing lightly on his feet in front of Ruslan and me. "All units are ready, My Emperor."

"Good. Join Savich and the Telivér on the western flank," Ruslan instructed.

Kriath brought his flattened palm to his forehead and offered Ruslan a sharp salute. His hands didn't even tremble as he returned them to his side and called on his bird form again. With one last look at us, he soared away toward the far side of our army.

With a nod at Artur, Ruslan signaled the Dragons to shift and take to the skies. The giant red Dragon roared his fury as the shift tore through him, and he used the hilltop like a launchpad to spear into the air. The spikes on his tail smacked against the ground, sending dirt flying forward and toward the surprised Night Fae. Shouts rang out as more and more Dragons took to the sky, the dying sun glittering against their scales.

"Put up your mental shield now," Ruslan reminded me.

Tapping into the white fire-wrapped crystal in my chest, I blocked out everyone around me, not wanting a repeat of the emotional pain I'd experienced when we popped into the middle of chaos the last time.

Across the battlefield, unit after unit crested the hills, Félvér archers taking aim and firing in rapid succession, covering the infantry as they charged forward. My best friend disappeared from view, and I tore my attention back to Ruslan, who watched on, ensuring everything unfolded according to plan. Zuriel hopped onto the Fehérmedve's back, settling between his shoulders and fisting his fur. He leaned down as Ruslan yelled, "Charge!" and we raced forward as a unit.

My two swords were heavy as adrenaline blew through me, and every nerve was alight with anticipation.

On the other side of this hill, my destiny, or my death, awaited.

The revolting smell of burnt flesh hit me first, a line of charred Fae collapsed on the ground from where the Dragons had burned a path forward. But already, another line of soldiers waited to oppose us, undeterred by their brethren's deaths.

The scream that tore from my chest promised violence as I engaged the first male to dare approach me. A haughty gleam brightened his eyes, and he barely flicked his sword at me, thinking he could so easily disarm me.

A manic smile spread across my lips, and I hoped it appeared as crazed as I felt. "That was your first mistake," I laughed, and only then did something else flicker in his eyes.

With black flaring in my chest, I launched forward.

Our blades met in a clash of steel that reverberated up my arms and rang in my ears. Using both blades together, I flung his sword to the side, attempting to knock him off balance. He stumbled over a half-melted pommel, and I did not hesitate to bring my swords back around and slice him in the side with one while I stabbed the other into his belly. With a hefty kick, I ripped my blades free and flattened him on the ground. Using his chest like a stone, I leaped over him, on my way to my next opponent.

The first of many my blades would drink from.

Ruslan fought mercilessly mere feet away, blood spraying in all directions as he pushed forward, putting a dent into the fiercely held line. On my other side, Zuriel rode the Fehérmedve, whose growls were nearly as terrifying as those of the Dragons roaring overhead.

I sank into the rhythm of the battle, all fears and worries melting away as my only thoughts became slice, dodge, attack, parry, blast. No space for other thought remained, not when a horde of Night Fae waited for us, continuing to rise as their comrades were slain. We were outnumbered, and for every one of us they killed, we needed to kill three of them.

Gritting my teeth, I braced my blade against a large male's, his mouth set in a firm line as he put his weight behind it. Sweat poured from my temples, and my arms trembled beneath his weight.

"You will not win," I spat out, slipping to the side and allowing his weight to fall forward. My blade lingered in the open space and bit into his side.

The deep gash gushed blood, and he spun, holding his weeping wound with one hand, still brandishing his blade with the other. "You bitch. How dare you choose *him* over your own people. We loved you." Faster than I anticipated, he lunged. A sharp pain blossomed on my upper arm, and I cried out, dropping a sword. Hot blood seeped from the slice, but I had no time to examine it as the male came forward again.

I flung my remaining blade up, causing his next strike to glance off it. The awkward impact sent me stumbling, and I tripped over a fallen soldier, my ass smacking the ground with a painful thud. Slightly disoriented, everything slowed to a crawl as he arced his blade toward my chest.

A rainshower of ruby scattered across my face, the male's torso flayed open. He crumpled to the side, revealing Zuriel and the Fehérmedve, his claws dripping blood and gore. My cousin leaped from the beast's back and rushed to my side. "Are you hurt?"

"My shoulder," I managed to say through clenched teeth as I sat upright.

The Félvér in our unit raced around us, providing us with much needed cover.

Zuriel crouched on the grassy hillside, examining the wound. White light flared beneath his palms, and the throbbing in my shoulder abated. Ruslan's raspy voice rang out over the din of battle, giving orders to hold the line while he raced to my side.

"I'm okay," I reassured him before he'd even reached us.

"Thank fuck," he swore, checking me over anyway. "Stay

closer." His tone left no room for argument as he hauled me to my feet.

"Thank you, Zuriel," I said, and the Angel nodded, racing to his steed to return to the fray.

We ate up ground on our next push, claiming another hillside and closing in on the encampment. Ruslan and I stood at the top of it, trying to catch our breath and survey the area. His eyesight was better than mine, so it was no surprise when he found our target first.

"He's there," Ruslan confirmed, pointing toward the back of the army.

I followed his line of sight, finally spotting an ornate tent erected among a series of interconnected ones. A flash of dark hair caught my attention first, the tent flaps flying as Kazimir entered the dusky air. The light was quickly fading, and fires – not started by the Iron Realm – popped up throughout the camp.

"It's like they don't even care that we can see where everyone is, even in the dark," I murmured, chewing my lip as a wrongness slithered through my belly.

A horn sounded in the distance, drawing my attention toward Kazimir once again. He blew the carved instrument repeatedly, and thousands of wings burst into existence as the rear guard prepared to launch their assault. The sound as they erupted into the air was akin to an explosion, and a shockwave from their wings swept across the battlefield. Bows gripped in hands, they notched dripping arrows and drew the string, preparing to fire.

"Archers!" I screamed, trying to warn my people of the incoming danger.

Dragons dove toward the advancing fliers, picking off a few before the Night Fae aimed and littered a purple Dragon with arrows. She careened to the ground, flailing her one good wing toward the encampment so as not to land on her own people. Even knowing she would not survive, she tried to help in whatever way she could.

A wave of gratitude and sadness swept through me as she collided with the ground, skidded, and then released her final breath and returned to her Fae form.

Thinking better of an attack with claws, the Dragons flew higher, trying to stay out of range while blasting the Fae below them with a rainbow of fire. As the battle in the sky raged on, more and more Night Fae joined it, leaving the ground to aid their brethren above.

And then the sun slipped below the horizon.

Blasts of silvery magic soon filled the sky, sending Iron Fae and Félvér scattering in every direction, only to be shot with an arrow a moment later.

"Their magic is stronger now that night has fallen," I said, gripping Ruslan's arm as a flicker of fear dimmed the white fire burning in my chest.

With predatory slowness, he turned his head and revealed the sinister smirk spreading over his face. "We need to retreat."

I opened my mouth to protest, but his low laugh cut me off. "We all know their magic is stronger now. By retreating, they will follow us into the mountains where we have the advantage."

"You planned this all along, didn't you?" I replied, wiping my brow and likely smearing blood in the process.

"I told you to trust me," he purred, reaching out and brushing a sweaty tendril of hair away from my face. "I needed our soldiers to believe that this was the place where we'd make our stand, to make a dent in the army. Now that we have, we need to entice them to follow us."

My brilliant mate.

"Then what are we waiting for?" I grinned, giddiness rushing through my veins alongside a new wave of adrenaline.

Ruslan winked, then shouted orders to retreat. Zuriel relayed them to Drazen and the Demons telepathically, and the message passed quickly across the battlefield.

The Night Realm's archers dropped from the skies, watching us race into the narrow, rocky paths that led toward the Iron Realm's border in the mountains. A cheer rose through their army as they were told to stand down, and when Ruslan took my hand, I allowed him to move us ahead of the others and into Zherzha Pass, where I'd started to fall in love with him.

48

KAZIMIR

One of the commanders jogged up to my position at the rear of the army. "They're retreating, My King," he panted, wiping sweat from his brow despite the chilly night air.

"Retreating?" I questioned, accepting his outstretched spyglass and training it across the battlefield. Sure enough, through the dim light of the fires and the sliver of moon, tens of thousands of soldiers raced toward the rocky cliffs and narrow paths that led into the Agrenak Mountains. The Dragons that had relentlessly flown overhead followed them, some stopping to pick up riders before soaring away. A wicked grin rolled off my face, and I strode forward in search of my generals.

I found Vadim and Viktor covered in blood and surrounded by limping infantry, most dropping onto logs around roaring fires. Healers tended to the wounded, the most injured carried in the arms of their uninjured brethren and settled side by side.

"Why is everyone relaxing? We need to follow them into the mountains. We can't let them get away," I insisted, running a hand over my face in frustration.

Vadim and Viktor exchanged a look.

"We will. But they're on the run now, and sending scouts to search for them will help us plan our attack better," Viktor explained.

"It should only be a few hours before we attack again, and in the meantime, our soldiers could use some rest and a hot meal," Vadim added in a rush.

I nodded, scanning the area. Already, cooks were handing out hot bowls of stew and bread. Blood coated the hands and faces of my legions, but they didn't care as they sucked down every morsel.

"Fine," I relented, but the binding magic in my chest beat its protest against my ribcage, thirsting for release. I'd yet to let it play in battle, and it hated me for it. But tonight, I would unleash it and let it eat to its fill. "When you send the scout, have them search for Ruslan specifically. It's time he dies."

"Consider it done," Vadim said, striding off quickly, hopefully to relay my orders. Viktor dipped his chin and then raced after him.

I wasn't alone for long. Desmond sauntered up, his hands tucked behind his back. "My King, what a great victory you have won. You're going to rule this continent before tomorrow night, I think."

I hummed my acknowledgement, looking up to the stars and moon. Their light caressed my face, and my name echoed in my ears.

Kazimir...

Kazimir...

Kazimir...

Three haunted voices wove together, and I closed my eyes, allowing the Fates to fill me. The last time they'd done this, I'd been gifted this binding magic that made me the king of the Night Realm.

Yes, our pet, you must use it to fight...

The voices wrapped around my ears like slithering snakes.

You are our chosen one...

Because I was a hero, no doubt. I would save all of Északi from the ruin Ruslan and Izidora promised. Goddess's Prophecy be damned, I would not be a fallen king.

A touch on my arm brought me back to the present, and Desmond looked at me like he had asked a question.

"What was that?" I snapped, irritated that the Mage had interrupted my time with the Fates.

"My King, I asked if you need to rest or anything to eat."

I waved him off. "No, but you may fetch all leaders of the army and bring them to the war tent. We have the next wave of our attack to plan."

He sketched a bow, then hurried off. I spun on my heel and strode, shoulders back and chin proud, toward my accommodations, relishing the victory I had won and the metallic sting of blood against my nostrils.

More blood would be shed by morning.

And with the breaking of dawn, I would be king of the whole continent.

"THE IRON REALM has retreated to just inside the line of mountains, where the cliffs start steeper and the path begins to narrow." The scout swiped a towel across his sweaty face, accepting a waterskin from Vadim. "There are some flat spots, and the path leading up to it is wide enough to fight about five hundred across."

"Sounds like they didn't go very far," Viktor mused, bracing his hands on the wood table in front of him. "What if we send some troops on the ground, and have the rest fly in from various directions?"

The scout sipped the water, then swiped his forearm across his mouth. "I think it would be doable. I couldn't see their entire camp, but it's bare bones at best. They had fires scattered throughout the area, so they're not concentrated in one location."

Viktor nodded slowly, running his hands across his dark hair to smooth it into place. It was clear he was thinking through all options and potential obstacles. "How many archers do we have left?"

Vadim shrugged, tugging on his tangled beard and uncrossing his legs to lean forward. "We lost a lot to the Dragons, so our bow supplies are limited. But we can arm anyone with a halfway decent shot."

"See that the remaining ones are passed out, along with the poison to dip the arrows in," Viktor instructed the scout, who understood the dismissal and took his leave.

"Where would you like to be among the army, Kazimir?" Vadim asked, not meeting my gaze.

"It is time I show the Iron Realm the true might of the Night Realm," I declared. "I'll be flying in toward the front."

Vadim's lips twitched up at the corners. "I think that is a brilliant idea, My King."

"I agree," Viktor hurriedly added, rapping the table with his knuckles. "It will be good for the males to see you in action. Inspiring them to continue the battle."

I nodded, chest swelling as they complimented my fighting skills. "Dawn is fast approaching, and we need to engage them before the day breaks. We are stronger at night. Let's finish this."

Pushing back from my seat, I strode toward the exit, the cold night air kissing my cheeks as the moon greeted me. Vadim and Viktor split off behind me, hurrying to gather and organize our forces to move out. The low hum of activity soon turned into a roar, the cacophony of clanking metal, sizzling fires, and heavy footfalls satisfying the part of me that thirsted for the blood of my enemies.

The first few groups of fliers departed not even half an hour later, taking off in two directions to loop around and attack in opposite directions. Footsoldiers winked out of existence by the unit, the Mage power taught by Desmond coming in handy time and time again. When Viktor returned to me, his face was set with grim determination.

"It is time," he said, unfurling his wings and taking to the sky.

I did the same, allowing an updraft to lift me higher as I raced after him, falling in behind a group headed straight toward the path that led into the Agrenak Mountains. Zherzha Pass waited for us, and the irony that the most dangerous border crossing in all of Északi was where the last battle would occur was not lost on me.

It would only ensure my legacy lived on for millenia, speaking of the prowess of the Night Realm defeating the Iron Realm in their own territory.

The thought filled me with vicious glee.

We flew over the infantry moving silently, stealthily, as they crept toward the new battlefield. In the air, no one spoke as we approached. The leader of the unit flew higher, and Viktor and I followed, a chill passing over us as we broke through some low-hanging clouds.

The fires grew larger as we approached, and I glanced to either side, searching for the telltale shimmer of feathered wings. We boxed in the Iron Realm's army, and the clouds thickened, covering the moon and blotting out the stars. The night couldn't have gotten any darker right as we prepared to attack. I smiled to myself as I dove.

The Fates had blessed me, and they were ensuring I would win.

49

RUSLAN

Izidora, Zuriel, and I tucked ourselves into tight balls, trying to remain unseen. The retinue of soldiers accompanying us did the same, keeping their crossbows tight to their chests. The iron bolts, notched and ready to shoot, would render the Night Fae unable to fly, even from just a scratch, as they slowly leeched their magic. Scattered across the mountainsides, other groups like ours waited, though with our low supply of crossbows, they wielded iron-tipped whips to attack from a distance. No one around us had one, because I refused to allow them near my mate, not when I needed her to be sharp for this battle.

As if she sensed my thoughts of her, she flicked her gorgeous aquamarine eyes to the side.

She was so damn beautiful.

Especially as the moonlight ghosted across her full lips and the stars twinkled around her head.

The first whisper of wings had us stiffening, and beside me, Izidora sucked in a breath. Against the powdery snow, we looked like a spill of small boulders, and I hoped they wouldn't notice us until they were nearly upon us.

A fat, angry cloud covered the moon, stealing what little light the night had to offer. My blood thrummed with anticipation, and I let the bloodlust rise in me, the darkness that haunted me since childhood ready and waiting to play.

Pain – that was all I thought life had to offer me until Izidora swept into it like a wildfire.

After this was all over, I wanted to be free of it – wanted *her* to be free of it, too.

Exhaling slowly, I raised my hand, signaling the archers to take aim. They were more than ready to end this, and with a full quiver slung across each of their backs, I hoped they could send thousands of Night Fae crashing from the skies.

Izidora closed her eyes, tuning into her magic and readying a shield for us once the first volley was loosed. The bolts would give away our position, and with how many archers they had before the retreat, I wasn't taking any chances on the return fire that would rain down on us.

The Night Fae closed in on three sides, but the ones coming from the west were our main concern. Drazen and the others were out there, preparing for their assault, and with one last glance around to ensure we were properly positioned, I whispered, "Fire."

The whooshing of bolts filled the air around us, shattering the silence before the discord of broken cries signaled the start of the battle.

Immediately, a shield of white energy surrounded us, and the males quickly reloaded their weapons. Above us, the Night Fae swooped and scattered, searching for their attackers. The smarter ones found us immediately and shouted for the others to regroup. As they dove, swords ripped from their sheaths, and bows took aim, their wielders tugging on the thick strings.

"Ready!" Izidora called out, trying to time her shield with the next volley. "Aim!" The males tipped their crossbows toward the sky. "Fire!"

The white disappeared a heartbeat before the bolts would have rebounded off of it, soaring upward to their targets. A blink later, we were covered again, and the answering arrows bounced harmlessly off the shield, falling to the ground around us.

Curses flew down along with the Night Fae, and they landed a dozen paces away, ready to attack when their feet touched the ground.

Rising slowly, we turned to face our enemies. Izidora stifled a groan as she shook a leg to get blood flowing through it again. Sitting so still in the cold was terrible, but the number of broken bodies littering the mountainside was worth it.

The sound of the continued screams of falling males was almost like a soothing lullaby to my ears.

Izidora's shield expanded outward to cover everyone as our positions changed. But we didn't have long to ease all the ache from our limbs as the Night Fae charged.

Whatever magic they possessed flickered into existence as they made their intent clear – they were going to break Izidora's shield. But my mate was ready. The moment they were too focused on her magic, she let it drop, and another volley shot out, impaling a dozen in the throat and sending more scattering as they tried to dodge the iron projectiles.

The sharp zing of my sword against its scabbard imbued my muscles with adrenaline as I sprinted forward, Izidora right beside me. Her two short swords left garnet gashes in their wake as she sliced the males into ribbons while my own blade sank through shoulders and stomachs. Blood sprays dotted the otherwise pristine snow as we killed. More and more bodies fell, sliding down the steep slopes and piling up behind boulders and trees.

"Watch out!" I shouted at Izidora, who had gotten too far

away from me and didn't see the male trying to drop down behind her.

Her aquamarine eyes flashed to me before she ducked the blow in her periphery, forcing her two opponents into each other. With a hard kick, she swept the newcomer's feet out from under him, sending him pinwheeling backward and off the edge of the cliff. She threw a hand toward the other male, white fire setting his leathers ablaze before he rose from the snow. His screams pressed against her back as the third flapped his wings and adjusted his position, malice filling his eyes.

With a flick of my wrist, the three males blocking my path to her were engulfed in black fire, and I paid them no mind as I stalked toward my mate and that male. "Finish him, Izidora," I growled, throwing my sword up at a charging Night Fae to allow her space.

"Gladly." She returned the venom in my tone, eyes alighting on the male landing in front of her.

He scoffed and drew his sword. "When I'm finished with you, your precious mate will be next."

The laugh that erupted from her made me grin like a madman. "I do love when they underestimate me."

I didn't bother giving my opponents my full attention as I watched my mate. These farmhands were no match for my strength and skill.

Izidora took a menacing step forward, and my cock twitched as the moonlight cast her in a haunting relief. The white of the snow highlighted an insidious grin. She feigned a strike, and the male fell right into it, allowing her to slip closer to him and slice deep into his thigh. He stumbled, dropping to one knee, and braced his hand against the ground. She wasted no time slicing up his arm, and with a grunt, he attempted to rise, only to be kicked into the ground with her boot.

She stood over him, blades pointed in two directions. "Not so tough now, are you?" she taunted him, and fuck, I wanted to have her right there. The rage she displayed as she toyed with her opponents was intoxicating, and memories of us fucking after we'd killed her captors in the cave flooded my mind.

"P-p-lease," he stammered, and she tsked.

"Mercy? Is that what you want?" She lifted a brow at the same time she flicked a sword toward his dick.

"I'm just doing as I was told," he whimpered, and the scent of piss assaulted my nostrils.

Pathetic.

"I had to do the same thing," she crooned, tracing the tip of her sword up his abdomen. "But you know the difference between you and me? I thought every day about how to get out of it. You are a sheep who never had the guts to stand up for what you believed in."

Before he could protest, she stabbed him in the chest. His hands clasped involuntarily around the blade before he collapsed backward.

The last of the Night Fae that dared to confront us fell under my blade next, and in three strides, I had Izidora in my arms, kissing her fiercely as my blood heated with desire. She kissed me back with equal ferocity, and it was hotter than any fire I breathed in my Dragon form.

"You are so fucking sexy when you taunt them, sprite," I groaned, pushing images of what I wanted to do to her into her mind.

Her aquamarine orbs glittered with delight. *"It feels good. The darkness. The power. Holding their lives in my hands and deciding when they should end."*

Setting her on her feet once again, I tucked an errant strand of chestnut behind her ear. *"Don't ever be ashamed of who you are and what you desire."*

She scoffed, shoving lightly at my chest. "Now why would I do that when being me is so fun?"

A wild grin twisted my lips as I followed her back to the huddle of our remaining soldiers. "Where is our next spot?" she asked Zuriel, who stood perched on the edge of the boulder, scanning the area below.

"There," he pointed, and I hopped up to join him and follow his line of sight.

Across the mountains, small groups fought fiercely, but just down the cliff from our spot, a legion of Night Fae were overpowering a group of Iron Fae and Félvér.

We leaped to the ground, landing lightly, as I commanded, "On me."

Our group closed ranks, and I uttered the spell to move us to that spot. When we popped into existence, our soldiers immediately broke apart, firing bolts into the backs of the Night Fae. With renewed vigor, the other group fought forward, and we made quick work of finishing them off.

The first streaks of blue swept across the sky as we moved on to the next landing, losing and gaining soldiers along the way. The stars winked out of existence one by one, the sky brightening and revealing the true cost of the battle. Bodies littered most available surfaces, and some resorted to shoving the deceased off the edge to give themselves a fighting change.

Our strategy was working, and as we made our way down the mountain, the frozen waterfalls melted, hot reds mixing with icy blues. But as I scanned the battlefield, taking a momentary reprieve to drink some water, I still couldn't find the one male I wanted to see bloody and broken in a ravine.

Kazimir.

50

LILIANA

Blood coated my armor and streaked my face, mixing with sweat before freezing on my skin. At this high altitude, it was hard to breathe, but I fought relentlessly anyway, back to back with Endre. Drazen and a dozen other winged Félvér were with us, our little unit fighting fiercely in spots that were harder to reach.

When I landed on a narrow path beside a group of Night Fae archers raining down arrows on soldiers below, I slipped a little on the ice, cursing and trying to use my wings to right myself. My sudden appearance shocked the closest male, but he recovered more quickly than I did, drawing a dagger and swiping at me.

The slice in my forearm stung, and I cursed him before blasting him backward with my silvery magic. He stumbled, nearly knocking his companion over, and then both a sword and an arrow were trained on me.

"Traitor," the archer swore, pulling back his arm.

"At least my emperor isn't insane," I quipped, readying to block the projectile.

Before he could release, a gush of ruby sprouted from his

neck, and I whirled, Endre poised with his open hand outstretched. The other male charged, and I thrust my sword out, catching him under the ribs. With a forceful yank, I ripped it out and sent him tumbling down the mountain.

"Thanks," I panted, swiping at my forehead.

"I've got you, Liliana." His peridot eyes were hard with that promise, and I believed him entirely.

"Let's get moving," I said, not wanting to linger, not when there were so many Night Fae and so few of us.

Drazen and another Dragon blasted past us, only partially shifted so they could move faster. With a look, Endre and I dove after them, black feathered wings unfurling behind us and carrying us off toward another set of archers.

The cut on my arm grew more bothersome the more I swung my sword, and I was irritated that the one part of me that wasn't fully protected was the one part that had been cut. But I said nothing because I knew Endre would insist on healing it, and we didn't have time for that, not as the sun finally crested the horizon.

It glittered off the mutilated snow, making our targets easier to spot but also increasing the accuracy of their shots. I flew toward a group at the base of the mountain, tucked conveniently beneath an overhang. One noticed my approach, and I had to snap my wings shut to avoid his projectile. Endre swooped in behind me, landing and jumping into a fight against them. Drazen touched down shortly after, the two working as a team to dispatch them.

I was too busy paying attention to them to notice the Night Fae beneath me grabbing one of the fallen Iron Fae's whips and coiling it up. The crack hit my ears a moment before pain wrapped around my thigh, and I cried out as my leg was yanked out from under me.

"Fuck!" I screeched as I hit the ground, tumbling over myself and trying to dodge the incoming kicks and punches. I tried to stand, but the male still held the whip, maintaining his control over me. I crashed down once again, a frustrated snarl tearing from my throat. Thinking quickly, I reached along it and wrapped it around my hand, then pulled with all my might. He stumbled forward, then realized his mistake and dropped the weapon.

I wasted no time pushing to my feet, holding out a hand as I backstepped to ensure he wouldn't race forward. The leather unwound from my leg, the air stinging my skin where it had bit into my body.

Fuck, that hurt.

My sword was only a few feet away, and I lunged for it, rolling over a body and grabbing the pommel as I flipped into a crouch. My thigh *throbbed* from the movement, but I didn't have the luxury of listening to my body when it protested.

The male charged forward, and I braced for impact as he swung. Our blades collided in a clash that reverberated through my whole body, and I gritted my teeth and pushed back as hard as I could, using the force to come into a stand.

He backed away, leaving me off balance, but I quickly recovered and sank into my stance. Before he could come forward again, I lunged, but he handily parried my blade. We danced around each other, striking hard and fast as I worked to steer him toward a large rock.

If I could just position him a little to the left of it...

To my delight, he never looked behind him as I herded him in that direction, sidestepping and striking in such a way that he kept having to chase my next move. With a blast of silver, I sent him stumbling backward, his leg breaking over the stone with a satisfying crunch. As he impacted the ground, I followed him, stabbing him in the chest and ending his life.

I felt nothing as I pulled my blade free and wiped it clean on his leathers.

"Liliana?"

I whipped around, blade poised to strike. Vadim stood there, his long hair and beard both an utter mess, and his evergreen eyes shone with a mixture of pain and relief.

"Oh thank fuck, Lil," he said, racing toward me and scooping me into his arms for an embrace.

I squirmed against him, trying to break his hold. "Let me go, Vadim."

"I didn't know if you were alive or dead," he said, releasing me and allowing me my space.

"Well, I'm very much alive. And we're very much enemies right now," I hissed, raising my weapon. Without warning, I lunged for him, despite the heaviness in my heart and the voice in the back of my mind screaming at me to stop. I'd sworn to Ruslan I was loyal to the Északi Empire, and I couldn't waver in that again..

He easily swept my sword to the side, not even attempting to fight back. I struck again, and he merely sidestepped, waiting for me to twist and face him once more. On my third attempt, I cut him, momentarily horrified at the sight of his lifeblood trickling down his arm, nearly a twin wound to my own.

With a growl, he charged, and finally, he fought me back.

My brother trained me to fight, which meant he knew all my moves – but I also knew all of his. The past year of training with the Iron Fae and Félvér had taught me a few new tricks, and I called on one just as Vadim arced his sword toward me. Instead of leaping backward and out of the way of his lethal blade, I rolled over my shoulder, hooking my legs around his and using them to send him crashing to the ground. With an oomph, he flattened, and I leaped to my feet immediately, jumping on his chest and pinning him down.

He raised both hands, the pommel of his sword slipping from his grip as he opened them. "I don't want to fight with you."

Still poised over him, I hissed, "You chose the wrong side."

"I know."

In a flash, he had me on my back, pinned beneath him. I thrashed and struggled in his hold, but he gripped my wrists and pressed them tightly against my chest.

"I should have listened to you and Domi last year. Lil, I've been so worried about you since then. Mother and father were furious when I returned without you. Mother has been heartbroken since that day, and she barely gets out of bed anymore, worried that something has happened to you."

His words were sincere, and guilt settled in my gut, a heavier weight than my brother pinning me down. I stilled, waiting for him to continue.

"We know this is a losing battle – me and Viktor and Kaztar. Someone has to kill Kazimir to make it stop. We're doing everything we can to put him in harm's way. Please, Lil, stop fighting me and start helping me." The plea in his voice was as apparent as the concern in his eyes.

Releasing a breath, I nodded, and he released my wrists, straightening to his full height. He offered me a hand to help me up – the olive branch we both needed. My palm collided with his, and his muscles corded and flexed as he hauled me upright. Our blood mixed together from the cuts on our forearms, and I nearly laughed at the absurdity of the situation.

But then, I blinked, and something hot splashed against my face. My brother's jaw slackened in a silent scream.

"Vadim!" I shrieked, stumbling into him and catching my brother as he fell to the ground. The sharp tip of an iron arrow pinged off my chest plate, but I didn't notice or care as I lowered him to the ground, tears spilling over my face.

He coughed, misting the air with garnet. "Vadim, no, please,

please, no," I wailed, my hands scrambling across his chest as I fought against the tide of death.

"Liliana... I love you," he managed to wheeze out.

"No, don't you give up on me!" I screamed at him, holding pressure around his wound, careful to avoid the bolt.

"You can't save me," he rasped, his voice growing fainter and his evergreen eyes dimming.

"No, I love you, Vadim, you can't leave me, not yet," I sobbed, my tears slipping down my face and onto his chest.

Two heavy thuds shook the ground, and I glanced up to find Endre and Drazen racing toward me. Endre slid to his knees, careening to a stop at Vadim's side and pressing his hands into Vadim's chest.

My brother gave a weak shake of his head. "Let me go, Endre."

Mirror tears poured down Endre's cheeks. "I can't lose you, too."

"The Nighthounds are done," Vadim coughed. "You have to kill him."

My heart shattered into a million tiny pieces at the pain that etched both of their faces. Endre leaned down, touching foreheads with Vadim. "You were the best brother I could have asked for."

"Me too," I choked out, joining their little huddle. "I'm so sorry."

"Nothing to be sorry for... so proud... of you."

My world splintered then, and it wasn't until Drazen hauled me backward that I realized my brother had died. The battle raged on around us, but grief pounded in my ears, drowning out all other sound.

Vadim was dead.

Sob after sob wracked my chest as I remained caught between Endre and Drazen. My vision was a swirl of red, white, and black, and I collapsed again, unable to support myself under the massive weight of his death. I couldn't get enough air, and what little I did was like razor blades to my lungs.

"Let's get you away from here," Drazen murmured finally, and I allowed him to scoop me into his arms. My head lolled back, all energy sucked from my body. We shot into the sky, Endre staying right with us as we navigated the peaks to the small camp that had been erected away from the battlefield to tend to the wounded.

Numbness had overtaken me by the time Drazen laid me on a cot inside a warm tent. The fire burning in the brazier mere feet away did nothing to chase away the chill that sank into my bones. Endre crawled behind me, wrapping himself around me as I started to shake uncontrollably.

"I'll stay here," he murmured to Drazen, though his words sounded distant, like they were muffled beneath water.

"Thank you. I need to get back," Drazen replied, also sounding like an echo through the mountains.

"Stay whole," Endre murmured, reaching out. The two clasped arms, their camaraderie solidified by my love for both of them.

I never got to tell Vadim that.

Drazen's ocean blue eyes held an endless depth of sorrow, and he brushed the backs of his knuckles against my cheek before leaving us. I scarcely felt the touch, nor Endre's, despite how we were positioned.

"Everything will be okay," Endre reassured me with a gentle squeeze.

But everything was not okay.

And I wasn't sure it would be ever again.

51

ENDRE

Liliana vacillated between sobbing uncontrollably in my arms and trembling like a newborn deer. Slowly, I stripped out of my armor, tossing it away before hooking my leg over hers and holding her closer. A healer stopped by to make sure we were okay, but I waved her off. She returned with a blanket, and once she departed for the second time, I pushed Liliana up and peeled the metal from her body, then wrapped the thick fur around her.

"I'm the worst sister in the history of Északi," she hiccuped, tightening her grip on the soft brown and gray fur.

"You're not. He worried about you the whole time you were separated. He never stopped loving you or held it against you that you stayed behind. You are as loyal as Vadim is..." My throat thickened, and I swallowed down my own grief to comfort the female I was desperately in love with, "...was, and he knew your loyalties were with Izidora first."

She turned into me, burying her face in my shoulder. I wrapped my arms tight around her and pulled her backward until we nestled together on the cot. "And you," she whimpered, clearing her throat before continuing, "you are hurting too. I'm so selfish."

"Shh," I murmured, stroking her matted, braided hair. We were both filthy, but the wound in my heart was so fresh I didn't give a fuck about it.

Kriztof.

Zekari.

Krigin.

Vadim.

All gone. All my brothers, gone.

And Kazimir?

He was next.

Would both Viktor and I be left standing at the end of this?

Or would one, or both, of us be dead?

Vadim's last request filled my ears. *"You have to kill him."*

Had he and Viktor had a change of heart?

"Yes," Liliana whispered, and I realized then that I had voiced my thoughts out loud. "He told me I was right and that he should have listened to me last year, when we were all still together. Vadim said that he, Viktor, and Kaztar were working to put Kazimir in harm's way... so he would be killed."

I gritted my teeth and pushed myself to sit. "Then we have to honor his last wish and ensure that happens."

Liliana joined me, her seafoam green eyes red rimmed and watery. "What do you mean?"

I swiped a tear that tracked down her cheek, cleaning away a mix of blood and sweat with it. "We can save thousands of lives by killing Kazimir. If he dies, Viktor and Kaztar will stop the battle."

A slight squaring of Liliana's shoulders told me I'd lit something in her – something that mirrored the anger rising to mask my grief like a wall of smoke. "What are we lying here for? We have to tell Izidora and Ruslan."

"Get dressed," I told her, already rushing around her to grab my own armor.

She didn't protest, hurriedly fastening the metal plates all over her body. Before she could race into the sunshine, I grabbed her hand and pulled her to me, capturing her mouth for a kiss. Her scent overwhelmed me, the sweet berries and hint of spice cutting through the pain and relieving a tiny ache in my heart. "I love you, Liliana. You are the most incredible female I've ever met, and I am choosing you right now like I will choose you every day for the rest of our lives."

"Stop," she whimpered, her eyes flooding again.

"No, I need to say it, because I may never get a chance to," I snapped, a little too forcefully. My grip on her hip tightened, and she sucked in a sharp breath. Her eyes went from brilliant green to black as her pupils dilated.

"Have me, have Drazen, have more than us. I don't care. I choose you, no matter what."

"Thank you," she whispered, and then I sucked her bottom lip into my mouth, nipping it with my teeth and eliciting another delicious whimper from her. With wild eyes, we broke apart, breathless.

"Let's go."

———

THE SUN ROSE above the mountain peaks, and we soared among them, searching for a trio of black, chestnut, and white hair. They had gone to the western front, opposite of us, and from deep within Zherzha Pass, we flew in that direction. I made the mistake of glancing down, only to spot the ruby river flowing forcefully in the ravine thousands and thousands of feet below. My stomach churned again as we flew over a mess of tangled bodies piled up and pinned between heavy boulders and snow-dusted pine trees.

Miniature skirmishes played out at varying altitudes, and groups of fighters popped in and out of existence as they moved across the field.

"There!" Liliana shouted over the wind, pointing further to our left.

She banked, and I followed her, racing toward Ruslan, Zuriel, and Izidora. The three fought fiercely with an amalgamation of warriors – Iron Fae, Félvér, and Telivér – against a large group of Night Fae.

Liliana and I dropped from the sky, joining the fray.

"Why are you over here?" Ruslan snapped, ripping through the tough leathers of a Night Fae with only his giant Dragon talons.

But then Izidora noticed us. "Oh, shit, what's wrong?"

Liliana shook her head, throat working as she was unable to speak.

"Cover me!" Izidora shouted, dropping back and taking us with her. The soldiers closed ranks and continued to swing at their opponents.

Her eyes darted between Liliana and me. "Tell me."

"Vadim... he's dead," Liliana choked out, and Izidora swept her into a tight embrace, making soothing noises as she reached for my hand. I let her take it, and the grief ebbed as she siphoned it away.

Ruslan was by our side moments later. Clenching my teeth around what remained of my grief, I conveyed what Vadim had said. "If we kill Kazimir, the battle is over. Viktor and Kaztar will surrender."

"You're certain?" he growled, his eyes narrowing on me.

Would he ever trust me?

"He's telling the truth," Liliana defended me, though her voice was slightly muffled in Izidora's neck.

"Then we need to find him. And fast," Izidora pronounced, straightening. Her eyes held a fire reminiscent of our first encounter, when she had fought against us despite the fact that we were trying to rescue her from her chains.

The female before me was formidable, a dark, powerful aura surrounding her, and by the firm set of her jaw, I knew she was not to be messed with – not when it came to this. After everything that had happened to her, she deserved to take whatever vengeance she sought.

I certainly wasn't going to interfere with that.

"How can we help?" I asked, my heart sinking to the pit of my stomach, even as I meant the words passing my lips.

"I will maintain a mental connection with everyone," Zuriel offered, nearly making me jump at his sudden appearance. "Simply shout in your mind that you have found him, and I will dispatch the others."

Ruslan crooked a brow at him. "Not only can you read minds, but you can read them across the entire battlefield?"

The Angel shrugged. "I block everyone out, most of the time."

"We'll talk about your powers in *extensive, truthful* detail when this is over," Ruslan snarled, cracking his neck, then his knuckles.

"Of course," Zuriel replied, but there was a sadness to his tone I couldn't quite place.

The others had finished off the Night Fae during our discussion, leaving us momentarily protected on the top of the cliff. Ruslan assigned us directions to travel and ordered us to relay the information to all commanders we came across. The Demons took off first, flying fast and hard toward the center of the battle, while Liliana and I returned to our earlier section in the east.

Ruslan, Izidora, and Zuriel carved a path high above, eventually disappearing from view.

As we wove among the clouds, I gave Liliana's hand a reassuring squeeze.

We'd make it out alive, at least.

The emotional wounds would take longer to heal.

52

KAZIMIR

My perch high in the mountains gave me a perfect vantage point to fling my binding magic and observe the battle, but it came at a cost. I watched Vadim fall to an iron bolt through the chest. Liliana, Endre, and Drazen had sped off, over the jagged peaks, and disappeared into the distance. "Send scouts over there. I want to know where they went."

"Yes, My King," Desmond said, using his Mage magic to relay the message.

When his form became solid once more, I told him to remain where he was. Carefully cloaking myself, I called on my wings and swooped through the chaos to the path below, where Vadim's broken and bloodied body had been abandoned. Hefting him into my arms, I returned to my earlier spot, settling his body across a smooth, bare stone nearby.

His lifeless eyes stared at the brilliant blue sky overhead.

I felt nothing as I softly closed his lids.

Desmond appeared beside me. "I am so sorry."

"For what? His sister was a traitor," I stated, stepping back.

"But he was your general, and a very good friend from my understanding," Desmond said, almost like a reminder.

Not even the chill of the altitude could make me feel anything. I was utterly numb.

"He was," I murmured, spinning on my heel and leaving him lying there.

I returned to my perch, the binding magic in my chest begging to be fully unleashed.

Kazimir...

Kazimir...

Kazimir...

The voices echoed in my brain again.

"I will, soon." I ran a hand over my face, trying to find an area to focus on. I still searched for Ruslan and Izidora, and I wasn't going to waste too much of my magic before I found them. I needed every ounce of it to destroy what they both held most dear.

Each other.

"What was that, sir?" Desmond asked.

"What? I didn't say anything," I grumbled, waving a hand at him. He must have heard something from below. Even from up high, the screams of pain and rage were audible, assaulting my ears with their cacophony. The sun tracked higher into the sky, nearly blinding me as it shone against the white snow. With a frustrated sigh, I turned in another direction, scanning and scanning, waiting for the scout's return.

He appeared, first like a black dot sweeping through the rocks, then larger as he soared upward, skimming the face of the cliff before landing in front of me. He swept into a deep bow. "My King, there is a healing camp beyond those mountains. No fighters."

"You are dismissed," I said, returning my attention to the area, waiting for Drazen, Endre, and Liliana to reappear.

But they didn't.

Shifting my weight from foot to foot and repeatedly clenching and unclenching my fists, I made a decision.

"Desmond," I barked, and the Mage immediately appeared at my side.

"Yes?" he questioned, ready for his orders.

"I am going there. If I cannot find them, I will make them find me."

I didn't wait for him to respond before I brought my wings forth and shot into the sky. I flew a straight path beyond the peaks, still scanning for any sign of the traitors. The battlefield was large and complex, especially since we were waging war on the sides of Goddess-damned mountains, but I had no doubt that if their healers were attacked, Ruslan and Izidora would come running.

If I couldn't find them, I'd make them come to me.

The tents appeared like gray beacons among the cleared dirt along the path, and I cloaked myself, mixing the black ropes of my binding magic with the tendrils of moonlight that remained in my chest. Noiselessly, I dropped to the ground, then crept among the structures.

It wasn't long before I found what I was looking for.

A dozen healers tended to rows and rows of beds filled with wounded soldiers. All rushed about or shouted for herbs and salves from their attendants, paying no attention to anything beyond what was right in front of their faces.

Dropping my magic, I startled the nearest one, having suddenly appeared in her tent.

She shrieked, but I silenced her quickly with a length of rope wrapping around her throat. The enclosure turned to chaos as healers fled and injured soldiers jumped into action. But the beast had taken over, and more slithering rope exploded from me, wrapping around anyone and anything in its path.

All I saw was black as I advanced, ending the lives of those who dared to stand against me.

And when I was finished, there was silence.

53

IZIDORA

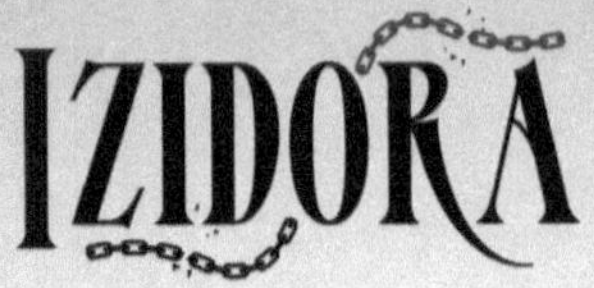

Zuriel whipped his head to the side, drawing my attention. "What is it?" I asked, heart thudding in my chest from the panicked expression drawn on his normally stoic face.

"The healers are in trouble," was his strained reply, and he twisted in the air, heading to the narrow, harrowing pass where we'd stashed them.

"Wait! I'm coming with you," I called out, stopping him midair.

Ruslan pulled up beside me, his large, black wings buffeting the air around us. "You two go, I will continue searching. I can contact you if I find anything."

"Stay safe," I pleaded, searching my mate's smoky gray eyes. There was a weariness there, one that I felt in my bones. We'd been fighting nearly nonstop for the better part of a day, and I was exhausted. Ruslan was exhausted. And if I was being honest, I needed a break from all the death and despair hanging in the air like a fine mist. My emotions were a wreck, and I was struggling more and more to maintain my mental barrier when it was constantly battered with agony.

The grief of others also sapped at the hatred I needed to fuel this darkness, and *that* was my priority in all of this.

"Get some rest," Ruslan hummed, kissing my forehead swiftly before backing away.

"Have I ever told you that you take such good care of me?" I spoke into his mind.

"I'll never tire of hearing you say it, mate."

Zuriel had already taken off, and I followed him, flapping my wings to catch up. I kept my eyes straight forward, tracking his movements, not wanting to look down at the distant ground or the gore that littered it.

It didn't take us long to traverse the distance, and as we crested the ridge, I frowned.

Nothing looked amiss.

"Zuriel–" I started, but he held up a closed fist. I snapped my mouth shut, wondering what he knew that I did not. Slowly, we started to descend, the ground growing closer and the promise of food, water, and a seat increasing.

We landed lightly, but Zuriel was tense in a way I'd never seen before.

"What is it, cousin?" I reached out to him, trying to understand the tight set of his shoulders.

"There is no movement, no sound. It's like everyone here vanished."

"Then we need to search these tents. What did you sense before?"

"Terror. There are no fighters back here, and no one should have seen the healers. They would have to know..."

We crept forward, slipping into a tent with its flaps tied back. No one was there, but half-empty jars were knocked askew. A trail of blood led us into the next tent, and the one after that, until we came to one lined with healing beds.

Each male on them looked like his neck had been broken,

their faces purple and contorted with pain. Among them, scattered on the floor, were the healers, in similar states of death.

"Oh fuck," I whispered, hand covering my mouth as I stared at them, frozen in horror.

"Izidora!" Zuriel's voice was laced with panic, and the yank on my hand tore me back to reality. With a strong grip on my arm, he hauled me from the tent, racing toward the open space beyond, his head whipping in every direction.

A low, sinister laugh sent chills skittering across my skin. I felt eyes on me, and I jerked myself free from Zuriel, spinning around and searching for the voice. White fire immediately filled my palms, ready to strike at a moment's notice.

"Show yourself!" Zuriel shouted, and the hairs on the back of my neck rose.

Ten paces away, Kazimir emerged from seemingly nowhere, striding toward us with malice in his steps. His eyes were completely black, like when he'd kidnapped me and directed a knife toward my heart.

"We found Kazimir," I shot down the bond toward Ruslan. Rage, so hot that it nearly burned me up, exploded through my veins, and I hurled a ball of white fire at him.

With another perverse laugh, he blocked my attack with a shield of silver, scattering the flames in all directions. Hatred flared like a wildfire, and I drank every drop of magic the extreme emotion allowed me and channeled it into my next attack.

This was exactly what I had practiced for.

With a snarl, I launched myself at his mind, trying to force him to still so that Zuriel and I could kill him.

Kazimir's mind was like a black hole, filled with nothing but twisted ideas and unprocessed rage. Those black ropes he'd bound me with before caged his mind in a tight weave, forcing me to focus more intently to slip past them. I was only half-conscious of his proximity as I worked my way inside his mind, absently circling with Zuriel by my side.

With a sharp flick of his wrist, Kazimir tossed his binding magic in our direction. Zuriel anticipated his move – whether by reading Kazimir's mind or drawing on two millennia of training – and threw up a shield of magic around us. The dark ropes fizzled out on impact.

"When I'm through killing your mate, I'm going to chain you to my bed and fuck you until you bear me a child, Izidora," Kazimir grunted, drawing his sword and dropping into his fighting stance.

I scoffed, my hatred rising again and fueling my attack on his mind. A tendril of my magic slipped through, and smothered any sort of celebration I would have otherwise taken at the accomplishment. He couldn't know my next move, not until it was too late. "You won't walk away from this encounter alive," I hissed, fingers curling into my palms.

He cocked his head, the total blackout of his eyes unnerving. "The Fates favor me, Izidora. They want me to win."

Zuriel took a half step forward, drawing Kazimir's attention away from me long enough to slip another tendril past the barrier of his mind. The crystal flared to life inside me, filling with black smoke as every last bit of hatred and rage from years and years of abuse melded together.

With a furious scream, I flung my arms wide, fueling my magic as Zuriel leaped forward to engage him in combat. A flurry of white tendrils assaulted Kazimir's mind as I forced his movements to slow, but the binding magic rebelled against me, yanking on bits of my own and sucking them into its endless void.

The clash of blades rang in my ears, and I tried to keep Zuriel between me and Kazimir so I could focus on the delicate balance of preventing my magic from tangling with his.

But Kazimir battled us on two fronts, seemingly empowered by his dark gift and able to handle a mental and physical attack simultaneously. Gritting my teeth, I pushed harder.

With his free hand, Kazimir tossed another sinister rope in my direction, and once again, Zuriel blocked it.

"C'mon, Angel, is that the best you can do?" Kazimir taunted, flinging another round at both of us. "You've lived for millennia. You should be able to fight circles around me."

Zuriel remained cool, his icy blue eyes hard and focused on the challenge before him.

Kazimir tsked. "Not even going to dignify a king with a response? How classless you are."

Still, Zuriel said nothing. In a flurry of movement, he drove forward, pummeling Kazimir backward and toward the precarious edge of the cliff. The ravine beyond was thousands of feet deep and raged with an angry river, still flowing despite the freezing temperatures around us. Kazimir dug his heel in and fought back, sweat pouring from his temples as he did so. My white magic thrashed with his, and no matter how much force I put into it, I was still falling short of my goal.

I was so focused on my task that I didn't realize Kazimir had fallen backward until his arms began pinwheeling, and our connection was broken when he fell out of sight. I rushed toward Zuriel, my breath catching in my throat.

But Kazimir burst from beneath the ledge a moment later. His black wings unfurled and flapped furiously as he towered over us.

I tried to slide to a stop, but it was too late.

A black rope that spelled my death flew toward me, aimed straight for my neck. Time slowed to a crawl, the scream tearing from my throat sounding disjointed as I watched with horror as the binding magic drew closer. White magic rose from my fingers like the breaking dawn, too slow to defend me.

Somehow, in the space of a heartbeat, I managed to say three last words to Ruslan.

"I love you."

"I'm coming, don't you fucking give up on me," Ruslan snarled back.

My eyes screwed shut, and I sucked in a breath, prepared to die. It was, after all, what I deserved, wasn't it? Why else would my life have been filled with so much pain?

The choked sound that hit my ears didn't come from me. Wrenching my eyes open, a flash of white hair flooded my vision before I was knocked backward, and a heavy male body landed on top of me.

"Zuriel!" I screamed, trying to wiggle out from beneath him. His hands scrambled at his neck, his gasps weakening and growing fainter.

"No!" I screeched, finally free, and my nails clawed along with Zuriel's at his neck.

Kazimir laughed, a crazed sound that I knew would haunt me for what remained of my life. "Come with me willingly, and he can live."

"Zuriel," I sobbed, looking between my cousin and the male I'd loved first. But there was nothing left of the Kazimir who'd rescued me in this sinister shell.

"You motherfucker!" I screamed, a blast of white energy magic bursting from me that was so intense it knocked Kazimir's smug face from the sky. His concentration broken, the rope disappeared from around Zuriel's neck, and he sucked down ragged breaths, pushing upright to grab his sword immediately.

"You're hurt," I pleaded with my cousin, but he shook his head.

Kazimir rose again, like a disease that couldn't be eradicated. He yanked two daggers from sheaths on his thighs, his sword discarded like he didn't need it to defend himself.

A ring of purple bruises was already forming around Zuriel's neck, and I hastily unsheathed my swords, ready to fight alongside my cousin.

I needed to kill Kazimir and end this fucking war.

The roar of an enormous black Dragon tore our attention away from the tense moment, and that was all Zuriel needed to fling himself forward at Kazimir.

"Zuriel, no!" I screamed, realizing what Kazimir had intended to do a moment before my cousin did.

A choked sound escaped the Angel's chest as one dagger went under his ribs, and the other came down on his shoulder. Kazimir ripped them out simultaneously, and Zuriel collapsed at his feet.

Without a care for myself, I raced forward, toward the last remaining family member I had – the only one I'd ever known. My heart was shattering, fracturing in a way I didn't know was possible after all the abuse I had experienced. I didn't think there was anything else that could break me, but watching my cousin bleed out did.

The sun was blotted out above me, and black fire spewed overhead, narrowly missing my hair as I flung myself over Zuriel's body.

Kazimir shot into the sky, disappearing entirely as Ruslan snapped his maw at the place he had occupied. Wind from strong wings buffeted me, whipping the loose strands of my hair about as Ruslan raced away in pursuit of my cousin's killer.

"Zuriel," I whimpered, holding him so tightly I wondered if it was him or myself I was trying to hold together.

"Izidora," he moaned, his chest jerking.

With a start, I realized I was crushing him. White magic filled my palms, and I pressed them to his bloodstained skin.

I would heal him, and then I wouldn't lose him.

His firm grip stopped me, yanking my hand away with more

strength than a dying male should have. "Don't," he whispered, his melodic voice as ragged as his breathing.

"But I can't lose you," I sobbed, my vision blurring.

He winced as he tried to pick his head up to look at me, then thought better of it. "I never told you... I lost my wife during the war between the Angels and Demons."

In that moment, I dropped away every barrier I'd erected to protect me. I needed to experience these last moments with my cousin without a filter on them. His sadness slammed into me, nearly stealing my breath. A new cascade of tears fell from my eyes, dripping too loudly on his wheezing chest.

"She is the one who spoke the prophecy," he managed to say in a rush.

I gasped, inching closer to my dying cousin. "Zuriel, why didn't–"

"Because, that day, she spoke of another... that predicted this. I had to be here, to die for you, in order to save the world." His icy blue eyes pleaded with me to understand, but I couldn't, wouldn't believe this.

I was drowning in grief – mine, Zuriel's, that of everyone around me.

"You lived without her for two thousand years?" I whimpered, cupping his face.

He nodded, then winced at the pain. "I want to go to her now. So, please, let me go, Izidora."

A sob wracked my chest, but I nodded, gripping his hands tightly. They were cold, so cold. I held them over my heart, the one that was shredding into a million pieces, as his eyes, so full of life and love for me, grew cloudy. "Thank you for everything, Zuriel. Go to your wife. I love you."

"Love you... cousin." With one last slow blink, my cousin joined his love in whatever waited for us beyond this life.

A scream tore from my throat, ripping it raw and bloody as

my grief swept over me like a tidal wave, crashing through every piece of me until it had shattered my soul along with my bones. I couldn't breathe, couldn't process that I'd never hear his voice again, never learn mind magic with him again, never hear all the secrets he kept in his head. I didn't ask enough questions about our family. I didn't know enough about him. How would I even find distant relations if I didn't know our real family name?

Everything heaved with pain, and each breath was like a thousand stabs to the chest. "Zuriel, Zuriel, Zuriel," I chanted over and over and over, as if saying his name could bring him back to me.

I didn't know how long I sprawled across his body, but it wasn't until a roar tore through my grief that I remembered I was on a battlefield and my mate chased a maniac through the skies.

Sucking in a serrated breath, I rose from the ashes of my pain, rolled my shoulders back, and told myself that I was an insidious bloom. That I had the power to bring males to their knees. That I was a survivor.

And survivors were the most dangerous ones of them all.

54

RUSLAN

Kazimir forced my massive Dragon body to twist and turn in complicated maneuvers as I chased him in the sky. Izidora's grief was like a white hot poker through our bond, and it took every bit of self control I possessed to fight the need to race to her side and relieve her pain. Not that mine was much better. Zuriel and I had never been anything more than cordial until after Kazimir had tried to kill her, and over the months that we'd all taken turns sitting by her beside, we'd grown close enough to call each other friends. But to Izidora, he was *family*, and that, to her, was the most precious gift. That loss for her hurt me more than anything.

I gnashed my teeth on empty air again, furious that Kazimir kept slipping through them. I needed to shred this male who continued to make her suffer.

He was fucking dead.

No one hurt my mate and lived to tell the tale.

A roar tore from my throat as something sliced into my side, and with a jerk of my tail, I smacked at the spot, connecting with something. The glancing blow didn't faze Kazimir, and he darted away from me again, much more agile as a Fae than I was as a Dragon.

Snapping my wings shut, I dropped into the ravine, hoping he'd follow me down. The arrogant prick did, and as we swept by Izidora, she rose, her aquamarine eyes filled with hate and rage and every other powerful emotion that fueled her to keep going when others would give up.

"I'm so sorry, sprite. Stay there with Zuriel. I can handle Kazimir on my own. You didn't deserve to lose the only blood you had left."

"No. Kazimir's death is fucking mine."

Pride bloomed in my chest, and I nearly grinned in my Dragon form. *"There's my sprite. Come fucking get him."*

Flaring my wings, I slowed my descent, hoping my sudden change in direction would throw Kazimir into my spikes. But at the last moment, he dodged, rolling over and slipping beneath the massive membrane, giving it a deep slice on his way. A snarl of pain escaped me, and I gnashed my teeth at him, but he was already out of reach.

A feminine shriek reached my sensitive ears, and a moment later, a thud landed on my back. I grinned to myself as my mate settled between the deadly ridges. Together, we chased after Kazimir, returning to the peaks above. Izidora launched blasts of white flame from my back, one managing to singe Kazimir's feathered wings.

He snarled, then hurled another dagger at us. Izidora blocked it with a silvery shield, and it fell thousands of feet into the river running red below.

"We can't fight him up here," I told Izidora down our bond.

"I know, we need to land. But where is your armor?"

"Don't worry about me, sprite. Focus on killing him and getting your revenge."

On our next pass near the healer's tents, I swooped low. A light weight lifted from my back, and I shifted back into my

Félvér form, grateful Izidora understood what I intended to do. Her white wings glittered in the sunlight, and covered in dark metal armor, she looked like a fallen Angel, hell bent on vengeance.

Which was exactly what she was.

Blood raced to my dick at the worst time as I watched her draw her swords and bathe them in flames.

I raced into the nearest tent, searching for clothes and a sword. Bodies were scattered everywhere, necks broken and twisted to odd angles. Cursing, I stripped one of his pants and boots, profusely apologizing to the Goddess and hoping she'd forgive me since I had bigger fucking problems than burning our dead at the moment.

Bare chested, I grabbed a sword as I raced from the tent and into the bright sun, finding Izidora and Kazimir locked in battle. My mate's jaw was set in a firm, determined line, and hatred directed at the male in front of her speared down our bond. She allowed that darkness to imbue her muscles, and I sent her more of my own, fueling her for the fight. Kazimir was eating up the ground between them, and with a string of curses, I ceased my admiration and raced back to Izidora's side.

We had to put a stop to his madness.

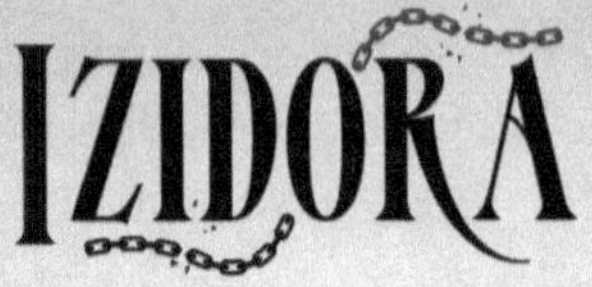 IZIDORA

"First you tried to kill me, and then you killed the last person in my family," I screeched, hurling white fire at the black feathers of his wings.

A crazed smile crossed Kazimir's lips, the blackness that overtook his eyes swirling with amusement. "To think, those bastards guarding you tried to break you, and all it took was some daggers from me."

"I will fucking kill you for what you did to me!" I swore, then swung with all my might. Our blades collided, sending sparks flying in all directions.

With a mighty shove, he forced me back, tracing his blade in a lazy circle before squaring up again. My heart thundered against my ribs as I fought to keep control of my emotions.

I needed all this hatred to kill him.

Zuriel's advice floated through my ears, a whisper from beyond this life. *"You have to let the emotions flow through you."*

Clenching my teeth, I let go of the white-knuckled grip and opened the floodgates, freeing every ounce of grief, fury, despair, and heartache I'd ever felt. The depth of the agony stole my breath, but I didn't let it consume me. No, I drank it all like it was the most decadent wine, allowing it to intoxicate me. The pain turned into delicious pleasure, and I basked in the power it offered and the black that filled the crystal at the center of my magic.

Tears pricked my eyes, and I let them fall, keeping my gaze firmly on Kazimir as I circled him. My body was somehow lighter and stronger, and my next flurry of attack was faster and more agile than ever before. This renewed vigor encouraged me to continue to open, and memory after memory of torture and abuse I'd experienced flashed through my mind with lightning speed. The swing of my sword was fueled by it, and as the sound of whips cracking the air surfaced in my mind, I dug a flaming blade into Kazimir's arm.

"You bitch," he spat out, letting it go limp by his side and tossing his sword to his other hand.

"You've called me that before, but I never did anything to you," I hissed, aiming another strike at his good shoulder. He parried it away, though more slowly than before.

"You manipulated me."

I arced my sword to his thigh, only to be blocked.

"You lied to me."

The tip raced up toward his abdomen, only to be swept away.

"You are *insane*."

My second sword sliced forward, joining the first to block his blow.

"I would rather *die* than have you touch me again."

That last statement enraged him further, and he pounded forward, his strikes heavy and brutal. Even as I tried to dig my heel in and defend, he backed me up, and my heart thrashed wildly in my chest.

He would not kill me.

My mind flooded with more images and sounds – a poem, a

cold bath, rotten meat – and I used each one to hold myself in place. Kazimir's strikes slowed, blood pouring from the wound on his arm, and I took the opportunity to slip past his blades and come around to his back. Along the way, I landed a hard punch in his side, forcing the breath from his lungs.

But he whirled, catching me with his bloodied arm, moving faster than I had ever seen him move before. "Your precious mate left you here to fight me, alone. He doesn't even want you. He'd rather see you die or be captured by me than spend one more minute with your whore mouth."

Over his shoulder, Ruslan approached, quickening his pace when he saw my position. His chest was bare, leaving his tattoos on full display, and should anyone creep up behind him, they'd revel at the perfect circle marking his back – the sign we had been mated.

He glistened with a sheen of sweat in the sunlight. *"Keep your attention on him. Not on me."*

I ripped my attention back to Kazimir, his hot breath ghosting over me and making my skin crawl.

"You were always mine, Izidora. Why did you never see that? When this battle is over, I'll have you, whether you like it or not. It's time for you to come home with me," Kazimir hissed, his black eyes reflecting the ferocity in mine.

I spit in his face, causing him to rear back and drop his hold on me. Without hesitation, I kicked out, digging my toes into his stomach and forcing him backward, right into Ruslan's waiting arms.

My mate snaked them around Kazimir's throat, holding him tight and cutting off his air. Black ropes burst from Kazimir's hands, forcing Ruslan to drop him so that he could burn them with his black fire. Kazimir sprinted away, and I chased after him, the two of us closing in on the edge of the ravine.

He whirled to face me, his sword slashing out behind him. I ducked, narrowly dodging the blade, then sprang forward, catching him around the middle and sending us careening over the lip. Ruslan called my name, but I didn't hear him, not as Kazimir and I plummeted toward the icy, violent waters thousands of feet below.

The force of my assault knocked his sword free, and it fell beside us, just out of reach. He grasped for it, and I quickly stabbed through his wings with my own blades, rendering him unable to fly.

"I loved you, you know. Once," I snarled, snapping my own wings shut so I had enough force to finish this. Releasing my grip on one sword, I grasped the other with both hands, tip pointed into his chest. White fire burst along its length, and Kazimir wrapped his hands around the blade as if he were trying to stop it from slicing into him. Blood soaked his hands and the scent of burnt flesh filled my nostrils as we battled for control of it. "But you became like every other asshole who tried to hurt me, to use me, to get what they wanted. I am no one's toy, no one's pet, no one's doll. I am Izidora Valynor, future empress of Északi, and you will die by my hand."

With a scream that held every last bit of unfiltered emotion inside me, I shoved with all my might. The blade pierced his chest, and he caved inward at the pain, his face contorting and a grunt ripping from his throat.

He opened his mouth and moved his lips like he wanted to say something, but no sound emerged. Still, I pressed, using my weight and my fire to ensure this fucking ended. The ground closed in, and I did not surrender my position and provide him any opportunity to escape.

At the last moment, I flared my wings, the wind catching me and keeping me aloft while Kazimir plummeted the remaining distance, utterly alone and destroyed. The jagged rocks snapped his body with a satisfying crunch. Frothy red water washed over his body, pinned by all the pointed tips.

I hovered there for a moment, watching, waiting for him to rise. Blood rushed in my ears, overtaking the sound of the crashing water beneath me. Trembling, I landed beside him, careful not to slip on the wet river stones.

I toed him with the tip of my boot, searching for any sign of response. The black in his eyes had faded away, leaving only a deep emerald green that stared, unblinking, at the brilliant blue sky.

I clasped my hands over my mouth, a choked sob catching in my chest as reality settled over me.

Kazimir was finally dead.

He would never hurt me again.

"Sprite," a voice said softly, and I ripped my gaze away from Kazimir to find Ruslan hovering nearby.

A heartbeat later, I threw myself into his arms, clutching at his bare skin as I tried to ground myself against the piercing pain. "Zuriel," I managed to gasp out, trying to explain why even though Kazimir was dead, I wasn't yet free of his torment.

He wrapped himself so tightly around me. I struggled to breathe, but in that moment, I needed it. Needed *him*.

"He was my only family," I sobbed, chest heaving with the force of my cries. Ruslan's sweat-soaked skin grew saltier as my tears mixed in, but he didn't relent.

"I know, sprite, I know," he choked out, and then I wriggled free, swiping at my eyes to find Ruslan's just as blurry. "Zuriel loved you very much."

"He wanted to die so he could be with his wife," I murmured, trembling from head to toe. Then, I clutched at Ruslan's chest, a frantic energy overtaking me. "I want to be joined with you in every way, Ruslan. I never want to live without you."

He crushed me against him, a growl rumbling from his chest

as his tongue parted my lips and swept through my mouth. *"Then you will fucking marry me the moment this mess is all cleaned up. You will have me in every way you want from this moment until our dying breaths. Because make no mistake, Izidora. There is no me without you, nor you without me. We die together or not at all."*

A fresh wave of hot tears tracked down my cheeks, but I couldn't stop kissing Ruslan, desperate to be closer to him, to fuse our bodies as one just like our souls. *"Us against the world."*

With that, he broke our kiss, his chest pressing against mine as we heaved down icy breaths. "Come, sprite. Let's prevent any further unnecessary deaths."

I glanced sidelong as Kazimir. "What should we do with his body?"

Ruslan did not deign to give him any attention. "Leave it."

I accepted his outstretched hand, and together, we took to the sky, returning to the battlefield and preparing to usher in a new world for all the residents of Északi.

INTERLUDE

Bodies lined the sides of the steep mountains, some broken over boulders, others staining the snow red. The heat from the cooling bodies melted what laid beneath them, creating rivers of ruby to trickle down the slopes and join the one raging below. The cries had died down as the survivors granted mercy to those who could not be saved, though the healers' tents overflowed with wounded warriors. Thousands of beating wings filled the air as bodies were collected on both sides, piled together for the pyres that would ferry them to the Goddess and the Fates.

A group of three sisters dressed in flowing black robes floated across from an ethereal lady in white. They surveyed the damage of one of the greatest conflicts to grace the shores of Északi – a conflict they had caused.

"Ezi, Kari, Riza," the Goddess greeted the Fates. "Are you satisfied with how everything unfolded?"

"Yes," they hissed in unison, their voices twining together in a haunting way.

On this plane, those below could not hear them, nor could they see them unless they chose to reveal themselves.

"My children are hurting," the Goddess said, sweeping an arm to the side and pulling the sisters to hover over her prophesied ones. The chestnut-haired female sobbed over the body of the Angel who had waited nearly two millennia to carry out his task, while her mate rubbed circles in her back, pinching the bridge of his nose to stem his own grief.

How he had grown, the Goddess thought.

The Fates' robes billowed on an invisible breeze, and they tucked their arms together, hiding their hands as they assessed the rest of the group. A female with chocolate brown hair was in a similar state of despair, thrown over her brother while his living friends sat in a ring around his body, tears flowing freely and without shame.

"Their pain will not last forever," they replied. "They will have a happy life, eventually."

"What's most important is that the worlds will survive," the middle one spoke, breaking away from her sisters and staring at the Goddess with an intensity that left no room for argument.

"As you said when we made our exchange." She looked away from the three, surveying the rest of her creation. The mountains that pierced the air, the river that ran with blood, the clear blue sky that covered this entire world.

Shooting into the sky, the four studied the rest of the continent – the loving queen and king cradling their babe on the grassy plains, the burned fields in the realm of lakes and greenery, the churned earth between it and the wooded realm. Then, they turned their attention beyond, to the other continents of Ravasz, where millions of others remained oblivious to the carnage on Északi.

Stories would soon spread as the world began to change, prompted by what had happened there. With a sigh, the Goddess closed her eyes and breathed her last breath into the world, renewing it with the last of her strength. This would be her greatest gift to her children, one that would prolong their lives here until the next prophesied ones were born.

She blinked slowly, the Fates coming into focus as she herself began to fade.

"The promise will be kept." The three voices twisted together, then followed the Goddess into oblivion.

VI

THE AFTERMATH

56

RUSLAN

Izidora and I sat at the head of a long table, both still dressed in armor despite the fighting having stopped not long after she killed Kazimir. After the battle, the entire continent knew that Izidora and I were the two most powerful Fae on it, and our Félvér powers were superior to those of pure-blooded Fae. But strife remained between the Night Fae, and with Kazimir's slaughter of King Aiire and Queen Immonen of the Crystal Realm, there was a void of power there as well.

Since I was the emperor of Északi, our victory came with the responsibility of restoring order. Though Izidora was not yet crowned empress, I included her in these decisions. After all, she would be marrying me not too long after this meeting adjourned. The extent to which she wanted to be involved in ruling the continent was still uncertain, but I knew she'd be fantastic once she believed in herself. She just needed some time to process everything without the threat of something else happening.

So, we called a conclave of all noble houses from every realm to carve a path forward. Izidora and I didn't want to restore what had been; we wanted to build a new, better world for all.

The rest of the table was lined with every race of Fae, along with the noble Félvér from the Iron Realm, and all stared in our direction. I picked my head up off my fist and uncrossed my ankle from my knee before scraping back my chair and standing. Beside me, Izidora rose on her own, wings glittering and flaring behind her as she lifted her chin and crossed her arms.

Silence fell.

"We have made our decision." The words dropped like a hammer on an anvil, and each noble straightened a little in their seat, no doubt vying for a last minute bid for attention just in case we changed our minds.

"Endre of House Zadik will rule the Night Realm." The brow of the male in question furrowed as if he couldn't comprehend his sudden launch to being a king. Izidora had argued passionately on his behalf and refused to let me consider anyone else. But honestly, no one was better suited for the role in the entire Night Realm. He'd betrayed his best friend to save us all, and despite our rocky, rough start, I had grown to respect him.

Endre pushed to his feet, his peridot eyes glistening as the reality of his responsibility settled over him.

"I think he wishes his parents were here. He has a lot of mixed feelings right now," Izidora spoke in my mind. It was only a few days ago that he learned that Kazimir had executed them for *his* actions, and from what Izidora and Liliana had told me, that guilt weighed more heavily on him than the Night Crown would in a short time.

"Emperor Ruslan, I am honored to be chosen." He cleared his throat and then opened his mouth to speak again. "I will do my best to steer the Night Realm in a better direction."

A smattering of light applause filled the room, and he dipped his head in the direction of Queen Viktoria and King

Consort Geza before turning to the surviving nobles of the Night Realm.

Fuck, so few of the High Houses remained.

Houses Luzak and Valintin were eradicated under Kazimir's rule, leaving only Houses Zadik, Arzeni, Adimik, Rass, and Volak behind. House Arzeni was one of the only ones left fully intact, though the name would die out after Liliana finally settled down. House Adimik was survived by Viktor and his mother, and if Viktor did not object to my next announcement, his line would continue as well. Domi and Kaztar would have a child or two someday, and House Volak was well on its way to securing its line well into the future. The Lower Houses in the distance were just as broken, but their succession did not concern me as much as the others.

Endre could reestablish the noble lines as he saw fit when he returned to Este Castle.

"If there are no objections, we have a few other announcements," I said, lifting a brow and waiting for a challenge. None come.

"Viktor Adimik, we propose a match for you with Natasha Bakal of the Iron Realm in order to promote further peace among our peoples," Izidora announced, her voice strong and steady. The dark-haired Félvér female straightened in her seat beside her parents, looking to Viktor for confirmation. The two had already been acquainted during Béke, and with both being offspring from High Houses of two different realms, their marriage would strengthen the peace we sought to build.

Viktor blew out a breath, then nodded. "I accept."

Natasha grinned, and both were congratulated by those around them.

"As for the matter of who will rule the Crystal Realm," I started, and everyone went silent again. "I have chosen High Lord Slavian Romanuk of the Iron Realm. He has agreed to marry one of the daughters of the nobles of the Crystal Realm to promote harmony with the Crystal Fae. You may decide among yourselves, but the wedding will take place in a year's time, as a gesture of good faith."

Frowns and crossed arms rippled through the gathered Crystal Fae, making their displeasure as clear as they dared. Izidora sent a pulse of support down our bond. *"Us against the world."*

"Us against the world," I echoed.

"If anyone disagrees or would like to protest, now is your chance to speak." Izidora flattened her palms on the table and stared down each group of Fae individually, daring them to challenge her. I schooled my features to hide my amusement. Her petite frame did nothing to back up her intimidation tactic, but that was why I had given her the nickname sprite in the first place. She was adorable when she was spitting fire, but never would I underestimate her because of that. She'd proven that she was as deadly as any male and as ruthless as me, especially since she had awoken after Kazimir tried to kill her.

High Lord Soma rapped his knuckles on the table, drawing the attention of the room. He glanced to his queen and king, then said, "I too wish to have a marriage arranged for me, to support the empire's new vision."

Queen Viktoria spoke her agreement. "High Lord Soma has our blessing with whomever he chooses or is chosen for him."

"We shall arrange it, High Lord Soma," Izidora promised, her features softening as she locked eyes with each of the Day Fae.

"It really feels like we did it, like they want to be part of this new world," Izidora said only to me, and she gave me unobstructed insight into her unbridled joy. The emotion filled me as well, and I struggled to keep the grin off my face. Our work was not quite finished.

"Tell them what else we have," I encouraged her.

Izidora had woken in the middle of the night two days after the last battle, gasping for breath. At first I panicked, thinking we were under attack again, but she grabbed my arm and sent soothing emotions into me. An idea had pulled her from sleep, and once she whispered it to me with hope in her voice, I vowed to make it happen.

And as she cleared her throat to make her last announcement, I allowed beaming pride to fill my face.

"I will be opening a trauma center to help anyone impacted by the war. Whether they are a refugee returning to the shores of Északi, from a noble house or a rural village, all will be welcome to receive treatment and heal. I am also seeking volunteers to train to help those in need."

Liliana, of course, was the first to volunteer, and around the room, nearly a dozen hands raised, all offering assistance. Tears spilled over Izidora's aquamarine eyes, and I caught one with the tip of my finger before it rolled off her cheek and into the table. My sprite would never have to hide her emotions again, not with me, not with anyone.

"I love you. I'm so proud of you."

"Thank you all very much for volunteering. We will be in touch regarding training and the location of the center," she said, her voice thick. I flattened a palm on her lower back and stroked my thumb soothingly across it.

"That concludes our conclave," I announced. "You are welcome to remain in the Iron Realm for as long as you like, though we hope you will stay for at least a few more days to attend our wedding and coronation. If there are further questions or issues, speak with High Lord Drazen, who will pass your messages along to me. Whenever you are ready to return home, the Mages will assist you."

Izidora and I stepped back from the table, and one by one,

each noble greeted and thanked us on their way out of the ballroom.

Drazen, Liliana, Endre, and Viktor all hung back, waiting until the very last of the Low Houses had departed before closing the doors behind them and leaving the six of us alone in the giant space.

"Who needs a drink? Because I sure as shit do," Liliana pronounced, lifting a bottle of amber liquor off a table that had been pushed against the nearest wall. She yanked the cork, then took a long swing straight from the neck.

Izidora laughed and lifted the bottle from her friend, mimicking her and exaggerating the hiss after she swallowed. "Thank you for being the first to volunteer, Lil."

I snagged the alcohol from Izidora's hands right before the two collided, tears and laughs and kind words slipping between them. Offering them a moment of privacy, I turned to the new king of the Night Realm.

"To Endre," I said, lifting the bottle then swigging from it before proffering it to Viktor. He repeated my phrase, then drank and passed the liquor along.

"I really don't know why you chose me," he said, shoving a lock of hair out of his face. "Why not Drazen? You've already made Slavian king of the Crystal Realm."

Drazen answered for me. "I don't want that level of responsibility. I much prefer fighting to ruling. Besides, after everything that has happened with the Night Realm, I think there needs to be a Night Fae on the throne. Kazimir did some serious damage, and King Zalan before him. The Night Realm needs an empathetic, level-headed ruler who can lead them forward. And that's you."

"Are you coming with us?" Endre asked Drazen with a glance in the females' direction.

"You are free to come and go as you please, Drazen. Don't

stay here on my account," I said to my cousin, my general, and my best friend.

The Dragon Shifter Félvér looked between Endre, Liliana, and me, then nodded. "The three of us will return to the Night Realm together." He took a step toward me, then clapped me on the shoulder. "But with those two," he jerked his head in Izidora and Liliana's direction, "I think I'll probably see you daily anyway. One of them better fucking be able to move like you do, or the Mages are going to constantly be drained."

The four of us shared a laugh, drawing the females' attention. "Hey! What was that about?" Liliana questioned, dragging Izidora back into our little circle.

"Probably stupid male stuff," my mate commented, earning a laugh and an eye-roll from Liliana.

"When isn't it stupid male stuff?" she retorted with a flick of her hair.

"Never," Izidora quipped, smiling sweetly at me. She bit her bottom lip, and with a playful growl, I yanked her to me and captured it between my fingers, pulling it free.

"You, sprite, were magnificent. After you get your center up and running, I'm taking you on a nice long trip to the Day Realm."

"What are you going to name your trauma center, Izidora?" Endre asked, swirling the amber liquor and then sipping.

I released her, though she remained tucked against my side, banishing her wings so she could wrap an arm around my waist. "The Angel Center. After Zuriel."

Fuck, even my eyes burned, and Izidora didn't bother to mask her pain from me. Losing Zuriel was heartbreaking for her, and I knew she needed the place just as much as anyone else. What he'd taught her would help countless others who lost their homes or loved ones during the war. And from what

Izidora told me, he was happy to move on from this life and return to his wife in whatever waited for us after death.

I squeezed her harder against me, wanting her to feel how safe and loved she was.

Liliana dipped behind us and grabbed six glasses, passing them all around. Drazen poured us each a healthy measure of alcohol, and then Liliana raised hers high in the air. "To Zuriel."

"To Zuriel," we all echoed.

57

IZIDORA

THREE DAYS LATER

The first day of spring broke with the clearest skies and a kaleidoscope of color falling over the trees in the valley surrounding Radence. Liliana burst into our room at the crack of dawn, shooing a very naked Ruslan out and throwing clothes at him as he protested her early arrival. I fell into giggles as they argued back and forth, Ruslan's bulk in no way intimidating my best friend. Eventually he stormed out with a growl, leaving me and Liliana with the day to prepare for the wedding and coronation.

"I kept your dress hidden from those dumb males all this time," Liliana squealed as she dragged in a white bag that I assumed held the dress I'd had made during Béke. "It will probably work out better that it's warmer today than it would have been in the winter. Pretty sure you might have frozen in it."

"Beauty is pain, is it not?" I quipped, opening the bag to reveal the beautiful gown and glittering gemstones that accompanied it.

"That's right," she laughed, flicking her long chocolate

brown hair over her shoulder. "Will you braid my hair before we get started? Mine are never as good as yours."

"Throw the bag on the bed and we'll set up in the bathroom," I said, slipping into a robe that wouldn't mess up the intricate braids I planned on weaving into my waist-length locks.

The early morning light was perfect, and Liliana perched on a plush stool pulled from beneath the luxurious marble countertop. In the mirror, her eyes gleamed with excitement, nearly matching my own. Using my fingers to shake out her locks, I teased out several sections, securing them away from each other as I began to twist and braid. "Up or down?"

"Down if you're planning on wearing yours up," she replied, and I altered my course slightly so that her hair would tumble down her back.

Soon, small braids dotted her hair, mixing with the straight pieces, and others were woven into a single thick braid down the back, giving her a free spirit vibe that perfectly suited her. A knock sounded on the outer door, and I jogged through the suite to answer it. Cedomir, Roc Palace's chef, stood there with a cart laden with food, and I opened the door wider to allow him entry.

"My Empress, you look stunning already. I am so pleased this day has finally arrived for you and Emperor Ruslan." He smiled warmly, arranging the feast on the dining table. I snatched a bottle of bubbly wine and some glasses for Liliana and myself, since my friend was never one to turn it down, no matter the hour. Especially if there was a reason to celebrate, and today definitely deserved it. If there was one thing I had learned from her, it was that no victory was too small for cheers. That attitude was one I desperately needed after everything that had happened over the past year.

"Thank you, Cedomir. I hope to see you in the temple later."

"It would be my honor to gain admittance, though I have a feeling those seats will be hard won." With a bow, he swept from the room, and I returned to the bathroom to find Liliana spilling colorful creams and fluffy brushes all over the counter.

"Oh! You brought wine," she said, leaving her mess and snatching the bottle from me. In true Liliana fashion, she popped the cork, making me both jump and laugh because I knew it was coming and still startled. I held out the glasses to her, and she poured enough wine in both to fill them to the brim.

"To finally marrying my mate and becoming empress," I toasted, a giddy feeling bubbling in my chest. I hadn't even tasted the wine yet and I was already drunk on pure, unbridled joy.

"Took you two long enough. I thought with the list of requirements stacking up, it would never happen," Liliana teased, clinking her glass with mine.

I smiled around the chilled liquid that ghosted over my tongue, leaving tingles in its wake. If there was even the slightest wisp of a thought that I didn't deserve this happiness, it was banished as the wine loosened me.

Ruslan and I would be wed, and I would be crowned empress.

"And then I will fuck you senseless all night, mate." Ruslan's voice echoed in my mind, causing my smile to widen and my heart to flutter with excitement. I hadn't realized I'd sent those thoughts wide enough for him to hear, though I suppose there was really no secrecy when we were constantly in each other's heads.

"My dress is really so pretty. It would be a shame to destroy it."

"I don't give a fuck. It will be in the way of me ravishing you."

"You guys are talking down the bond again aren't you?" Liliana sighed wistfully.

Sheepishly, I sipped from my drink and nodded. "Being mated is the best."

"You two disgust me with how sweet you are. But also he literally kills people for hurting you and doesn't lose sleep over it. So I'm pretty sure he's crazy," she pronounced, cocking her head in a teasing way.

"I wouldn't want him any other way," I laughed. I thought he was insane in our first conversations, but then, I discovered that underneath his ruthless, crazed exterior was a male as desperate to be loved as I was, who would shoulder responsibility that was not his own simply because he cared for me. Guilt still clung to him over his lack of awareness of my circumstances, and he hadn't forgiven himself for being unable to stop the harm befalling me. Fucking him while we were covered in blood, then accepting the mating bond after, was perfectly on track for us. Not to mention all the sex we'd had over the last week and a half while we relived our battles in our joined minds.

We were light and dark, but when we came together, we were the most brilliant shade of gray, like the moment just before breaking dawn where the stars still lived and the first rays of sun flitted through the sky. Ruslan understood me, empowered me, and allowed me to explore all the sides of me I never got to discover while I was chained. And yet he was ruthlessly protective of me in a way that made my toes curl and my core throb. No one laid a harmful hand on me and lived. He was my dark God, my fierce Dragon, the male who lived in the darkness and laughed in its face when it tried to consume him.

Together we were invincible, and in a few hours, we'd be joined in every way possible.

While Liliana painted her face, making her already feminine features even more striking, I plaited my hair, ensuring it was off my neck to accommodate the jewels I would wear, then pulled a few strands loose around my face. Finally I fluffed up the thick braids until I looked ethereal in the mirror. Scanning my face from side to side until I was satisfied, I adjusted pieces here and there until my heart-shaped face was framed perfectly by the loose tendrils.

"How does it look?" I asked Liliana, who was in the process of swiping a thick coating of black across her already dark lashes.

"Absolutely perfect." Her eyes glittered as they roamed over my hair. "Okay, let me at your face."

"Can I at least eat first?" I laughed, my stomach rumbling in protest. All I'd had was wine, and dizziness greeted me as I rose from the stool.

"Bring me some fruit," she called out as I returned to the living space. I rolled my eyes and piled two identical plates with food, both with extra fruit. They clattered against the marble as I placed them amid the haphazard array of makeup.

Settling cross-legged onto the stool, I dug my fork into the eggs and semi-cold cinnamon rolls before consuming the fruit and cheese. I didn't realize how hungry I was until I looked at my empty plate and wanted more. "I'm still hungry, but that dress was tight when I had it made," I laughed, and Liliana joined me around a mouthful of food.

"Beauty is pain," she managed to say, covering her mouth with her hand. She chewed and swallowed, then drained the last of her wine. "Now, let's fix your face. I'm thinking sultry."

"When are you not?" I bantered, spinning to face her. "But yes, I want Ruslan to think of nothing else when he sees me."

Liliana scoffed and unscrewed the lid of one of her jars. "Pretty sure he would do the same regardless of when, where, or who was around."

"True," I replied. A smile pulled up the corners of my mouth despite my attempts to smooth my face so Liliana could work her magic. The depth of devotion Ruslan offered me with each glance in my direction was nearly indescribable, solidifying the utter safety I felt when I was with him.

Obediently, I followed Liliana's directions as she painted my face, accentuating the bright blues of my eyes with heavy dark makeup around them, then sharpening my cheekbones and dusting them with a shimmer that caught the light no matter which way I looked. Her final touch was a glossy lip stain that made me afraid to drink or eat anything.

Her brows pinched ever so slightly as she made a few adjustments, and I had to smother the smile as her bottom lip popped open. Why her face frozen in concentration was so amusing, I had no clue. Perhaps it was the wine, or perhaps I was drunk on the excitement of the day. Either way, she snapped at me to hold still more than once.

When she was finally satisfied, she stepped back and then spun me so I faced the mirror again. Crouching, she bent her head toward mine, and we gazed at our reflections together. Our styles were similar, but each of our unique personalities shone.

"We're definitely going to be the most fuckable females there," I whispered, that smile finally breaking.

My comment earned a laugh from her, and shook her head. "As if we weren't already."

"Have I ever told you how much I love your self confidence?" I said as I rose from the stool and made my way to the bedroom where the intricate dress rested on the bed. We worked together to shimmy it out of the bag, careful not to snag the jewels sewn into the fabric on anything. As I drank in the exquisite gown with a sheer waist with thick boning, I regretted that last cinnamon roll I'd eaten.

"Hopefully I don't break it," I said, patting my belly.

"Oh shut up, you'll be fine," Liliana snorted, unhooking the buttons on the back and shaking out the wispy skirt. The train was long enough to cover the bedroom end to end if we stretched it out. My robe dropped from my shoulders, and I took great care in avoiding the white fabric as I readied myself to pull it on. Using Liliana for balance, I stepped into the puddle. I exhaled all the air from my lungs, and she shimmied the dress up over my legs. When the cups that supported my breasts reached my chest, I clasped them against my body, allowing Liliana to work to close the dress around my torso. The dress fit perfectly, even after all this time, and I breathed a sigh of relief when Liliana stepped back.

"All done!" she exclaimed, gingerly bunching the white fabric around my feet so she could circle me, searching for anything out of place. I adjusted my breasts in the top, then the sheer sleeves that started just above my elbows and billowed out until they cinched at my wrists.

Glancing down at myself, I admired the fine fabric, its sheerness leaving almost nothing to the imagination, but the softness held an almost romantic quality. And because it was the Iron Realm, there were gemstones galore. None of the tiny diamonds sewn into the skirt compared to the bodice Liliana lifted from the bed.

The glittering metal overlay made it look like I was quite literally dripping in gems, and Liliana managed to fasten the collar of the piece around my neck without catching my hair. From there, she adjusted the layers of chains covered in glittering diamonds and smoky gray stones, fastening the last of them around my waist, just above where the flowing skirts tumbled down my hips in every direction. The metal was cold against the bare parts of my back, and I hobbled to the mirror to get a better look at myself.

The female in the mirror looked like a goddess – sexy, romantic, and powerful. Metal armor had become my preferred attire, but this, this was an outfit of war just as much, if not more, than what I strapped on to spar. The dress commanded attention and respect, and the fierce look on the female wearing it? Well, that was enough to send any male's knees quaking.

"Insidious bloom," I said to myself in the mirror, turning this way and that as the white fire in my chest flared with the heady thrum of my thoughts.

Liliana slipped into her dress, a sultry garnet piece with a slit so high in the leg that one forceful breeze would expose her. The bodice had boning that matched mine, keeping with the style of the Iron Realm to show a lot of skin. Glancing at the large clock on the wall, I noticed it was nearly time for the procession to begin, which meant Ruslan would be returning at any moment.

"Ready?" Liliana asked, using silver tendrils of her magic to lift my skirts and arrange them in a neat bundle that would allow me to walk. We waddled over to where a pair of white slippers waited for me, and I stepped into them, not loving the pinch around my toes.

"Now I am," I grinned, my stomach turning over as I felt Ruslan drawing nearer.

Liliana's eyes shone as we held each other's gazes, and a crooked smile twisted her features. All her emotions washed over me, drawing tears to my eyes, too. "You look so beautiful, Izidora. You deserve this so much."

I clasped her hands in mine, giving them a light squeeze. "You will have this too, with Endre and Drazen. Now reel back your emotions, otherwise I might cry and ruin all your hard work."

"You're the empath, can't you do that?" Her laugh was watery as we embraced. I was so grateful to have my best friend by my side for one of the most important days of my life. Goddess, I was grateful to have everyone in my life when I had gone twenty-one years without a true friend or family.

Ruslan, Drazen, Liliana, Endre, the other Félvér... they were my family. The Iron Realm was my home. And my mate was steps away from seeing me.

The doors to our suite opened, revealing Ruslan in a sharp

black suit perfectly molded to his muscular frame, the newly minted Empire Crown resting atop his head. Garnets the color of blood dotted the thick band of black metal covered in intricate filigree that spoke of the unity of Északi as it wound its way around. A matching one had been crafted for me, though I would receive it from Ruslan later.

Never had he felt so large and imposing as he did the moment he stepped into the room, looking every bit the emperor of all the Fae realms. The air fled my lungs as our gazes collided, and it was as if the world stopped turning, just for us. We remained frozen, raking our eyes over one another, until finally he broke our trance and crossed the room in three strides, capturing me against his body and running his nose along what little bare skin remained around my neck.

"This fucking dress and those fucking jewels, Izidora... are you trying to kill me with lust?" His raspy voice was thick with it, and I didn't have to imagine just how aroused he was with his erection digging into my stomach.

I clutched the lapels of his jacket as I tried to ground myself against the overwhelming urges coming down our bond. The tide of Ruslan's emotion shattered the loose mental shield I maintained to block out the emotions of those around me.

"Don't you dare ruin this before the world gets to see me in it," I admonished him, throat thickening from the all-consuming happiness pooling between us.

"Why not? Then they'll know just how *mine* you already are." He flattened a palm against my lower back while another dipped between my breasts.

"Because I am a powerful Félvér and I want everyone to see that. They will fear me, they will respect me, and everyone will speak of how the Angelic empress will destroy all who dare challenge her." I flattened my hands against his chest and gave him a playful shove.

"Mmm, when you talk like that, it only makes me want you more," he groaned, but he relented and stepped back. His smoky eyes swirled with desire, and he didn't remove them from me for a moment as Liliana and I combined our magic to gather my skirts and make our way to the lift that would carry us down the mountain.

"You look even better from behind."

I shot a heated look over my shoulder at Ruslan, and Liliana rolled her eyes, obviously catching on to our internal conversation. "I wonder if we'll even get through the ceremonies with the way you two are eye fucking each other."

Several carriages awaited us when we finally emerged from Roc Palace, and with the utmost care, Liliana helped me into the first one. The journey to the temple on the outskirts of Radence would be a long one, especially as the streets would be lined with Fae and Félvér eager to glimpse their emperor and future empress. The High Priestess would marry us before the Goddess, and afterward, Ruslan would crown me as his empress.

The midday sun cast much needed warmth over us as the black horses trotted forward, leading the procession through the capital of the Iron Realm. In the carriages behind us, Drazen and Endre rode with Liliana, Anton, and Slavian. Beyond them, line after line of Iron Realm nobility brought up the rear of the procession. Ruslan grasped my hand, linking his fingers with mine, and brought it to his lips.

The kiss he planted there was hungry, sensual, and reverent. "You are stunning, mate."

A chill swept through me at his tone, painting goosebumps on my skin.

Ruslan examined the rings adorning my hand, the large rectangular ruby surrounded by a pointed diamond standing out among the bands of silver and black that circled the rest of my knuckles. "A ruby so dark it reminds me of blood, and you,

Izidora, have spilled enough blood for a lifetime. We will know peace for the remainder of our lives."

The promise in his words poured into my muscles, relaxing them as I took the opportunity to remind myself that I was safe. No one would hurt me ever again.

"Never," he emphasized, and I lost myself in the severity of his smoky gray eyes.

He released my hand from his purview to rest on the seat between us. The throng of people thickened around us as we entered the busiest part of Radence, and I beamed at my people, waving to them and sharing my joy. Even Ruslan cracked a smile, breaking the ruthless facade he carefully cultivated to hide his hurt from the world. I was lucky enough to be one of the people who saw the true ends he would go to to protect those he loved, and to be privy to the darkest thoughts and desires he had. He was my mate, lost in the darkness until my light shone a way forward, and together, we had proven how unstoppable we were.

The glass temple came into view as we rounded a corner, the clopping of the horses' hooves against the stone streets indistinguishable over the roar of the onlookers who managed to squeeze themselves along the best street to view the wedding and coronation. Flowers that had to have been cut that morning rained down on us as Fae tossed them along with their well-wishes.

"Are you ready?" Ruslan asked me, giving my hand a squeeze.

"Absolutely," I grinned back, excitement bubbling in my chest – almost painfully – as I tried to remain still instead of bouncing in my seat.

Our carriage rolled to a stop in front of the stoic temple. The entire building was glass, save for the metal frame holding the wide panes together. Through the windows, rows and rows of seats, mostly filled with attendees already, waited, while white flowers cascaded over every available surface. Mixed in among them were glittering black gemstones, creating balance in the way that Ruslan and I did for each other.

He stepped from the carriage, holding out his hand to assist me in my descent. Calling on my magic to help me, I lifted the long train of my dress, hovering it above the earth so it would not get dirty before entering the temple. Liliana trotted over from her carriage to help me, shooing Drazen and Endre away as she assisted me in entering the building. Through a side door, the nobles who accompanied us on our parade through Radence took their seats, the air buzzing with anticipation. Those who remained after the conclave clustered in row after row together, and joy filled my heart as I counted each and every one of them.

The glass doors closed behind us, and with one last flourish, Liliana settled the long, white, wispy strands of my skirt and flashed me a teary smile before hurrying to her seat at the front. The High Priestess stood at the center of the temple, black robes floating around her as she waited for our arrival. I slipped my hand into the crook of Ruslan's arm, my own eyes pricking with hot tears as the hour we would be wed was finally upon us. Drums beat a steady, slow rhythm as we approached the dais in the center of the room.

The platform was high above the seating, and with a forceful step, I managed to rise to it gracefully. Liliana darted forward to arrange my skirts, and then Ruslan faced me, shooting me a devastating smirk that had my core heating in the best way.

A hush fell over the room as every important Fae, Félvér, and Telivér in all of Északi waited for the rites to begin. The drums softened until they were barely audible, but the beating of my heart in my chest drowned them out regardless.

Taking my hands in his, Ruslan nodded to the High Priestess, and she tipped her head back to look at the brilliant, cloudless blue sky. With a flick of her wrists, fire burst into existence on the edges of the temple. Raising her arms overhead, the ground beneath our feet shook as she called on her power.

"Goddess, we beckon you to join us during this time of celebration." Her voice was fierce and heavy as she began chanting, joined by her acolytes scattered throughout the temple.

"Goddess, you have offered your children the ultimate gift – a mating bond." The drums beat louder as the acolytes' chants quickened. Goosebumps broke out across my flesh as magic seemed to rise from all around us, and I was grateful for the sleeves that covered my arms, preventing me from shivering.

"Join us now as we unite them in marriage and crown," the High Priestess shouted toward the sky, her fires flaring brighter as she summoned the mother of all nature.

The chants and beats reached a crescendo, then fell silent all at once, like an otherworldly force had sucked the sound from the room. My heart lurched as power settled across my shoulders. Silence reigned, so quiet that the silk cloth the High Priestess pulled from her robes was audible as she began looping it over mine and Ruslan's joined hands.

"My blood is your blood. My body is your body. My life is your life," Ruslan began, reciting the lines we'd memorized for this moment.

"My blood is your blood. My body is your body. My life is your life," I repeated, my voice unwavering as I locked eyes with my mate.

The world fell away as we uttered the last line simultaneously, reserved only for those who had been mated. "My soul is your soul."

The High Priestess finished her weaving as we spoke, tying an intricate knot around our hands and tightening it to the point that my fingers went numb. With a nod of his head, Ruslan indicated we should begin. Tendrils of white magic slipped through the knot just as black fire arced into the sky, and all around us, our magics undulated together, blending into a brilliant gray that sparkled like the polished glass of the temple. For the first time, the crowd broke its silence, gasps of awe filling the room as they witnessed the force of our combined powers.

We let the magic dissipate on its own, reserving a wisp to settle over our hands and burn away the silk, officially uniting Ruslan and me. The fire that remained in his eyes made me weak at the knees, and I was grateful for his powerful hands grasping mine.

"Seal your union with an unbreakable kiss," the High Priestess commanded, and my husband wasted no time in yanking me flush against his hard body and capturing my mouth in one of the most fervent kisses he had ever given me. Promises, vows, and emotions flowed between us as our lips and tongues tangled, and all around us, enthusiasm erupted from the crowd.

But their cheers melted away as there was only him – only us – in that infinite moment. Ruslan stole my breath as much as he had stolen my heart, my soul, and I let him, falling deeper into the safety of his arms. He kissed me as if I was his salvation and he would be damned without me, his grip tightening on my lower back, the heat from his hands burning my skin through the thin fabric of my dress.

"Now, forever, always, sprite."

He broke our kiss, leaving my lips bruised and red and a bit less glossy than they had been. The triumphant smirk he wore as he gazed down at me was worth every bit of it.

"I love you, Ruslan."

"I love you more, Izidora."

Stepping away, he strode to the pedestal where a delicate black diadem encrusted with glittering red gemstones rested on a plush velvet pillow. Dropping to one knee before my mate, my husband, I bowed my head, heart hammering in my chest as the weight of my responsibility settled over me.

Was I ready for this? Could I be an empress after everything I'd been through? Would I be good enough to my people?

"Izidora Valynor Drakkar, do you swear to uphold the laws of the Északi Empire, to care for its people, and to make every effort to defend its sovereign territories?" Ruslan asked, his raspy voice taking on a serious and solemn air.

Dragging in a serrated breath, I swore my oath. "I do." My voice managed to come out steady, and I braced myself for the moment Ruslan would place the diadem over my intricately woven braids. The piece was not as heavy as I'd anticipated, but the metaphor of it was.

"Rise," he commanded, grasping my hand to assist me.

I lifted my gaze, the diadem thankfully remaining in place, and the High Priestess stepped forward once more. "Goddess, witness the union of Emperor Ruslan and Empress Izidora and know they serve you and all of your creation."

The ground trembled beneath our feet, and the fires she had been fueling speared upward again before vanishing like they had never existed. Ruslan raised our joined hands overhead in celebration and victory, and I worried the glass temple would implode with the force of excitement reverberating within it.

Even outside the temple, our people celebrated, their cheers and cries adding to those bursting from those within. Liliana swiped furiously at the tears spilling from her eyes, and Endre flashed us a triumphant grin. Drazen, Anton, Slavian, and the other Félvér clapped furiously, shouting at us, the two young High Lords tossing out obscene and highly suggestive ideas about what would happen after we left the temple. Ruslan growled in their direction, which only made them laugh harder. Xorrek and Gozzak slapped them on the shoulders and howled.

Queen Viktoria beamed up at me, Princess Gizela wrapped protectively in her arms, while King Consort Geza whooped and joined Anton and Slavian in their remarks. The queen of the Day Realm smacked her husband on the thigh, making me giggle.

The mosaic of sounds rose to a crescendo as the whole of Radence erupted with joy. In that moment, I knew that all the pain, all the trauma, was worth it, because not only was I a symbol for them, but also for all who had suffered.

And I planned on showing everyone else just how strong a survivor could be.

58

RUSLAN

That evening

I didn't even wait for the formal dinner at Ryza Citadel to finish before I snatched Izidora and ferried her to our apartment at the top of the spire. The revelry around the city and in the citadel were loud enough to drown out any sounds she'd be making.

That fucking dress.

She glittered like a diamond mined only for me, and as I circled her in the middle of our bedroom, she lifted her chin and grinned deviously at me.

"Mate, emperor, husband," she purred, batting her black-coated lashes at me.

I stopped behind her, forcing her to look at me over her shoulder. The black surrounding her eyes made them pop like gemstones, and the diadem resting in her braided hair squeezed my heart, making it pump harder and sending all that blood straight to my groin. I reached for the collar that held the jewels to her body, finding the latch and hesitating. Then I closed the distance between us, letting her feel just how fucking hard I was. "Mmm, I'm going to leave these jewels on while I fuck you, *wife*, but that means I'll have to shred this." My hand drifted to her skirt, bunching it between my fingers and revealing her legs.

Her breath hitched as I shifted one finger into a talon and skimmed it along her thigh. The sound of ripping fabric filled the air as I sank it into the dress, peeling it from her body piece by piece. First, the skirt fell away, and the scent that wafted from between her thighs nearly had me falling to my knees to worship the ethereal being before me. The sheer sleeves were next, leaving only the transparent bodice covered by gemstones. I circled around again, drinking in the sight of her dripping diamonds.

I shucked my jacket off and threw it to the side, not caring where it landed. Then, button by button, I removed my shirt, baring my tattooed torso to my wife. Her gaze raked across my muscles and down to my hardness, straining to break free of my black pants. I kicked off my shoes and then returned to my empress. Her hands hovered by her waist, and I separated them, then fell to my knees and gripped her thighs. Looking up at her, I smirked, then shoved them apart and sank my tongue into her core. Immediately, her fingers twined in my hair and dug into my scalp, pulling me closer to her. Throwing one leg over my shoulder, I deepened the angle, drinking from the most decadent liquid I had ever tasted.

"Ruslan," she moaned, throwing her head back in ecstasy. The rubies glinted from the light streaming into the room, and an idea struck me that had my dick throbbing.

Without warning, I lifted her and directed her toward the window, pressing her back firmly against it. Every gemstone adorning her exquisite figure came to life, and I couldn't tear my eyes away from them as I licked her again.

My inner Dragon purred contentedly, and I moaned against

Izidora's pussy. "You're going to come for me a dozen times before this night is over, sprite."

"Keep doing that and you'll have the first one shortly," she panted, hips grinding shamelessly against my face.

Hooking both legs over my shoulders, I pressed her into the glass, and she splayed her hands on either side to keep her balance. One finger, then two, found their way to her folds and pushed inside, tearing a cry from her lips. I curled them against that spongy spot and nipped her clit at the same time, and she was falling apart around me. Wetness gushed over my face, but I kept going, driving her higher and higher into the pleasure only I could give her. White sparks, much like the ones from the rites earlier, burst from her, and my own magic rose to the surface to meet hers. The light cast by the combination made her fucking shine, and I could wait no longer to be inside her.

Her bare feet hit the floor, and I ripped off my pants, my cock bobbing and pointing straight toward her. Before I could lift her onto it, she fell to her knees and wrapped her glossy pink lips around it, swallowing me down like I was her favorite dessert. "Fuck, sprite," I moaned, abs tightening when she gagged on me.

Watching her head bob and the crown sparkle with it nearly had me exploding down her throat after only a minute. I braced my hands against the window, focusing on breathing through my nose to keep my composure. She hummed around me, and my balls tightened. *"I love the power I have over you when I'm on my knees."*

"You have enough power to bring the whole damn world to its knees, Izidora. But I love when you're on yours for me. You take my cock so fucking well, and I love how your throat tightens around me when you go too far." She obliged me by taking me all the way again, and I had to close my eyes to block out the sight that would make me come.

Deciding I could take no more, I grasped the back of her neck and pulled her off me with a pop. "On your hands and knees," I ordered her. "I want you to look over our empire while you come around my cock."

She whimpered, then did as I bid, her ass pointing in the air and looking delectable. I couldn't help but sink my teeth into her flesh, earning a gasp and a moan as my fingers stroked her at the same time. I repeated my action on the other side, marking her as mine even more than the circle between her shoulder blades did.

"Please," she begged, and I tsked.

"Please what?"

"Take me. I need you to fill me up." Her words were breathy, wanton, and how could anyone expect me to refuse when my wife, my empress, my mate spoke like that.

My hands dug into her ass as I lined myself with her entrance. "Say it," I commanded, and she knew exactly what I meant.

"I love you, Ruslan, my mate, my husband, my emperor."

With a groan, I sank into her wet heat, and the way she gripped me felt like coming home. It was as if her pussy was perfectly molded for my cock, and as I moved inside her, her walls stroked me in turn.

Our skin slapped as I quickened the pace, and wetness dripped down both our thighs. Without her long braid to guide her head, I could only dig my fingers into her hips and force her to take me deeper. But she took me like she was crafted to do just that, and her body turned into a kaleidoscope of light as the sun dipped over the horizon and softened in the room.

"You are exquisite, sprite," I said, tracing one finger through the trails of gemstones lining her back, brushing against her bare skin. Stopping at the collar on her throat, I lifted her up by it, trapping her body against mine. She moaned at the new angle, and I banded a corded forearm across her belly. The shell of her ear was bare, and I traced my tongue across it before nipping at her earlobe.

"Ruslan," she panted, a question hovering in her voice.

"Yes, sprite?" The hand on her belly dipped lower until my finger brushed against the sensitive bundle of nerves at the apex of her thighs.

"I loved killing him." Her core clenched around me as the words slipped from her lips.

A string of curses fled my lips before I rasped out, "What about it?"

Images of Kazimir's bloody and broken body flooded our bond, and Izidora's pussy clenched again. Fuck, I loved that the violence of the act turned her on, and I flexed my hips, driving into her slowly while the scene played out in our minds.

Izidora stilled, then shimmied out of my hold and faced me. Her aquamarine eyes flamed with a mixture of lust and ferocity, and fuck, if that didn't make me want to yank her to me again. Instead, she flattened her palm against my chest and pushed me backward slowly. I took her hint and settled back on the floor.

She straddled me, gripping my shaft and hovering over it for a moment as she stared down at me. Gone was the female who held any ounce of fear toward the males that had hurt her. Instead, the fiery goddess I witnessed when she'd challenged me on our first day together emerged, only this time, all light she clung to had vanished.

Sinking down, she threw her head back and moaned. "The feel of my blade separating his ribs." Her hips circled, and my abs tightened. "The heat from his lifeblood spilling from the wound." She rocked back and forth, her pace quickening, and I gripped her thighs, encouraging her. "The sound of his body cracking against the rocks."

Wetness dripped down my balls, and whatever she was

going to say next had me very intrigued. "The lines I cut into his flesh as we fought, so he could feel even one ounce of my agony. I wish I could have peeled his skin away, let him suffer every time the breeze brushed his skin. I wouldn't have let him die until I was satisfied that he had suffered even a fraction of what I had. I would have kept him like that for months, healing him just to repeat it all over again, until the time he took away from me was repaid."

My fucking sprite.

Her hips rocked faster, and I let her ride me with everything she had, drawing her pleasure to a peak. Her breath came faster and more erratically, and my nostrils flared as her arousal flooded them. Yanking her down by the neck, I crashed my lips against hers, claiming her mouth with a fervor that would never cease, not when we shared this bond and the desire to exact revenge. She tasted like the wine we'd had with dinner, her own rose and plum scent shining through, a scent that would follow me across lifetimes. My tongue swept against hers, and I stole her air as I shoved her down on my dick. She gasped into my mouth, and I stole that sound too.

"Fuck, I love you so much," I swore, my own release closing in fast. "Your light may have called to me first, but I love watching you truly embrace the dark, Izidora. I love to see just how powerful you are when you let go. But now, I want to see your head thrown back as you come for me, and I want to hear you call me your God."

"Yes," she hissed, her hips moving faster and faster as she closed in on the edge of her orgasm.

"Good girl, take all of me deep in that sweet pussy of yours," I praised, gritting my teeth and trying to hold off until she was ready.

"Ruslan," she whimpered, then kissed me again, ass bouncing up and down. I pinned her face to mine with a firm grip on the back of her neck, the other hand finding her lower back and forcing her lower on me. She could barely breathe as I licked and sucked her lips, and I held her there until I was certain she was about to fall off the edge. The moment her walls clenched, I released her so she could ride the wave of her release. Her brows pinched and she threw her head back, whole body trembling as she came. "Fuck, yes, Ruslan, you are my God."

"That's it," I growled, finding her hips and keeping her in place while I dragged out her orgasm. "Keep taking my cock. That's my good girl."

She cried out, my praise taking her over the edge again, and this time, I followed her over it. My balls tightened, and then I throbbed inside her, body jerking until I was utterly spent. She collapsed over my chest, sweat slicking both our bodies. Our hearts beat in sync, slowing at the same pace as we laid there in utter bliss.

It had been a big day – fuck, a big year – for both of us, and down the bond, I sensed that Izidora was exhausted. Gingerly, I picked us up from the ground and carried her to our bed. "You might need help taking this off," I smirked, hands reaching around the back of her neck to unclasp the collar that held the jewels to her chest.

"Thank you," she sighed, allowing me to take care of her. My mate was strong and powerful on her own, and the fact that she trusted me enough to surrender to my ministrations spoke volumes about how far she had come since our first meeting.

Kissing her on the forehead, I removed the gems, then the remainder of the fabric left beneath them. Her aquamarine orbs glittered up at me, and a smile spread across her heart-shaped face. "I love you, Ruslan."

59

ENDRE

One Month Later

"My King," a servant called, racing down the halls of Este Castle. The male wore the new livery with House Zadik's emblem, a wolf howling at the crescent moon.

"Yes?" I said, pausing my walk and allowing him to catch up to me.

The shock from Izidora and Ruslan naming me king of the Night Realm at the conclave hadn't worn off yet. Reuniting with Viktor and Kaztar hadn't helped either, especially as we shared our grief over the loss of Vadim. But the pain of his loss was nothing compared to the news of my parents' execution under Kazimir's orders in response to my leaving the Night Realm.

Even now, tears pricked my eyes at the thought of everyone I had lost in the past year and a half. War had torn Északi apart, and now we were trying to piece it back together, to heal as a people, rather than four separate realms.

The male skidded to a stop, his dark skin and golden hair

signaling his Day Fae heritage. "Taya needs to speak with you, urgently."

Sighing, I pushed my messy locks out of my face and nodded. "Lead the way."

The halls were quiet at this time of the evening, most having retired after dinner. It wasn't a huge affair, informal at best most evenings. I couldn't bear to have all eyes on me, not when I was still processing everything that had happened.

We slipped into a sitting room reserved for nobility, but not often used. "Thank you, you may go," I told the servant, and he shut the door behind us softly.

"Taya." I greeted Kazimir's former lover with ice in my tone.

Her red hair was tied back, and her golden eyes were swollen and watery. She nervously smoothed her hands over her dress. "My King," she said finally, dipping into a quick curtsey.

"Did you need something?" I asked, exhaustion weighing down my bones.

She twisted her fingers together before smoothing them over her stomach again. "I'm pregnant," she declared. "So are the others."

My brows shot up my forehead. "How many?"

"Five, total," she admitted, looking down at her feet before meeting my gaze again. "We need to leave the continent. Go somewhere else and start over."

That was a plan I could agree with. I hadn't been sure how to deal with Kazimir's harem when I returned to Vaenor, so I'd sent them to live in the city, hoping they'd move on with their lives.

"How much gold do you need?" I asked. There wasn't an amount I wouldn't give to have them out of here.

She told me her number, and I promised to send it to her, along with arranging passage on the first ship that could carry them to another continent.

With a watery sniff, she departed, and I sank into a chair, needing a moment alone.

Still fucking cleaning up Kazimir's messes.

At least Ruslan had executed Desmond immediately after Viktor surrendered, and I didn't have to deal with the devious Mage. Just the fucking harem.

Rubbing my eyes, I gathered myself and slipped back into the halls in search of a few discreet servants. I sent three to the docks to secure passage, then wound my way to the Royal Treasury, unlocking the vault and taking the money I knew I could spare and slipping it into five leather pouches.

THE DOCKS WERE EERILY quiet in the early morning, and the ships rocked lazily in the bay, waiting to be sailed into the deep blue waters. The five pregnant females descended the steps to the water carefully, a breeze lifting off the briny water and blowing their skirts around their legs. I watched them, wondering how the hell Kazimir had managed to sire five babes at once.

Taya led the group, her shoulders squared and golden eyes hard. "Where are we going?" she asked after rising from a polite curtsey.

"Keleti." I paused my survey of the group of females who looked so similar to Izidora. "There is enough gold in each pouch to get you started in a new life. Please, don't come back."

And with that, I deposited a bag in each of their outstretched hands, then strode past, not bothering to look back until I crested the cliffs and the shouts of the sailors readying to depart drifted into my ears. Standing on the edge with the wind whipping at my hair, I waited until the sun rose higher and the ship disappeared into the distance, carrying the heirs to the Vaszoly line with it.

When I returned to my apartments at Este Castle, Liliana propped herself up in the bed, the sheets slipping down her bare torso and revealing her full breasts.

"Come here," she begged, crawling toward me and sitting on her knees at the edge. Drazen stirred behind her, groaning as he rolled over to face us. Our gazes met, and he must have seen the harried determination in my face, because his brows dipped together.

My cock twitched in my pants, as I returned my attention to Liliana. I wanted nothing more than to forget what I had learned and bury myself inside her, but I had something important to say.

"Marry me." It wasn't a question, and I gripped her long hair in my hand and tugged her head back.

Her seafoam green eyes slid to Drazen, and I released her so she could face him. But his focus was locked on me. His sharp scrutiny slid over me, and I lifted my chin, not backing down. I hoped he sensed that even if I wanted Liliana as my queen, I didn't want him to be banished from her life.

Liliana opened her mouth to speak, but the Dragon Shifter cut her off. "Endre needs a queen, little vixen. I won't be going anywhere."

"Are you certain?" she breathed, glancing between the two of us.

A rumble emanated from his chest, and he propped up on an elbow, using his other arm to turn her back to me. The tension in my ribs loosened, and I offered him a grateful look before grasping Liliana's waist and hauling her to me. Her back bowed as she stared deeply into my eyes.

"Then yes," she whispered, and I crashed my lips against

hers, inhaling her scent like it was the only thing I needed to survive.

Because, right now, my soul was shattered, as was Liliana's, and the three of us needed each other to heal from the trauma of the past year.

Breaking our kiss, I rested my forehead against hers, staring into the depths of her seafoam green eyes. "I love you, Liliana."

"And I love you, Endre."

60

IZIDORA

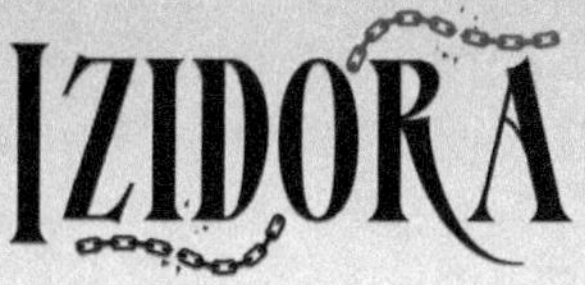

ONE MONTH LATER

"Come to the water, sprite," Ruslan called, the waves lapping around his trim hips in an incredibly enticing way.

Setting aside my book, I strode across the wet sand to the ocean's edge. "But I'm dressed," I pouted playfully, gesturing down to the breezy, colorful attire I wore.

My mate looked from side to side and then up and down before throwing me a salacious wink. "Even if there were people around, I wouldn't care. My empress is the most beautiful female in all of Északi, and they should all be jealous of what I have."

Without shame, Ruslan strode from the water, revealing his hardness already dripping for me. Falling into giggles, I stripped out of my clothes, tossing them behind me, and met him halfway.

"I love to hear you laugh, so carefree," he purred, nuzzling into my neck.

I sighed, melting into his embrace. "This is the first time I've ever truly relaxed."

"I will ensure there is plenty of time for you to relax when we return home," he promised, pulling me deeper into the water.

It was crystal clear and bright blue, and around my feet swam schools of little silvery fish. In the Iron Realm, the first sprigs of green were peeking through the snow, but in the Day Realm, it felt like summer. Queen Viktoria had offered up the royal's seaside residence for our use after our wedding and coronation. Once all the nobles of Északi departed the Iron Realm, we'd followed the Day Realm's queen and king consort home, then taken a carriage to the getaway.

"I feel like I can breathe, deeply, for the first time," I admitted, paddling beside him.

I loved being in the water, but not knowing how to swim was tricky business when the ocean liked to toss me this way and that. Ruslan held onto me the whole time, letting my muscles grow accustomed to swimming so that eventually I'd be able to venture further on my own. He had told me of other creatures that lived beneath the surface, and excitement raced through me as he explained ways to explore the water's depths.

"It will take time for you to fully feel safe in our everyday lives. But we'll work on it. Together," he promised.

I flipped to my back, floating with my hair loose and flowing in every direction. "It's a good thing we have such long lives to share all these experiences with each other."

"I want you to experience everything in this life, sprite. If there is something you want, I'll buy it. If there is somewhere you want to go, I'll take you. If you want someone killed, I'll be your executioner." I grinned, but he stole my smile with a press of his lips. Threading my fingers in his hair, I pulled myself upright and wrapped my legs around his waist. His hardness dug into my core, throbbing and wanting despite staying in bed for far too long this morning making love.

"And I want you to know that I will love you always. You need reassurance? I will tell you a million times. You need someone to share your burdens? I will listen. We're a team, and we do everything together." I ground myself against him, earning a low warning growl that sent delicious goosebumps across my skin.

"Us against the world," he repeated the phrase we said to each other over and over.

"Us against the world," I echoed.

Beneath the brilliant sun and among the salty ocean waves, we kissed, falling into each other with unrivaled passion, knowing truly, that we were both loved, wanted, and needed.

And it was in that moment, I realized I was no longer afraid.

I was free.

Want to know more about Ruslan's life prior Izidora's rescue? Read chapters of Broken, an A Choice of Light and Dark prequel novella on Patreon! https://www.patreon.com/laceylehotzky.

If you enjoyed Freed, please consider rating or reviewing on Amazon, Goodreads, BookBub, or any other platform you prefer to use! Your support means everything, and taking a few moments of your time to let others know how much you liked the book is appreciated.

Subscribe to my newsletter for a spicy bonus scene featuring four of the Nighthounds and one very lucky lady! And if you need some therapy after that ending, join the discussion in

Lacey's Insidious Blooms Facebook Group or <u>Discord - Lacey's Insidious Blooms</u>.

Where to connect with Lacey:
Patreon - early chapters & exclusive art
<u>Instagram - @laceylehotzkyauthor</u>
<u>TikTok - @laceylehotzkyauthor</u>
<u>Discord - Lacey's Insidious Blooms</u>
Lacey's Insidious Blooms Facebook Group
<u>Goodreads - Lacey Lehotzky</u>
<u>Amazon - Lacey Lehotzky</u>
<u>Pinterest - Lacey Lehotzky</u>

Merch & Signed Copies:
<u>www.laceylehotzky.com</u>

AUTHOR'S NOTE

If you've ever been in an abusive relationship, you know that at first, everything is perfect. They say all the right things, treat you like a queen, take care of you. But then, things start to slip. They want you to change to please them. Stressors happen, and they start to take it out on you. Maybe you see the signs then and are able to get out. Maybe you're like me and forgive and move on so many times that the violence starts. Maybe you continue to stay because you're so dependent on this other person for your self-worth and validation. The cycle continues, on and on, unless we can break it. And even if we manage to free ourselves, they might not let go.

Then, someone amazing comes along and shows you every way that you are perfect the way you are. That you are so worthy of love without having to earn it. Their devotion never wavers, even in the face of adversity. You are an unbreakable team, and you wonder how you ever tolerated being treated like you were before.

If you've found that person, I am so happy for you. And if you haven't yet, know they are coming. Because you deserve that fairytale love, where you are safe, secure, and empowered.

Where you are free.

United States
USA Suicide and Crisis Lifeline: dial 988
Crisis Text Line: Text REASON to 741741

United Kingdom
SHOUT: text SHOUT to 85258
Samaritans: call 116 123 (free from any phone), email jo@samaritans.org, or visit some branches in person
National Suicide Prevention Helpline UK: call 0800 689 5652

Australia
Lifeline: call 13 11 14 , text, or chat online 24/7

ACKNOWLEDGMENTS

Finishing this series, my heart series, has been an emotional ride. I cannot believe how my life has changed in a little over a year. From debut author to tens of thousands of books sold, I am so grateful for this journey and thrilled about what the future holds.

I couldn't have done this without you, my amazing readers, my insidious blooms. Your love of this series propelled it to the bestsellers lists and kept it there. Your unhinged DMs made me smile on the hard days. Your messages about connecting with Izidora's story made me cry. That's why I wrote A Choice of Light and Dark – for everyone who has had significant trauma in their life to feel seen. From the bottom of my heart, thank you.

To my betas - Alex, Ashley, Courtney thank you for all your feedback on the final installment of Izidora's story. You helped take it to the next level and deliver the emotional impact it needed.

To my content team & influencer friends - thank you for your enthusiastic support all over socials and spreading the word about ACOLAD! Nicole, thank you for your continued support of this series. Brit, Kimberly, Lexi, Merritt, thank you all for sharing ACOLAD and squealing over PR boxes! Thea, thank you for bringing Izidora to life in your cosplays. I can't wait to see what you make for Freed! Lisa, thank you for all the creative ways you've promoted this series, I will never forget the "fuck your boyfriend he's a bitch" one you made about Kazimir and Ruslan. Cracking up thinking about it now!

Sleep Token - you guys will probably never see this but I couldn't have written this book without the Take Me Back To Eden album on repeat.

Kristina - Thank you for everything you gave this series. Thank you for taking a chance on me after Matt said I needed someone to read Chained. Thank you for reading it like a million and twenty times since then. Thank you for helping me proof the audiobook, find quotes and content, and give me instant feedback with your insanely fast reading skills. Thank you for coming to work with me and helping me grow this business. This is just the beginning and I'm so excited for our future. Sorry not sorry for how many times I made you cry. You like it.

Kat - I cannot wait to be neighbors. Thank you for being the first one to raise their hand when I needed TikTok help. Thank you for listening to me talk out random business stuff. Thank you for your enthusiasm with putting together a content team. Thank you for everything you've given ACOLAD and me. I seriously could not do this without you and I am so dang proud of how you've grown Inkspire.

Courtney - Thank you for all your beta feedback, you are truly one of the best betas out there. But more than that, thank you for your friendship. For all the laughs we've shared, the heartfelt moments, the bitching sessions when we were both struggling. You are incredible, so dedicated to this book community, and I am so lucky to have you on my team.

Kaitlin - we started this crazy journey together a year and a half ago and I am so so grateful for that. I'm also so dang proud of how far you've come in your own mental health journey in that time.

Bobby - Without your marketing method, I wouldn't have gotten this series in front of so many readers who needed to hear Izidora's story. Thank you for helping me launch my author career with a bang!

Author friends - Kaela, Kat, Amarah, Logan, Harmony, Vee, Sara, Chloe, Melissa, Breanne, Isa, Inez, Blake, Rosa, Susan, Annie, HL, Rachel, Nikki... I couldn't do this without you guys. Special shout out to Samantha Amstutz for beta reading Dark and Freed, going in the TikTok trenches with me, and being an all around amazing friend.

Andrew - Thank you for loving the dark parts of me. The parts of me that struggle. The parts of me that are relentless and don't know when to quit. Thank you for being my safe place, for showing me that no matter what sort of craziness I've concocted in my brain, that you love me no matter what and you're not going anywhere. Thank you for telling me I should write in the first place and believing in me even when I doubted myself. My blood is your blood. My body is your body. My life is your life. My soul is your soul. Love you always, fated mate.

ABOUT THE AUTHOR

Lacey is a writer, photographer, and author of the international bestselling dark fantasy romance series, A Choice of Light and Dark. She is most often found with her nose in a book when she isn't training to be a fighter like her main characters. Lacey has her best ideas while traveling, where she finds inspiration for people and places in her books. She especially loves exploring the dark side, writing characters with deep flaws and even deeper trauma, and strapping her readers in for an emotional roller coaster that will leave them begging for more.